Acknowledgements

I was knocked down when I was twenty and I've always wanted to tell that story but instead of a simple car-hit-pedestrian scenario, I wanted to write about an incredible accident, one that the reader would question whether or not it was possible. I wasn't having much luck until one day in the TV3 dressing room I asked producer Tom Fabozzi if he knew of anyone who would have a story to share. He then proceeded to tell me about the accident he and his girlfriend had been involved in one late night in Sligo in the early 90's and it was incredible. In fact so incredible that every aspect of the accident has been recreated on the page here including, unbelievably, some of the dialogue. I replaced my character Eve for Tom and wrote it exactly as he told it. He shared x-rays and reports with me, talked me through every detail of his recovery, and we both reminisced about hospital life and the monotony that comes with being broken and bed-bound. Tom's kindness, patience and his ability to recall the most horrific night of his life with such clarity and humour has been invaluable and I am so grateful to him because the rest of the story and its tone came from there. Thanks so much, Tom, we'll all miss you in the halls of TV3 and wish you every success in your new role with Fine Gael.

Speaking of TV3, I'd like to thank all the team and the ladies I've met through *The Midday Show* – it's been an honour and a pleasure working with you all.

Thank you to Dr Thomas in the Ayurvedic spa in the Carlton Atlantic Coast Hotel in Westport for his invaluable advice.

To all my pals and family – after five books you know who you are. I love you all.

To my husband Donal for always being there and taking care of me so well. I'm grateful for you every day.

And sincerest apologies to the people who went hungry when I locked myself away for months on end: Hallie, Jo, John, Enda, Tracy, Lainey C, Eimear, The D'Oracle, Gamo . . . Loosen up your belt buckles because the feeder is back.

POOLBEG FICTION

'Enormously readable, funny and emotionally engaging'
Irish Times

The Space Between Us

If you knew you'd leave this
world so soon, would you do
it all differently?

Anna
McPartlin

The Space Between Us

Anna McPartlin

CANCELLED

523 175 40 X

This novel is entirely a work of fiction. The names, characters and incidents portrayed in it are the work of the author's imagination. Any resemblance to actual persons, living or dead, events or localities is entirely coincidental.

Published 2012
by Poolbeg Press Ltd
123 Grange Hill, Baldoyle
Dublin 13, Ireland
E-mail: poolbeg@poolbeg.com
www.poolbeg.com

© Anna McPartlin 2011

Copyright for typesetting, layout, design
© Poolbeg Press Ltd

The moral right of the author has been asserted.

1

A catalogue record for this book is available from the British Library.

ISBN 978-1-84223-500-3

All rights reserved. No part of this publication may be reproduced or transmitted in any form or by any means, electronic or mechanical, including photography, recording, or any information storage or retrieval system, without permission in writing from the publisher. The book is sold subject to the condition that it shall not, by way of trade or otherwise, be lent, resold or otherwise circulated without the publisher's prior consent in any form of binding or cover other than that in which it is published and without a similar condition, including this condition, being imposed on the subsequent purchaser.

Typeset by Patricia Hope
Printed and bound by CPI Group (UK) Ltd, Croydon, CR0 4YY

www.poolbeg.com

About the author

Anna's debut novel *Pack Up The Moon* was published in January 2006. It went on to be a bestseller both here and abroad and earned her a nomination for best newcomer at the Irish Book Awards. *The Space Between Us* is Anna's fifth novel. She is published in Ireland, Germany, America, Russia, the UK, NZ, Australia, Portugal, Spain and India. She's currently working on her first film. She's also written *School Run*, a TV comedy-drama for TV3 which was nominated for both an IFTA and a TV award. Anna has lived many kinds of lives in this short lifetime. Her parents separated when she was five and her mother was diagnosed with MS when she was six. She lived with and cared for her mum and her gran until the age of eleven and was then fostered by her aunt and uncle who lived in Kenmare, County Kerry. She was lucky not to have lost her own life when she was hit by a car aged twenty. Surviving loss and being faced with death inspires Anna to write about the darker side of life but, because she has been lucky enough to be surrounded by joyful people, her work and life is brimming with hope and laughter.

Also by Anna McPartlin

Pack Up The Moon
Apart From The Crowd
The Truth Will Out
So What If I'm Broken

Published by Poolbeg

PRAISE FOR ANNA MCPARTLIN

"Enormously readable, funny and emotionally engaging"
The Irish Times

"Anna McPartlin delivers the goods again"   *Cosmopolitan*

"Anna McPartlin radiates an amazing life-affirming humour and
positivity . . . a superb writer"   *Sunday Independent*

"Captures the pain of loss and longing . . . but her background in
stand up comedy spills on to every page, making this touching novel
so funny"   *Irish Independent*

"McPartlin ranks up there with Marian Keyes and Melissa Hill in terms
of how well she writes and how good she is at crafting a story"
Chick Lit Reviews Website

"I loved every page of it . . . It so impressed me that I will be reading
it again"   *Mail On Sunday*

"A wonderful book that's refreshingly honest in its delivery with
great characters, a great storyline and a clever conclusion . . . a must
for all McPartlin fans"   www.femalefirst.co.uk

"Insightful and moving . . . defiantly irreverent" *Sunday Independent*

To all my friends, this world would be a
sorry place without you.

Chapter 1

Introducing the one and only Eve Hayes

Sunday 1st July 1990

Dear Lily,

You've been away a week and it feels like a year! So what's been happening on the home front? Well, not too much really. You know the weirdo who works at the bowling alley? (The one who looks like Glen Medeiros, not the one who picks his nose and eats it.) Well, he followed me from the chipper to the harbour and I could feel him behind me but I didn't let on until I realised that it was getting dark and there was no one else around so I turned on him and said what do you want? He pointed to his bike which was chained up just ahead of me and said I want my bike. MORTIFIED. Anyway we got talking about music, he's an REM fan (yawn, isn't everyone) and out of nowhere he said he liked me! Just like that. I said he was too short for me to like that way. Was that a mean thing to say? You are my filter when it comes to social contact with plebs. He looked hurt but for God's sake I'm 5 foot 11.

1

What's he – about 5 foot 6? We'd look so stupid together plus there is that issue of him being weird. He said and I'm not joking, we'll be the same height when we lie down!!! Think about it, Lily . . . he's talking about sex! The cheek of him. So I mentioned his weirdness and he denied being weird. Instead he said he was different and being different was sexy. Can you believe it? I said yeah maybe if being different is being fantastically good at something or being totally original and having some sort of vision instead of getting a perm, wearing his sister's blouses and standing on street corners shouting out really bad poems. That really seemed to knock him. He wasn't pushed about the perm or the blouse comments but the poetry hit hard. I felt bad because he looked like I'd stuck a pin in him. I said sorry but he looked like he was about to start crying then he called me a stuck-up blonde bitch and stormed off. I sat on the wall and tried to eat my chips which were now cold so I ended up giving most of them away to a dog that had been licking another dog's shit on the beach. Then Gar, Declan and Paul arrived. Declan seems to be in an awful way without you. He was asking me if I'd heard from you. I said just that call you made from the phone box on Wed night and he said you'd rung him then too.

How is everything in Dingle? Is waitressing getting any better? Is the money good enough to stay? I really miss you. It's so lonely here without you. Gar keeps trying to get back with me and I've no intention but, and don't kill me, I did kiss him last night. It was stupid and I was a bit drunk and he was nice and told me my eyes were so green they shone like emeralds. I know – puke – but when you're drunk that kind of thing makes you feel amazing. Well, at least it made me feel amazing until we kissed and I realised I just don't want to go back there. I really like Gar as a friend but that's it. I made some stupid excuse that I had to go so now I have to face him and talk to him sober!

Do you think if the tips are good and you do well down

there that you can come home for the month of August? I just can't believe this could be our last summer together and you are down there and I'm up here and it's so completely boring without you. I know your mother is broke but couldn't she ask your father for some money? How much does it cost to phone Greece to remind him he has a kid in Ireland who wants to go to college and needs help with the fees? It's not like he's been there for anything else in your life and I know it hurts so sorry for bringing it up but it has to be said. He owes you.

I'm using my time to research. I spend a lot of my days in the library. The lads think I've lost it but I love the library. I've been reading about fashion through the ages and it's really interesting. Dad bought me a new and much better sewing machine to make up for you leaving and on Thursday I bought loads of oversized clothes in the charity shop so that I can rip them apart and start again. I wouldn't be caught dead in anything I've made to date - the material is way too naff but it's something to do.

Clooney is never really home and when I do see him he's with a different girl every time. Dad seems amused by it. I'm not. He's changing and since he started in that stupid college radio he goes around the place like he's Bono or something. It's pathetic. The one he was with last night was a state. She had big wild black hair like Kate Bush gone wrong, a million bangles and her T-shirt hadn't been washed in about a year. They slept in his room because Dad was away. I wonder if Dad would be amused by that. That will cost my bro! The next time he annoys me I'll charge him 20 quid for my silence. Anyway she calls him my fluffy Cloudy!!!! Can you believe it? It's sickening. Watched Young Guns 2 (with TV up loud) again last night. OK, so name who you'd go out with in order of preference:

Emilio Estevez, Kiefer Sutherland, Lou Diamond Philips, Christian Slater?

I'd go for
1. Emilio Estevez (Really cute in a serious way)
2. Lou Diamond Philips (Exotic)
3. Kiefer Sutherland. (I liked him in Lost Boys but in YG2 he was just there)
4. Christian Slater. (Does he really talk like that?)

Right, have to go, I'm pulling apart a size 16 pair of dungarees. Don't know what I'm going to make yet but I'm hoping for at least three pieces out of it.
MISS YOU, MISS YOU, LOVE YOU.

Your best friend,
Eve

P.S. Paul told me that Glen Medeiros from the bowling alley (his real name is Ben Logan) writes those poems about his dead sister. Now I feel really bad. She died when she was 10. That's what that poem (the one he keeps repeating in the funny voice) - 10,10, never again - is about. I still think it's weird. I miss my mum but I don't make up poems about her death.

I was 5 she was alive,
I was 7 she was in heaven!

P.P.S. What's the weather like down there? It's been raining here for 3 days solid. Sick of wet hair. Thinking about doing a Sinéad O'Connor. So much for summer.

* * *

On the 1st July 2010 and twenty years after eighteen-year-old Eve Hayes sat down at her bedroom desk one rainy Sunday afternoon to write a letter to her best friend Lily, a much older and wiser Eve

sat at that same old desk. It was raining just like it had been all
those years before. Eve's mind drifted back to that day as it often
did when she felt sad or lonely. At the time a week felt like an entire
year. She smiled at the memory of her unreasonable desperation.
She had missed her pal so much that her heart hurt and she walked
around like a zombie because she'd lost sleep engaging in all-night
conversations with Lily in her head. Eve would say something like
Hey, Lil, this time next year we'll . . . and Imaginary Lily would
finish Eve's sentence . . . *be millionaires.* They were both big fans of
Only Fools & Horses and had the dialogue down. Eve would call
Lily a *plonker*. Imaginary Lily would call Eve *a saucy old git*. When
Eve got bored of basically calling herself names, she'd tell
Imaginary Lily about her everyday happenings and annoyances like
for example the morning she'd thought that her brother Clooney
had died on the toilet because he didn't respond when she'd banged
on the door and swore at him while cupping her crotch in her hand
and considering whether it would be better to pee in the kitchen
sink or under the tree in her own back garden. The sink won. *Can
you believe it, Lily? I peed in my own kitchen sink. I couldn't really
do it in the garden because it's overlooked by the Noonans' and we
all know that Terry 'The Tourist' Noonan is a perv with a set of
binoculars and a second-hand Polaroid camera which he carries at
all times. So not risking my rear end hanging on his wall!* Eve
remembered that Clooney had emerged from the bathroom ten
minutes after she'd peed in the sink, with a girl and a smug look on
his face, while she was up to her elbows in bleach and fairy liquid.
She wanted to punch him badly but then eighteen-year-old Eve had
often wanted to punch twenty-year-old Clooney. Instead she'd just
screamed that she was straight telling Dad when he got home. He
had laughed at her and in her head when she told Imaginary Lily
she had laughed too. Lily and Clooney were thick as thieves.

Back then and on the advice of their guidance counsellor Mrs
Moriarty, Lily had decided to go to medical school and become a
GP. She liked the notion of being a doctor but not cutting people up
and there was no way she was going to be a gynaecologist because
she and Eve both agreed that fannies were disgusting. Besides a GP
practice was child-friendly and Lily had always wanted to be a

mother even as far back as Eve could remember and they had been friends since they were in nappies. Lily toted around a doll until she was ten. She called her Layla and treated her like a person. When Lily's teacher Mrs Marsh began to worry that Layla was some sort of psychological crutch for Lily, her mother put a stop to any more nonsense talk by giving the doll to charity. Lily cried for one week solid and Eve tried to soothe her by giving her a present of her own precious monkey but, even as she handed Monkey over, she knew Layla was irreplaceable to Lily. And so, having confirmed that to be the case, she took Monkey home, cuddled him all night and promised she'd never let him go again.

Eve had always been determined to be a designer. She'd been sewing since she was twelve. She loved sourcing material, drawing and making clothes. Not to mention she had the perfect model in Lily who was so tiny and petite she looked like a perfect little doll and, no matter how bad the design or ensemble was, she would always wear Eve's creations. As the years went by Eve's work got better and better. In fifth year she won a design award and following her win she was commissioned to make four Debs dresses and a Communion dress for a second cousin of her dad's. Even before receiving her Leaving Cert results and on the basis of her portfolio, she had secured herself a place in St Martin's College of Design in London. Lily was the smartest girl in the class. She sailed through school and never had to work too hard, which meant that she could take extra classes in photography, art and piano. She was good at everything, even sewing, much to Eve's disgust. She didn't have Eve's flair though so that was good.

"You're going to make it," Lily would say to Eve.

"Yeah," Eve would agree, "Coco Channel is somewhere shitting herself."

They both knew that bar a sudden brain injury Lily would get medicine in the university of her choosing. She based her first preference on her boyfriend Declan's and that annoyed Eve because Lily had never talked about leaving Dublin to go to college but Declan favoured Cork. Eve thought that was an excuse. Everyone knew that UCC was easier to get into than UCD. Lily would have sailed into UCD or Trinity or even College of Surgeons but Declan would have to fight tooth and nail to get Cork. They had fought over that when filling out the CAO forms but Lily was stubborn and insisted she was going to the same college as Declan and as Eve was going to London anyway it was none of her business and so she gave up. *But still . . .*

It was an exciting time, full of promise, and the only real difference between the girls was that Lily was desperate to grow up while Eve was slow to embrace change. Twenty years ago, that summer was supposed to be the girls' last one spent together but as it turned out Lily needed to earn money for college and the only way to do it was to leave and work for her uncle in his restaurant 228 miles and a world away. Eve often wondered in the years that followed what would have happened if she had followed Lily. *Would we still be friends?* Eve smiled to herself as she remembered the little mantra she'd say every night before she fell asleep. *Goodnight, Lily, I miss you, I miss you, I love you.* And she conceded to herself that teenagers were mental.

The old familiar desk looked out onto her back garden and past her back garden to the large old trees and swing-set and toward Terry the Tourist's empty bedroom window. It had been years since she'd seen him. His family moved after Leaving Cert but Eve's friend Gar had heard he was a press photographer in the UK which made a lot of sense. Why go take pictures of death in a war zone when you can look up some celebrity's dress outside The Ivy? Eve absentmindedly traced the faded etching of BGML she'd spent a good hour or two carving into the table. Ben 'Glen Medeiros' Logan had come into Eve's life as Lily had exited. That summer twenty years ago Eve had fallen in love, made a huge mistake, told the truth, lost her best friend and grew up.

The house was empty and the old desk was the last of the furniture being taken by the movers. They were on a break, sitting at the back of their van eating sausage sandwiches from the local Centra shop, and Eve was left to roam around the house she grew up in one last time. She left her old bedroom and made her way downstairs. The red paint had faded, leaving intermittent vibrant red squares on the parts of wall that were once covered and protected by family photos. They were all gone but Eve could see them as clearly as if they were still hanging there. There was one of her mother, father, Clooney, Eve and Lily. She was two years old, sitting on her father's shoulders. Eve's mother had her arms wrapped around four-year-old Clooney and Lily was holding Clooney's hand. It was summer in the seventies and they were standing, freckled by the sun, under a big blue sky and everyone bar Eve was grinning like a Cheshire Cat. The oval shape was once covered by a picture of Clooney and Eve hugging in their school uniforms on the first day she joined him in primary school. He seemed to be delighted and was squeezing her tightly but the effect was that of a gristly bear constricting its prey. Eve was miserable and battling to escape. The largest square of vibrant paint once held the family portrait that Eve's father had commissioned when her mother got sick. The family sat in a line on the sofa in their best clothes. Mum sat at one end, Dad at the other and Clooney and Eve in between them, Clooney was holding his sister's hand and, although the rest of the family were smiling, Eve looked annoyed. She was six, Clooney was eight and she remembered the photographer getting annoyed because she refused to smile when he uttered the word '*cheese*'.

"You can't help but smile when you say the word *cheese*," he said.

"That doesn't make sense," Eve said.

"Why won't you smile?"

"I don't feel like it."

"I can't take your picture if you don't."

"Yes, you can. Just press the button."

"It'll only be for a second. I assure you it won't break your face."

"Why won't he just do his job and go away, Mum?"

Her mother told the man that for some reason she hated getting her photo taken.

"We all have our issues," she said as a way of explaining Eve's petulance.

"Look, love, I'm not asking the child to take over the controls of a plane or jump into the damn River Liffey. I'm just asking her to move the corners of her mouth up toward her eyes."

Her father told Eve to smile in a voice that he always used when he meant business. The photographer poised the camera and just as it clicked she stuck out her tongue. He was unimpressed. Clooney thought it was funny. Her father warned her to be good but Eve was having none of it and her mother was tired so the photographer was ordered to take another shot whether Eve was smiling or not. He did as he was told: the three others looked like they'd just won the lottery and Eve looked like her pet dog had just died. The rest of the photos were pretty much the same and from those photographs it would be easy to think that Eve had grown up a miserable little sod, but the opposite was true. She was mostly delighted with life, herself and the world around her. The only time she stopped being delighted was when there was a camera pointed in her direction. After her mother died that was a rare occurrence because it turned out her father hated the camera every bit as much as his daughter did and so every cloud . . .

Eve moved from room to room across the old wooden floors and as she did memories floated in and out of her mind. Even though the kitchen had been refurbished, when she stood still in its centre where the large dining table used to be and closed her eyes, she went back in time. She could smell her father's attempt at tomato-and-chilli sauce burning. She could see him standing over it, stirring vigorously and wearing a ladybug apron. He was covered in sauce and flinging pasta at the wall, insisting when it stuck it was ready to eat.

"Kids, we have lift-off!"

Clooney, Eve and Lily were sitting at the dinner table. Her dad was taking apart an old radio he'd found in a skip and eating his dinner with one hand. In her head she could hear the radio he'd magically fixed while clearing his plate of burnt sauce and sticky pasta. Eve's father had always done his best and his kids didn't really know any better because their mother was no chef either. Eve once overheard her aunt say to her Uncle Rory: "God love them, those kids would eat fried dog-shit if their daddy served it with a smile." She was right, and poor Lily, well, she thought the sun, moon and stars shone out of Eve's dad. He was kind to her and made her a part of his family without question or reason. She called him Danny not just because his name was Danny but because it sounded like Daddy and for as long as Eve could remember she had copied her friend so Dad became Danny early on. There wasn't a memory in that house that Lily wasn't in some way a part of.

As she moved to the glass doors that led to the stone patio, she began humming along to the memory of Paul Young and Zucchero singing '*Senza Una Madonna*'. Clooney used to insist on singing the words 'Scent of Madonna' to make Lily laugh and annoy Eve. Eve was easy to annoy as a teenager.

"*Scent of Madonna, gives me pain and some sorrow, scent of Madonna, she'll still smell bad tomorrow!*"

"Dick."

"Evey, don't call your brother a dick!"

"Well, tell him to stop acting like one."

"Clooney, stop annoying your sister."

"I'm only singing."

"No, you're just doing my head in!" Eve said.

"It's hardly the end of the world, Evey."

The back garden was overgrown, the old tree-house was long gone, but the big old oak tree was still there. Eve leaned against it and looked at the house she grew up in. She remembered her mother living in her bedroom for months before she died. Eve was allowed visit once a day and for a few minutes at a time near the end. She always brought Lily who would stay silent and stroke Eve's mother's hand.

"How are you, Mum?"

"I'm good," she'd say with a big smile.

"You don't look good."

"No."

"You look weird."

"Don't be scared."

"I'm not scared, I'm sad."

Eve's dad often tried to explain to her that saying everything that entered her head wasn't necessarily the best idea in the world especially when it made her sick mother cry. Eve never did quite learn the art of subtlety.

She sat on the old wooden swing-set, the one she and Lily sat on nearly every dry day until they were twelve and too cool for swings.

After thirty years it should have been falling apart and unsafe but her father had maintained it over the years. It was rooted into the ground with cement foundations and it was as much a part of the landscape as the big old trees. She started to swing a little, remembering their squeals when each girl tried to beat the other by going higher and higher until their feet were touching the sky.

"The one who swings highest gets a wish!" Eve would call out and Lily freaked out every time because she could think of so many things she wanted that it was hard to make just one wish.

"I can't think, I can't think!" Lily would say frantically as though it was the first time making a wish was ever suggested.

As they climbed and climbed and when they couldn't swing any higher, Lily would call out at the top of her lungs: "I love you, Eve Hayes!"

"I love you, Lily Brennan!" Eve would scream back and they'd giggle and kick their legs wildly.

It had been a long time since Eve had swung or indeed done anything with abandon and so she just sat on the swing and stared at the ground in front of her, at the patch of grass where she spent time lying on her back with Lily at her side battling with the sun to look up towards the sky and toward her mother's window. They were doing just that on the day she died, just lying on the grass talking about this and that. There was a lot of commotion, adults coming and going, Eve's aunt was crying and her uncle talking on the phone. Eve's father called Clooney and then something happened. People stopped moving around the house, everything became still and then someone unseen inside Eve's mother's room closed the curtains. Lily held Eve's hand and even though they were only six years old at the time they both knew that Eve's mother was gone.

Eve shielded her eyes from the sun that shone brightly despite the falling rain and she looked up at the room that stole so much from her. It was the only room she hadn't visited one last time. The pain was still too raw because it was the same room her dad had died in only eleven months before. That time she was in the room and the hand she was holding was her dad's.

He died on an October morning after a short illness. He was sixty-two years old and up to the day he was diagnosed with cancer he was the happy, healthy, busy man he'd always been. He was still working as an investment banker, he was still mad about boats and golf and he did both every chance he got. He was dating Jean, a woman in her mid-fifties, and it was early days but they had a lot in common and he really liked her. He still travelled and visited Eve in New York at least three times a year. On his last visit he brought Jean and they looked like they were in love. His back had been at him for a while. He had been diagnosed as a Type 2 diabetic a few years before and initially he had managed to control the disease but recently his blood sugars were all over the place and he was starting to begin and end his days feeling nauseous, so finally and only on Jean's insistence he went to his local GP. Two weeks later on 16th August he was diagnosed with terminal pancreatic cancer. It was Jean who phoned Eve in New York.

"Hello, Eve?"

"Yes, hello?"

"It's Jean . . . McCormack . . . your father's . . . ah hmm friend."

"Oh Jean, hello, how are you?"

"Well, I'm well. Thank you. Thank you for asking." She sounded weird and it didn't take a genius to work out she wasn't making a social call.

"What's wrong, Jean?"

"It's your dad, dear." She sounded like she was trying not to cry.

"What about him?" Eve's heart rate increased, her temperature rose and the blood that had previously been in her head rushed to her toes. She held on to her chair. *Get to the point, Jean, for Christ sake.*

"He has cancer."

"Oh no."

"In his pancreas."

"Oh no."

"You need to come home, dear."

"What about Clooney?"

"You need to get him to come home too." She broke down then and cried and Eve listened to herself comfort Jean and it was as though she was in another room and listening to strangers' converse through a wall.

"All right, Jean, it's going to be all right. I'll call Clooney and we'll come home and we'll take care of him and he will be fine because I have money and I can pay whatever it costs so you just relax because I will sort it. OK?"

"OK, dear," she said. "OK." But she had known better, that no amount of money was going to save Eve's father and the only thing that could be done she was doing and that was surrounding him with the people he loved and who loved him until he died two months later. Once diagnosed, Eve's father's health declined incredibly quickly and so those two months had been very special. Eve and Clooney hadn't lived in that house since that summer in 1990. Their father didn't want to be in hospital or a hospice and so it made sense that they live the short time he had left, together. Eve's money couldn't save him but it could pay for the kind of round-the-clock care he required.

Clooney arrived home two days after Eve. Despite his tan he looked grey-faced and new lines were forming around his eyes even as they hugged in the airport. He got drunk that night and cried like a baby. Eve made lists of things that needed doing and got busy fitting the room that her mother had died in with all the conveniences necessary to ensure that her father died more comfortably. Within one week the room was kitted out like a state-of-the-art hospital. Eve's father was cheerful and if he was angry or bitter he pretended he wasn't and he was sincere and believable but every now and then when he thought that he was alone in the house he'd scream, roar and sometimes he'd sob so much that Eve would have to hold her brother back from his door.

"He needs this," she'd said.

"He needs us," he'd replied.

"When was the last time you were grateful to have an audience when you cried?" she asked and Clooney nodded and let his dad be.

When they were with him and he wasn't in pain he revelled in those moments. The nights were dark, gloomy, and rain pelted against his window, but he had always loved the sound of rain. Jean was there from beginning to end but not so that she was invasive. She was a lady through and through. She was always appropriate. Even though Eve and Clooney thought it was odd that she often prayed silently, moving her fingers up and down her rosary beads, whilst sitting at an atheist's deathbed. Eve mentioned it to her over coffee one day.

"You know my dad's agnostic."

"Yes, dear, I do."

"And yet you pray."

"I know. Selfish, isn't it?"

"I've lost you."

"Well, I'm praying for me."

"Oh."

"And you? Are you an agnostic?"

"Until the Virgin Mary, a jolly Buddha, Allah or Brahman come to sit on the end of my bed and tell me any different," Eve said.

"It will be hard to let him go," Jean said.

"Yeah," Eve agreed and she couldn't expand because her nose burned and her tear ducts itched.

"I pray for him because it makes me feel better and I pray for me that when he's gone I'll have the strength to go on."

"You just will," Eve said with the confidence that came with experience, even though the thought of it made her heart ache.

"And you?" Jean asked.

"People live and then they die, Jean," Eve said as a matter of fact and she left Jean alone to finish her coffee.

When they were alone Jean and Eve's dad flirted and laughed and even with a catheter and a bowel-bag he was a smooth operator. Jean brought light into his darkened room and he wasn't the only Hayes grateful to her.

Eve and Clooney spent days together in that room. He loved crosswords and watching re-runs of *Who Wants To Be A Millionaire*. Clooney would answer the questions loudly and with authority as though he knew what he was talking about. More often than not he'd get the answer wrong, making the others laugh. On one occasion Chris Tennant asked the question. "Which legendary German scholar sold his soul to the devil?" He then gave four names.

Eve looked at her dad and shrugged. He did the same.

"Tannhauser," Clooney said confidently.

It went to 50:50. Faust and Tannhauser were the two names left.

14

Clooney looked over at them and nodded smugly. The contestant picked Faust.

"Oops, you've just blown it."

Chris Tennant paused for what seemed to be eternity before he smiled and announced that the contestant had just won £16,000.

Everyone celebrated except Clooney who pretended to be put out by his dad's laughter.

"Faust. Damn it, Faust, of course."

"'Of course' my rectum, you didn't have a clue!" Eve said.

"Fair enough," he admitted, "but if that was poker I would have won the hand."

"Sap!" Eve said.

"Yeah, well, at least I'm not a Big Foot!" Clooney said and laughed at himself. Because of Eve's height she had been christened Big Foot by a boy called Eoin Shaw in first class and it had caught on so much that she really didn't rid herself of the name until she moved into secondary school.

"Danny!" Eve shouted in a tone that suggested her indignity at the injustice of Clooney bringing up the name that dared not be spoken under the Hayes roof.

Eve's dad laughed and repeated "Big Foot," under his breath. He scratched his tired face and reminisced about the song the kids in Eve's class would sing, all but Lily of course.

"'*Big Foot Hayes doesn't do Sundays. We go to Mass, she eats grass. Big Foot Hayes . . .*' What was the end of it?"

"Danny!" Eve repeated in the same voice although her smile suggested she wasn't as aggrieved as she'd first let on.

Clooney thought about it for a second before raising his hand: "*Big Foot Hayes blocks out sun rays.*"

Eve's dad giggled. "No future Poet Laureates in that bunch." He went to sleep smiling that night and it was one of the last times his slumber wasn't drug-induced.

Some afternoons they would play Monopoly together. Eve rarely failed to win. Clooney suggested this was due to her cold, detached, industrialist Ming the Merciless personality.

"Ah come on, Evey, don't take Shrewsbury Road! You always get it!" her dad said when it looked like she was going to win again.

15

"Take comfort that it isn't worth what it used to be, Danny."

"Just give it to him, Ming."

"Can't do it, Clooney."

"I'd be happy to part with Shannon Airport, Dad?" he offered but his dad just laughed.

"Of course you would, son."

When he was still able for conversation they talked about everything and anything but they never once mentioned he was dying. Jean took care of his last will and testament and she was the one who talked to him about his funeral plans. She had a pen and paper and wrote out his wishes as he spoke them. The Hayes family were agnostic, Eve's mother's death hadn't changed their perspective nor would their father's. He had no truck with religion of any kind. He didn't believe in an afterlife, at least not the one sold by the various organisations. He didn't look forward to kicking it up on a cloud in Heaven nor did he fear burning in an eternal Hell. He wasn't expecting to see Eve's mum – it would be nice if it happened but he didn't fear a complete full stop. Even as he grew worse and his pain became more difficult to manage, they continued to pretend that Clooney and Eve were staying for an extended visit and that all was well.

When he began to slip away from them, Clooney couldn't bear it and Eve finally let go the pretence. As he battled to breathe his last laboured breath, she held his hand and whispered in his ear. "It's OK to let go, Danny," she said and he gently squeezed her hand before closing his eyes and he was gone.

Jean sat by the door with her head bowed, twisting her well-worn rosary beads in her hand. Clooney stood by the window facing out. He didn't turn around for the longest time. Eve just held her dad's hand and with her free hand she made notes of what she would need to attend to.

He wanted to keep it simple in a nice funeral home with a few words from Clooney and Eve although he understood if Eve didn't want to talk because he knew what she was like. He wanted his old friend Lenny to play the guitar and sing a few Bob Dylan songs and after they'd said their few words, sang a few songs, ate a few rolls and drank some tea he wanted them to take his ashes out to sea on his beloved sail-boat before dumping him ceremoniously.

"Is that even legal?" Clooney had asked Jean.

"Who cares?" Eve said.

So that's exactly what they did. Eve packed a picnic, including a bottle of expensive wine. Jean, Clooney and Eve stood on the deck, each lost in their own thoughts and memories. They made sure they knew which way the wind was blowing because he had been adamant that they shouldn't risk wearing or eating him.

"Wind direction is the key, Jean," he had warned.

"Got it."

"It's the key," he repeated before licking his finger and raising it into the air.

"Understood."

"And don't dump the urn in."

"Righto."

"That's littering."

"Got it."

"But don't keep the urn either."

"Well, what would you like me to do?"

"Recycle it."

"Okey dokey."

"I wish I had more time to love you, Jean," he said and he smiled at her. "I'm so very sorry about that."

"Me too," she said, allowing a tear to fall silently as she went on ticking down his list of requests.

When the wind direction was assessed, Eve handed Clooney the urn and then the three of them stood for a minute or so before he tossed the ashes overboard. Eve poured three glasses of wine and they toasted him. Jean cried the whole way back, quietly and into a large hankie so as not to make too much of a fuss. Clooney was silent and barely touched his drink. Eve had most of the bottle drunk by the time they hit the harbour.

In the eleven months since her father's passing a lot had changed. It was time to leave the house and her childhood behind. She was looking forward to a new chapter in her life, a slower-paced one. It was time for Eve to stop and smell the roses.

She closed the dark-blue glossy front door behind her and when she'd walked down the short tree-lined avenue she turned to take one last look at the large white house covered in vines and a pink flowered creeper and the big oak tree and the bench underneath it in the centre of her front garden. *Goodbye, old house – goodbye, childhood – goodbye, Mum – goodbye, Danny. You were amazing, we were lucky to have you both. I miss you. I love you. If I never see you again, thank you.* She didn't dally about or shed a tear. Eve was not one for making a fuss and her mother and Jean had taught her that a lady always knows the right time to leave. She nodded to the guys in the van as they finished their lunches. She crossed over the road and got into her car. She put the key in and drove away from the street she'd grown up on, believing it to be for the final time.

Eve had spoken to Clooney briefly that morning on the phone. He was in some hellhole in Afghanistan feeding orphans and strays and he didn't much care about the details of the house sale.

"I need your bank details."

"For what?"

"For the money from the sale of the house."

"Just give my share to a cancer charity."

"Please don't make it difficult."

"I'm making it easy."

"No. You're making it difficult. I'm not going to give away your money."

"What if I said please?"

"Fine, I'll set up an account in your name."

"Ah, does that mean I have to deal with tax?"

"You don't give away money because you don't want to deal with tax."

"*You* don't. I do." He changed the subject after that. "You sound tired."

"Yeah, well, of course I'm tired. I'm the one doing everything while you swan around Afghanistan."

"People don't swan around war zones."

"No. I suppose they don't," she conceded.

"You must be happy to be home again."

"Yeah," she agreed a little half-heartedly, "it's great."

"Maybe I'll come visit you soon," he said and she laughed.

"I won't hold my breath," she said. "A person has to be dying to get you home." He didn't argue. Instead he just ended the conversation by telling her to do what she wanted with the money. "I don't need it, Eve, and I don't want it."

Clooney had always been strange about money. He had never really cared for it. Even as a kid material things never impressed him. He'd been living on expenses and banking money for years. He lived the life of a nomad with no dependants. He didn't even know what was in his account, he never looked. He fed the poor in the worst conditions known to man and he didn't need a suit or an expensive car to do that. Eve often thought that her brother was probably the most dependable person you could ever meet in a crisis but the minute that crisis has passed he was gone and moved on because he didn't feel much use if he wasn't needed.

Clooney had left home when he was twenty. In September 1990 he was due to go into his third year in college. He was studying engineering but he'd somehow managed to secure himself a spot on college radio six months into his first year. He co-hosted a show with a girl called Vera Kilpatrick. They hosted an evening spot from eight to ten Monday to Friday. Clooney never liked his name. His mum had seen it in a name book and even though his parents had agreed on calling him Matthew, the second she saw him with one eye open resting in her arms she changed her mind.

"He's not a Matthew. He's a Clooney."

His father wasn't so sure he liked the idea but she was determined. "It's Gaelic for a rogue. And this one is most definitely a rogue."

And she wasn't wrong about her son. Most people had never heard the name before and he was often asked to repeat and spell it – that is, until 1994 when George Clooney played Dr Doug Ross on ER and suddenly the whole western world knew the name Clooney and on the rare Christmas he'd come home the associated commentary made Eve's poor brother miserable.

"Clooney? You fancy yourself."

"Clooney. I need CPR. Stat."

"Clooney? You're cute but not that cute."

"Here, Clooney, you were a shit Batman."

His dad used to joke that the reason he chose to live and work in third-world countries had nothing to do with his altruism and everything to do with escaping the curse of the actor George Clooney. Before George and the call of the starving, in the late 80's and early 90's, a lot of DJ's gave themselves stupid names and he was no exception. Clooney Hayes became Cloudy Dayz and his sidekick Vera Kilpatrick was simply known as V Kill P. She'd play Kylie and Jason's 'Especially For You', he'd play Simple Minds 'Belfast Child'. She'd play The Bangles 'Eternal Flame' and he'd play Guns N' Roses 'Paradise City' and between their musical tug of war, they'd introduce their audience to sex, drugs and rock 'n' roll. They'd argue from the male and female perspective. They'd talk about everything, no holds barred, and they made a good team. They celebrated and explained the impact of the 1988 decision to decriminalise homosexual acts carried out by consenting adults by the European Court Of Human Rights as a result of a case taken by David Norris against Ireland and its draconian and unfair laws. They canvassed to appeal the 1989 Supreme Court's finding which prevented students from providing leaflets and contact information on abortion services in the UK. They discussed the 1990 Criminal Law Amendment Act on Rape and explained what the abolishment of the marital exemption meant. They had great passion and chemistry and, although at the time Eve would never have admitted it, the show was pretty good.

Clooney could have gone into radio if he'd wanted to and he would have made a fine engineer but it was his bleeding heart that claimed his future. Clooney was fourteen when Bob Geldof's Live Aid changed the world and it had a massive impact on him. Millions were dying in the worst of circumstances and, long after the concert was over, the faces of the starving that crossed the screens across the world lived on in his head. When he was presented with the opportunity to join a group of peace corps volunteers going to Africa, he abandoned his degree and his promising radio career and left as soon as he'd received his vaccinations and he'd broken his father's will to stop him. In the intervening years he had worked as an NGO with many organisations across three continents and the two months spent with his dying father was the longest time Clooney had spent in Ireland since he was twenty.

Eve had left for St Martin's that same September. For the first year she studied for a BA Honours in Fashion but, when she realised she was never going to be as talented as some of her peers, she changed to a BA Honours degree in Jewellery Design and in doing so she found her niche. The course lasted three years and, although she enjoyed her time in London, she took a job with a jewellery design house in Paris as soon as she graduated and spent another three years living there. Eve wasn't much of a party girl. She had a work ethic and commitment and determination to succeed. To achieve her goal she worked endless hours and, unwilling to take drugs to stimulate her enough to party all night and work all day, she remembered little of the high life that she was expected to experience. But it didn't matter because she loved what she did and she learnt enough to go to America to design her own line and create an international business. America and her own business left little room for a work/life balance but life was good and she was grateful and content, that is until her dad died. Those precious two months had changed everything. She had slowed down and reconnected with her dad, her brother, her old friends and her home.

After a long silence of many years Eve had reconnected with friends via Facebook. Her old teenage boyfriend Gar Lynch contacted her first and as a result of their friendship she'd reconnected with their mutual pal Paul Doyle a few weeks later. Gar had gone on to marry Gina McCarthy. Gina was two years older than Eve but they grew up around the corner from one another and had been good friends up until the age of twelve when the two-year gap seemed to make a big difference to Gina and so she ended their friendship by telling Eve and Lily that she'd moved on and slamming the door in their faces when they had been so bold as to ask her if she wanted to come out and play. Despite being dumped by Gina as a prepubescent, Eve had always liked her. They had reconnected that summer of '90 just before Eve left Ireland and she was so pleased to learn that Gar had ended up with her. Through the power of Facebook she learned that they were happy with two kids, two dogs, one cat and a boat. They had stayed in the same area because Gar couldn't think of any reason to move.

"Sea air, good schools, great restaurants, the best pub in Ireland

and it's on the DART line. It's perfect here," he'd said via personal message, but then Gar had always seemed content just to be where he was and to be fair he was at least half right. Eve's old hometown was as close to perfect as any place she'd been.

She learned that following college, Paul had moved away to the UK but he returned home during the boom years and despite a strained relationship with his parents he stayed local too. Gar explained that Paul had come out during his second year at Trinity College and no one saw it coming. He just didn't seem like the type. He was a brilliant rugby player, hard as nails and always with girls. Eve had noticed he never really went out with anyone in her village. It was always some girl a bus journey away. He didn't stay with a girl longer than five minutes but there was always a girl. The lads thought he was a legend. Eve thought he was a major slut, a nice one though, but the word was if you wanted to retain any dignity or your virginity it was best to steer clear of Paul Doyle. She was in London when he came out and, distanced from her old group, she missed all the drama at the time. She later heard through Gar and then Gina that there had been plenty of that. Paul's father went on a bender for three days and nights before ending up in the A&E department with a split head and no memory of how it happened. His mother threatened to swallow an entire packet of sleeping pills only to be talked out of it by the local priest who promised to pray that her son would escape eternal damnation. He later turned out to be a paedophile, news which Mrs Doyle seemed to take better than her son's sexuality. Paul lived with a guy called Paddy for years and the first anyone knew of the relationship ending was Paul's change of status on his Facebook. Paul was great company but he never talked about his personal life and so in the three years since Paddy mysteriously vanished from his life no one knew what Paul was doing, who he was doing it with or if he was doing anything with anyone at all. On one particular evening over dinner twelve months previously Eve had tried to extort information, using her dying father as emotional blackmail.

"No."

"Ah, come on, tell me something."

"No."

"I need distraction."

"No."

"Why not?"

"Because I don't want to."

"You're a crap gay."

"You've no idea."

He smiled at her and nodded his agreement then he changed to a subject sure to distract from his personal life and so for the rest of the evening they spoke about Eve.

During her short stay in Ireland she even managed to catch up with Ben Logan. He'd contacted her through Facebook six months before her dad's diagnosis. She'd thought about whether or not to accept his friendship long and hard before making the decision. She'd even polled some of her American friends.

"Never *ever* befriend an ex," Debbie said.

"Absolutely befriend him – it's not like you've anything going on here," Marsha countered.

"It's dangerous," Debbie said.

"How is it dangerous?" Marsha said. "He lives there, you live here, and it's just a little flirting on the net. God knows she needs to do something."

"So why can't she just buy a dress, clean herself up and go on a date?"

"I'm in the room," Eve reminded them both.

Despite Debbie's warning, curiosity was always going to win out, so having procrastinated just enough to ensure no-one, most especially Ben himself, thought she was too eager, she accepted his request and immediately trawled through his photos and updates. *Still short and still a total ride.* His hair was tight and he was tanned and healthy. *Oh Ben, you'll always be Glen Medeiros to me.* It was clear he went to the gym and his eyes still shone when he beamed down the camera lens. He owned a chain of organic posh food supermarkets across Dublin, Wicklow, Galway and Cork. He was married to a woman named Fiona. From the photos it appeared that despite his mini-supermarket empire they went on lots of holidays and they had no children. He messaged Eve a few hours after she'd accepted his friendship.

Hey, Blondie,

Didn't know if you'd accept, glad you did. Congrats on all your success. I always knew you'd do it although surprised you ended up in jewellery but then again I thought I was going to be a rock star and ended up in the food biz. How's life? Do you ever get home?

Ben AKA Glen M. XXX

She'd responded friendlily enough, congratulating him on his supermarket success and his marriage. She told him she hadn't been home in years, wished him well and politely signed off. After that they made comments on one another's updates, tagged each other on photos from the past or funny YouTube videos and every now and then they conveyed that they liked something the other one had posted and that was that until Eve's dad got sick.

Eve was home one week when he rang the house and asked her if she wanted to meet for coffee. At that stage she'd spent most of that week in and out of the hospital while trying to set up her dad's room at home and organise his home help. When she wasn't running around she was alone in the house waiting for Clooney to come home. She hadn't yet contacted Gar or Paul and then out of nowhere Ben tracked her down.

"How did you know I was here?" she asked incredulously.

"I thought I saw you in Donnybrook so I said I'd try and call."

"I was nowhere near Donnybrook."

"Well, then, it must be fate," he said and he sounded like the boy she had loved and lost one summer twenty years ago.

Her heart skipped. *He's married, Eve, so just behave.*

They met for coffee near the hospital and even though she worried that it would begin awkwardly it wasn't that way at all. They fell back into an easy relationship, neither pulling any punches but yet neither bringing up much about the past either.

"So, posh supermarkets," she said.

"So, cheap costume jewellery."

"That's only a tiny portion of the business and I prefer the term *affordable* and weren't you supposed to be a tortured poet turned rock star?"

"It turns out you were right and I was crap, but weren't you supposed to be the next Coco Channel?"

"Things change."

"But you haven't changed a bit."

He looked at her approvingly and Eve's heart skipped another beat.

Eve didn't melt easily. She wasn't a conceited or particularly vain woman and she rarely felt beautiful, but she saw beauty in the strangest faces and working in high-end fashion for many years didn't change that. The reality was that to most of those close to her Eve was considered to be quite beautiful. At 5 foot 11 inches, she was a natural blonde with a face that could carry a pixie cut. She was thin with an athletic build, creamy skin, blonde hair and green eyes. Eve could have been a model if she hadn't despised cameras. She always felt quite boyish. She cut her hair into a short crop in her early twenties and she wore a version of that crop since, not because it was trendy but because it was handy. Much to the disgust of her friends in America she lived in jeans, vest tops and blazer jackets and rarely wore make-up. She was never girly, she didn't have millions of shoes, and for someone who made jewellery the only thing she wore was a gold disk around her neck with her mother's name written on it. She spent a lot of her time looking down and as a result she had to watch her posture because on rare occasions when she let herself go she slouched. So despite the general consensus, when Eve looked in the mirror she just didn't see what others saw. In fact the only time Eve Hayes felt beautiful was when she saw herself through Ben Logan's eyes. Sitting in a coffee shop in Dublin, twenty years after they split up on the worst night of Eve's life, she blushed because for an hour she felt beautiful again.

After that initial successful reunion they met regularly, at first for coffee, then lunch, then dinner, drinks at a bar and when they slept together it was on the understanding that he loved his wife and she loved her life and neither of them wanted anything from each other aside from a little distraction. They both knew that her time in Ireland was finite. They both felt the same way. They both wanted the same thing. They were absolutely confident that no one would get hurt.

Eve hadn't considered that her time at home and her father's death could change her and that the non-stop working life she'd built in America would no longer sustain her nor, more importantly, could she sustain it.

At first she denied that she wanted or needed a different life and she tried desperately to return to form. She was tired and she didn't want to be a captain of industry any more. She didn't want to design jewellery. She didn't want to promote or sell it either. Her life had been very stressful for so long that she hadn't noticed that she was a workaholic with little or no quality of life. Being around her father, Clooney and her old friends reminded her of that and it had occurred to her that if she died no one would really notice and that scared her. *I'm so sick of being alone.* Her board of directors were happy to buy her out. They had plans for the company that she had attempted to block so her change of heart was like a dream come true for them. America had treated Eve very well but her hometown was calling and six months after they had buried her father at sea she moved home. All she had to show for twenty years away from Ireland was two suitcases and a crate of books on design. *Clooney isn't the only one who travels light.* She did have a fat bank balance which was something nobody else seemed to have in Ireland, two brownstone buildings and an apartment overlooking Central Park. Eve's accountant was responsible for those purchases. She'd lived in the penthouse and rented out the brownstones and had never even visited them. Clooney and Eve were very different in many respects but one of the few things that made them similar was their lack of interest in accumulating things.

She rented a house overlooking the sea and only ten minutes from the house she grew up in. She joined a local gym and signed up for yoga classes.

She'd meet Gina for a coffee but only when her kids were in school because Eve never liked kids. As far as she was concerned they were noisy little people who constantly interrupted interesting conversations with banal stupid little comments like:

"Mom, mom, mom, mom, mom."

"Mom is talking."

"Mom, mom, mom, mom, mom."

"*What?*"

"I, I, I, am . . . I like cheese."

Eve was never the kind of person who pretended to like children just because it was the socially acceptable thing to do. Some people valued her honesty, others did not. She hung around with the people who did. So the first time Gina suggested Eve met her and the kids, she made it clear she did not do children. Happily Gina accepted Eve's position and was actually grateful for a morning chat without the 'I like cheese or my friend Reece has a dog named Bones' interruptions.

She played golf with Gar and talked about the banking crisis, the consequences of an IMF deal and whether or not Ireland should burn bondholders. He was sure Ireland would recover but it would take about twenty years. He worked in exports so had one of the few relatively safe jobs but he was considering moving his family to Australia anyway.

"Whatever happened to this place?"

"We got greedy and messed it up," he said sadly.

He didn't want to go but he was worried about mortgage increases and taxation, he worried about his children's future and his and Gina's. Their pensions were all but gone. He wanted to live in a country where his kids had half a chance of getting a job when they grew up.

So typical I get back and my pals leave.

She played tennis with Paul once a week, afterwards they'd have dinner and sometimes they'd take a walk on the cliff on a Sunday. He didn't share Gar's concerns. He was resolutely positive about everything. It would be hard for a few years and then we'd right ourselves and be better than ever. Paul was ever the optimist but then he, like Eve, had no kids to worry about and although he'd taken heavy pay cuts in the Justice Department, his four-bed semi-detached house was nearly paid for, he hadn't amassed personal debt during the boom years, and he still had a few quid in the bank for a rainy day. Paul was not typical but then Eve knew that Paul was never typical.

One day as they walked the cliff he pointed out towards the sea. "You don't need to spend money to have a good time," he said.

"Yeah," she said, "you don't have to spend money to kill yourself

27

either." She was referring to the local investment banker in his forties who jumped off the cliff the week before.

"You always have to bring things down." He shook his head.

"Just keeping it real," she said, hunching her shoulders.

"It's not like you to think of the little people, Eve," he said and he was right. Eve was more often than not too wrapped up in her own world to notice or care about the people around her.

"Maybe I'm finally growing up."

"It's too late for that," he said and they walked on.

Paul was right about that. She often behaved like a spoilt madam, she was used to getting her own way and, especially when it came to Ben, Eve couldn't help but act like a stupid teenager.

She was home one month before she contacted him. Their affair had been based on Eve having an exit date and before she left it was clear his business was in trouble. Posh supermarkets do not do well in a recession. Eve told herself that she just wanted to know how he was doing and that she was happy to be his friend. They met in another coffee shop and this time he was drawn and fidgeted a little. He was uncomfortable around Eve and it made her sad. She told him she wasn't looking for anything and that she only wanted to catch up. It eased tensions slightly but not completely. He spoke about the difficulty he was in. He had closed two shops and if he couldn't turn things around in the other three he would face bankruptcy. He couldn't afford to pay off the suppliers and close the shops. All he could hope to do was trade through but it was becoming more and more difficult and he was running out of ideas. He was a mess and she sympathised. He needed to focus on his business, restructure, negotiate with dying banks and prepare his wife for the possible loss of their livelihood. She told him she'd be there for him if he needed a friend. He thanked her and left.

After that they spoke on the phone a few times. Things were up and down. He'd found an investor but then the investor fell through. He had various plans all of which were doable but only if he could secure credit. He was a fighter, he'd find a way. They only talked shop. She gave him advice and he was grateful. She listened to him and made suggestions. She offered to look at the books. After declining he called her back and asked her if she would. She picked them up from his accountant. She spent a week making notes and working out how the business could restructure and survive. She thought she'd found a way of changing the business model to suit the climate so she left a message to talk to him about it. The plan would involve a big change she wasn't sure he was ready for, but it was nice to feel like she was offering a solution. She desperately wanted to help. He didn't get back to her right away and she didn't want to press him. Their relationship had changed. She accepted that. Besides, she was busy resting and de-stressing – after all, that's why she'd walked out on her life.

There were days she was so bored and lonely that she believed she'd made a huge mistake. On those days she'd often think of Lily. She'd rehash that summer all those years ago and who did and said what to whom and where it all went wrong. A combination of bad memories and regrets made her head hurt, her stomach turn and her heart beat too fast, so she'd lie down on her hard white sofa and look out her floor-to-ceiling windows and onto the sea her dad's ashes floated in. She'd stare at a passing ship moving ever so slowly in the distance and by the time the ship was out of sight she was sound asleep.

Naps were becoming Eve's new ritual. Her new life was all about relaxation and yet she was still suffering from the stress headaches and an anxiety that she'd been suffering ever since her dad died. Her head often felt like it was going to burst and there was a hole in her heart tearing a little wider every day. She thought it might be a brain tumour or heart problem or both so she saw a doctor.

"You're in perfect health."

"Tell that to the pharmacist who practically accused me of drug-seeking behaviour because I tried to buy my fourth box of Solpadeine in a month."

"When is the last time you had an eye test?"

"Years."

"Well, then, it's time for another one."

"What about the hole in my heart?"

"You don't have a hole in your heart."

"Well, it certainly feels like I do."

"Have you ever considered that what you are experiencing is grief?"

"My symptoms are physical not emotional."

"You've lost your father, you've walked away from your business and life in New York, and you're starting again in an alien environment during a recession."

"My father is dead almost a year. My business was my life in New York and I've no intention of starting anything here. Instead I'm enjoying a well-earned if slightly ahead-of-schedule retirement."

"People can grieve for years, you know."

"I'm not people. There is something wrong with me."

After that she booked herself into a private facility to have a battery of tests performed. She was checked head to toe, inside and out and, except for the necessity to wear glasses when reading or working on a computer, she was given a clean bill of health. *Stupid doctors, what the hell do they know?*

She spent a lot of time reading or on the internet. Sometimes she'd stalk people she knew on Facebook. One day she tentatively tried to find Lily. She keyed her married and maiden names in but she wasn't there. Even if she was, Eve probably wouldn't have done anything about it. There was a moment at her father's funeral when she thought she saw Lily but as the woman drew closer it was clear she was nothing like her at all. Gar had mentioned Lily and her husband Declan once when Eve returned home first. He'd told her that Declan was a heart surgeon and they had two kids but he didn't know much else. They went to college in Cork and literally disappeared off the scene after that summer. Paul had heard that in recent years they'd moved to Killiney which was really only up the road, give or take half an hour in traffic, but they were never seen around. Eve pretended she wasn't particularly interested but she was and when she went home she googled Declan Donovan. A few articles came up regarding a particular heart surgery he was associated with. His private practice details and the hospital he was associated with came up a lot but after that there was nothing. There was a picture. He was older but the same. Eve wanted to print off the picture and burn it but that would have been childish so instead she gave the screen the fingers. *Screw you, Dicknose Donovan. I hope you die roaring.* She googled Lily but nothing came up. She wondered if Lily had ever googled her or if Lily ever thought about her the way she thought about and missed Lily. Probably not. After all, Lily had a full life with kids and a husband and Eve was pretty convinced that Lily couldn't have cared less if she lived or died.

After leaving the removal company to finish up packing her father's furniture into their van Eve returned to her apartment with her head pounding. She put two painkillers in a glass and poured water over them. She swished them around absentmindedly and she didn't notice the water spill over the top of the glass until she slipped on it and nearly broke her leg. *Close. That's all I need. To be alone in this place with a broken leg.* When the tablets had dissolved, she drank them down. She felt hot even though it wasn't a particularly warm day and she'd turned the under-floor heating off at the end of May. The gleaming white porcelain tiles were cool under her feet. She rested the glass on the counter and sat on the floor in the lotus position. She stretched her arms over her head and leaned forward, resting her face against the cool tiles and hugging herself tight. The cold tiles felt good against her cheek so she lay there for the longest time until her hips hurt and her feet were so numb she felt footless.

She was dancing around the kitchen trying to shake off a particularly intense case of pins and needles when the phone rang. It was Ben and he sounded down. He'd had a massive fight with his wife and she'd stormed off to her mother's for the night. He wanted to come over. The headache had subsided, she'd just spent an undisturbed hour lying on her kitchen floor, it was early, she had nothing she wanted to do as she wasn't much of a TV person, it was the first phone call she'd received in three days, she was so lonely and bored she could taste it and besides she missed him so much it hurt. She willingly agreed. *Yipeeeeeee, Ben's coming!*

She took a long shower and dried her short-cropped hair in five minutes. She put on her lucky underwear, sprayed herself in perfume and put on one of the only two dresses she owned. It was a black jersey wrap dress that was comfortable and easy to take off. She really, really hoped that Ben wouldn't want to discuss her business proposals but was instead looking for a little distraction, because they both needed it.

If Eve could have known how things would turn out she would have told Ben to chase after his wife. She'd have told him never to contact her again. She'd have hung up on him. But that was always Eve's problem. She spent little time thinking of consequences.

Chapter 2

Will the real Lily Donovan please stand up?

Wednesday 4th July 1990
4:30 pm

Dear Eve,

Holy Moley, I can't believe you spoke to Glen Medeiros! Laughed hard when you asked him what he wanted and he pointed to his bike. Still it's curious that he just blurted out that he likes you. I mean that takes real guts. I like that. He has been looking at you for ages so it was obvious but seriously how ballsy do you have to be just to come out with it, especially to a girl like you and you know what I mean by that. (As in Eve AKA what a bitch haha!) And yes, bringing up his perm, blouses and bad poetry wasn't necessarily the best thing you could have done but at least you didn't reduce him to tears so that's good. I'm proud of you. Speaking of which I cannot believe that you kissed Gar AGAIN what is wrong with you? And yes I promise I won't give out although I'm itching to. I'm glad you've decided to stay away from him for good and glory and please do, regardless of how many bottles of Ritz you've drunk. And when you are breaking his heart please remember he's soft and he's still into you so please DO NOT mention that you think he kisses like a goose or whatever it is you say. Just tell him that you've thought about it and as you are going to London in September and he's going to Dublin you think you'd both be better off staying as friends and leave it at that. Don't expand. OK?

So things are really improving here. I'm way happier than I was when I arrived. The restaurant is lovely. The people are really cool. It's always packed so the hours just fly by and the tips are really, really good. I work six nights a week but it's only from 6 pm to 11:30 pm and then we all have a few drinks in the back kitchen. There's a local late bar and a nightclub and they are both a great laugh. I've become really good friends with two of the staff around my age. Ellen is 19, she's just finished her first year in college in Cork and has so many stories. I know you're annoyed I'm following Declan there in the autumn but he's desperate to go to Cork and Trinity would be awful without him and I seriously don't know why you care so much. You're going to be in London and now I'll know Ellen which is fantastic. Colm is 17 – he's going into Leaving Cert next year. You would love him – he's 6 foot 4 and built like a brick shithouse. He has dark hair and brown eyes and he's so funny. Honestly, I laugh all the time. He's a Gaelic footballer (don't make bogger jokes) but he's supposed to be very good at it.

You know me, I'm an early bird so I'm doing a lot of reading in the mornings. I borrowed Ned Linney's first-year biology, physics & chemistry books. You know Ned, he's the son of the woman who lives on the hill, the posh one that my mum cleans for? Well, anyway he's a medical student (third year) and the books are OK, I'm getting through them. (I know I'm boring!) Aside from reading during the days, I meet Colm and Ellen for coffee at around 11 and then if it's a nice day we buy sandwiches and head down to the beach where we pretty much hang out all day. If it's dull or raining we go to Ellen's and listen to music and talk about this and that. And I know it's been raining up there a lot but down here it's mostly sunny which is amazing. You should see me, I'm so dark my own mother wouldn't recognise me. By the way, have you seen her? I've tried to call a few times but she's never there.

Speaking of my colour and regarding my absent father, I would never ever ask him for a single penny. It's out of the question so please never ever bring it up again. Besides, I'm making really good money here but still, Eve, I have to stay for the whole summer. I need to make as much as I can and I know it's hard but there is nothing I can do about it. I'm really sorry. I do really miss you and I know you'd love Ellen and Colm and they would love you.

Look, there's one more thing and it's a bit sensitive. I know I promised I'd ring you once a week but I have only allotted so much money for the public phone and, well, Declan is really suffering up there without me. He has begged me to phone him every day and he talks and talks and it's costing a fortune so I can't really afford to call you too. So how about we stick to our letters? You write to me every Sunday and I'll write to you every Wednesday? I know it's not ideal and please don't give out about Declan – you know what he's like and I do love him so please understand.

OK, I'd better go. I'm in work soon and Colm is coming to collect me. Oh that's another thing – please don't mention that I'm friends with Colm to Declan. I know it sounds strange and I'm sure he wouldn't mind but he's so upset I don't want him to think that there's anything going on because there's not and he's having a hard enough time with me being down here anyway so I don't want to make it worse for him. Thanks.

I miss you too and I love you and I promise we'll have many more summers together.

Lily XXXOOOXXXOOO

P.S. Be nice to Glen Medeiros and DO NOT KISS GAR AGAIN

P.P.P.S. Forgot to answer you on Young Guns. Can't believe you'd go for Emilio Estevez first and Lou Diamond Philips second, are you nuts? In fact my list is the direct opposite of yours.

1. Christian Slater (I love the way he talks)
2. Kiefer Sutherland (In brown leather, are you nuts???)

3. Lou Diamond Philips (Alright but I wouldn't be running after him)

4. Emilio Estevez (He'll always be the weirdo Kirby Keger to me)

But that's probably a good thing – at least we'll never fight over men. XXX

* * *

Lily always woke at 7 a.m. on the dot regardless of the time she fell into bed. 7 a.m. struck and *bing* – Lily Donovan was awake. She often tried to fight it but in the end her restless legs and busy brain won out and so she rose up to face the long day ahead. Lily's husband Declan said that Lily was keenly in tune with her body. He declared it to be a good thing but she disagreed. Sometimes she just wished her brain and body could disengage even for a short time. Even in sleep she was restless which meant that more often than not her husband would abandon the bed in favour of the spare room. She liked it when he was gone and enjoyed every second of having the bed to herself, stretching out, unencumbered and free.

On the morning of the 1st July 2010 Lily woke up in a bad mood. She was fighting her mind and body and stubbornly keeping her eyes tightly shut and her breathing steady and even. Declan was walking around the room. The clock hit 7:01 am and he started to whistle.

"I know you're awake," he said.

"Asleep."

"Awake." He threw one of her loose cushions at her.

"Fine."

She moved to stand and her insides ached. When he leaned over to kiss her she battled the urge to push him away. She didn't need to as instead he ruffled her hair and told her that her breath needed freshening. He continued whistling and she could hear him drying himself off in the bathroom. She swung her feet around to the side of the bed and threw her head back so that she could stare at the ceiling she had stared at the night before. *Morning, ceiling. Any new cracks? No? Good for you.*

The previous evening Declan had returned home in a good mood. He'd had no surgeries scheduled and miracle of miracles nothing unexpected came in. He had time to catch up on paperwork and with patient's charts. He was energised and frisky. She knew it the second he walked in the door. He winked at her and he was all over her while she was trying to put his dinner on the table. She didn't mind as it had been a while. He had been very stressed and tired and if he didn't initiate sex they didn't have it. That was for two reasons: 1. If he didn't initiate he didn't want it and was turned off by her advances. 2. She hadn't particularly enjoyed sex in many years. Lily figured it was an age thing. She and Declan had been together so long it was bound to be boring and predictable and when it wasn't it seemed so contrived and sometimes when he was most turned on she was uncomfortable or it was sore. The previous night had been both uncomfortable and sore. He had handcuffed her to the bed with some stupid cuffs he was given as a joke Christmas present. The headboard was high and Lily was so short and petite that the part of the headboard that separated into bars was too high for her to be handcuffed to without her dangling slightly. This put pressure on her shoulders and wrists and, because Declan seemed to have the stamina of an eighteen-year-old, she found her head banging against the board, her arms and shoulders pulling and aching and for some reason the way he had entered her felt like he was tearing her inside out. She didn't complain though because, if she had, one of two things would have happened: 1. He would have banged the wall and stormed off leaving her in cuffs until his huff wore off and God knows how long that would take. 2. He'd ignore her and keep going as though he hadn't heard her but at least when he did that he came quicker. The previous night she made all the sounds he expected to hear and, although it wasn't over as soon as she'd hoped for and her insides were red raw, she knew it would be a while before she'd have to endure that particular brand of passion again.

She got up and moved around, stretching her arms out in front of her. Her left shoulder was really aching. *Damn it. I've pulled something*. Lily didn't have time for injury so she decided to ignore it as long as possible in the hope that it would simply go away. She brushed her teeth and got into the shower and idly dreamed of drowning under it. Lily wasn't a negative person in the least – in fact, she was known to all who loved her as Little Miss Sunshine. She laughed at the notion of drowning in her own shower. *Only Lily Donovan could do such a thing*. She arrived back into the bedroom in a towel in time to greet Declan who appeared from their walk-in wardrobe fully dressed and smelling of her favourite aftershave. He was handsome when he wasn't ripping her apart.

"Hey, Lily, why don't we take a break this month? Maybe we could head to Paris or Rome? What do you think?"

"I think we're both too busy."

"You're probably right. Maybe when things slow down." He pulled her into him and kissed her. "Last night was great."

"Yeah, it was," she agreed and when she moved away he grabbed her arm to pull her back to him and she moaned a little.

"Are you alright?" he asked, filled with concern.

"I'm fine." She pulled him in close and kissed him deeply. "Everything's fine."

"Last night really was amazing," he said again, grinning from ear to ear. "I love it when you're bad."

Yeah, well, I wish to hell you were any good. Lily smiled and wished he'd just shut up and go away. She had too much to do and was far too tired and sore to pretend her husband was anything other than mediocre in bed at best and horrible at worst. *Still, there's more to marriage than sex*.

In the kitchen, Lily's nineteen-year-old son Scott and her twelve-year-old daughter Daisy sat around the table with their father, all drinking juice and waiting patiently to be served. Declan was reading the newspaper. Scott was quiet and staring into space, clearly daydreaming that he was still in bed, and Daisy was practising her piano scales on the table. Lily wasn't sure why her children were up at seven thirty on a summer's morning. Scott had just finished his college exams and Daisy was usually a late sleeper.

"What's this?" Lily asked.

"I'm looking for a job," Scott said.

"I'm going to practise for my piano recital. Are you coming, Dad?"

"When is it, Princess?" he asked.

"Tomorrow." She pointed to the large circle on the calendar.

"We'll see," he said and everyone at the table knew it was unlikely and so they moved on without a fuss.

"I'm impressed," Lily said to Scott.

"Yeah, well, the early bird," he said. "Besides, every guy in my year is looking for something so the competition is fierce."

"You'll get something," Lily said.

"In this economy, you'll be lucky," Declan said.

"Don't be so negative," she said, smiling. "Who could say no to that cute face?" She walked over to the oven and turned it on.

Declan put down his paper and rubbed his hands together. "What are you in the humour for, kids? Omelettes? A mixed grill? How about Eggs Benedict? In fact, I think I'll have that."

Scott wanted a mixed grill, Daisy wanted a plain omelette so Lily got to work boiling the water for Declan's poached eggs, cracking eggs into the frying-pan for Daisy and putting the various meats and puddings under the grill for her son. She was making the hollandaise sauce when Declan received a call from the hospital. It was an emergency case and so he didn't have time for his eggs. He left his paper unread on the table and picked up a piece of fresh fruit from the bowel.

"Damn it, I was looking forward to that," he said before kissing her on the cheek.

He ran out the door and Lily binned the hollandaise sauce before serving the mixed grill and omelette. She sat with them at the table. She drank coffee while they ate. This was her morning ritual for as long as she could remember. At some point after the kids were born Lily's meals had reduced from three down to two and sometimes down to one depending on how busy she was.

"I was thinking maybe Granddad might let me work in his garage," Scott said when halfway through his breakfast.

"Oh, I don't know," Lily said.

"Why can't I ask?" He knew the answer to the question which was why he hadn't brought it up in front of his father.

"You know how your dad feels about his father."

"It's a job and you heard him – they're hard to come by in this economy. I don't want to go to college without a cent in my pocket."

"That won't happen."

"He worked there when he was my age and I know Granddad would love to have me there. It's only down the road in the car."

"I've talked to your dad about a reasonable allowance," she said.

"I don't want to rely on you for everything. Look, I know he and Dad don't really get on but we do."

"And that's great."

"So!"

"So I'll talk to Dad."

"Really?"

"Really."

"Thanks, Mum." He got up and headed up the stairs, taking off his T-shirt as he walked.

Lily walked out of the kitchen and looked up after him with hands on hips.

"I thought you were going out looking for a job!" she said.

"Well, let's just see what Dad says about me working for Granddad first," he said, grinning.

"You've already discussed this with your grandfather, haven't you?"

He nodded to confirm her suspicion. "Thanks, Mum," he said, before running back to bed. She smiled to herself. Scott knew how to play both his parents but his mother especially. *You'd make a good politician, son. You're just about sneaky enough.*

Daisy was always a slow eater – even as a baby she'd take hours to feed – she played with her food and nibbled on tiny morsels and still she'd never get up and leave a plate with food on it. Everyone else in the family would be on dessert while she'd still be on her starter. It was just the way she was. Lily sat down with her daughter and poured herself a second cup of coffee. Daisy practiced her invisible scales and hummed a little. Lily hummed along and joined her, mimicking her daughter's hand moves until they appeared to be playing the piece with four hands. They watched one another and they were in unison.

"Perfect," Lily said.

Daisy grinned. She was very like her mother in that she demanded perfection from herself and didn't tolerate failure. Daisy wasn't as naturally intelligent as Lily had been and she wasn't as gifted, but she had brains, talent and her father's work ethic and drive and that more than compensated. Daisy continued to pick at her omelette and told Lily a story about a boy in her class that had been mean to her and a few of her friends during the year and who was now in care.

"It's awful, isn't it, Mum?"

"Terrible."

"He was horrible to Tess – he even threatened to pull down her tracksuit pants once."

"But he didn't. Did he?"

"No but she was freaked and walked around holding them up all day."

"He sounds like a nasty piece of work."

"He is but Tess says his father used to beat him badly."

"It's no excuse."

"He broke his arm once."

"He could have broken his back – it still doesn't give him to the right to go around pulling girls' tracksuits down."

"OK. Take a chill pill, Mum."

Lily laughed at her daughter. "'Chill pill' – who do you think you are, The Fresh Prince of Bel Air?"

"I don't even know who that is," Daisy said, finishing her eggs and handing up her plate to her mother who took it without question or remark.

Daisy got up and went into the dining room to play piano for real and Lily got busy cleaning the kitchen. She knew she'd been obtuse about the poor boy who had been put into care. After all, he hadn't pulled down Tess's tracksuit and clearly he had a very difficult life, but Lily was sick of people's excuses for bad behaviour. Bad things happened to people every day and it was no excuse to become selfish or twisted, violent or sinister. Lily believed in sucking it up, internalising pain and turning that frown upside down and she couldn't for the life of her work out why other people couldn't just do the same. Lily had always been that way. As a child she grew up with a woman who resented her for being born.

Lily's mother May wasn't in the slightest bit maternal. She had never wanted children. Lily was an unhappy mistake. May was twenty-two and had a good job in a bank in Dublin. She loved her job and she was good at it, having been promoted twice since she'd started three years before. She'd gone on three sun holidays with bank friends before people from Ireland really could afford sun holidays in foreign destinations. She was going to make something of herself. She was a single, hardworking fun-loving girl who one night met a Greek sailor in a bar in Dublin. He was on one month's leave and they spent every evening and her weekends off together for his entire stay. She didn't know she was pregnant until two months after he'd left. Although he'd promised to write he didn't and her only means of tracking him down was through his ship's captain. She didn't have the option to abort and, coming from an uptight and upright Catholic family, she was disowned. He chose to ignore his duty and although she ended up corresponding with his mother who sent money every now and again in exchange for photos and letters on Lily's development, Lily's father never did make any sincere effort to know his daughter despite going through the motions once in a blue moon. When the pregnancy was revealed, Lily's mother was fired from her dream job. Her parents weren't going to let her back into their house so she ended up on welfare back in the small town she'd come from. The exotic life she had lived for such a short time was over and she couldn't seem to look at her daughter's pretty face and see past that fact.

Lily had tried to please her mother from the time she could walk but nothing really did the trick. She could say "Look, Mummy, look!" until the cows came home and her mother wouldn't even bother to pretend she was interested.

"Go away, I'm busy."

"But, Mummy!"

"Don't make me tell you twice."

The first time Lily remembered her mother being genuinely happy or impressed was when she won an Irish dancing contest. Her mother stood up and clapped and afterwards she heard her tell one of the other women that Lily was her daughter. Finally, after five years of doing everything bar turning herself inside out to please her mother, she had succeeded and when that smile lighted up her mother's face Lily was hooked. After that she did everything she could to please her dismissive parent. Everything she did she did with careful execution and aplomb, failure was not an option, and because she was such a smart little thing good grades came easily, giving her the precious time needed to notch up other achievements, all in a bid to please a woman that really didn't care that much. Lily's successes became boring and, worse, reminded her mother of the successful life she could have led instead of the stigmatised, part-time, low-paid single parent she had inadvertently become. She did try to be a good mother. Lily was always presented beautifully. She ate well and no matter how little money her mother had hidden in the shoebox in her wardrobe, Lily always got to participate in everything she wanted to do. May wanted the world for her – she just couldn't disguise her disappointment and pain that she had lost her own world to Lily. She never told Lily that she'd tried to throw herself down a flight of stairs when she was four months gone or that she'd drunk a bottle of brandy in a hot bath at six months. Every now and then she'd mutter that Lily was most definitely a fighter, that's for sure, and she'd often mention her regret that she hadn't given Lily up for adoption and the only reason she didn't was because she'd have to move into a convent for the duration of her pregnancy and she'd heard the rumours about the horrors those girls went through.

"It would have only been a few months, I could have taken it, and don't think you wouldn't have been better off either because you would have," she said once when she was drunk and distraught that yet another man had simply walked away from her. "One day when you were older you'd walk up to my door and thank me and I'd have welcomed you and we'd talk about our perfect lives before saying goodbye."

Lily scrubbed the counter until it gleamed. She checked it by leaning her head to the side in an attempt to catch a glimpse of a hidden mark on the marble under the sunlight steaming in from the big window that opened onto her beautifully kept garden. It was unblemished and so she could move on to stripping the beds. It was the day before she returned to work for a week – she worked one week on and one week off – and so it was one of her busiest days, ensuring the house was spotless and all the following week's dinners were made and frozen. Declan didn't like to eat past seven thirty in the evening and she didn't get in until just after eight and, to be fair to him, she had always insisted on cooking from scratch and depending on his taste that evening he could have to wait up until ten for his dinner. That just wouldn't work. In her head she made a list of ingredients necessary to feed her family for the week ahead. As a nurse she worked days, 7:30 am to 7:30 pm, so it was important to ensure her house ran with military precision and over the years she had managed to make it all work quite beautifully. Of course it was hard, but Lily learned at an early age that nothing that was worthwhile was easy.

In the past, when the kids were younger, she and Declan had often rowed over her job. When he finally passed all his exams and went into residency in the Regional Hospital in Cork, he approached her to give up her job working down the road in the Bons Secours. She had been supporting the family up to that point and it hadn't helped that Declan had hated Cork and their time there was extended because he was forced to repeat two years of university. The first year he failed he blamed his young son's incessant crying and Lily's inability to soothe him. He was awake all night and studying all day and it was all too much. She tried her best to help but it just made him angrier.

"How can you help?" he'd roared one night when he was studying for his first-year finals; Scott was only six weeks old and suffering from colic. She tried everything to soothe the child but he just cried and cried and when Declan was so exhausted and incapable of thinking straight she tried to talk him into moving out of their little one-bedroom flat for the duration of the exams.

"Where the hell do you want me to go?" he shouted.

"Anywhere," she said quietly.

"Are you trying to chase me out of my own home?"

"No," she said, "of course not. I just want you to be able to study. Couldn't you stay with one of the lads in your lectures?"

He was exhausted, he was unreasonable and paranoid.

"So the baby's in and I'm out, is that it?" he said, shaking his head from side to side and gritting his teeth.

She decided to change tack. "I'll do questions with you," she offered in a bid to curb his paranoia before it manifested itself as unbridled rage.

"Great," he said. "Well, if there's a question on how to make beds I'll let you know."

"I read a lot of the books on your course last summer," she said, knowing that it would piss him off, but after his comments belittling her nursing training she didn't much care. He was the one who had talked her out of medicine and into nursing for the sake of their family life. *Asshole*. The baby started to cry just as he turned to say something that was no doubt mean and vicious. He stopped in his tracks and listened with his hand to his ear.

"Why don't you focus on settling that crying child. Maybe you could read some books on that because, let's face it, motherhood certainly isn't coming naturally, now is it?" he said, content that he couldn't have said anything that would wound her more.

"Nice! You're a prick, you know that?" she said and in her head she warned herself not to cry.

"I've got exams in a week, Lil! I can't remember my own name never mind what the hell the parietal pleura is!" he said, shouting and throwing his book at the wall.

"Any chance you'd forget where we lived for a few days?" she'd said.

That was the first time he grabbed her by the hair and pushed her against the wall. He held her tightly for maybe a minute or two while he breathed in and out slowly and steadily in a desperate bid to calm himself down. When he let her go she turned slowly to face him, terrified of what was coming next, but he just looked at her strangely and sadly.

"You're destroying me," he said and he walked out the door.

Declan Donovan always did have a dramatic side to his personality. He probably would have made a good actor; he certainly could play a convincing villain. Lily let the baby cry, she poured a cup of coffee and sat at her kitchen table staring at the cup, afraid to pick it up because as soon as the fear and shock began to dissipate her hands trembled, her heart tightened in her chest and her eyes threatened to burn holes into her face. After a few minutes of silence and grief, she clasped her hands together and said to the wall: "The parietal pleura is the name given to the cavity that surrounds the lungs, Dicknose." It took a while for her heart rate to settle and for the trembling to stop but she didn't cry. Instead she smiled and for two reasons: 1. She knew what the parietal pleura was and 2. Her only real friend Eve had nicknamed Declan 'Dicknose Donovan' the first time they met him and that morning and for the first time Lily realised her ex-best friend was right. *You do have a dick of a nose.*

He passed second year, third year he failed again. He didn't have a child to blame so instead he blamed his responsibilities as a young father and husband. Lily didn't entertain him much that time. Having lived with him for three years, she had learned to pick her battles. She was working her nursing shifts and bringing up a two-year-old she didn't have time for his bullshit and so she let him roar and scream and act the fool and when he later apologised and tried to make it up to her with dinner and flowers she accepted with good humour and grace because what else could she do. Declan wouldn't accept her help. He wasn't a good student but when the drudgery of book-learning was behind him, he was quite brilliant from the practical point of view so after that third year he sailed through. His anger and frustration dissipated and life got better even though with every success he achieved he couldn't help but make Lily feel smaller.

"What the hell do you need to stay nursing for?"

"Because I like it and I'm good at it."

"Oh for God's sake, Lily, it's embarrassing."

"Embarrassing?"

"You know what I mean," he said.

"No, Declan, I really don't."

"I'm a heart surgeon for God's sake."

"Congratulations."

"Don't try to be smart, Lily, you know it's a turn-off."

"Oh good, stay turned off for both our sakes."

When she was pregnant with Daisy he was outraged that she wouldn't even consider giving up her job following maternity leave.

"Look how easy it is for you to take care of the family when you're out of work," he'd pointed out.

"If I'd wanted an easy life I'd have never married you, my darling," she'd joked in an attempt to get him off her back.

"You've always thought you were funnier than you actually are."

"Why are you such an asshole, Declan?"

"Don't push me, Lily."

"*Or what?*"

Declan had never pushed her into a wall after that day when Scott was only six weeks old but every now and then he was slightly rougher than he should have been. He'd push her out of his way as opposed to asking her to move. He'd hold her tiny arm and squeeze it so tightly she thought it might snap. He once pulled her back into a room by her hair but after that he did instantly apologise. Lily wasn't a domestic-abuse victim – she just lived with a man who teetered on the edge of controlling a temper that rarely showed its face but when it did it was a safe bet to evacuate so that's what she did. After over twenty years together, she knew which buttons to push and which ones were off limits. Lily knew the line and she walked it diligently.

She ripped the sheets off their bed and threw them into the clothes hamper. Using a stool, she pulled out the clean duvet set from the top of the hot press. She started to cover the duvet but her shoulder hurt and so she decided she deserved a break and a hot bath might help with the pain. She ran it and lay there disappearing under the bubbles and enjoying the water jets. There were still beds to be stripped and made and shopping to be got and an entire week's menu to be cooked but she didn't care. She was enjoying a short half an hour before she got back to work and her kids got back up and began making demands. Lily was looking forward to going back to work because a week at home was nice but long. She preferred her time on the ward where she was truly needed, people were mostly grateful and time passed in the blink of an eye. She loved helping people, no matter who was put in front of her or what was wrong with them. Lily was capable and understanding and fun and she never failed to make someone better, happier and more hopeful, no matter how scared or traumatised they were.

Lily Donovan was an excellent nurse. Her dream of becoming a doctor changed as soon as she said yes to marrying Declan and, despite the fact that she had brains to burn and could have got through the course in her sleep, Lily realised early on that nursing was a calling and it suited her caring, outgoing, perfectionist, controlling, kind, giving personality perfectly. It occurred to her that the only reason she was doing medicine was to be with Declan and because kids with her testing scores were encouraged in that direction. Before she got all As in her Intercert exams aged fourteen, she'd wanted to be a beautician and if she was honest it was still something she was interested in. She was a slave to beauty magazines, she loved hair and make-up, and if she had her time again that's what she would have gone into – beauty for fashion shoots and high-end fashion. Despite her unfulfilled ambitions, she was happy to leave the cutting to a man like her husband who had a way with a knife but the bedside manner of brick. He might save a life but her care would make those early days worth living and she was proud of that. Besides, her mother had warned her from an early age that as soon as she turned eighteen she was on her own. University cost money and medicine was a long course. They were both abandoned financially by their parents. If she was a nurse her salary would kick in quicker and anyway children were her real dream and doing medicine would mean she'd have to wait longer than she cared to. It made perfect sense.

Lily had always yearned to be part of a family. When she was five she asked her mother if she would think about giving her a brother or sister.

"I'd rather be hit by a bus," her mother said and that was the end of that conversation.

Lily had met her father a few times over the years. He visited her twice in Ireland and for no more than a few hours despite being in the country for over a week at a time. She spent a month in Greece the summer she was sixteen, staying with her grandmother who had very little English, and her father's new wife and their three children. Her father had left the navy and was a fisherman. He disappeared for days on end and when he returned they spoke very little. It was a long month and she was happy to leave and never return. She used to envy Eve with a mother and father who loved each other and most importantly who wanted and loved Eve. She envied her with a brother as lovely, sweet, funny and cool as Clooney. She felt bad when Eve's mother got sick because for a while she worried that it could be as a result of her jealousy. *How come Eve gets to have a brilliant mum and dad who love her and a brilliant brother. Why not me?* Envy was a mortal sin and she prayed that God would save Mrs Hayes and at the same time save herself from hell.

Lily's mother spent a lot of time talking about hell. Everything she did, whether it was wash dishes or stub her toe, she offered it up as penance for her sins. Lily had grown up in a very holy house. Her mother had fallen from grace by having her and she spent Lily's childhood trying to make up for her terrible sin. She often told Lily that she had gone to three priests before she could find one that would baptise her. Lily never did find out if her mother was just lying to make her feel bad or not because no one else seemed to have difficulty baptising their illegitimate children.

"But I persisted to save your soul and what thanks do I get for it?" she'd ask.

Lily didn't know what her mother wanted her to say.

She wasn't sure her mother was a particularly good example of a good person but she was her mother and she loved her despite her failings and of course there were kindnesses too. May wasn't all bad. She just didn't know how to be a mother, that's all. She wanted the best for Lily and she didn't want her making the same mistakes as she had. She tried to be a good Catholic but she was good at bending the rules to suit her particular needs at the time. When Lily turned fifteen she used Lily's extremely painful and sickening periods as an excuse to talk the local GP into putting her on the pill. She warned Lily against having sex, telling her it was a sin from which her soul might never recover, but at the same time she slept soundly knowing that if Lily did decide to engage in premarital sex she would be doing so to the detriment of her afterlife as opposed to her future on earth. She was also as proud as she was jealous and occasionally, when Lily said something smart or funny that made her laugh, she'd hug her tight. "Thank you, sunshine," she'd say. Lily might not have had a father who loved her, a mother who was grateful for her or a brother to mess with her but she had that. *Thank you, sunshine.*

Lily lost track of time and it was nearly ten thirty when she scrambled out of the bath. She tied up her hair, put on a pair of old leggings and a threadbare Alley McBeal T-Shirt, an old house-coat and some fluffy slippers. She made up her marital bed and then proceeded down the corridor to see whose bed she could strip. Scott was passed out cold so she made her way into Daisy's room. She began stripping the bedclothes and by the time she was finished in there Scott was up and although zombie-like he was moving about. She got through his room quickly, without looking around too much for fear she'd find something she didn't like. Once the rooms were done she turned on the vacuum cleaner and ran around vacuuming with the skill, speed and dexterity of an Olympian. When she was finished hovering, she dusted and then she started on the toilets. By the time the toilets were done it was one o'clock and time to feed the kids lunch. Scott's friend Josh had arrived sometime between her dusting the banisters and scrubbing a toilet. She kept lunch simple, making ham and cheese paninis with a little home-made coleslaw and relish. Daisy was still practising and wanted hers by the piano. Scott and Josh were in the sitting room on PlayStation which suited Lily fine.

"Thanks, Lily," Josh said, grinning widely.

Lily was sorry she hadn't been stricter about kids calling her Mrs Donovan when they were younger.

"You're welcome, Josh," she said and quickly left.

She started making a list and checked the store cupboard for the ingredients she'd need to do a week's menu. Josh's inane grin reminded her that she needed basil since Scott had eaten her entire plant for a bet when they were both out of their minds on weed although they both vehemently denied it.

"Crack is whack, Lily," Josh had said.

"We're not talking about crack though, are we, Josh? We're talking about weed."

"Weed is . . ." He looked at her grinning son who was sitting on the counter and still munching on the basil plant.

"Freed . . ." Scott said.

". . . dom!" Josh finished and they both burst out laughing.

She sent them to Scott's room and turned to her husband who shrugged his shoulders. "They're just letting some steam off," he said. "We all did it."

"Yes, Declan, but we had the decency to do it behind our parents' backs. We can't be seen to support this type of behaviour and besides I *don't* support it and neither should you. There are plenty of studies that suggest cannabis and hash are not as benign as we'd like to think they are."

Declan laughed. "Oh look at the nurse who knows everything!" And on that note the conversation was over.

Later she went up to Scott's room to discuss the implications of smoking weed under his parents' roof but before she could launch into her prepared speech Josh told her she was a prize-winning MILF, her son feigned puking and then Josh hugged her and smelt her hair. She left, confused, and feeling slightly violated. She later discovered that MILF meant Mom I'd Like to Fuck. And since then Lily found it hard to look little Josh, whose nappy she'd changed on more than one occasion, straight in the face.

The list was made and Lily was heading up the stairs to change into something suitable to wear outdoors when the doorbell rang. She answered and it was Rachel from across the road. Rachel's face was frozen and she had a wild look in her eyes.

"Rachel?"

Rachel seemed to find her voice but instead of verbalising a problem she screamed straight into Lily's face without taking a break.

"What's wrong?"

She screamed louder.

"Rachel, talk to me!"

She screamed ever louder.

Lily shook her. "*Rachel!*"

Her scream was now so high-pitched Lily could imagine random dogs around the country perking up their ears and Forest Gumping their way towards their cul de sac.

Rachel turned, pointed, and ran, still screaming, so Lily followed her to her house and there she found Nancy, Rachel's five-year-old daughter lying on the patio in the back yard with an arrow sticking straight out of her eye. Rachel's scream seemed to increase by another full decibel, threatening to pierce all ears present.

"Rachel. Shut up. Do you hear me? Shut your mouth." Lily made a closing gesture with her hand.

Rachel looked at Lily's hand closing in front of her face. She stopped shouting. Instead she pointed at the ground and to her daughter who was starting to move a little.

"Well done. Now stay like that." Lily put her fingers to her lips and Rachel nodded. Lily turned to Nancy. "Hi, Nancy."

"Hi, Lily, I think I have something in my eye," the child said before raising her hand to try to pull the arrow out.

Lily caught Nancy's hands in time to save her from herself but not in time to save Rachel from passing out cold and hitting her head on the oversized pottery plant pot.

"Oh, fudge cake!" Lily exclaimed. "OK, Nancy, look at Lily."

She didn't know how far the arrow had gone inside the child's head or if it had penetrated her brain. Nancy was talking and alert so that was positive. She wrestled with Lily, trying to free her hands so that she could take the arrow out.

"You can't do that, baby. Look at Lily. You cannot pull out the arrow. If you do you will blind yourself and you don't want to do that. OK?"

Nancy nodded.

"Are you with me, Nancy?"

"Yes."

"Do you feel pain?"

"No."

"Good girl, now I need to look at your mother and then I'm going to call an ambulance but I need you to stay lying down exactly as you are. OK?"

"OK."

"You must not touch the arrow. OK?"

"OK."

"Good girl, you are the best and bravest girl. Lily is here and I'm not leaving you. OK?"

"OK."

Lily got up and went over to Rachel who was still out cold. Still watching Nancy, she placed her hand on Rachel's forehead and called to her. Her airway wasn't constricted but the back of her head was bleeding profusely. Rachel woke up. Lily kept her hand on her forehead and gently held her down.

"Rachel. Don't move. You've hit your head. Your breathing and colour is good. Do you feel any numbness?"

"No."

"Good. I want you to stay where you are just in case, so don't move. OK."

"OK." Rachel grabbed Lily's hand. "Nancy?"

"She'll be fine. Stay there."

Lily ran to the house and grabbed the phone and a clean sheet out of the dryer. She ran back outside. Both her patients were immobile. She phoned an ambulance and then wrapped the sheet tightly around Rachel's head. Rachel looked like a whacked-out sheik when the ambulance arrived eight minutes later but it was the best that Lily could do in difficult circumstances. The two paramedics loaded Nancy and Rachel on board but when it looked like Lily wasn't getting into the bus Nancy started to scream. She wanted her there. She reached out her hand and begged her.

"Please Lily, please Lily, please, don't leave me!"

Lily looked down at her twigs for legs in greyish black leggings, her threadbare Ally McBeal T-Shirt, horrible housecoat and her fluffy slippers.

"Fudge cake," she said, shaking her head from side to side. She couldn't say no to a begging child with a ruddy arrow in her eye so she jumped aboard with no phone and a full shop to do, not to mention an entire week's worth of meals to cook.

Fudge cake was something Lily said instead of the word *fuck* which she found quite aggressive and unnecessary. She sometimes said *fudging*. Every now and again she told someone that they could shine up their buttons with brasso, emphasising the words *shine* and *buttons* and *brasso* in such a way that the statement became quite menacing. She also liked *bugger* or *bugger-balls* and sometimes she added a side of fries. Lily was not one for cursing, it just wasn't her style.

In the ambulance Rachel was clearly concussed. She was

confused and babbling about leaving the keys in the car and asking Lily if she'd put the shopping away.

"Did I put the shopping away?"

"Yes, you put it away."

"Good, it's important to put the shopping away because Nero will eat everything in sight. Did you put the shopping away?"

"Ah ha. It's all in the presses."

"Good because there's a lot of frozen food there. Did you put the shopping away?" she asked the paramedic.

"Yip. It's all away, chicken."

"Good. The last time Nero ate two M&S goat's-cheese tarts, a half a packet of chocolate digestives and a roast duck. For days afterwards his farts would knock you sideways. Jim threw up. Did I put the shopping away?"

"All put away."

When the paramedics had finished setting Nancy up, Lily held her hand and told the scared, sleepy little girl a story about a princess and a dragon and she was halfway through the story when Nancy asked where her eight-year-old brother Dylan was.

"I don't know, sweetheart? He wasn't home."

"Yes, he was. He's hiding down the garden."

"Why would he do that?"

"Because he hit me in the eye with a bow and arrow."

"Bugger-balls and a side of flaming fries!"

Rachel was too busy throwing up to react. They got to the hospital and as Nancy was taken one way and Rachel the other Lily went up on the lift to the third floor and found Marion in the corridor wheeling the medicine trolley.

"What are you doing here? Thought you weren't in till tomorrow?" she said, meanwhile taking in Lily's strange attire.

"I'm not. There's been an accident in the neighbour's place. A little girl and her mother. I need to use the phone."

"I hope they're OK," Marion said and she pottered away down the hall.

Lily phoned the house. No answer so she phoned Scott's mobile phone which rang out the first two times but on the third he picked up.

"God, Mum. *What?* "

"Don't you dare *what* me and pick up your fudging phone when I call you! There's been an accident in Rachel's next door and I need you to go across the road and hike over the wall into the back garden."

"*What?*"

"I'm in the hospital with Rachel and Nancy. Dylan is hiding somewhere in the back garden."

"So what am I supposed to do?"

"Find him, the back door is on the latch, bring him through the house or unlock the side gate and go out that way – just tell him his mother and sister will be fine and bring him to our place."

"OK. But, Mum, *are* they OK?"

"Well, Rachel has a concussion and Nancy has an arrow in her eye."

"Wow!"

"Yeah, wow. I have to go."

"And, Mum?"

"What?"

"What's happening about dinner?"

"Don't annoy me, Scott."

Lily sat with Rachel while Nancy was in surgery. Rachel received three staples to the back of her head. She was being observed for a brain injury but she was feeling a good deal better.

"Thank you so much, Lily. I'm so sorry I lost it."

"It's no problem, Rachel."

She started to cry. "Do you think she'll lose the eye?"

"I don't know," Lily said honestly. Rachel looked like she was about to cry harder so in a bid to lighten the moment, she added, "But what's an eye between friends?"

Rachel looked at her strangely. She didn't really get Lily's sense of humour.

"Oh, God Almighty! Dylan!"

"It's OK – he's in my house with Scott and Daisy."

"He didn't mean it."

"I know."

"I'm going to kill Jim. I told him not to buy a bow and arrow for an eight-year-old. He might as well have brought a gun into the house. I swear to God I'm going to get that bow and arrow and shove it so far up his arse he –"

The doctor treating her came in. Lily knew his face but couldn't put a name to it. He was just some kid out of college. He asked Rachel if it would be all right to examine her and Lily used it as an excuse to check up on Nancy. She looked at the wall clock and registered that it was after four. She hadn't noticed time passing and she had so much to do. She walked into her husband's office and was leaving a message on his notepad about dinner when he walked in.

"What the hell are you doing here dressed like that?"

"Well, that's a nice greeting!"

"You're wearing a pair of bunnies on your feet, that T-shirt is a disgrace and we both know you're far to skinny to wear leggings anywhere outside the house. In fact, I'd prefer if you didn't wear them *in* the house but I suppose that's an argument I lost years ago."

"You know, Declan, sometimes I think you belong in a nuthouse. Did you consider for a second why I *might* be here dressed like this?"

Clearly it hadn't occurred to him at all. His colour changed. He didn't say a word. He just waited for Lily to spit it out. She thought about letting him suffer for a moment but decided it was too cruel. As soon as he realised it was a neighbour and her child that had brought Lily to the hospital in that state he lost interest. She tried to talk to him about Nancy's eye but he reminded her he was a heart not an eye man.

"You're more dick than heart surely, darling," she said, smiling at him benignly.

"Not in the humour for your attempts at funny."

Then he looked at his watch and said he hoped to hell she'd managed to get to the shops. He'd been looking forward to chicken cacciatore all day.

"You are joking."

"I never joke about dinner," he said.

"Declan."

"What?"

"Why don't you go and *shine* up your *buttons* with *brasso?*"

"Will do as soon as you go home and make my dinner," he said.

She stood there, shaking her head.

"Seven thirty sharp," he said.

He fixed his tie and eyed her before sitting down at his desk. He shook his head slowly, showing his silent disapproval. He opened a file and it was Lily's cue to leave.

She walked out simmering because she had the misfortune of marrying an ignorant pig. She was so annoyed and too busy seeing red as opposed to the person approaching her. She walked straight into Adam Wallace. He was the orthopaedic surgeon that worked on Lily's ward. He held her out in front of him and beamed at her

"Well, Lily, you never fail to dazzle me."

"Haha."

"What's your story?"

She told him about Rachel and Nancy and, unlike her husband, he seemed concerned.

"I was going to get a coffee, join me," he said.

It was at that point she realised she was light-headed from lack of food so she agreed. He drank his coffee and she tucked into a croissant and they talked about how lucky Nancy was and he complimented her on her quick thinking which embarrassed her because she'd done nothing really. They talked for a while more and then she had to admit that time was ticking by and she needed to check on Rachel before she went to the supermarket. Then she remembered she was still wearing the stupid bunny slippers, the threadbare Ally McBeal T-Shirt and the unflattering leggings.

"I can't go to the supermarket like this."

"You look great."

"That's a very kind lie."

He laughed and shook his head. "There are a million women who would kill to look like you do."

"Just a million? I must be losing my touch."

She walked away smiling. Kind, sweet, sad Adam always managed to cheer Lily up.

Nancy still wasn't out of surgery but Jim was with Rachel. It was clear he'd just had the face chewed off him. He looked contrite and terrified. Lily felt sorry for him. She hugged him and ignored Rachel's disapproving look.

Lily said she had to go home and make dinner and of course Dylan was in the pot and if they wanted her to keep him that night she'd be more than happy to. She asked Jim to call her as soon as Nancy came out of surgery and he promised he would. She ran around Tesco like a hare. Luckily she didn't meet anyone she knew and, apart from the odd raised eyebrow here and there, no one really seemed to notice her ridiculous garb.

It was after six when she made it home and chicken cacciatore takes between forty and fifty-five minutes to cook, never mind prepare, so she was hopeful that her inconsiderate, ignorant pig of a husband would be late. Dylan started crying when he saw Lily so she hugged him tight and took him into the kitchen and told him about the cool staples in his mother's head.

"Oh," he said with a trembling lip, "she won't like that."

"Are you kidding me? How many people do you know with staples in their head?"

"None," he said.

"Exactly," she said, "that's what makes it cool."

He was eight and eight-year-olds aren't as gullible as they were when Lily was his age. He wasn't buying her cool staples line.

"OK, so guess who's in trouble?" she said.

"Me," he said, about to cry.

"Nope," she said, shaking her head.

"Who then?"

"Your dad."

"Why?"

"Because he bought the bow and arrow."

"Oh. Is he in big trouble?" His tone suggested he was hopeful the answer would be positive.

"Oh yes."

"Thanks, Lily," he said with a grin that suggested he had cheered up considerably and he ran out of the kitchen to join Daisy and her friend Tess in the sitting room watching TV.

Lily prepared her chicken cacciatore in record time. When it was in the oven she showered and changed for dinner. Declan liked her to change for dinner – he was old-fashioned that way. The kids were due to eat at six so by six forty-five they were starving. The kids always ate half an hour to an hour before their father and mostly it was different menus but that night due to time constrictions they were all eating the same thing.

"Ah, I hate chicken cacciatore!" Daisy grumbled as loudly as her stomach. She plonked herself down at the table.

Tess sat in beside her and opposite Scott and Dylan who were already eating.

"You do not hate it," said Lily. "You loved it as a baby."

"Seriously, Mum. I'm twelve not a brain donor."

"Yeah, well, shove it down your neck or starve."

Scott wolfed it down in two minutes, burped, said thanks and got up to go out.

"Where are you going?" Lily asked.

"Do you really want to know?"

"I do now."

"It involves nudity," he said, grinning.

"Get out," she said and when he'd gone she allowed herself a smile.

Dylan loved Lily's chicken cacciatore. "Yum," he kept saying. "I wish you lived at our house."

I wish I lived there too, Lily thought to herself.

Tess was a huge fan of Lily's cooking too. She often came for dinner because her mother worked late and her father had been off the scene for years. Lily took extra special care of her and always included Tess in everything the family did, so much so that even Daisy noticed and commented upon it.

"Why is Tess coming to France with us?" she'd asked the first year they took Tess away with them.

"Don't you want her there?" Lily asked.

"Of course I do but why is she coming?"

"Because she's your friend."

"Cool, can Josh, Cedric and Ethan come?" Scott said.

"No."

"OK, just Josh."

"No."

"Why not? How come Tess gets to come?"

"Because I said so."

"So unfair," he said and walked out, slamming the door, and it was true it was unfair but life was unfair and nobody understood that better than Lily.

It was nice to have some grateful children in the house.

"Thanks so much, Lily. It was really lovely," Tess said.

"You're welcome, sweetheart. How about you, Daisy?"

"I'm shoving it down, amn't I?"

"Yes, my angel, you are," Lily said and Tess and Dylan laughed.

Declan arrived home at seven thirty. He was tired and grumpy because he was delayed. He sat at the dinner table and she served them both their meals.

"I only have an hour. I have to go back to the hospital to check on a patient."

"Fine."

"You look nice," he said.

"Thank you." *Eat me.*

"Is that new?"

"No." *Yes.*

"I don't remember seeing it before."

"Really? Maybe you're suffering from early onset dementia." *Fingers crossed.*

He smiled. "Oh, you're a riot today."

He ate and left.

Lily cleaned up and put the dishes in the dishwasher. *What a knob. It's not like this dress is coming out of your bank account, you tight bastard.*

Lily and Declan had never shared a bank account, well, except when she was the sole earner. Lodged into Lily's bank account were her nurse's wages and the Children's Allowance and lodged into Declan's bank account was the salary of a top heart surgeon. He paid for the mortgage and utility bills and she paid for the groceries, her needs and those of the children. Lily's kids had expensive taste and for them she always tried to buy nothing but the best. When it came to shopping for herself, Lily bought in second-hand designer stores and bought material. She may not have been a designer but she was handy with a sewing machine. The black dress was a recent purchase in an actual high-street shop. It was going out of business and, at 70% off, priced to sell. She treated herself after a particularly brutal day and she wasn't going to let her husband, who had all his suits custom-made by Louis Copeland, berate her for spending money on herself that she should be spending on the kids.

"Well, don't come crying to me when Scott wants new trainers," he would say on such occasions.

"God no, of course not, after all you're only his father."

"I've told you before, Lily, if you want to live off me give up your job."

The conversation would descend into a row about the two times in twenty years his dinner was late to the table or why it was important for her to continue working which would then lead into an uncomfortable conversation about her need to be all things to all people and why she felt she had to flirt her way through life. This conversation would invariably end with him insulting her.

"I mean, a woman of your age. It's pathetic. The younger girls must laugh at you!" or "You're not half as cute as you act, Lily."

They'd both shout and slam doors. He'd leave and cool off with his pals over a game of golf or bridge. She'd take a bath and talk herself out of crying. The truth was, she did try to be all things to all people. *So what? Why is that a bad thing? Why can't you just love me and let me be?*

When Lily got married she was barely nineteen years old and she cooked a little but not the way she felt a wife should. Of course she breezed through nursing school and so, although she attended class that first year, she never had to open a book and instead of studying she took cooking lessons and when her teacher told her she had a flair for it she took more and more lessons until she could compete with any gourmet cook. She ran her kitchen like a hotel. In part because her husband was a demanding man and in part because she set herself up for high expectations early in their marriage and, however unachievable, being the perfect wife and mother was still her goal.

Of course she also attempted to excel as nurse and neighbour.

Nursing was easy. People were sick and sad and she was the difference between them feeling better or worse. The results were there to be seen. She had to work harder at her neighbouring skills. She was always the one to turn to and the one that could always be relied upon to help anyone with anything whether it was snaking out a drain, pinning up a hem or performing CPR. But she also had a way of getting some of her female neighbours' backs up. The term Little Miss Sunshine wasn't always said as a compliment. Lily had a quick wit, she was game for a laugh, and she always got on easily with men and they all liked her, some a little too much. Petite, beautiful, delicate, doll-faced, 5 foot 3 Lily, with her shiny dark bobbed brown hair, brown eyes, soft lips and silky cappuccino-coloured skin thanks to her Greek absent father, was always the belle of the ball. Every man in the room followed her with their eyes when she moved apologetically past them, when she laughed they all eagerly laughed with her, when she spoke they listened intently while taking her in and fantasising about what they would do to her if she'd only let them. The women on the road noticed it, her husband noticed it, her fellow nurses noticed, any woman she had ever tried to make a real connection with after Eve noticed it. The only one who didn't seem to notice was Lily. When she looked in the mirror she saw a thirty-eight-year-old woman who often shopped in the children's department. She had twigs for legs, tiny breasts, and big eyes and even though she'd worked for twenty years and borne two children, the gasman once arrived at her door and asked her if her mummy was home. *Hardly sexy, is it?* What Lily perceived as friendly banter, her husband and the rest of the world perceived as flirting. This enraged him and estranged the women on the road but it was not a conscious decision. She meant nothing by it; it was just part of who she was and how she related to people. Sometimes, when her husband disapproved of her most, she'd see herself through his eyes and she'd hate herself. In a second she'd be reduced from his wife and the mother of his children to a flighty, insignificant, giddy, annoying, silly woman who not only looked like a child but acted like one too. She'd feel less than a woman, just like she used to feel less than a daughter, tragic and doomed. Then she'd get a grip and realise her mother was a bitch and she married a prick and that she'd just have to suck it up and soldier on. Lily did love her husband. He was the only man who really needed and wanted her.

There were moments of great tenderness between them and, when he found her funny and he often did despite his comments to the contrary, his laughter lifted her to a place where her spirit could soar.

Yes, Lily was the go-to person in times of trouble but the last person on the list when it came to coffee mornings or afternoon gossips. Lily wasn't good at gossip, she wasn't trusted around the ladies' men and anyway who would they talk about if she was there? Lily was a popular acquaintance amongst her work colleagues but she had no real friends. As hard as she worked to please and as much as she pretended to be in control, deep down she was still an outsider in her own life and the niggling voice that constantly whispered to her, telling her she was an unlovable loser, grew a little louder with each year that passed.

Lily was halfway through cooking food for the week ahead when the phone rang. It was Jim. Nancy was out of surgery, they were hopeful that they could save the eye, and there was no brain damage.

"Oh Jim, I'm so pleased!"

"If it wasn't for you, Lily, I don't know what I'd do."

"Oh, don't be silly. Of course I'd be there."

"Honestly, Lily, I'm so grateful. If there was something, anything I can do?"

"I'm just glad she's OK."

He sounded like he'd been crying. He was vulnerable and tired.

"Maybe a drink sometime? You and me?" he said.

Is he coming on to me? No. Don't be stupid, Lily. Of course he's not.

"I don't think Declan would be too happy with that."

"So don't tell him."

Oh no. This is uncomfortable.

"And Rachel, how is she?"

"Giving out."

"She'll get over it."

"Yeah, maybe when I'm dead and buried and she's finished dancing on my grave," he said and Lily laughed.

"Seriously, I know Declan's hard work too so if you ever want to have a drink?" he said.

Oh my God. Lily didn't respond. She knew her husband could appear aloof around the neighbours and sometimes when he drank he got a little narky with her, especially if the other men in the room were too complimentary. He liked to remind them he was boss and that she was his wife. She made light of it and, when necessary to save face, she was smart and funny enough to diffuse him and show them that she was a match for him, without darkening the mood or causing a fuss. Jim was their first neighbour ever to comment on it and it stung.

"Dylan's fine," she said and looked at her watch. "He's exhausted so I'll put him to bed if that's alright."

"No, that's fine, thanks. What time should I pick him up?"

"Well, I'll be gone by seven but Declan will be here until eight and Scott and Daisy will be here too, so whenever suits you."

"Thanks."

"You're welcome."

"Lily?"

"Yes."

Silence followed and she thought she heard him inhale and sniffle.

"Thanks again."

"OK."

She hung up and went back to cooking a shepherd's pie, a lasagne, a lamb stew and a large pot of tomato and basil soup. It was after midnight when she stopped. She covered the dishes in cellophane and sat them on top of the counter. She fell asleep on the sofa while waiting for them to get cool enough to separate into single dinners and freeze. She woke after two in the morning with a crick in her neck. She dished out the meals into the plastic Tupperware tubs that had Declan, Scott and Daisy's names written on them and popped them into the freezer, stacking them so that they were easy to read. She fell into bed and was grateful that her husband was sound asleep. Her shoulder still ached but at least her crotch had cooled down. She heard Scott come in and she could tell by how loudly and how long it took him to get from the front door to the fridge that he was drunk. Too exhausted to deal with him, she closed her eyes and hoped that her son didn't burn the house down.

Chapter 3

The Strangest thing happened

Dear Lily,

I'm not even going to talk about how annoyed I am that Declan is being such a dicknose and I can't believe you're letting him away with it. In fact, I'm really hurt. I'd call you if we could arrange a time for you to be at the telephone box and, even though I'm so monumentally pissed off with you, I'd still do it — if of course Declan doesn't mind and you can spare five minutes. Oh and don't worry, I haven't said anything to precious Declan about Colm or the other one (can't remember her name and too pissed off to fish out your letter) but seriously, if you can't tell your boyfriend that you've made friends it's a bit sad. I mean what does he expect? Would he be happy if all you did was work and moon over him? And don't answer that because we both know what your answer will be and I also don't want any excuses. As you said in your letter, you love him so that's that. I just wish that you loved me half as much (and no, not being a lesbian about it) but where was he when you were bullied in primary school? I was the one who pulled Megan Murphy's hair out of her head and pinched her so hard she still has the marks! (Which she showed me at the disco last Easter - they were really small across her knuckles but seriously how bad is that? MORTIFIED.) I was the one who carried you home and put you in bed when you were so drunk you didn't even know where you lived and I managed to do it unseen while your mother was still in the sitting room doing a crossword. She would have disowned you if she'd found you in that state and as a result of my efforts you got away with an event which would have seriously changed your life for the worst. I'm the one that's there for every little drama you have with Declan. I'm the one who picks up the pieces when you fight. I'm the one who's always on your side. I'm the one who wants nothing for you but happiness. I'm the one who really loves you and again not in a lesbian way. Although if I was a lesbian and you were my girlfriend, I wouldn't insist that you spend ALL of your money calling me because I may be a bitch but I'm not a selfish dicknose and that is all I have to say on the matter.

Now for my news and you are not going to believe this. Gar, Dicknose, Paul and I went to the pub the other night and guess who was there with a brand new look? GLEN MEDEIROS!!!! And he's only cut off the horrible perm and instead of wearing one of those stupid-looking blousy shirts he was wearing a Bruce Springsteen T-Shirt and Jeans and he looks really, really good. Like a different person. It's like a Fairy Godmother came down and waved a magic wand over him. I had a drink with Gar and Paul (steadfastly ignoring Dicknose but of course he was too up his own bum to notice so don't worry about it) and then I went over to Glen. He was sitting at the bar with two boys I don't know. I know it sounds stupid, bearing in mind up until very recently I thought he was a freak, but I was really nervous and every time I caught him looking at me before I went over (which was a lot) I pretended I hadn't but seriously you'd have to be Helen Keller not to notice him. He'd never make it in the CIA that's for sure. Anyway every time I caught him looking at me my stomach flipped and flopped so much so I felt a little sick. (I SWEAR TO GOD) So I went up to him and of course I was trying to act cool so I kept it short and sweet because I knew if I said too much I might actually vomit. So I walked up to him just like Tom Cruise walked up to Kelly McGillis in Top Gun. (Don't get me wrong, still think that film is embarrassing but it's a good reference point) He turned around from his friends to face me and he did look a bit smug but that's OK, he deserved to feel a little smug. I looked him up and down slowly and then I said you're welcome and walked off. His friends were in hysterics. I didn't look back but when I went over to our group Paul said he'd watched the whole thing and Glen was grinning. Eve Hughes "Is" Glen Medeiros "Love". Anyway I went outside with Gar when he was having a smoke. (He still refuses to smoke inside in case Mr Duffy spots him and tells his father - what a baby!) And before I had a chance to mention the fact that I thought that because I was going to London and he was going to be in Dublin we shouldn't get involved (exactly as you said) he told me that he was really into a girl from Bray. CAN YOU BELIEVE IT? I didn't know whether to be relieved or insulted. In the end I went with option 1. Relieved. So I wished him luck on getting together with her and he was actually really sweet about it. I'd had three bottles of Ritz by then and thought it might be a good idea to tell him not to peck, peck, peck her like a chicken (NOT A GOOSE) but then I remembered what you said and didn't say a word. When he went in I said I needed some air and stayed outside just to see if Glen would notice. He was out like a hot snot. THRILLED. Of course he was mortified because I was sitting on the wall watching him run out and look up and down the street. He sat on the wall with me and when I called him Glen he reminded me his name was Ben Logan and so I told him that no matter how cute he was now he'd always be Glen Medeiros to me. He laughed and of course focused on how cute I thought he was but I changed the subject and warned him that I'd find him most unattractive if he kept standing on corners saying those poems. (I know, don't freak out but I believe honesty is the best policy.) Anyway he didn't take it too badly. He said is it alright if I continue with my band? I didn't even know he was in a band. Anyway I said that was fine as long as his band was a good deal better than his poetry. He told me they were and then out of nowhere he kissed me and I NEARLY DIED. He is an amazing kisser. I can't even describe it. And it was so romantic. The moon was out and even though we were in a carpark I could see it glint off the sea in the distance. And the way he looked at me as he was moving in and out for kisses. Well, let's just say Glen Medeiros is intense. Anyway we stayed outside for at least an hour. Paul came out to look for me and when he saw us together I called out and asked him to say nothing to Gar and he gave me the thumbs-up. So I presume he's happy to say nothing to Gar which is nice of him but then again he is a slut so there's probably some sort of slut code he's obeying. Either way I'm grateful. I've met Glen twice since and I'm going to his gig in town on Saturday so I'll fill you in next Sunday, that is if you don't give me a telephone number and time to call you so that we could actually talk. I know it's mad and this time last week I thought he was weird but I'm really into him. When he looks at me I feel like jelly and I know there is a serious height difference but I really don't care. I've always said I'm not the kind of person who falls in love but Lily I think I could fall in love with him. He makes the world feel like a better place. I KNOW IT'S HORRIFYING. I'm seeing him tonight and I'm counting down the hours. It's pathetic but can't wait.

Anyway what other news do I have? Clooney dropped that yoke with the big hair. I think he's having a fling with V Kill P which is pretty dangerous, bearing in mind I'm totally convinced she's a lesbian and if it doesn't work out it could mess up their radio show. Not a massive loss to the world but still he can have any girl he wants so why does he have to be stupid about it? Anyway she's been hanging around the house a lot lately and although they don't make it as obvious as he was with the yoke, they do seem to have got a little flirtier. She hasn't stayed over but then again Dad is home and I haven't caught them kissing all over the house but then again V Kill P is way cooler than the yoke and so she probably wouldn't be on for that, but anyway watch this space.

I met Paul the other day and he was on his way into town to meet a girl. His rugby team are playing on Friday and I promised I'd go and watch. Maybe I'll get to meet his latest girl. He's in good form but he's nervous about the results and whether or not he'll get law. I told him not to worry he'll fly through it but he said he's not like you. He said you will get medicine without breaking a sweat but he had to work his balls off and even then he's not sure how he's done. I told him that I had no doubt you'd both be in university doing your highfalutin subjects while I'll be in London behind a sewing machine. He laughed at that. He did say he wasn't entirely convinced that Dicknose would get medicine (even in Cork never mind Trinity) either. (I promise I'll stop calling him that in my next letter – just give me this one to vent – I think it's the least you could do under the circumstances.) I didn't say anything but it would be insane if you got medicine and Dicknose didn't.

Anyway only a matter of weeks to go before we'll all know what lies ahead of us and speaking of which I met Gina Daly in the coffee shop on Monday. She's home from college in Galway and she asked me if I'd like to join her so I did and she was talking about living there in the college accommodation and the balls and the students' nights out and it all sounded amazing. So between your new friend down there having a blast in Cork, Gina loving Galway and Clooney living like a rock star, the reports on the college experience are all good. I just hope it's as good in London. Getting a little anxious but I'll be fine. I always am. Anyway Gina and I had a great time together and it reminded me of how much fun we had when we were younger and before she decided she was too old to hang around with us. She's working for her dad in the bar for the summer so we're meeting for coffee again tomorrow and she's thinking about going into town to see Glen's band on Saturday. (I'm going to have to stop calling him Glen – I've got Gina at it now.)

Tell me more about your life. How is Colm? He sounds interesting and your type and no I'm not saying you should be with him but having said that it's not like you are married or anything so it mightn't be the end of the world either, just a thought.

I have to go and beautify myself for Glen. Talk soon I HOPE.

Your best friend,
Eve

P.S. Dicknose does really miss you and he's talking about you all the time – even Gar has a pain in his face listening to him.

P.P.S. I DO LOVE YOU.

P.P.P.S. I cannot believe your taste is always the direct opposite of mine. Christian Slater first and Emilio last just isn't right.

* * *

Eve's unexpected date with Ben had helped rid her of her headache and put enough pep in her step to make the usual decision to cook, so she nipped to the supermarket and bought half the shop to give herself enough food to really work with. She'd proven to herself long ago that she was far too impatient, mistrustful and possibly arrogant to follow recipes.

Four hours? That's ridiculous! I could be in another country in four hours. I'll see what it's like after two. What the hell is a fenugreek leaf? Screw it, basil will work just as well.

She kept the menu plain and hearty and she still managed to burn everything when she went online to search for a potato recipe and got caught up watching a YouTube video and forgot she was cooking. As it turned out Ben was over an hour late so the house was cleaned and the smoke evacuated before he even got to the door. It was seven when she answered the door with take-away leaflets in her hand. He walked into the apartment and without breaking stride he wrapped his arms around her, lifted her up so that she was sitting on his hips with her legs wrapped around him and before she knew it she was leaning against a wall and he was kissing her. He started stripping her and then he carried her to the bedroom and aside from weaving a little from left to right and bumping her against the doorframe they made it to the bed intact and without having spoken one word. With Ben she felt safe and free and warm and beautiful. Eve could look into his brown eyes forever. When he touched her she tingled and when he held her and moved inside her she felt abandon.

Eve often enjoyed sex and over the years she'd had many men come and go – some she was simply attracted to, some she liked, some she really liked – but there was only ever one that she thought she could love and he was Ben Logan. *You're just living in the past, Eve, because you just don't want to let go*, she'd tell herself but her body wasn't listening.

They lay together on the bed facing one another, sated, still, calm, lost in their own little universe. He was tracing Eve's collarbone with his finger and she was cupping his cheek in her hand. She knew his world was collapsing, his wife was somewhere crying and what they had was a fantasy and merely his way of escaping the pressure cooker that had become his life and her way of escaping herself and her own head. She didn't talk business. She didn't say anything that would burst their bubble. Instead they lay there comfortable in each other's arms, talking about the past as a means of avoiding the present.

"Call me Glen," he said.

"Glen," she said.

"I remember the first time you called me by my actual name," he said.

"We were fooling around in a park," she said, remembering with a smile.

"It was the night I knew you were mine."

She laughed. "You always did have a head too big for your body."

He pulled her into his arms. "I loved you then, Blondie."

Eve felt like crying so instead of ruining the mood she changed the subject.

"Gulliver Stood On My Son," she said and laughed.

"What?" Ben said, feigning disbelief. "That was a great band name!"

"Yeah, it had Hall Of Fame written all over it," she giggled.

Ben loved to hear Eve giggle.

"I remember that gig where you went from 'Long Way Back,' to a rendition of 'Nothing's Gonna Change My Love For You' as I walked into the club. It was so cheesy," she said.

"It was funny," he said.

"It was awful."

"You loved it."

"Yeah, I did."

Ben remembered he had to fight with the band all day to get them to do it. They were rehearsing in Billy's dad's garage when he floated the idea.

"No way," Mark said and put down his sticks.

"No fucking way," Finbarr said from behind his keyboard.

"I'd rather cut my knob off than do anything by Glen Medeiros," Billy said, taking his bass off and lighting up a cigarette.

"Ah come on, it's for my girlfriend," he pleaded. It was the first time Ben had called Eve his girlfriend and he liked the sound of it.

"Rusty knife," Billy said, pointing to a toolbox in his dad's garage. "Knob." He pointed to his penis.

"What about you, Tom?"

"Yeah, whatever."

"Nice one."

"No, no, no and fuck no," Finbarr said.

Billy just kept on pointing to his penis and making a snipping gesture with his hand. After a long discussion and Billy threatening to take it out and start cutting, they agreed on the basis that Ben would do all the gear after gigs for the rest of the summer. He was desperate for it to be spontaneous and he knew Eve's bus wouldn't get her there until at least five minutes after they were already on stage so he had asked Terry 'The Tourist' Noonan for a picture of Eve.

"I don't have one."

"Liar."

"I swear."

"I saw you taking one the other day."

"I was looking past her."

"Give me the picture."

"No."

"Give me the picture or I'm going to report you for being a pervert."

"I'm not a pervert."

"Yeah, well, they don't know that and frankly neither do I."

"Fine," Terry had said and he'd gone up to his room and brought down a collection.

Eve leaning on a wall at school. Eve on a bike. Eve lying out in her garden. Eve sitting by the harbour. The one that was clearest and head on was the one where she was leaning against a wall.

Ben took the picture from him.

"If I ever see you taking a picture of my girlfriend again I'll throw a bowling ball at your head and call it an accident," he said.

Terry 'The Tourist' Noonan just nodded. "Fair enough," he said.

Ben had given the picture to the guy at the door. As soon as Eve entered and received a stamp to her head, he radioed the stage hand who signalled Mark on drums. He changed tempo and by the time she was standing in the middle of the room, Ben was belting out the Glen Medeiros classic to her as if she was the only girl in the room. He could still see her eyes light up, the smile that crossed her face, and way she hid her face and then raised her hands into the air. She had loved it and it was worth doing all the gear by himself for the entire summer just for that moment.

"What are you thinking about?" she asked now, bringing him back to her.

"You," he said.

"Sing me the song you wrote for me," she said.

"No."

"Ah come on!"

"I'm not a singer any more."

She pretended to sulk.

"I'll say it."

"Oh, like those bad poems."

"Exactly."

"OK."

"*She's the one to avoid, strong, beautiful, a living android. She talks, I flinch, she makes me think. She chews me up and spits me out; she makes me scream, bleed and shout. This battle's lost but I'll return, when she is mine my war is won.*"

Eve sang the chorus loudly and badly while waving her arms in the air. "*It's a long way back, you know I'll keep on coming, it's a long way back, without you I'm nothing.*"

On cue they both burst into Glen Medeiros, 'Nothing's Going Change My Love For You'.

"You'll always be Glen Medeiros to me," she said.

He seemed sad. "I do love my wife."

"I know."

"But you're the one that got away."

"No," she said.

"Yes," he said, nodding. "That last night together I told you I loved you. You burst out laughing in my face and it was like I was being knifed."

"I didn't mean it. I was nervous and drunk and scared."

"Scared of what?"

"I don't know. You? Love? Leaving? I just wasn't ready."

"Billy told me," he said.

"I guessed," she said.

"If I could do it again I'd have known better."

"I don't want to talk about it," she said sternly and he knew she meant it.

He nodded sadly. They'd never spoken about what happened that night and they never would. They lay in silence. He held her hand. His eyes were full. She pursed her lips and he wiped away a stray tear. They stared at each other and engaged in a full conversation without saying one word.

Around ten they were hungry and neither of them wanted take-out. Eve rang a local bistro and she was promised a table if they made it there for last orders at half ten. They jumped into the shower, got dressed and instead of taking the car and because it was a fine night they decided to walk so that they could have a little wine with dinner. They walked along the small dirt road that led from Eve's house toward the village. It was quiet and dark. They were alone and wrapped up in one another. Every now and then they would stop in some little nook in the old stone wall that separated a farmer's field from the narrow track. He'd pull her into him and they'd kiss and touch each other and hold on tight before kissing again.

"We'll miss our reservation," she said.

"I wish we could just stop here and now in this moment forever," he said, stroking her cheek.

"Time to go," she said, pulling him away from the wall and they began walking hand and hand down the road again. He was pensive and she could feel his thoughts slipping away from her and back to life and his wife. "Don't leave me yet," she said to him and he smiled.

"I'm right here," he said.

The car came toward them and Eve could see its lights. She didn't hear anything or see anything then. Suddenly her legs were buckling and Ben's hand being ripped from hers. She didn't black out but it was all so surreal, like a pleasant dream morphing into a nightmare. One second she was looking at Ben and the next second she was sitting in the passenger seat of a car with her two broken legs poking out through the smashed windscreen. Her shoulder felt strange and when she looked at it, it seemed to have disappeared somewhere under her skin. She couldn't move her arm. She looked back from her shoulder to her twisted legs and the road ahead and then toward the drunken man who was driving the car. She smelt the stale odour of whiskey before she saw him. She had to focus hard to do that. He was weaving all over the road and her broken body rocked with every weave and tilt. He was mumbling to himself as though he was alone and she wasn't even there. *Where's Ben?* She tried to turn to look in the back seat to see if he was there but she couldn't seem to turn her body. *Where's Ben?* She tried to talk but she couldn't seem to connect mind and mouth. She tried desperately to find her voice and focused hard to be heard.

She heard herself whisper. "Where's Ben?"

He didn't respond, instead he turned on the radio. Eve's heart was beating so loudly it seemed to reverberate in her eardrums. Still she felt no pain but looking at her twisted legs straight ahead of her resting on the bonnet of his car she knew it was coming. She remembered what her yoga teacher had said about breathing and control so she took in a deep breath and then she let it go and in her head she said one word over and over. *Stop. Stop. Stop. Stop. Stop.* Until it finally reached her mouth in a whisper. "Stop."

He looked away from the road he was driving all over and toward Eve and he was angry.

"You wanted a lift, I gave you one," he said.

She was confused. *Did we ask for a lift?* Once again she looked straight ahead just to confirm one more time that her broken limbs were hanging out of his missing windshield window.

"Ben?" she said.

"You were in the middle of the road!" he shouted at her before wiping his nose on the sleeve of his woollen jumper. It was too dark and she couldn't make out its colour.

Lights flashed in front of them. The car swerved from left to right even though the driver seemed so focused on the road ahead. She wondered if he noticed her broken limbs. On the steering wheel she noticed the emblem for Nissan. When they passed under a street light or an oncoming car she could see that the bonnet of the car was red that he had a red beard and huge hands. On his left hand he wore a large gold Claddagh ring

"Stop, stop, stop, stop, STOP!" she said until her whispers became a shout.

He steadfastly ignored her, continuing to mumble while turning the sound on the radio up. She realised her right arm was undamaged; she could use it so she grabbed at his jumper and pulled and dragged at it.

"*Please!*" she screamed. "*Stop!*" She couldn't think of or bring herself to say anything else.

"You wanted a lift!" he shouted at her. "I'm giving you a lift. What more do you want?"

"To stop," she said, in a voice and tone that sounded foreign to her.

"Fine," he shouted, "bloody women, never know what you want!"

He stopped the car in the middle of the road. He got out of the driver's seat, arguing with himself. He passed his smashed windscreen and her twisted legs and made his way to the passenger door. He opened it with a jerk and she felt herself falling. *Oh God, he's going to drag me.* She steeled herself for the agony that was coming. He grabbed her by the arm that was now missing its shoulder. He pulled her and she screamed and begged, using only one word over and over. "*Please!*"

He let the arm with the missing shoulder go and, grabbing her by the back of her neck, he pulled again and she felt the glass cut deep into her burning, pounding legs.

"Please."

Her legs were so long that he had to twist her to get them through the hole in his windscreen. She could see them bend and she felt another snap.

"Please."

He had a good grip on her now and pulled from under her arms. He pushed on the place under her shoulder-blade where her shoulder now rested and for a moment she thought and hoped she would die.

"Please."

She felt her legs thudding to the ground. He dropped her upper torso so that she was lying facing up at the stars. It was a clear night, beautiful, the same night that she had been with Ben kissing against a wall like teenagers.

"Ben?" she said.

He ignored her. "You wanted a lift," he said, pointing at her.

She lay motionless.

"I gave you a lift," he said, pointing to his car before once again rubbing his nose.

She remained motionless.

"And it's the last lift you'll get from me," he said and got into his car and disappeared, leaving Eve in the middle of the road.

She realised quickly that if she stayed on the road she'd be killed. She also knew that three limbs were badly damaged but she had one good arm. *You can do this, Eve. You're strong, remember? It's either pull yourself to the side of the road or become road kill. Simple. No choice. Just do it.* Eve began to slowly pull herself toward the ditch at the side of the road. Every move was torture, every minute seemed like an hour and she cried all the way. When she was out of the middle of the road she lay once again looking at stars and hoping that any car that could have killed her minutes before would now come and find her. *Where's Ben?*

Eve heard a car pass but it didn't see her and then another one and another one. She tried to wave with the one arm that still worked but she couldn't do it. She was so tired. *This is where I die. I hope you're OK, Ben. I'm so sorry about that night. It was my biggest and stupidest mistake. I think I love you. I think I've always loved you.* She closed her eyes and she let go.

Big lights shone down on Eve and she heard voices before she could open her eyes and when she did it was hard to focus on the faces looking down at her. She could hear a conversation but it was muffled and as though she was on the phone and it was a bad signal. One of the faces she was trying to focus on was talking to her and with every blink he was becoming clearer. The other one was sticking her with something and it felt good. Suddenly it was as though the signal cleared.

"You're OK now, love. We've got you. Can you hear me?"

"Yes," she said.

"Nice one," he said, smiling down at her before turning away, "She's back with us, Brendan."

Brendan said something that Eve couldn't make out.

"What's your name, love?" said the other.

"Eve," she said.

"Well, Eve, we're going to move you now." And the memories of her being dragged out of the car and crawling across the road flashed into her mind and every nerve seemed to scream in preparation for pain like she'd never before known.

"No," she begged.

"It's OK," he soothed her. "You're in good hands. We won't let anything else bad happen. Isn't that right, Brendan?"

Another face appeared. "That's right, Tony."

Eve opened her eyes and focused on the white roof of the ambulance. She could feel that she was tied to a board. Although she couldn't see the wires and tubes she knew they were there. There was a mask over her mouth and she felt the cold crisp oxygen move in through her nose and her warm breath escaping through her lips.

"There you are!" Tony said, removing the mask for a second. "Back with us."

"Yes."

"Do you believe in God?" he asked.

"No."

"Well, we were on the way to another accident when we saw you and that's a miracle in my book," he said.

"Luck," she said and she searched her mind because she knew she was forgetting something important. *Something, something, something.*

He laughed. "Maybe," he said and moved to put the oxygen mask back on her face.

Another accident. She stopped him with her good arm.

"My boyfriend," she said and suddenly she was eighteen again, she was a girl and Ben was the boy she loved.

"Who's your boyfriend, love?" she heard him say.

"Glen Medeiros," she said, although in her head she was saying the words *Ben* and *Logan*.

He smiled at her. "We'll do this pick-up and then we'll find Glen." And he placed the mask back over her mouth and she disappeared again.

The ambulance stopped and when the doors opened Eve could hear people talking loudly and hurriedly.

"We did what we could."

"We did our best."

"Is he alive?"

"We weren't sure what to do."

Eve knew it was Ben and she waited for what seemed like an eternity. *Come on, Ben. You can do it. You're strong too. You can do it. You can do anything and you will be fine.* They loaded him onto the ambulance. She couldn't see him.

"Is he OK?" she asked.

"Just worry about yourself, love," Tony said.

"Is he OK?" she asked again.

"Just relax," Tony said.

"*He's mine!*" she shouted. "*He's with me, he's mine!*"

"Alright, OK, I understand, he's OK, relax now."

And Eve disappeared for the final time on that journey.

In A&E she became alert again and all of a sudden under glaring lights and surrounded by people. They were all busy and she was trying to work out if she was in pain or dead from the neck down. Someone lifted her arm and she heard herself scream. *Not dead from the neck down then. That's positive.* She was still secured onto a body board and it was suffocating. Voices came and went.

"Hang in there, Eve."

"Well done."

"We're going to give you more pain meds – you're doing great."

"OK, we're going to move you to X-Ray."

"Good girl."

"I'll be in the other room and just outside. OK? Stay still. I know you will."

"Well done. Now I'm going to take you back. It's OK, Eve, stop screaming, we're going to get you more pain meds."

She saw the first policeman at 3 a.m., according to the notes. He asked her if she could remember any details of the incident. He apologised immediately after he asked the question and told her that if she didn't remember anything it was perfectly fine, he could talk to her another time, but she didn't want him to go anywhere because she remembered so much and she wanted him to know it before she forgot an important detail or died.

"He was driving a red Nissan. I know it was a Nissan because I saw the emblem was on the steering wheel. He was taller than me and I'm 5 foot 11, so maybe he was 6 foot 1 or 2. He had red hair and a beard and when I say red I mean ginger. He had allergies, his nose was constantly running. He had big rough workman's hands. He was wearing a Claddagh ring and his breath stunk of whiskey." She was pleased that she had regained the power to speak in the form of sentences.

He was scribbling down everything she said. "Hold on, I thought you were a pedestrian?"

"I was."

"So how could you see the Nissan emblem on the steering wheel?"

"Because I landed in the passenger seat of the car. Through the front windscreen."

His eyes widened in amazement but he didn't comment. He closed his notepad. "Maybe we should talk again tomorrow."

She knew there was something more.

I'm missing something, what is it?

"Something else," she said. She focused for a minute or two.

The policeman stood up to leave.

"He was wearing a navy woollen jumper," she said.

The policeman smiled. "If you were in that car it must have been pitch dark – how could you see the colour of his jumper?"

She held up her good arm and showed him her hand. "Because the wool is stuck under my fingernails," she said and he looked sideways at her with some degree of fascination before he took her hand in his and slowly took the wool from under her nails.

Then she asked him about Ben.

"I'll ask the doctors and get back to you."

"When?" she said.

"Soon."

"Now," she said as though she was in a position to make demands.

"Just a few more questions."

"I don't know anything more. I helped you, help me."

He agreed to find out. He disappeared. He didn't come back.

Eve went into shock officially at 4:30 a.m. and disappeared for the final time that horrific night.

Lily had the strangest dream she was in a military aircraft carrier dressed in fatigues and going to war. She spent a few seconds looking around at all the boys on the carrier with her. They were all talking amongst themselves. She wondered what the hell she was doing there. *This isn't flower-arranging class.* Then she wondered if she was there because she was a nurse. *Damn it anyway, why did I sign up for this?* There was a boy around Scott's age, maybe a little older, sitting beside her. He was pumped up and excited.

"Is this your first time?" he asked.

"Yeah. You?"

"Oh yeah. I've been waiting to do this for a long time."

"You're a kid. You don't know what a long time is," she said.

"Whatever." He smiled at her and rocked excitedly. She noticed the engines were getting louder, meaning they had to shout instead of speak. *I hate shouting.*

"I'm getting married," he said.

"It's not all it's cracked up to be."

"We're going to have a house and a dog and some kids and a rabbit," he said, "but first I'm going to kill some bad guys."

"Get a rabbit or a dog, do not get both."

"Why not?"

"Because the dog will eat the rabbit. It's nature."

"Nah, they'll love one another," he said and he was confident he was right.

"If they told you I was your enemy, would you kill me?" she asked.

"Who is they?"

"The people who've put us on this plane," she said.

"No."

"Why not?"

"Because you're a friendly."

"But how do you know?"

"You look friendly," he said.

"Not that friendly," she said and she took out a gun and shot him in the head.

She sat watching the blood tumble out of the hole in his face, mesmerised by his fixed stare. *All I wanted to do was a flower-arranging class.* Lily woke up in a cold sweat.

"Lily, are you OK?" Marion asked after the change-over meeting. It was clear Lily hadn't been listening to a word said about any of the patients she'd be taking charge of for the next twelve hours.

"I'm sorry, I didn't sleep very well."

"You're pale. Would you like to lie down?"

"Are you nuts?" She almost laughed. "We're short-staffed and overworked as it is."

"Why do you keep pulling at your shoulder and guarding your chest?"

Lily hadn't noticed she was doing that. "It's nothing – my shoulder's at me," she said just as Adam walked in.

"Let me look at it," he said with concern.

She was embarrassed. "No, it's fine, honestly."

"She's been pulling at it since she got here, she's pale and off form," Marion said to him as though Lily was a patient she was reporting on.

"I'm just tired," she said.

"Follow me," he said.

"Bugger-balls."

"What was that?" he asked, smiling.

"Nothing."

She followed him into his consultation room.

"Take off your top," he said.

"In your dreams," she said in a tone that suggested that she was joking and yet they both knew her top wasn't coming off.

"I'm a doctor," he said.

"Congratulations. Your mother must be so proud."

Adam Wallace shook his head and laughed. Adam was the closest thing Lily had to a real friend and as long as she was clothed she was at her most comfortable in his presence. He was a forty-year-old man who had never married but had most definitely had his share of beautiful women on his arm over the years. The last woman he was with was called Caroline. She was a broker and seemed nice when Lily met her at the various hospital events, dinners and charity balls. They were together four years. She left when she realised he would never marry her. He was really down when Caroline left and he and Lily had become really friendly after a particularly boring charity dinner. Declan was drunk and lording it over everyone at the table and Adam was vulnerable and sad. Declan thought it was funny to suggest that Adam had paid off his latest beard and queried whether it would be cheaper just to come out as everyone knew he was gay anyway. That joke went down like a lead balloon and when Lily tried to make Declan sit down he pushed her, not forcefully but enough to cause embarrassment. She laughed it off and told him to pick on someone his own size. Later Adam and Lily met on the hotel balcony and she apologised for her husband's behaviour, explaining he drank so rarely that he couldn't hold the smallest amount with any dignity.

"It's no excuse," he said. "There are mean drunks and entertaining drunks. You married a mean one."

She nodded. "I married a sleeper. He'll be passed out by the time the band starts to play."

"Can I ask you a personal question?"

"Depends."

"Are you happy you married him?"

"I was eighteen."

"Not an answer."

"Happiness is a feeling not a result."

"How are you feeling tonight?" he asked earnestly.

"Tipsy," she said and grinned.

He laughed before becoming serious. "Why is getting married such a big deal to women?"

"Ah, Caroline," she said

He nodded.

"Why is *not* getting married such a big deal to you?" she asked.

He smiled. "Good question."

"And none of my business," she said, drained her glass, placed it on the table and placed her hand on his shoulder. "You might not marry but a man like you will never end up alone," she said before she walked away.

He called her back.

"One last question," he said.

"OK."

"If you could do it all again, would you marry at eighteen?"

"Not a chance," she said honestly and she walked away.

That was the night Adam Wallace fell for Lily Donovan.

Now he placed his arm on her shoulder, and he was fiddling under her horrible pink nurse's tunic.

"You don't make life easy," he said.

"Funny, that's what Declan says."

"Declan doesn't know he's born. Do you play tennis or swim?"

"I like to swim when I get time."

"When was the last time?"

"1991," she said, smiling.

"Seriously," he said.

"I don't do sports or exercise."

He leaned his head to the side and looked at her quizzically. "So how do you stay so slim?"

"I binge and purge."

"I'm serious."

"Honestly, I eat when I have time and I don't always have time."

"Caroline lived on leaves and seeds and she weighed more than you do."

"Can we get back to my shoulder?" she said, remembering she had to call in on Rachel and Nancy before she started her shift.

"OK," he said, removing his hand from under her top. "Try to move your arm inwards and across your chest. I'm going to provide a little resistance."

She couldn't do it.

"OK, try to rotate your arm inwards," he said. He pressed on her chest. "Is that painful?" "No."

"OK. It looks like you've done a bit of damage to the pectoralis major muscle – the connecting tendon seems inflamed. Do you know how it could have happened?"

"Not a clue," she said innocently. *Flaming Declan and his S&M fantasies.*

Adam prescribed Ibuprofen and told her to apply heat. If it didn't settle with rest, he ordered her to come back to him so that he could refer her to a physio.

"I know them all," she laughed.

"Just come back to me and make sure you eat something today," he said, feigning weariness.

She thanked him and told him she would and left him to stare after her as she bounced down the hall like a teenager.

Lily walked into Nancy's room just as Jim was coming out with Dylan by the hand. It could have been awkward but Lily didn't do awkward so instead she acted as though he hadn't pretty much propositioned her on the phone the previous night.

"Jim, how are you?"

"Good, thanks, better. Thanks so much for having Dylan over last night. I picked him up after you'd left for work."

"You're welcome," she said before bending down to Dylan. "How are you doing, soldier?" The question reminded of her dream. *I just wanted to do a little flower-arranging.*

"Nancy has a big plaster over her eye, she looks like a pirate," he said.

Lily smiled. "Cool."

He nodded to agree that it was indeed cool and he grinned. He was clearly proud of the part he had to play in her new look.

Rachel came to the door. "Well, are you going to sign the papers or are you going to stand in the doorway talking all day?" she said to Jim.

He sighed and left.

Lily pretended she didn't notice the tension and entered the room.

"Hi, Nancy, how are you feeling, darling?"

"Great," she said and smiled a big wide smile.

"Great," Lily said. "That's good news."

"She's a trooper," Rachel said. "We're so proud of her."

"Well, I'm thrilled you're feeling better, Nancy," Lily said. "Well, I must get back to work. See you soon."

Nancy started to open one of three lucky bags.

Rachel took Lily aside.

"We really are so grateful," she repeated unnecessarily. "They think she's going to keep the sight but obviously there will be scarring on the eye. We don't know how much yet."

"Try not to worry about it – it might be almost impossible to notice. Trust me, kids heal so much better and quicker than adults do."

"You're right," Rachel said and nodded to herself.

"Dylan seems happier?"

"Dylan's lucky my father's in his grave because he would have taken a large stick to him."

"Accidents happen," Lily said, uncomfortable with the way the conversation was going and she wondered where the empathy Rachel had displayed the previous day had gone.

"Not if people act responsibly," Rachel said.

"Jesus, Rachel, he's eight years old!" Lily said and instantly regretted it when Rachel gave her a look that could kill. It was clear to anyone outside looking in, that Nancy was Rachel's mini-me and princess all rolled into one. Lily felt sorry for Dylan who seemed to watch their love-fest from a distance. At least he had Jim but then Jim was always either working or, as Rachel often said herself, 'making a bollocks of it'.

Lily made her excuses and left them to it and with her shoulder seen to and her neighbourly duty done, she looked forward to the shift ahead.

Her first duty was to escort a patient who had been involved in a road-traffic accident to theatre. She arrived onto the ward in time to meet Bob rolling the woman down the corridor.

"Ward 5?" she asked.

"Ward 5," he confirmed.

She picked up the woman's chart, smiled at the poor mangled woman lying on the trolley and walked alongside it heading towards theatre.

Eve didn't remember waking but she was awake, well, at least her eyes were open and her brain half-engaged. She was on a trolley looking at a white ceiling and moving. Seeing was more difficult than it had been before she slept. When she closed her right eye she realised that she couldn't see out of her left at all. She tried to work out if her eyelid was swollen or her eye was gone. *My face? What's happened to my face?* The right eye leaked and speaking was difficult once again. Eve's words seemed lodged in the back of her head and she was mentally trying to force them into her mouth but she couldn't. She wondered if this was as a result of drugs or head trauma. She couldn't seem to ask about her face so she tried to work out how it felt. It felt foreign. She tried to focus on the nurse but she was standing on her left side so it was difficult.

They stopped at the lift and the nurse switched sides and tucked in the blanket covering her.

"Just waiting for the lift, we'll be there soon," the nurse said.

Eve's lips were bigger than she remembered; she started to purse them and they were swollen and sore. She ran her tongue over her teeth and they were all intact. *That's something*. She licked her lips and instantly felt the stitching and tasted blood. *Damn*. They moved into the lift. Her face seemed to roast when she hit the wall of heat and the smell of decay inside. She heard the button being pushed again and she heard the two women, who had stood aside to allow them in, talking beside her.

"I told Mike that if I wanted that kind of commitment I'd get pregnant but he just doesn't listen. Not to mention the fact that I'd hinted heavily in the direction of an iPod."

"What are you going to do?"

"I'm going to let him take care of it."

"And he's OK with that?"

"Oh, he loves it."

"So really he bought the dog for himself?"

"Exactly."

"And you hate dogs."

"Correct."

"So now you've got a dog in your house that you don't like."

"Well, I've had a man in my house that I don't like for two years so might as well have a dog too."

"Well, you're a better person that I am."

"Not really. I stole his banklink card and bought myself an iPod."

The lift stopped and they got out. The nurse leaned over Eve and brushed a piece of bloody matted hair off her forehead.

"Nearly there," she said but Eve was somewhere else thinking about Ben. *Where is he?*

The lift stopped and they were on the move again down a corridor and for some reason the pace had been picked up, the lights on the ceiling seemed to be flashing past.

Suddenly and abruptly they stopped and she heard the man tell the nurse he'd see what was going on. Eve heard the nurse push down the brake on the trolley with her foot and she felt the trolley jerk slightly.

"It shouldn't be too long now. I know it doesn't feel like it but you will be OK," the nurse said.

Eve thought her voice sounded familiar like a song she knew and could sing along to but she couldn't quite place the singer. Silence followed and her mind drifted back to Ben. *I saw him. He was with me.* She remembered that Ben had a wife and that she'd be worried for him. If they'd found his phone and called her she'd wonder what he was doing on that road. There were police involved. It would be hard for them to conceal the truth. Lying on the trolley, waiting to go into surgery, it dawned on Eve that her no-strings-attached secret affair that was never intended to hurt anyone could potentially devastate Ben, his wife and family.

The man returned and Eve's trolley started to move and as she did the nurse quickened her step and took Eve's good hand in hers. Eve looked up at her and focused on her face and it was so strange because she looked a lot like her old friend Lily. *Is that you, Lily? Couldn't be. Could it? It looks so like you. Your hair is different but if it is you then a bob suits you and you're still beautiful. That's nice. If it's her surely she'd recognise me but maybe not, maybe I'm unrecognisable.*

They arrived at a door and the trolley stopped. Lily leaned down and smiled at her patient. "Don't be scared. I know the guy who's operating and he's the best," she said and winked.

"Lily?" the woman whispered.

Lily looked at her patient. "Yes?"

"Eve," the woman said, pointing to her chest.

Oh my God. Eve.

Lily covered her mouth.

"That bad," Eve said.

"No," Lily said, recovering. "No, not that bad, Eve, not that bad at all."

"I missed you," Eve said.

"I missed you too," Lily said and she felt like crying.

They reached the door to the theatre.

"Ben?" Eve said.

"Ben?" Lily repeated.

"Ben Logan."

"Ben Glen Medeiros Logan?" Lily asked in shock. *What the hell?*

"Please find him, Lily," Eve said and Lily nodded.

"I will," she promised.

The theatre doors opened and Adam stood waiting in his scrubs. He waved at Lily. Bob pushed the bed through the door and Eve was gone.

Chapter 4

Only the lonely

Dear Eve,

OK, I'm a bad friend. I feel horrible and I did try to call you twice last week after I sent the letter but there was no answer. Besides, I've got a question – are any of you Hayeses ever at home? And have you people ever heard of an answering machine? On Friday I walked to the phone box in the pouring rain (so much for it being mostly sunny here) and stood outside it for twenty-five minutes while the town gossip called every dog and duck she knows to fill them in on the exploits of a woman named Lucille Thomas who discovered her foreign boyfriend Benito kissing her brother in the back garden. Initially she was whispering but when I pushed my face up to the window in a bid to get her to hurry up which obviously didn't work she stopped whispering and by the time she was on her fourth phone call she was shouting because apparently the person on the end of the line was partially deaf. I think she saw my tan and thought I was a foreigner who couldn't speak English. It's happening a lot here – when I go into the local newsagent's, to buy a Mars bar or something, the woman speaks slowly and shouts that the Mars will cost 45p. Colm was with me yesterday and he burst out laughing and spent the rest of the day speaking slowly and shouting at me. He had the whole kitchen staff at it by seven o'clock. Anyway, the point of that story is that I shouldn't have said that I couldn't call you and I'm sorry I missed you, especially as by the time I got into the phonebox I was like a drowned rat. I'll try again later today or maybe tomorrow, it just depends on time.

And now onto more important matters – you and Glen Medeiros! I can't believe it. Not that you kissed but that you actually think you could have feelings for him and that's not because he's not cute because even with the perm and the stupid blouses he was cute but because it's you and you said you'd never fall in love and now after one kiss . . . It's just so unlike you but I am happy for you and I hope it's going well and that you haven't changed your mind about him since Sunday. And Gar with the girl from Bray is a turn-up for the books. I'm so happy that you were nice to him about it. He deserves to be happy and he's mooned over you long enough, so good for him and well done. I know it sounds condescending and I don't mean it to be but you really are changing for the better. I've just read that back and it is condescending – I'm sorry but you know what I mean, at least I hope you do.

Work is crazy busy and the craic is 90. We all get on so well and have such good fun and living away from home is a blast. You are going to love it so don't worry about London because you will have such a good time. There's a great freedom that comes with living in a bed-sit and away from parents. I thought I'd be lonely but I'm happy as a clam but then again I suppose Mum isn't around a lot so it's not so different and the fact that I don't have to cook is a real bonus because I get all my real food in the restaurant and it's beautiful. In fact I've decided that as soon as I get settled in Cork I'm going to do a cooking course at the weekends or evenings or something. Anyway, I have a coffee for breakfast. I buy a sandwich in one of the local cafés for lunch and then

I have an amazing dinner at six when we open. Perfect.

Colm and Ellen are great. Ellen met a Spanish boy in the local pub. He's a chef in a hotel close by. He speaks perfect English and he's really nice. They are a nice couple, at least that's if they are a couple – at the moment they are just seeing each other casually. Ellen just broke up with a boy in college and it was a bad break-up. She doesn't want to talk about it so I don't know the details. Colm is really kind and we've been hanging around a lot lately because Ellen is off with her Spanish chef. He brought me to a GAA game and I met his friends and they all seem nice but a few of them were slagging him about me but he told them to shut up and that we were just friends and I had a boyfriend so I feel better about things because I was starting to worry that we were spending too much time together and that maybe he thought something would happen. It's not really anything he has said or done, it's just a feeling. I'm probably mad. Declan says I have too high an opinion of myself – he's probably right.

It's not so strange that Paul mentioned to you that Declan mightn't get the points for medicine. Declan probably said something to him. He's really upset at the moment and I know you are annoyed at him but don't be. I was the one who decided to call him rather than you. Please be nice to him, he's having a really hard time. The other night on the phone he burst out crying because if he has to repeat it will kill him. He's really worried about it. He's been poring over the exam papers since I left and second-guessing every answer he gave. I told him to relax and not to worry. He did well in the mocks. He'll be fine. I felt so sorry for him, he really is stressed out, and Gar is always in Bray (and now I know why) and Paul is always slutting around in town so he's really lonely. He mentioned he might come down to see me if his dad will give him some time off in the garage but in the meantime please, please, please just be nice. He has noticed you ignoring him and he overheard you calling him Dicknose to Gina in the coffee shop – apparently he was standing behind the coat rack waiting for a table and walked out before you could see him. He's wondering what he could have done to offend you and he's only pretending not to notice that you're pissed off because he doesn't want to get on the wrong side of you. So I'm begging you as my friend to make up with him. He could do with a shoulder to lean on.

How's Clooney these days? Are he and V Kill P still seeing one another? I was really shocked to hear that. I was so sure she was a lesbian. Although if anyone could change a girl's mind, he could, and I know you hate to hear me talking about Clooney like that but seriously he is one in a million.

I'm listening to a lot of The Beautiful South at the moment – they are one of Ellen's favourite bands and I love both their albums, Welcome to and Choke, and I think you'd really like them too. When I listen to Song For Whoever I always think of you because it's clever. It makes me smile the way you do when you just say it like it is, no matter how blunt. I love that about you.

I'm glad you're hanging around with Gina again. Tell her I was asking for her. And I'm really glad you're seeing Glen Medeiros and can't even tell you how happy I am that you might be in love because maybe now you'll get off my back about Declan and now that I think about it I'm disgusted you'd even think that I would do anything with Colm. Declan and I have been together two years! And even though everything is changing, we are forever, just like you will always be my best friend.

Now I have to go. Colm and I are going for a hike with Ellen and the Spanish chef. I can never remember his name, it's something like Oreo like those American biscuits that Mary Walsh talked endlessly about when she came home from Florida last year. He's bringing a picnic basket.

I swear this living on your own stuff is easy peasy. Did I tell you that there is an electricity meter in my bed-sit? It's brilliant, it means I just have to fill it with 50p's and the electricity stays on and there's no bill at the end of the month. I just have to remember to have enough 50p's lying around and that's easy because I can keep them from my share of the tips so it's really handy.

Love you. And I'll try and call you again on Friday at around 4pm?

Lily XXXOOOXXXOOO
P.S. Top Gun is one of the best films of all time so stop slagging it off

and I loved when you went up to GM and said 'You're welcome' – that's so funny.

P.P.S. Out of U2 who would you date first to last? I'd go for
1. Larry Mullen
2. Bono
3. The Edge
4. Adam

TRY AND BE THERE AT 4PM ON FRIDAY AND GIVE ME AT LEAST TILL 4:30 BEFORE LEAVING BECAUSE THAT GOSSIP COULD BE THERE AGAIN.

P.P.P.S. One last thing – I totally forgot to tell you about the fall-out from the girl who found her Italian boyfriend kissing her brother. The brother has been kicked out of the house because the mother was with her and they both saw the kissing and apparently there was more going on than kissing. In fact the gossip told the last caller that they had their hands firmly down each other's pants. Anyway he's left town with the Italian and nobody knows where they went. I don't know the girl but apparently she's a fantastic singer and leads the church choir. I'm tempted to go to Mass just to look at her. That's another brilliant thing about living on my own – I don't have my mother making me go to Mass. Oh and one last thing – I saw a man who looked just like Danny the other day and it reminded me to miss him. Tell him I said hi.

* * *

When Lily recovered enough to start moving she ran down the hall, got into the lift and pressed the ground floor. It seemed to take an eternity for the door to close. *Come on, come on, come on!* She ran to admissions and waited impatiently while the receptionist gave a visiting couple directions to St Claire's Ward on 4. *Come on, come on, come on!* When they moved out of her way she leaned in.

"I need to find a Ben Logan," she said.

The receptionist typed in the name and shook her head.

"Nope, nobody by that name here," she said.

"Are you sure?"

"No Grogans."

"It's Logan. L.O.G.A.N."

"OK. Logan. Ah yeah, here he is."

"Where?" Lily asked.

"ICU."

Lily nodded slowly and silently walked away and when she was out of the receptionist's line of sight she started to run again. She didn't have time to wait for the lift which was already going to be full judging by the amount of people waiting in the hall. *Buggerballs and a side order of flaming fries!* She ran up the stairs taking two at a time and she made it in two minutes flat and without breaking stride.

Olivia Castle was on duty. She had transferred from Orthopaedics the previous year.

"Olivia," Lily said, glad to see a friendly face.

"Hey, stranger, what has you visiting ICU?"

"Ben Logan," she said.

"He's in 3. What's the connection?"

"None really. I knew him years ago."

"Oh."

"Well?" Lily asked.

"He took a serious blow to the head."

"How serious?"

"He's in coma and on a ventilator."

"Outlook?"

"Not good." She shook her head.

"Oh," Lily said and her heart sank. "Is it OK if I go in for a second?"

"Go ahead. And Lily, sorry about your friend."

"Thanks."

Lily walked into the room and instantly recognised Ben. He didn't have the facial injuries that Eve had. It was the back of his head that sustained the damage when Eve was ripped from his grasp and he was thrown head first into the stone wall he'd just been leaning against a short time before. He was surrounded by a wall of machines. Tubes poked out from under the bed linen, attached to various collection bags. Lily felt awkward standing there as though she was some sort of angel of doom. The room was stifling hot, the run up the stairs was the most exercise Lily had done in years, she hadn't slept well, she'd taken Ibuprofen on an empty stomach and so when she suddenly felt light-headed she thought *Fudge cake* and promptly fainted. She picked herself up before anyone saw and sat on the chair with her head between her knees. *After all this time, Eve Hayes and Ben Logan, what is going on?*

Olivia appeared with a woman who was distraught and silent. They walked into the room together. The woman stared at Lily sitting on the chair. Lily lifted her head and immediately jumped up, risking fainting for a second time.

"Lily used to be an old friend of Ben's, Fiona," Olivia explained to the woman who was pale-faced and trembling.

The woman redirected her gaze to Ben on the mention of his name. He was dying in front of her but she was the one who looked like a ghost. Lily was acutely aware she had no business being in the room.

"Really," Fiona said, with eyes fixed on her husband, "he never mentioned you."

"It was a long time ago," Lily said. "I was more of a passing acquaintance."

"Right," she said and Olivia pulled out another chair and sat her down. She hesitated before taking his hand in hers. His knuckles were scuffed but, apart from the fact that the back of his head seemed to be caved in, he looked perfect.

"We had a fight," she said.

"People fight," Olivia said.

Lily remained silent. She waited for the appropriate time to leave.

"It was a huge fight. I went to my mother's."

"You're here now," Olivia said.

"He's under a lot of pressure," she said. "Business is bad." She touched the wedding band on his finger. "I told him if he didn't get his act together I'd divorce him. I didn't mean it. I was just angry.

He'd let things get so bad and didn't tell me but he was only trying to protect me. I know that. I know he was doing everything he could to get out of the mess. I know he didn't want me to worry. He's my husband. I love him." Tears of overwhelming sadness and regret fell freely.

"I'm sure he knows that," Olivia said, putting her hand on Fiona's shoulder.

"I still don't know what really happened," Fiona said. "What was he doing there? It doesn't make any sense."

Olivia handed her tissue so that she could blow her nose.

"I don't understand," Fiona said.

Lily couldn't stand it any more. She made her apologies and left the room. *Oh Eve, what were you up to?*

Lily returned to her duties and watching the clock. One hour passed, then two, then three, then four. Declan appeared out of nowhere and nearly gave her a heart attack.

"I'm free for lunch if you're hungry later," he said.

"No. I can't," she said.

"Why not?"

"I had to take some time earlier to get my shoulder sorted. I'm running behind."

"What's wrong?" he asked, concerned.

"Adam took a look at it, it's fine – I'm taking Ibuprofen," she said and began walking toward the lift, hoping he'd follow her. She wanted him as far away from her floor as possible in case Eve came back.

"What happened?" he asked.

"You," she said and he clasped her hand to stop her in her tracks.

"Me?"

"And your games," she said and smiled so that he knew she wasn't accusing him of anything untoward.

"Ah," he said, "the time has come to set aside such childish things."

"Or buy a new headboard," she said.

He laughed and kissed her in the corridor and she knew their little flirtation would guarantee his good mood for the evening. *That's something.*

Another hour passed and then another one.

She saw Adam passing by the ward when she was taking out

Mrs Niven's catheter. She pulled the tube out so quickly poor Mrs Niven squealed.

"I'm sorry, did that hurt?" she asked while craning to try to work out where Adam was walking to.

"No pain although I did worry I'd open my eyes to find my fanny in your hand, dear," Mrs Niven said.

Lily smiled. "It's just the suction," she said and showed her hand to her. "You see, fanny free!"

When Mrs Niven was settled with her buzzer in hand and was enjoying an episode of *Midsomer Murders*, Lily went to find Adam. He was in his office.

He stood up, looking concerned.

"Are you OK?"

"Not really," she said.

He pulled the chair out and she sat. He sat opposite her.

"What's going on?" he asked.

"The woman you were operating on – Eve Hayes. How is she?"

"She's in recovery. Everything went well."

Lily nodded. "How bad were her injuries?"

"Can I ask why you want to know?"

"We used to be close," she said.

"Oh."

"It was a long time ago but . . ."

"I understand. Well, she has fractured the neck of her right fibula, a fractured left tibia and fibula, a fractured left shoulder, her glenoid was sheared off the scapula with a fracture of her coracoid and acromion. She has a fracture to her left cheekbone and a laceration over the left side of her face running into the lower portable part of her nose."

"Jesus," she said and she burst into tears.

Her reaction was as shocking for her as it was for Adam. He got up and walked around his desk, sat on it and patted her shoulder.

"She'll be OK," he said.

"I know – it was just shocking to see her like that," she said between sobs.

Adam didn't know where to place himself or what to do. He wanted to take her in his arms and cradle her like a baby but he thought it might be inappropriate so he continued to pat her on her arm, hoping that she felt comforted as opposed to awkward.

"I'm really sorry," she said, pulling herself together.

"Don't be," he said kindly.

"It's been a long day."

"I promise she'll be fine – I did some beautiful work in there," he said, grinning.

"I've no doubt," she said and she smiled and wiped away her last tear. "How long more in recovery?"

He looked at his watch. "She could be brought back any time now. She really did do well in surgery."

Lily looked at her watch. It was just after six. Her shift finished at seven thirty.

"OK. Thanks, Adam."

"You're welcome," he said, rising from his desk.

She stood up and he hugged her. She smelled like orange blossoms and her hair was soft when he leaned his chin on her head for just a split second. She patted his back in a friendly gesture and he berated himself for having a stupid crush on a married woman. *Get over it, Adam.* They parted.

Lily stood looking at him.

"One more thing," she said.

"Anything."

"Please don't mention Eve is here to Declan."

"OK."

"Thank you."

"You're welcome."

She moved to leave but turned back and hugged the door. "And Adam?"

"Yeah?"

"Thank you for not asking why."

He nodded and she left the room.

Eve woke up in pain. Her left leg was particularly bad. *My shoulder's on fire. Am I dreaming? This is a really painful dream. Holy crap, what's happening?* Her throat felt like she'd swallowed sandpaper and her lips were dry. When she licked her lower lip she felt the stitches with her tongue. *Oh, now I remember.* In her good hand she held something that felt like a remote control. She searched with her fingers for the button but before she could a nurse got off her chair and took it from her.

"Are you in pain?" she asked.

"Bad."

"OK."

She pressed on something and in that moment the fire in Eve's shoulder seemed to engulf her entire body but just as suddenly the pain drifted away and although she'd just woken she felt exhausted.

"There you go," Lily said and she handed Eve what felt like another remote control. "When it gets bad, press on it."

Eve registered Lily's voice and the memory of meeting her at the theatre door flooded back.

"You," she said.

"Me."

"A nurse?"

"A nurse."

"Good."

"Everything went well, Eve. You're going to be fine." Lily leaned in and fixed her pillow.

"Where's Ben?" Eve said, battling the urge to sleep.

"He's on another floor."

"How is he?" Eve said urgently, knowing she had only a little time before the drugs took over and she disappeared.

"He's OK."

And, although twenty years had passed since she'd last seen Lily and although she was doped up to high hell, Eve knew she was lying.

"Your voice still rises an octave when you lie," she said.

"OK," Lily said and she took Eve's good hand. "He's not so good, Eve."

"How bad?" she asked, battling to stay alert.

"He's in a coma."

"But he'll be OK," Eve insisted as opposed to asked.

"I don't know yet," Lily said and she was only half lying. He could still live and there was no need to tell her it would most likely be in a vegetative state.

"Oh God Almighty, Lily, he has to be OK," Eve said, beginning to slur, and big fat tears rolled down her face. Her head weighed heavy like a bowling ball and her burning eyes sealed shut.

When she was asleep Lily wiped her old friend's wet face gently with a tissue.

The next time that Eve woke it was to a rumpus. Lindsey Harrington in the bed opposite was a senile eighty-four-year-old who'd just had her hip reset following an accident in a park involving her mistaking a passing Bernese Mountain Dog called Prince for the pony she had by the same name as a young girl. Her daughter turned around in time to see her mother attempt to mount the confused animal which bolted leaving Lindsey Harrington on the ground with a broken hip and talking about sending him to the sausage factory. Eve heard the voices of the nurses as they tried to restrain Lindsey who was shouting loudly.

"Will you please let go! I have to find my handbag!"

Eve heard a nurse calmly telling Lindsey Harrington that she didn't have her handbag with her.

"Well, that's because it's been stolen! I'm surrounded by bloody peasants!"

"Nothing has been stolen, Mrs Harrington," another nurse said. "You have to stay still – you've just come out of theatre."

"Oh really," Lindsey Harrington said, relaxing, "I do love the theatre."

One of the nurses must have pushed a button because Lindsey Harrington disappeared after that and Eve soon followed.

Lily was too tired to face dinner when she got home. She was pale with exhaustion and her husband took pity on her and poured her a bath. He helped her in and sat on the toilet watching over her as she sank down into it.

"I haven't seen you this tired in years," he said and she nodded.

"Is it your shoulder?"

"It'll be fine."

"I didn't mean to hurt you. You know that."

"Of course I do."

"Why don't you take the rest of the week off?"

"No," she said and he heard the mild alarm in her voice.

"You're so desperate to get out of this house," he said sadly. "It's not like anyone will die without you."

Lily had learned to ignore her husband's disregard for her profession and professionalism.

"I'm fine," she said, "it was just a long day."

"OK."

"I have something for you," he said and he went into the bedroom and returned a minute later with a box.

Lily dried her hands with a towel and opened it to find a beautiful gold bangle inside. Declan didn't believe in a joint account but he was generous when buying his wife gifts. Lily often thought the reason she got away with second-hand and home-made clothes was because of the jewellery she wore with them. Declan had a habit of buying it when he felt bad about something. Her collection was extensive.

"It's beautiful," she said.

"So are you," he said, "and I should say it more often."

She sighed and smiled and took his hand in hers and with her heart in her mouth she seized the moment.

"I have a favour to ask," she said.

"What?" he said, placing the bangle on her arm and admiring it.

"Scott wants to work in the garage with your dad this summer."

Declan stopped gazing at the bangle and looked at his wife with a pained expression on his face. "I don't understand," he said.

"They must have talked about it when he was here for dinner a couple of weeks ago."

"And Scott wants to work in that garage?"

"Scott doesn't know the man you knew, Declan."

Declan was lost for words. He didn't know what to think. His relationship with his father had always been horrendous. When Declan was growing up his father was a malevolent, violent drunk. He chose to discipline Declan the way he had been disciplined as a young boy in a Christian Brothers boarding school outside Kildare. If Declan did anything his father considered to be breaking the rules, he would deliver him the worst and most brutal kind of beatings. Declan tried his hardest to be the best boy he could be but the problem was the rules changed depending on how much his father had to drink. Mostly he damaged Declan just enough so that the boy was horrified and terrified but not enough to invite suspicion. The Christian Brothers had taught him well. Declan's father was a haunted, angry and bitter man. His mother was a quiet and distant woman who tended to live on another plane of existence, one that was sustained by prescription drugs and an unhealthy ability to completely disengage from reality. She married a cold man and once when she had one too many glasses of wine she admitted to her fifteen-year-old son, much to his embarrassment, that it was a miracle he was born because she could recall on one hand the amount of times they'd made love. She was her husband's housemaid and mother to his child and although no one but the man himself could say if he ever loved her or not, in the eighteen years they were together he never once laid a violent hand on her. She turned away when her son was being disciplined, and pretended there was nothing sick or sordid happening on the occasions her husband really lost it.

When Declan was thirteen he joined his friends Gar and Paul for a smoke behind the bike shed in the schoolyard. Their teacher caught them and duly reported their misbehaviour to their parents. Gar was grounded for a week. Paul was grounded for two weeks and made to go to Confession. Declan was punched in the stomach, stripped of all his clothes and locked into the coal-shed deep in the garden behind his house. With only straw for heat he was kept there for twenty-four hours before his father freed him.

"Well, Smokey Joe, fancy a cigarette now, do you?" he had asked and laughed as Declan made his way back to the house blue with the cold and with straw hanging out of his arse. When he was fourteen his father kicked him so hard in the balls he had to wear a protective cup for two weeks. When he was sixteen he came home to find his father sitting at the dining-room table with a stick lying across it and Declan's report card in his hand. Declan had averaged

Bs in all subjects but he had only passed Irish. The teacher said he could do better and it was enough to warrant a beating. He smelt the whiskey on his father's breath as he shouted and roared and spit and when he grabbed the stick Declan punched him hard in the face. His father was shocked but still much stronger than his son. Declan received a broken collarbone and two cracked ribs on that occasion. He sat in the hospital waiting area listening to his mother tell the receptionist that he'd been playing rugby and when he was being patched up his doctor spent his time reliving his own glory days on the field.

"It's a hard game but worth it," he said. "It might feel like forever but you'll be back on the field in no time."

Declan just stayed silent while his mother smiled and thanked the doctor and told him what a promising rugby player Declan was and how proud she and his father were.

Afterwards he called to Lily. She was alone as per usual; her mother had taken a job working in a pub at night. She realised instantly what had happened and she took him inside and they lay together in her bed and she held him while he cried like a baby. He never told anyone else about what he went through at home but he told Lily everything, every beating, every humiliation, every emotion. They were so alike in a lot of ways, both only children who came from dysfunctional families, deprived of the parental love that was supposed to be bestowed naturally. They were both control freaks and overachievers. In their early years together Lily would have said that the only thing separating them was that, while she was emotionally neglected, she was never subjected to deliberate cruelty. In later years she realised that there was a second thing that separated them: she was a giver and her husband was a taker. He found strength in her acceptance, love and support of him and she found love in his dependence on her. They needed each other desperately. They fitted. They had their own little world that no one was privy to, even Eve. She would never have understood and Declan would have killed himself if anyone had found out – God knows he was close to it before they found each other.

Declan was desperate to go to university in Cork, not just because he wasn't sure he'd get the grades to follow Lily into

Trinity as Eve had suspected. He wanted to go to Cork to get away from the house that twenty years later he still had nightmares about, and Lily would have followed him to the moon to save him back then. When Declan got a place in Cork, he cut ties with both his parents and he never returned to the house again. The day after he left for college his mother moved out. She moved in with her sister who lived on a farm in Sligo and, although she and her son shared Christmas and Easter cards, she never accepted her culpability in Declan's maltreatment, she never apologised or tried to make it right. Maybe because she didn't feel it was necessary or maybe because she didn't care enough – either way their relationship had never progressed past those two cards per year.

Declan and Lily were married nine years and Scott was eight years old when his father knocked on his door. It was a Sunday and he shook his astounded son's hand, telling him that he had found their address in the phone book and took a chance on them being there. Lily was at first quite frightened and Declan was stunned but ready for a fight. And then the strangest thing happened. The ogre that had made Declan's life such a misery sat in their kitchen and pleaded for his son's forgiveness. He had been sober four years at that point. He was in AA and Declan was the last person on his list to attempt to make amends with.

"I hurt you worse than anyone else," he said.

"You were an animal," Declan had said.

"Yes," he admitted and he cried and tried to explain what had been done to him in his boarding school.

But Declan didn't want to hear it. "I don't want to know. I don't care. It's no excuse," he said, and his father didn't push it.

Lily often thought about that day and Declan telling his father that his torture at the hands of the brothers was no excuse and she agreed there was no excuse. If only he could realise the same reasoning applied to his own behaviour. Of course he was nothing like his father. He would never lay a hand on his children and although he carried anger and bitterness he battled with his demons every day. Lily knew that Declan did the best he could – she just wished he could do better.

Declan's father turned up often after that day. He was determined to make amends and when Declan realised that his father was serious about a relationship and he was utterly changed, he allowed him to visit once a month. The only time they saw each other was in Declan's house where he was in control because it was the only way he could have the man back in his life. Declan's dad had been in counselling and he was in a group partaking in a report being made on abuses by the church. He realised and admitted that his past was no excuse for his treatment of Declan. He had met many people who had suffered as he had and they had not turned into monsters. He was sorry and he meant it. Declan knew it but, despite that, he could just about tolerate the man who worked tirelessly to become a part of his son's new life. Scott had fallen in love with his grandfather from day one. He loved cars and trucks and racing bikes and was intrigued that his grandfather had his own garage. He loved to tinker and pull things apart. He liked the notion of building a car and when he was sixteen his granddad, with his father's permission, bought him a car that needed work and together they rebuilt its engine in Declan's garden and under his watchful eye. When the report on church abuses finally came out in 2009 the whole country gasped at what the children under the control of the church had gone through. Declan read it cover to cover and only then did he fully understand his father's past. They never spoke about it and, although it was strange, in reading that report he felt closer to his torturer as though they were kindred spirits in some way. He realised that his father was sexually abused, something he couldn't ever speak about nor would Declan ask him, and although their relationship remained fraught and difficult it had thawed considerably in the last year that had past.

Declan would never have considered letting his son work in the garage that was the scene of many a beating before that report came out but, sitting in his en-suite bathroom with his wife's hand in his, he found himself seriously considering it.

"He does love cars," he said.

"And if anything did happen and I know it won't, but if it did it would be different," she said.

"How's that?" Declan asked.

"Because he'd have you to come home to," she said and Declan nodded and his eyes filled and he squeezed her hand.

"I love you," he said.

"I love you too."

He didn't like to cry in front of his wife so he stifled a cough and left the bathroom. And maybe it was because Lily was reminded of her husband's painful past, or that she caught a glimpse of the boy she'd fallen in love with, or maybe it was seeing her old best friend battered and broken, or the ocean of grief she carried inside, or maybe it was all of those things because for the second time that day the tide she spent most days keeping at bay rolled back in and she sat in the bath quietly sobbing until she was empty and cold.

Eve woke up twice more during the night. The first time she woke screaming, having dreamt that she was on a rack, her arms and legs being torn apart. She could hear her arms dislocate and she saw the Ginger Monster throw her legs into an old wicker basket. She was wet and sweating profusely. Her heart was racing and she was crying out, begging him to stop and repeating loudly that she was sorry.

A nurse came running into the room.

"It's alright," she said in a soothing voice before she pressed the button and the fire ripped through Eve and she became still, warm and heavy.

The ceiling disappeared, revealing a perfect dark velvet navy-blue night sky complete with dazzling diamond stars and a pearl-coloured half moon. She was back on the dirt road leaning against the old stone wall separating a farmer's field from the passing traffic. Ben was eighteen again and wearing his Bruce Springsteen T-Shirt. He was sitting on the stone wall and she was standing between his legs, kissing his face and holding him close.

"I wish we could just stop here and live in this moment forever," he said, stroking her cheek.

"We can," she said and she hugged him tight, whispering in his ear that everything was going to be alright.

The second time she woke that night a nurse was standing over her fiddling with one of the various tubes or pipes attached to her.

She felt groggy and sick, the sharp pain she'd experienced earlier had dulled and she instantly knew where she was.

"What time is it?" she asked.

"It's just after 3 a.m.," the nurse said.

"Where's Lily?"

"She's at home. She'll be back on shift in the morning."

"OK."

"Can I get you anything?"

"Ben," Eve said and she drifted back to sleep.

Lily arrived into work early and checked in on Eve before heading to the nurses' station. She was asleep and comfortable. *Long may it last.* Post-operative Day 2 was often the worst day. *Hang in there, Eve.* She got to work and warned the other nurses to call her when Eve woke. As it turned out Eve waited until late morning and when Lily was at the bottom of her bed reading her chart before she opened her eyes.

"Good morning," Lily said, reading her chart. "You had a good night."

"Clearly we have different ideas on what constitutes a good night."

"Good to see you're coming back to us," Lily said and smiled.

"Ben?"

Lily's heart sank. She'd dropped by the ICU on her way to work and Ben did not have a good night.

"The same," she said.

"Can I see him?"

"No, Eve. Impossible."

"Because of his wife," Eve said in a tone that suggested her resignation. *Oh Jesus Christ, his wife.* "Does she know?" she asked, alarmed at the notion of the woman he married, and who'd she'd only ever seen smiling in holiday photos, making calls and freaking out trying to find her husband.

"She's with him," Lily confirmed.

Eve sighed with relief and then said, "I don't belong there."

"Not to mention that you've got two broken legs, a mangled shoulder and you've had enough hardware installed to give the Terminator a run for his money. You're going nowhere."

"But mostly I don't belong," Eve said and she was so desperately sad.

Lily remained silent.

"How long?" Eve said, pointing to the damage to her body.

"Weeks," Lily said vaguely.

"How many weeks?"

"Everyone heals in their own time. I can't answer that."

"Ballpark."

"Still pushy, I see."

"Please."

"Your shoulder is your worst injury. Adam basically rebuilt it and they might have to go back in and if they do it will be in another month or so. Your right leg is in a cast that's going to take about eight weeks, your left leg will take at least two months and physio."

"What about my face?" Eve asked.

"Well, you look a state now but you'll heal as good as new."

"Thank you."

"You're welcome." Lily sat down on the chair and pulled it close to the bed. "I found your phone. It was in the pocket of your jacket. I could call Danny for you."

"He died."

Lily's face fell, her heart sank and tears filled her eyes. It was as though she had been punched in the gut. When Eve and Lily parted company all those years ago, Lily had lost more than her best friend – she had lost the man who had been the closest thing to a father and Clooney too.

"Oh Eve, I'm so sorry."

"Thanks."

"If I had known . . ." Lily trailed off because she hadn't known and even if she had would she have had the guts to turn up to his funeral? *Maybe – after all, it was Danny*.

Lily fell silent. She needed time to compose herself. Eve saw the pain in her face. She understood it. Lily had loved Danny as surely as she had. A vision of Danny swinging tiny Lily around and around and Lily screaming "Faster, Danny, faster!" popped into Eve's head. They both were quiet for a minute or two.

"How about Clooney?" Lily said after a minute or two.

"He's in Afghanistan."

"What the hell is he doing there?" Lily asked, alarmed.

"Feeding people," Eve said.

Lily nodded. *Of course he is.*

"Have you a husband or children?" Lily asked.

"No."

"Who do I contact?"

"No one," Eve said and she was drifting off into sleep.

"Eve."

"What?"

"You can't go through this alone."

"Of course I can," Eve said.

She closed her eyes and when Lily was sure she was asleep she opened up the locker, pulled out her phone and went out into the corridor. She scanned through the contacts and found Clooney's name. She paused for a second or two before hitting the call button. Clooney's phone went to voicemail. She took a deep breath and waited for the beep.

"Hi, Clooney, this is Lily Donovan or, em, Brennan, I used to be Lily Brennan. Eve's friend? I'm ringing because she's been in a serious car accident. It's not fatal and she's going to be fine so please don't worry but she is badly hurt. She's going to need help. She's here in St Martin's Hospital. Ward 5 on the third floor. I hope you get this and I hope you can come. OK. Bye."

She switched off the phone, went back and put it back in Eve's locker. Her heart was racing. She didn't know if she had done the right thing or not. She was filled with anxiety because although she had no right to interfere Eve needed someone and, although they were on friendly terms and it was nice to see Eve, their friendship had died a long time ago and that someone could not be her. Lily was simply Eve's nurse and she didn't have the room in her life or the energy to be anything more. *I wish I could but I just can't, Eve.*

Eve was doubled over and throwing her guts up the next time Lily returned to the ward. Lily took over from another nurse she called Marion. She stabilised her while she threw her insides came out and cried with the pain the violent expulsion caused to her tender, taut, broken body. Spent and dizzy from discomfort, she lay back staring at the ceiling. It swirled and the figure 8 kept appearing and disappearing. She blinked and a rabbit jumped through the top circle of the figure 8 before burrowing into the bottom circle with his little button tail wagging.

Lily returned with Adam in time to hear Eve singing a verse of 'Bright Eyes' and waving her good arm at the ceiling.

"When we were kids we saw *Watership Down* eight times," Lily said.

Adam smiled and checked on Eve.

"Hi, Eve, I'm Adam. I'm your surgeon."

"There's a bunny on the ceiling."

"Hallucinations, tick," Adam said to Lily while making an invisible tick sign in the air.

"Lily says that you're good. Are you good, Adam?" Eve asked.

Adam laughed. "Yes, I'm good, Eve," he said. "I'm just going to check you for rash, OK?" He pulled down the sheet and checked her extremities.

Lily helped remove her paper nightgown so that he could check her body. She was free from rash. Lily made a mental note to buy her some nightclothes. *Please come home, Clooney.*

"Are you experiencing any tightness in your chest or difficulty breathing?" Adam asked.

"No. I'm experiencing rabbits," she said, pointing to the ceiling.

"No unusual swelling in your hands and feet?" he said, after examining them gently.

"So this is what doing drugs is like?" Eve said. "Because I'm not sure I like it."

"How about a headache?"

"Always have a headache. Life is one big headache."

When he finished the check-up and confirmed that she wasn't experiencing any dangerous side effects, he prescribed an anti-nausea injection which Lily gave her as soon as he left the room.

"What time is it?" Eve asked for the third time in the space of two hours.

"It's 4 p.m."

"How many bags and tubes are coming out of me?"

"Well, you have a bowel bag and a bladder bag, you have a tube inserted into your knee with a bottle attached to collect puss and the same for your shoulder. You have a drip in your right arm." She lifted Eve's good arm. "And this is a cannula – it means we can inject the drugs straight in here."

"So I just lie here, wee and crap myself and watch for rabbits."

"For today. Tomorrow will be a better day, I promise."

Before Lily left, she wet Eve's lips with some ice chips, trying to avoid the cut.

"Any news on Ben?"

"When there's news I'll tell you," Lily said, keeping her voice even-toned.

"OK."

At seven and before the change-over meeting, Lily called to see Eve for the last time that day. She was distressed and calling out in her sleep. Lily waited until she settled before joining the meeting.

Lily jogged around the shopping centre. It was an unscheduled trip and, as fast as she went about her business, she was still going to be late home. Her phone was out of juice and she knew that her delay would worry Declan and when he became anxious he became angry. She hoped he was still in the hospital. Her heart sank when she saw his car in the driveway. *Bugger-balls.*

"I tried to call you four times," he said, opening the front door as though he'd been waiting and watching through the glass.

"Sorry, my phone ran out of juice." She wasn't in the mood for an inquisition just because she dared to veer two hours off schedule.

"Where were you?"

"I got delayed."

"Where?"

"Are you the police?" She was annoyed by the limitations set by him. *Jesus Christ, just let me breathe.*

"Answer the question, Lily."

"Oh for God's sake, Declan, I was in the shopping centre. Are you happy?"

"What were you doing there?"

"I was looking for trainers for Scott," she said, putting her meal into the microwave.

"So where are they?"

"I couldn't find any worth buying," she said, sighing and leaning on the wall.

"You could have been dead."

But they both knew that Declan's first thought was never injury and always infidelity. He was obsessed, despite the fact that she'd never given him any reason. Of course he'd say that it was her fault he was the way he was because she couldn't help herself from flirting with every man she met. Lily felt terribly aggrieved by that because in all the years she'd been married she'd never even dreamed of straying even when things were at their worst.

"Does dead on my feet count?" she asked, attempting to lighten the mood.

She opened the microwave, took out her food and placed it on a plate. She sat at the dinner table, keenly aware her husband was looming and silent.

"Anything on the box?" she asked, hoping she could turn the tide.

"No," he said, sitting opposite her.

She started to eat. He sat silently.

"Where are the kids?" she said.

"Scott's out. Daisy's in the sitting room."

"How was your day?"

"Fine until I thought my wife was dead."

"What do you want me to say, Declan?"

"Say you'll never put me through that again."

"Oh for the love of God, I'm two hours late!"

Declan nodded before he picked up the plate she was eating off and threw it at the kitchen wall. The plate smashed and food went flying everywhere. Lily stared from the plate to her husband.

"Two hours is a lifetime," he said and he walked out of the room.

Lily sat at the kitchen table, resting her head in her hands for a few minutes before she cleaned up. She wondered what Eve would say. *I told you so? What did you expect? How could you pick that dicknose over me? Why didn't you give me a chance to explain myself? Why didn't you trust me? Everything could have been so different.* Maybe Eve had been right about Declan but Eve didn't know Declan the way she did. *Then again . . .*

She was cleaning the wall when Daisy appeared.

"What happened?" Daisy asked.

"I dropped my dinner," Lily said.

"Dad was really worried about you."

"Yeah, he told me."

"You didn't ask me how my recital went."

"Oh fudge cake! That was yesterday. I'm so sorry, Daisy."

"It's OK."

"How did you do?"

"I rocked it," she said, smiling.

"Did you tape it?"

"Of course."

"So why don't I make us some tea and you pull out some brownies and we'll watch it together?"

"Cool," Daisy said, grinning.

Lily sat with her arm around her daughter, drinking tea and eating a brownie for dinner, watching Daisy proudly play her piece perfectly. She thought about Eve being alone in the world. She thought about the nightdresses, underwear, perfumes and creams she had bought for her that were stashed away in the boot of the car. She thought about her husband's jealousy and temper. She wondered how long she could keep Eve's presence in the hospital away from him and mostly she feared the outcome if and when he found out.

Chapter 5

The things we do and don't say

Dear Lily,

I am so, so, so, so sorry that I wasn't there to take your phone call on Friday. I really did try to make it home but I was in town with Ben (I'm calling him by his name now because he's officially my boyfriend - more on that later) and his band rehearsal ran really late but Clooney said he picked up and you talked for about half an hour. What's that about? I thought you had no money for phone calls??? I asked him how you were and he said fine. I asked for your news but he just said you had no news. So what did you both talk about for that length of time? We haven't talked for five minutes since you left. Anyway I'm not going to complain because I should have been there but still I can't seem to get a word out of him unless he's annoying me. Anyway where do I start with my news? Ahhhhh, well, Ben is an AMAZING singer and guitar player. His band is so cool. There are five of them, Ben on vocals & acoustic guitar, Billy on bass, Mark on drums, Finbarr on keyboards and Tom on lead guitar. They're called Gulliver Stood On My Son and they're going to be as big as U2. The gig was brilliant last night. The band were already playing when Ben got on stage and he took the mike and screamed out that they were Gulliver Stood On My Son and he was Ben fucking Logan and the crowd roared and cheered. He says the f word because it's rock 'n' roll and it always gets the crowd going. And in the spirit of friendship and feeling a little like a numpty for being overheard calling Declan Dicknose, I did apologise and asked him to the gig. I went up to him in the bar and said, listen, I've been missing Lily and taking it out on you because she calls you all the time and she won't call me. He was actually very nice about it. He said that he was glad it was that because he was really worried he had done something to offend me and he'd hate to do that which was nice of him and then he bought me a drink. I made sure to buy him one back but it's the thought that counts. Anyway Declan came to the gig with Gar who brought the girl from Bray. She's really nice, she's just going into Leaving Cert in September, the poor cow. It's all ahead of her. Anyway, back to the gig. The band on before Gulliver Stood On My Son were called Bricking It and it was a good name for them because they were shit. I actually got quite stressed because even though the rehearsal had been good, I thought, what if they get so nervous they are shit too? It would be written all over my face and anyway I'd be doing him no favours just saying yeah you were brilliant when clearly they weren't brilliant but anyway it didn't matter because they were brilliant. They blew the roof off the place. I swear I was so excited and high I felt like crying. It was really weird and so unlike me. I don't know, Lily, I look in the mirror and I don't recognise myself any

117

more. (Oh don't freak out but I've cut my hair, it's in a bob now) I'm feeling and thinking so differently and it's so weird. And don't say I'm growing up or maturing or something else condescending. In a few weeks it feels like everything has completely changed and there's a part of me that wishes everything would just slow down a bit because I'm getting a little dizzy. Declan and Gar were really impressed by the band. Afterwards we all had drinks together in the bar a few doors down from the venue. You'd really like Ben's band. Billy is 21 and he's an electrician by day. He has a thick Dublin accent and he's really funny. He's always making jokes. He calls Ben Bono's Bollocks. HILARIOUS. Mark is 20, he's the quiet one but he's kind and really clever. His head is always stuck in a book and it's usually one I've never heard of but no doubt you'd know them all. He's in college doing Arts. He's still not sure what he wants to do besides the band. Finbarr looks really like your neighbour's dad, well, a younger version – he's doing history, he has horn-rimmed glasses but he's cute with a quiff. Tom is 19, the same age as Ben, and he's Ben's cousin. He lived in France for years, his mother is French and he speaks French fluently. They seemed to get on well with Declan and Gar. Ben and I left them drinking together in a pub and we walked around Grafton Street and around Stephen's Green and then he showed me a gap in the wall and I followed him into the park. It was really dark and a bit freaky to be honest. I said if he knew about the gap loads of others did and some of them could be perverts, rapists, murderers and junkies. He said I had a way of ruining a perfectly romantic gesture and I told him I didn't do romance. We found cover and talked for ages. He told me that his parents own the bowling alley. I didn't know that, did you? And that other weird boy that works there, the one who eats his own snot, well, he's the son of a friend of the family and he was perfect until he was

12 and then one day he started seizing and now he's a bit brain-damaged. It's awful, isn't it? I said, still, brain-damaged or not you'd have to have always had a taste for snot to eat it. He wasn't too happy with me saying that so we changed the subject. He told me that even though he likes college and marketing is OK he really just wants to sing and play the guitar. I told him that I had no doubt that's what he was meant for. He was happy then. We kissed and kissed and kissed until my face was sore and my chin was raw. He slipped his hand under my blouse and I didn't even feel him doing it until it felt good if that makes any sense? Not like poor Gar who nearly ripped my nipple off with his stupid hangnail. And then he started moving south and I held his hand and said NO WAY, not in a park, who do you think I am???? He said, I'm really sorry, I just got carried away and I'm so into you. I felt bad then so I gave him a hand job because he didn't seem to mind the fact that we were sitting under a bush. Oh and on our way out I found a stack of porn in plastic bags about two feet from where we were messing around, proving my point about perverts, rapists, murders and junkies. On the way to the bus stop he asked me if I was a virgin! Can you believe him, he really does have a nerve. I said it was none of his business and he stopped right then and there and grabbed me and pushed me against the railings. OK when I read that back it sounds like he attacked me but it wasn't like that at all, it was sexy and I hate to say it but he was firm but tender. (PUKING AS I'M WRITING) He looked at me straight in the eyes and I couldn't escape his stare even though I tried because I was embarrassed (ME EMBARRASSED IT'S UNBELIEVABLE) and he told me that it did matter because he was my boyfriend and he didn't care either way but it was an important detail! I nearly died. I mean it's so personal and I hadn't really considered that we were going out but then I suppose we are and I

want to be his girlfriend and I wish you were here because you are so much better than me at feelings. I feel like I want to run away but then I look at him and I want to stay and I'm scared. I know it sounds really stupid but I am. I don't get close to people. Aside from you, who knows me? Clooney a little bit but that's just because he lives with me and now when I think about it he doesn't really know me – I mean, I don't talk to him the way I do with you. Arrghhhhhh, it's so frustrating!!!! I just want to talk to you. I mean, what if he gets to know me and he doesn't like me any more? What if by the time he works out that he doesn't like me I like him so much that I'll want to die when he leaves. That's what was so great about Gar and he was nice and a distraction but if he decided to leave I didn't care. That was a real plus in our relationship.

Anyway back to the night by the railings. I turned the question around on him and of course he isn't a virgin, he's a 19-year-old college rocker! So I told him the truth. I said that Gar and I had tried it but it hadn't worked. He laughed which annoyed me so I walked on. He caught up and apologised and asked what I meant. I told him that we were in my room and I thought that Danny and Clooney would be out all evening. Gar was nervous and first the condom took ages because Gar was all fingers and thumbs and then when he got going and it was like I was being poked in all the wrong places and he was getting frustrated so I asked if I could help but he said no and then we heard the door and it was Clooney and he was shouting Danny's name and my name and just as Gar was finally pointed in the right direction Clooney came stamping up the stairs and Gar jumped up and out of the bed and that was pretty much the end of it. I didn't tell Ben that I'd been pretty much turned off after that and broke it off with Gar. I still feel a bit mean for not giving him a second

chance but seriously I was afraid he'd arrive with a
potholing helmet and a car jack. Ben said thanks for telling
him and I said you're welcome and then he said you won't
have to worry about that happening with me. COCKY OR
WHAT? I told him he needn't get any big ideas, I had no
plans to be with him like that in the near future. He just
smiled and said the best things are never planned. I told him
for a short boy he really does have a big head. He just
laughed. Anyway I've been thinking about it since and I'm
going to go for it with him. I mean so far so good and
let's face it I'm 18 and I don't want to go to London a
virgin. That would be a nightmare. I'll wait another week
or so and see how it goes but that's the decision made. I
know you probably think I'm rushing into it. I only know
him a few weeks etc but not everyone meets their soul
mate when they are 16 and you've being doing it for over a
year so I'm really falling behind here. I need to get going.
Oh and V Kill P is a lesbian. Apparently she and Clooney are
just friends and they've been spending more time together
because she's just split up with her girlfriend and he's
sworn off girls since Bushy Head started stalking him. I'm
not joking. He told Danny and me the other night over dinner
that she's everywhere he goes. She's always at the radio
station he's interning in. (He's a runner as opposed to host
which is a big comedown but it's a nice place to work and
it's only for the summer so he's happy enough.) She's at
the coffee shop he has lunch in and the bar he drinks in.
Danny told him that aside from the station he has to
change his haunts. Clooney's really upset but Danny says
change is better than rest anyway so it would do Clooney
good and if he sees her in the new places he'll have to go
to the guards. Can you believe it? Clooney didn't want to
do that - he said the whole place will be laughing at him
but Danny said, let them laugh, she's clearly not stable. I
agreed having met her - her hair alone confirms she's

121

definitely nuts. Anyway Clooney is hoping that making some changes will be enough to stop her and in the meantime I told him not to worry because he has a lesbian bodyguard. Danny and I thought that was really funny but Clooney failed to see the funny side, instead he stormed out and we didn't see him after that.

I met Gina for a drink. She's at a loose end because a lot of her friends went to the States to work in New Jersey for the summer. I asked her why she didn't go and she said she stayed to be with her boyfriend who then broke up with her when he got a chance to go to Germany with friends. I got a part-time job in Murray's coffee shop so she comes in and out when it's quiet and we catch up. She's going to come out for a drink with Declan, Gar, Paul and me on Friday. I'm going to meet Ben afterwards because he's working in the bowling alley late. Speaking of Paul, we're not seeing much of him. I went to his rugby game with the lads but his new girl wasn't there and after the game he chatted to us for five minutes and said he'd catch up with us later but he disappeared. I did run into him yesterday and we had a quick coffee. He was quiet and I asked him if he was OK and he said he had a lot on his mind. I thought he was still worried about his exam results but he said he wasn't and what will be will be. He's resigned to repeating if he has to. He asked me about Ben and I told him I really like him and he was really pleased for me. I asked him not to say anything to Gar but he told me that Gar would be fine and that I should just do what I want to do. He's right, I don't know why I'm being such a dick about it. I asked him to come to Ben's next gig and he said he'd try. So I hope he does. Before he left he told me out of nowhere that I was beautiful and I deserved to be with who I wanted to be with. I know it's NUTS. I don't know what he's been smoking or taking but it was really nice and I was embarrassed so I just said thanks, you too.

Oh did I tell you Clooney is going camping with some friends. I think it's to get away from his stalker but guess where they are going? Yeah, he's going to be heading to your neck of the woods. Don't know how big or small that town is but you might bump into him.

Right, I'm going. I bought a size 20 linen dress and I'm going to see what I can make out of it. I hope you are still having a good time and Colm hasn't tried anything yet because he will, I'd put money on it.

I'd love you to try to call me again this Friday at four. I promise I'll be there. Ben's working and I'm not meeting the lads until eight.

Miss you, love you,
Eve

P.S. My list isn't exactly opposite of yours which makes a nice change.
1. Adam (Because he's the coolest)
2. Bono (Because he's the singer)
3. Larry (Because The Edge looks like someone's dad)
4. The Edge (Because who wants to be with someone's dad?)

P.P.S. I know all I did was talk about myself (What's new?) but I just really needed to vent and I am looking forward to hearing your news.

And one last thing, I really am falling in love with Ben. TERRIFIED.

* * *

On Day 3 and for the first time since the accident Eve felt somewhat alert. The amount of morphine that was being pumped into her was being reduced and although sore and uncomfortable she felt brighter and less heavy-headed and hearted. Her morning started off with a bed bath given to her by Lily. She arrived with towels, fresh linen, toothpaste, lotions and swabs and placed them on the tray. She went off to fill a basin with warm water and it was the first time Eve realised that Lindsey Harrington had been joined by another woman in her seventies called Anne.

"Who's that?" Anne said.

"I'll be with you in a minute, Anne."

"Is that you, Abby?"

"No, Anne, it's Lily. Abby is off today. I'm just with another patient – I'll be with you in a while."

"OK, chicken. Not to worry. Not to worry. Is that girl any better, chicken?"

"Yes, Anne, she's much better," Lily said, appearing by Eve's side with the basin of water.

"Oh good, she was crying a lot last night. She's a noisy thing."

Lily smiled at Eve. "Yes, Anne, she is." She pulled the curtains around Eve's bed.

Lindsey Harrington shouted at Anne. "She's not the only noisy thing!"

"Jump off a building!" said Anne. "Do you remember what a roof is?"

"Peasant," Lindsey Harrington mumbled loud enough for all to hear.

Anne just shook her head and picked up a magazine.

Lily raised her eyebrows and Eve grinned. She braced herself when Lily pressed the button to raise the bed.

"It's OK," Lily said, taking the side rail down. "I've got you." She put on her gloves and placed a towel on Eve's chest.

She brushed Eve's teeth, being careful to avoid the stitches in her mouth. The fluoride burned and Eve sighed with relief when Lily offered her water to rinse with. Cleaning her mouth felt like an ordeal and now all she had to do was endure the rest of her tortured body being touched and tampered with. *Oh help me.*

"I'm going to take off that paper gown and place a bath blanket on you, OK?"

"OK."

Lily gently tore away the paper gown from Eve's battered body. She was covered head to toe in yellow, brown, blue and purple bruising. Her left leg and shoulder were both covered in brown iodine used to sterilise the areas that been operated on. Caked blood spilled out over the bandages. Lily placed the blanket on Eve. "We're going to take our time," she said and as terrified as Eve was she couldn't help but smile.

"Who's this *we* you're talking about?"

"Sorry, force of habit," Lily said, squeezing water from the facecloth before she gently washed Eve's face, careful to remove all the blood without dragging on the stitches.

Eve flinched once or twice but, although her eye and lip were still very swollen, when clean she started to look more like herself.

"Do you want to see?" Lily said.

"I don't know. Do I?"

"I promise it will get better," Lily said and she handed Eve a hand mirror.

Eve lifted it up and turned it and looked at her face.

"Holy crap," she said.

"It's not that bad."

"Easy for you to say," Eve said, dropping the mirror. "You still look like that beautiful teenager I used to know."

It was the first time either one of them verbally acknowledged that they had not been friends in a very long time.

Lily took the mirror from her. "Trust me she's long gone," she said.

"Nah," Eve said, "she's still in there somewhere."

"What about you, Eve? Are you still that girl?" And she couldn't disguise the edge in her voice.

"No, not exactly the same, you'll be happy to hear, but no one really changes that much – we are what we are."

Lily nodded and agreed with her old friend. "So, sleeping with a married man?" she said and Eve laughed a little.

"Not my best self . . ." Eve said.

"I read that you had a life in America," Lily said.

Ah, she has googled me. "I did. It consisted of work and nothing else. I got tired."

"And Ben Logan?" Lily asked.

Eve's eyes filled and Lily felt immediately sorry she'd brought the subject up.

"I tried to go back in time. It didn't work," Eve said and that ended the conversation.

Eve's shoulder was the biggest problem. She cried as Lily cleaned it because no matter how gentle she was, the slightest touch felt like she was being knifed. When Eve was finally clean and lying naked under the bath blanket, Lily placed the bags of stuff she'd bought in the shopping centre on the chair. She pulled out three nightdresses, two soft woollen shawls, and cotton underwear.

"You shouldn't have," Eve said.

"I'm not going to leave you dressed in paper. Danny would kill me." Lily said it as though she was doing it for a dead man as opposed to the woman in front of her.

"Thank you," Eve said, battling the urge to cry again.

Eve's right arm was pretty much immovable and so, in a bid to find her way around it, Lily had bought the nightdresses three sizes too big. She cut the narrow straps of one so that she could slip it over Eve without moving her shoulder or arm. She slipped it up under Eve's frozen arm and tied the straps at the back of her neck.

"Ingenious," Eve said.

"Ah but wait, there's more," Lily said and pulled out two large nappy pins. "It will look so much better when it's fitted."

She gathered the extra material at the sides and pinned it on both sides. She stood back and surveyed her work.

"Lovely," she said. "Would you like a wrap?" She held up a nice soft cotton wrap in charcoal black.

Eve nodded and Lily placed it around her shoulders.

"I'm really grateful," Eve said as Lily spritzed her with perfume.

"Glad to do it," she said and opened the curtains just as Clooney entered the ward.

"Clooney!" Eve said, clearly shocked, and it was clear to Lily by the look on Clooney's face that he was experiencing the exact same emotion.

"Oh Eve, what happened to you?"

"What are you doing here?" she said and she was crying again, not because she was worried for Ben or because of pain or desperation, but because she was really happy to see her brother.

He leaned over and kissed her forehead. He pulled up a chair and sat with her.

"As if I wouldn't come," he said.

"I must be dying!" she joked.

"Well, if you are it looks painful."

Eve looked from Clooney to Lily. "You shouldn't have but thank you," she said.

Clooney looked at Lily and he smiled a big wide smile. She smiled back before nodding goodbye and leaving them alone.

Clooney turned back to his sister, shaking his head.

"Of course she should have, she's your old friend and I'm your brother," he said and Eve looked into his haunted eyes and she was glad he was out of Afghanistan even if it took her nearly getting killed to get him home.

Clooney had picked up Lily's message the previous evening. He had been in meetings all day and his phone had been on silent. His driver was talking about a bombing which had taken place earlier that day. A woman approached American soldiers and blew herself up. Clearly the intention had been to take out the soldiers but for some reason the bomb didn't ignite as it should and while she managed to rip herself apart they were simply thrown clear. They were lucky, she was not so lucky. She didn't die on impact, instead she bled out slowly on the street. The soldiers and passers-by kept clear in case of a secondary detonation and so the rumour was that her only company on her journey to Allah was a stray dog who licked up the blood before cocking his leg. Inured by such stories, Clooney was tired from a day of endless repetitive frustrating meetings and so he wasn't particularly focused on what his driver was saying.

Clooney had been feeling restless for a while. Like Eve, his time in Ireland had instilled the need for change, but unlike his sister Clooney was familiar with the feeling because he never stayed in one place or doing one job for too long. He had been in

Afghanistan for two years and it was two years too long. He was sick of security checks, minders, restrictions, dust and death. He dreamt of an exotic climate, lush trees, white sands and blue sky and seas. He dreamt of rest and silence. He was tired of arguing about funding, figures and distribution channels. It was incredibly hard on the soul watching war destroy lives and livelihoods, reducing good people to beggars and thieves. Before his father died he had been involved in an incident in which he witnessed two American contractors being kidnapped. Their car was turned over by a roadside bomb, men seemed to appear from thin air and the scrambling security team was shot on sight. Clooney's car was three behind the car targeted for attack. As his driver manoeuvred to get them out of the area Clooney turned to look out the back window to see the injured men being dragged into a waiting van. The car sped off, the dust rose and the men were gone. Clooney knew that he was never in any real danger – the attack had been surgical – but it had a huge impact on him, especially when one of the men was later beheaded. Over the years he had become accustomed to being cautious but he had never before experienced real fear no matter how hairy the situation he had found himself in. That incident had acted like an injection of poison that was slowly spreading through his system. It stole away his sleep and that in turn was aging him. *I don't want to be here any more.* Clooney had been establishing an exit plan since he'd returned and part of that plan was to say goodbye to Stephanie, an American journalist who lived in the room down the hall. They had been seeing one another on and off for over a year. It was causal – she would disappear for days and weeks with George her ever-ready cameraman, chasing stories. When she was gone for over a month he thought she might have gone home but it turned out she'd followed a story into Pakistan. He liked her a lot, she was ballsy and fun. She had no business there, being a woman, but then again the same could be said for him and every other expat in the building. Stephanie came from a large family of boys and a military background – generations of her family had fought in wars around the world. She was born to be one of the guys and she seemed comfortable in chaos and far more so than Clooney who'd started off his career replacing shacks with houses by day and getting drunk and jumping into swimming pools at night.

He got back to the hotel and ate in his hotel room alone. Stephanie knocked on his door just as he was finishing up. She'd been MIA for over a week. He let her in and she kissed him.

"How did it go?" he asked.

"A bust."

"Sorry."

She hunched her shoulders. "Shit happens."

She kissed him again and he pushed her gently away.

"Exhausted?" she said, looking at his red-rimmed, steely, blue eyes watering.

"I feel like I've been hit by car," he said and she smiled.

"Me too. Why don't I run us a bath and we can lie down in it for a while before we hit the hay and lie down some more."

"Sounds good."

Stephanie went into the bathroom and turned on the tap. It came on after a couple of seconds' delay – at first it spluttered and the pipes could be heard groaning and then, as if someone unseen had given the system a good kick, it powered up and the hot water flowed freely. The tiles around the bath were cracked and broken. It was still a pretty room even though its best years were far behind it. The bath was discoloured, yellow in some places and black in others. The mirror over the sink was cracked from corner to corner and only held together by its golden thick frame. The hotel had once been one of the most beautiful in Kabul but like everything else its splendour had been eroded by its time spent in war. When it was filled, Clooney slipped in and she sat in between his legs and leaned back on him. The bath was deep and long enough for both of them and so they often unwound in it, usually with a gin and tonic but that night neither had a taste for alcohol. Clooney wrapped his arms around her and held her tight.

"Anything happen out there?" he asked her just as he always asked.

"Nope. All fine," she said as she always said and Clooney never knew whether to believe her or not because she was a risk-taker, arrogant and dangerous, and if he'd allowed himself to really care for her he would have gone insane worrying about the endless horrible things that could happen her. *Please don't die here, Steph.*

"There's more to life than war," he said.

"This again?"

"I'm going soon."

"You've been saying that for a while."

"Just finishing this project and going," he said. "You should think about getting out too."

"Nah. This is where I should be."

"Don't you want something else for yourself?"

"What, like a husband, house and kids? Is that what you want?"

"Hell no," he said. "I was thinking more like a hammock, a cold beer and a blowjob."

She laughed. "That's a pervert's holiday, not a life."

"It's better than this."

She turned and looked at his tired face. "I don't know," she said, "this is pretty nice." She kissed him and turned back around and slid further down into the warm water.

He stroked her arm. "There's less than two weeks left."

"And you're sure."

"Yeah."

"Where will you go?"

"I was thinking about the Galapagos Islands, maybe hang out in a beach hut for a while, then head into South America and take it from there."

"Are you thinking about looking for work there?"

"No," he said. "No work."

"All play. Good for you."

Clooney never lined anything up when he finished a contract but there was always something there when he wanted to return and usually his return was sparked by a major catastrophe. He worked best as an emergency response coordinator. He had led many teams into humanitarian disaster areas and in some cases they were the first international responders and so Clooney had in his lifetime witnessed the worst destruction and devastation that nature was capable of. He also saw first hand the strength of the human spirit, the best as well as the worst in people, as well as experiencing the best and worst of times. He celebrated the incredible highs when they had a win and a life was saved in extraordinary circumstances or because of the extraordinary risks taken. He wallowed in the lows when a three-year-girl starved to death in front of his eye because a food and medicine truck had broken down only a few miles away. He remembered every name and face of those he'd help to save and those for whom his help came too late. In the early days he'd work a six-month or yearly contract and then take a month or six off. During that time he'd live on a beach somewhere and always in a place where he could live like a king on a tiny budget. Of course Clooney's idea of living like a king was different to most. If he had sand under his toes, sun in the sky, a blue sea stretching out in front of him, a beer and food to eat, that's all he needed. It occurred to him recently that although he had been moving around, he had been working constantly since 2004. He landed in Indonesia two days after the 2004 Tsunami. In 2005 he left Indonesia to lead a team in New Orleans following Hurricane Katrina. In 2006 he returned to Indonesia and was based in Java following a powerful earthquake. He stayed in Java until 2008 when he'd been approached to carry out a food programme in Afghanistan.

Clooney had been used to death and destruction but it had always been as a result of a natural disaster. Afghanistan was his first war zone and he swore to himself it would be his last. However depressing and horrifying the loss of thousands were to a greater power, man willingly slaughtering man was not something Clooney could ever truly comprehend. Clooney lived by a simple ethos. The wrath of nature is inescapable, the wrath of man is avoidable. Clooney was about peace and love and all that good stuff. A tree-hugger at heart, he didn't belong in Afghanistan. The place, the ethos of those around him and the things he'd seen were slowly turning him into someone he'd never wished to be. He was becoming colder and more removed with each day that passed. *How can I give a shit about people who want me dead? And why wouldn't they? We've blown up your business, now here have a sandwich and a nice day.* Clooney was long overdue a break.

Those few months in Ireland with his father had been hard. Clooney was used to seeing the very worst this world had to offer and yet his designer-penthouse-dwelling sister was made of sterner stuff when it came to the end of his father's days. Clooney watched two parents die in that house and when the funeral was over he had thought about hightailing it to an exotic beach but a sense of duty prevented him from bailing on his work commitments.

He was just about finished and he was literally counting down the days. He'd miss Stephanie as he knew she would miss him although they were both confident that in each other they had found respite as opposed to enduring love and companionship. They were far too different for that. He was way too much of a happy-hearted hippy for her and she was a get-the-job-done, camera-toting military brat. They enjoyed one another but saying goodbye was never going to be difficult.

He'd noticed a burn on the back of her thigh when she was getting out of the bath.

"What happened?" he asked.

"Nothing," she said and gave him that look that told him that's the only answer she'd give.

He followed her into the room. She put on a light cotton long shirt and got under the covers. He threw on a pair of boxers and joined her in bed.

"I don't want you to die here," he said.

"It's as good as any place," she said. She kissed him and she fell asleep as soon as her head hit the pillow.

He would lie awake for another three hours before he'd join her and then it was only for an hour or two and upon waking he'd discovered Stephanie had left. He checked his phone to hear news that his sister had been seriously injured. Stephanie had left early. He packed and left a message saying goodbye at reception. He handed over the wrap-up duties to a colleague and he left Afghanistan without looking back.

Clooney sat on the chair looking at Eve and taking in the damage the Ginger Monster had done. She sighed.

"You look like you've been in a war," he said.

"Well, traffic was murder," she said, trying to make light of her situation but she wasn't convincing. Ben was constantly on her mind, making it difficult for her smile to make it to her eyes. "It is good to see you."

"I would have preferred to meet on a beach."

"Me too," she agreed. "Remember Bali?"

"How could I forget?"

"We should have done that more," she said.

"You were always working."

"Those days are over."

"So we'll do it again."

"Now *you're* always working."

"I'm finished," he said. "There were only two weeks left on that contract. Jerry's going to wrap it up. I'm done."

"Ah, I'm glad. War doesn't suit you."

"You're right."

"And so to a beach?"

"As soon as you can come with me."

"You don't have to do this, Clooney."

"I know."

"But it's really good to see you."

"Back at ya," he said. "Now tell me everything."

Clooney was the only person that Eve had confided in about seeing Ben when she was last home and he'd warned her of the dangers of sleeping with a married man, especially one who claimed to be happy. She had never involved Paul, Gar or Gina in their sordid secret. They didn't need to know and, if Clooney hadn't caught her exiting Ben's car around the corner from her house, she wouldn't have told him either. Ben was Eve's shameful secret. She didn't need to fear hell to embrace morality. She knew their affair was wrong. It worried her and it mattered to her.

Clooney was a lot more easy-going than his sister when it came to ethics. "As long as no one gets hurt it's nice to see you have a little fun," he had said.

"If it feels wrong, it is wrong," Danny used to say and even when it felt right it had felt wrong. Eve was a very matter-of-fact person and she always had been. She said it like it was regardless of the consequences. She got the job done. She was who she was without apology. She didn't like sneaking around, it didn't excite her. She abhorred the treachery involved in their seeing one another and the only thing that kept her going back was the drug that was his eyes when he looked at her. Since returning to Ireland she told herself their relationship had changed and she was only trying to help with his failing business. Then they had sex and were hit by a car. Eve may not have believed in a divinity or divine intervention but she did accept the possibility that the universe was telling them something. *If it feels wrong it is wrong.*

Eve spent the next hour telling Clooney about selling off her business and returning home and helping Ben and their once-off liaison culminating in the accident. She cried when she told him that Ben was on another floor in a coma with his wife by his bed. She begged him to find out some information because she was absolutely sure that Lily was hiding the extent of his injuries from her. He promised he'd find out. She gave him the keys to her apartment and told him to stay there. It had been four days since she'd been home so she warned him to stay away from the dairy in the fridge and that he'd have to clean up the knickers that Ben had ripped off her in her hall. She mentally berated herself for not being a more efficient housekeeper. That night when they'd got out of the shower and she'd put on a fresh pair, she'd momentarily considered going into the hall and picking the other pair up but then Ben kissed her neck and she forgot. Once again, as she passed them on the way to her front door, she considered it but then she looked at her watch and decided she couldn't afford the three seconds it would have taken to pick them up and pop them in the bin or wash basket, depending on whether or not they were salvageable. *That's what you get for wearing a string.* Then it occurred to her: *At least I was wearing fresh knickers when I was hit, that's something.*

Clooney had travelled through the night and he hadn't slept. Eve insisted that he go home.

"I don't want to leave you," he said.

"You smell."

He laughed. "OK. I'll go."

"Good."

He kissed her forehead and left.

Lindsey Harrington was first to speak.

"Who's that handsome man?" she asked.

"My brother."

"Do you think he'd go out with me?"

Anne piped up from behind her book. "If he was deaf, dumb and blind maybe you might have a chance, chicken."

"Tell him that my curfew is ten o'clock and he'll have to speak to my father," Lindsey said.

"Of course," Eve said.

Anne shook her head and sighed heavily. She had no time for the demented. "She shouldn't be here, she belongs in the nuthouse," she said.

There was an empty bed beside Eve. A nurse she didn't recognise came in and started to make it up.

"Are we getting another roommate, chicken?" Anne asked.

"Yes, she'll be joining you soon."

"I hope she's a young one. We need to bring down the average age in here." She pointed to Eve. "That poor girl must think she's been taken to an old folks' home."

Eve laughed a little.

"I'm afraid you're out of luck, Anne," said the nurse. "Beth is seventy-five."

"Another hip?" Anne said.

"Another hip."

"Is she nuts?" Anne asked while directing her eyes towards Lindsey whose eyes were open though she didn't appear to be listening.

"No, Anne, she's not."

"Well, that's something, chicken," Anne said to Eve and Eve smiled as a means of acknowledgement.

Anne Murray was seventy-two years old. She'd broken her hip when she'd tripped on her grandson's toy train that he'd left on the stairs. "It was lucky I didn't break my neck," she had told Eve, "and I'm not even going to tell you how close I came to putting my head through the glass window at the bottom of the stairs. The pup!"

"I have two Labrador puppies, Simple and Simon," Lindsey piped up. "Simple chases his own tail until he gets so dizzy he falls on his side then he rolls onto his back and waits for me to rub him. My daddy says that when I'm old enough I can take him for walks. Simon doesn't like to walk. He's very lazy. Daddy says he was born an old man."

"Oh Christ, she's off again!" Anne said.

Lindsey would soon be celebrating her eighty-fourth birthday and her father had died thirty years before. There were moments of lucidity and in those moments she was sometimes rude and abrasive and other times sad and teary but when she was lost in times gone by Eve found her quite sweet. Anne made it very clear that she did not share Eve's sentimentality, simply referring to Lindsey as a pain in the hole.

Beth was wheeled in soon after that. She was moaning and she cried when they moved her onto her bed. She was riddled with arthritis – even as she passed, Eve could see one hand was so badly affected it was like a claw. She cried a little when the nurse left. Anne shouted over to her that she'd be alright. She told her to settle down and sleep – it was the best thing for it. The woman disappeared soon after that.

Eve turned on her little TV for the first time. She watched some news. The dinner lady came around and for the first time since her accident Eve was hungry and ready to eat. The dinner lady cut up her food for her and using a spoon she ate a light salad complemented by a slice of brown bread. She drank a cup of tea and felt almost human again.

Clooney had managed to track Lily down before he left the hospital. She was busy but gave him five minutes in the visitor's room.

"I just wanted to say thanks for getting in touch," he said.

She told him she was happy to do it.

"It's really good to see you," he said and they gave one another an awkward hug.

"I often wondered what happened between you two," he said.

"You were never one to beat around the bush."

"Eve would never tell me."

"It was all a long time ago."

"You were so close."

136

"We were kids."

"And it had nothing to do with me."

"No." She shook her head.

"Good," he said.

After that they talked about Eve's prognosis, recovery time and of course Ben. Lily explained that it was looking increasingly unlikely that Ben would make it. Clooney wanted to tell Eve the truth but Lily wasn't sure it was the best course of action.

"She's not well enough," she said.

"She's stronger than she looks."

"I disagree," she said. "Not when it comes to this."

"She'll never forgive me if I lie."

"So blame me."

"I just wish she could say goodbye," he said. As someone who said goodbye to two parents and who witnessed hundreds and possibly thousands of people lose and mourn loved ones, Clooney knew how important that last goodbye was.

"He's a married man, Clooney," she said.

"I know," he nodded.

"And, besides, she's still bedridden."

"You mean on that bed with wheels."

She looked at him and shook her head. "He has a wife," she said.

Clooney nodded and left.

Lily called in to Eve just before she left for the evening.

"Do you need anything?" she said.

"No, thanks," Eve said, keenly aware that it was a flying visit and that since Clooney had walked in the door she had seen a lot less of Lily. *She's pulling away – but of course she is. Silly to think we could actually be friends after all this time.*

"OK then," Lily said, "see you tomorrow."

"Lily."

"Yes."

"Thanks again."

"You're welcome," Lily said and she was gone.

Adam called in to see her after Abby gave her something to relax her.

"How are you doing, Eve?"

"I'm OK."

"Good."

"Can I ask you a question?" she said.

"Of course."

"Am I ever going to be back to the way I was?"

"Yes . . ."

"But . . ."

"It's going to take a lot of work."

"When do I start?"

"Give it another few days."

"It's going to hurt," she said.

"Yes, it will."

"Life's a bitch," she said.

"And then you're dumped by one," he said and she grinned.

"Can I ask you something else?" she asked.

"Of course."

"Do you know Lily's husband?"

"Yes," he said tentatively.

"Is he still an asshole?"

Adam couldn't help but smile. "No comment," he said.

"Understood."

Adam walked out of the room after looking in on Beth. *I like Lily's friend.*

The taxi stopped outside Eve's apartment block. Clooney realised that he'd forgotten to get cash.

"Damn it. You don't by any chance take Afghani, do you?"

"Is that some sort of hash?"

"No."

"Pity."

Clooney laughed. "It's good to be home," he said, before asking to be taken to a bank machine.

He got out of the car in the village and, when he'd taken out his money and just as he was getting back into the cab, he heard his name being called.

"Clooney?"

It was Paul.

He shook Clooney's hand. "Welcome home, Eve didn't mention you were coming back."

It was clear Paul had no idea that something terrible had happened to Eve and, when Clooney explained he was home because of her accident, Paul joined him in the cab to hear the rest of the story.

Clooney let them in using Eve's key. He swiftly picked up her knickers from the floor and binned them before Paul even noticed. He was so stunned by the story that Clooney had told he was too distracted to notice much at all.

After washing his hands and wiping his mind, Clooney opened the fridge and found beer. He offered one to Paul who took it gratefully.

It was a nice warm evening so they sat on the balcony looking out to sea while Clooney explained Eve's relationship with Ben.

"And she accuses me of being a dark horse," Paul said, stunned that chatty, open Eve had wanted to keep it secret from him. He was also surprised to hear that Lily was nursing her. "I thought she'd done medicine," he said, shaking his head. "Jesus, she had the best exam results in the school."

"Nobody knows who they are at eighteen," Clooney said. "She's a nurse, wife and mother. She seems perfectly happy."

"I'd heard she'd married Declan but I haven't seen either of them since they left for Cork. They just seemed to cut everyone off," he said. "Did Eve ever tell you what happened between her and Lily?"

"No. You?"

"No. It's a mystery."

"Ah well, all in the past now. Lily is being really good to her."

"Jesus. Lily Brennan's back on the scene!"

"Lily Donovan now and by the way she's still a beauty."

Paul smiled. "Eve Hayes and Lily Brennan were the best-looking girls in our school and I wasn't with either of them." He shook his head sadly.

Clooney laughed. "I heard you had your pick of girls back then. Little did they know you preferred boys."

Paul smiled but didn't respond. Instead he focused on how attractive Clooney was. His blonde hair had silver highlights and he'd be grey soon. His face was brown and battered but the battering lent character as opposed to stealing from his looks. His steely blue eyes were still as piercing as they were when he was young but they were somehow sadder. He was a beautiful boy that Paul had often fantasised about but he was even more handsome as a man.

"Did you meet Declan?" Paul asked after a minute or two.

"No. To be honest, I wouldn't know him if I did."

"We were so close in school, at least I thought we were, but then he left for Cork and I was going through my own shit. Gar tried to keep in touch with him but he never responded. I heard rumours years later, about his dad, but I don't know – his father always seemed like a nice guy to me."

"I know one thing," Clooney said. "Eve hates him, and Eve doesn't hate without good reason."

"I can't believe she was with Ben Logan."

"Poor guy."

"His poor wife. Losing your husband is bad enough, never mind finding out he was having an affair."

This was not something Clooney had considered. "Oh no," he said. "I didn't think of that. Maybe she doesn't have to know."

"Eve is the only witness to the incident that has either brain-damaged or killed her husband. Why was he there? Why were they together?"

"Jesus, that's all she needs."

They had another beer together before Paul left Clooney to a well-earned night's sleep and for the first time in months he was asleep within two minutes of lying down.

Paul called Gar as soon as he got home. He told him about Eve's accident, her terrible injuries, the fact that she was with Ben Logan when it occurred, that he was in a coma with his wife by his bedside and that Lily Brennan was nursing Eve. Gar put him on speaker so that Gina could hear the conversation. The conversation was a series of shocks.

Eve could have died. Ben Logan was dying. Lily was a fucking nurse. They agreed that they would visit Eve together the next evening. Gina was hoping to see Lily but Paul told them that she worked days only.

"Damn it," she said. "I wonder what she looks like now."

"Still a beauty," Paul confirmed, confident in Clooney's assessment.

"And poor Eve!" Gina said.

"He said she's in an awful way but she will recover."

"Why didn't she call us?" Gina said.

"She didn't even call Clooney. Lily did."

"Lily Brennan," she said. "Whatever happened with those two?"

"No one knows."

Gar was silent, taking it all in.

His wife turned to him. "What do you think?" she asked.

"Whatever happened with all of us?" he said.

Declan was Gar's best friend, at least that's what he had thought growing up. When Declan left for Cork and cut off all communication it had really hurt him. He didn't understand why Declan had done that. When they were kids he never questioned Declan's stories about his injuries and Declan never let him in. He heard rumours after Declan's mother disappeared but he'd never believed them. He knew his dad, he was his family's mechanic and he always seemed like a lovely man. He had wondered why Declan and Lily had chosen to cut themselves off from their hometown and the people who cared about them. He wondered what he could have done to deserve to be dismissed in such a cruel manner. He grew up believing he would be Declan's best man at his wedding and Declan would reciprocate. He wasn't even invited when Declan married one year after he left and he only learned of the wedding eight years later when Declan's father mentioned it when he picked up his car after a service. He was too angry to ask questions. He didn't want to know. He didn't care. He felt bad for Eve and of course he would visit her but the thought of seeing Lily or God forbid Declan rankled him. *Fuck them both.*

Paul continued drinking beer in his house after he got off the phone to his friends. He was freaked that Eve had been in hospital alone for four days and she didn't think she could call him. He understood that their friendship had only been recently rekindled and he also understood her need for privacy – if anyone understood that, he did. He didn't care that she hadn't confided in him about Ben but he cared that she had nearly died and he wouldn't have known if he hadn't bumped into her brother at a bank machine. *I thought we were friends.* As recently as the drink after their last game of tennis, he had considered confiding in her. Paul was exceptionally private. He gave little of himself away but that night she had pushed and pushed. *All the while she was screwing Ben Logan on the sly, the cheeky bitch!* They were both pensive. The game had been robust and they had enjoyed the competition. He had won but only by a point. She noticed a cute guy at the bar and mentioned him but Paul didn't agree.

"He's too short."

"Nothing wrong with short," she'd said.

It all makes sense now – bloody Ben Logan.

"Are you seeing anyone?" she'd asked for the hundredth time and this time he had considered telling her but once again he balked. *Too many questions to answer.*

Paul grew up in a house where you grew up to be a hard worker, married, with kids and mortgage. When he was young he knew he was different but for a long time he couldn't work out what was different about him. He loved girls and he was tall and handsome and built and in a winning rugby team so he had his pick of girls. He went outside of his hometown, not because he was looking for beards as everyone suspected when he came out, but because the only girl he was interested in was Lily and she was with his friend. Eve was beautiful but he never felt that way about her. He could have married Lily. He wanted to tell Eve that night that he was sexually attracted to all those girls he was with back in the day and they did have a great time, and the only reason he came out was because, although he had great sex with those women and many boys at the time, he could take or leave them all until he met Paddy and fell head over heels in love.

Paddy was the one as far as he was concerned. They had met at a club and the first moment he saw him he knew. *I love you.* Paddy had long hair like Samson. He was broad and dark and basically he

142

was the male version of Lily. He had her softness, her openness and kindness. He was beautiful to look at and he had the soul of a saint. He was funny, positive, free-thinking, inspirational and most importantly he knew who he was. That was something that Paul could never really work out. When he fell for Paddy he was sure of himself for the first time. Paddy was a proudly open gay man and he demanded that of his partner. Paul came out to his parents to ensure that the relationship with the one he loved survived and, despite their close-mindedness and their ridiculous response, he didn't care because he was in love and as far as he was concerned it was forever and that meant he was gay. Except he still noticed a beautiful woman, her curves, her skin, her smell, her hair and the way she moved. He didn't covet any women, no matter how beautiful, for a long time but he always noticed. After he and Paddy were together for years and their sex lives became stale they were still best friends. Paul still loved Paddy but he no longer cared to share his bed. Paddy felt the same but because they shared a home and a dog and a life neither wanted to admit it. Until one Friday night when Paddy was away at a convention in Brighton for the weekend and Paul went to a pub in Dublin and met a girl called Simone.

Cappuccino-skin, brown eyes and silky brunette hair, she was Paul's type from the start. She sat next to him sipping on a beer and he couldn't help but watch her read an article in *Vanity Fair* as she was so consumed by it. He watched her react to what she was reading. One moment smiling, the next shocked, the next saddened. He could read every emotion on her face and her beauty and emotional openness intrigued him. When she was ready to leave, she leaned down to grab the bag that she'd left by her feet only to find that it was gone. She stood up and looked around disbelievingly. Paul had seen her bag and recognised it was a 'Mulberry' only because Emma the girl in the cubicle next to him was a 'Mulberry' fanatic and had at least five of them and talked about them endlessly as though they were her pets. He hadn't noticed anyone slope in to steal it, he was so busy focused on the story playing across her face. When she realised it was gone she looked so lost. He stood up and asked her if he could help. She explained that her bag had just been stolen and was so embarrassed that she couldn't pay for her beer.

Paul immediately offered to pay and then he walked her to the police station to make her complaint and insisted she use his phone to cancel her cards. When the complaint was made, her cards cancelled and evening had come, he asked her if she wanted dinner. She did. They ended up in bed together in his apartment for the entire weekend.

Paddy returned on the Monday and Paul sat him down and told him he'd met someone. Paddy couldn't believe his ears, most especially when Paul admitted it was a woman. He was devastated because for him the betrayal was worse with a woman rather than a man. Paul didn't want to hurt him and was devastated by the devastation he had caused. *It was time.* They fought, screamed and cried. Paul reminded Paddy that it was the most passionate they'd been in years. Before he left Paddy and their dog Samba he kissed them both and, grief-stricken, he left the house to move into a hotel. A week later he rented a house in his local town and a year later he bought that house.

Simone had been a fixture since. She was a model, spending a lot of time abroad. She was based in London and they had met when she was spending time in Ireland on a shoot. Their weekend had been a one-off as far as both were concerned. She was returning to London and he was returning home but something changed during their two days together and she couldn't simply go home and forget him so she called him as soon as she arrived in London. That first year they only saw each other a handful of times. He went to visit her in London twice, she came to Ireland twice and they met in Paris once. The second year she ended up doing more work in Ireland and they spent one month together in Cuba. That's when it became serious. Paul realised he was in love when saying goodbye became impossible. He had considered moving to London but Simone was tiring of the model scene – at twenty-nine she was considered ancient and the jobs were drying up. In five years she had taken up five courses. Styling, she didn't like it. Make-up, not for her. Hair, definitely not. Photography bored her in the end. Then by chance she ended up doing a dog-grooming course and she loved it. She met a photographer at a shoot who told her about a shoot he'd done in Cornwall. It was in a dog-grooming parlour which had a kennels and studio attached for photo-shoots. As a dog lover who had never had the stability in life to be able to own a dog, she was intrigued and after two sleepless nights in which she fantasised about her parlour-cum-kennels-cum-photography studio, she booked herself onto the first course she found and loved it. Simone had been coming and going from Ireland for months. She'd found the perfect location to set up her new business and she was moving in with Paul.

He just hadn't told his friends and family. As far as they were concerned he was gay. He had confided in Simone about his bisexuality and he did it that first day, mostly because he thought he'd never see her again. Simone hadn't made an issue of it – in fact she admitted having messed around with girls herself although she never went all the way. "It just wasn't me," she said. She understood why he hadn't introduced her to friends and family and didn't care when she lived abroad because their time together was precious. But now it was different, now she was coming to live with him in less than a month and they were becoming a family.

The morning she told him she suspected she was pregnant he was sitting in a hotel in London, enjoying breakfast in bed. She brought it up as though she was asking him to pass the butter.

"The crumpets are really good," she said.

"Aren't they?"

"I think I'm pregnant."

A grin spread across his face and she saw it before he even realised he was doing it.

"I'd really like that," he said, dropping his crumpet.

"Me too," she said.

They hugged and kissed and when they parted he asked her to marry him

"I'd love to," she said and that was it.

They bought a test in Boots, returned to the hotel, she peed on the stick while he waited anxiously, already behaving like an expectant father. The stick turned pink instantly. Simone was having Paul's baby and when she held it up and shouted the word "Score!" he cried like one.

They planned a simple wedding to be held in their favourite

hotel in Westport in September. She would be only a few months pregnant by then. Simone's family and friends had all met Paul. In fact he had spent so much time in London in recent years that they were all really shocked when they decided that she should move to Ireland and not the other way around, but then Paul had a good, high-paying, steady job and large house in a beautiful spot and she was pretty much out of a job, broke and looking to start up something new. She did worry how Paul's friends and family would take the news and he worried even more. *How do you go back into the closet?*

Paul was in his mid-twenties before he really confronted his bisexuality. He went to the library to read about it and when he couldn't find anything that really explained to him who he was and what he actually wanted, he went to a sexual counsellor who explained to him that he was a three on the Kinley Scale which meant he was equally attracted to both men and women and from his past behaviour she concluded he was an alternating bisexual, which meant that when a relationship with one sex ended he could find himself falling for and having a relationship with someone of another sex, and that is exactly what happened. He could have fallen for a guy just as easily but Paul Doyle realised that the sex didn't matter, it was the person he was attracted to that did.

And in Simone he had found someone who accepted him for exactly who he was. She wasn't jealous, she wasn't possessive, she didn't care about his past, she didn't care that he got a hard-on for other men. He was with her and she was confident in them. Simone wasn't a worrier. She lived in the moment. "When you're happy be grateful not greedy," she'd say. She did understand his reticence about explaining himself to friends and family, especially as he'd made such a big deal about coming out.

He felt foolish and worried his friends would think him a fool. As for his parents, although his father had come around in recent years, his relationship with his mother was extremely strained. They tolerated one another but she believed that all gay men and women were going to hell in a hand-basket and the only thing that she could offer her son in terms of support was her prayers. Of course she'd see his marriage and fatherhood as a win. She'd claim it was the power of prayer that saved him from himself and eternal damnation and it sickened him. Simone laughed at the notion but then she hadn't met his mother.

"You can say I used to be a man if it makes you feel any better," she said.

"If you weren't pregnant I probably would have."

"You're going to have to do it soon," she'd said when he was leaving her to return home for the final time without her.

"I will."

Then he'd gone back to work and put it off and put it off because he didn't want to have to go house to house explaining himself. Paul was so private, the notion made him feel nauseous. Now Eve was in a terrible condition. She was having an affair with Ben Logan and he, Gar and Gina would be visiting with her the next night. Lily was back on the scene and Gina Lynch was beside herself waiting for all the gossip. The heat was definitely off him and so it was the perfect time and place to tell them he was going to be a father and invite them to the wedding.

Cheers, Eve. Hello, Lily.

Chapter 6

If this is the end

Dear Eve,

I'm lying in my bed writing this to you. Had a really heavy night last night – we all ended up in the club and I don't even remember getting home. Colm dropped over at 10 this morning with a few scones. He told me he brought me home (and no, nothing happened) and said I was singing most of the way. We sat on the bridge for a while and talked. I told him about Declan and our lives at home and plans for Cork. (Don't remember any of that conversation!) Before he left he hugged me and told me that I had no idea how amazing I was and he hoped I would see it some day. I was embarrassed. I didn't know what to say. He said Declan was very lucky to have me and he hoped he knew it, which I thought was very cheeky, but because I couldn't remember what I'd said I wasn't able to answer him. He looked concerned (if that's the right word, maybe troubled would describe it better) and the vibe was weird. I feel a bit sad now and I don't know why. I hate this feeling, I should never have got so drunk. It's pathetic. I'm thinking of staying in bed all day. I have a stack of books I want to read. It's just me, my bed, music and books.

OK, to cheer myself up a bit here are my top 2 reasons why living on my own is amazing:

1. Independence
2. Peace

I can get up when I want. I can eat or not eat what I want. I can come and go as I please. I'm free! It's an amazing feeling. There's no shouting, no fighting. I haven't been to Mass since I got here and I was thinking about going to Confession when I arrived just to confess having sex with Declan just so I could promise not to do it again (at least for the summer) but I got as far as the church and didn't go in. I know, can you believe it? My mother was whispering in my ear, if you die in an accident have a clean pair of knickers and a pure soul, but I ignored her – except for the clean knickers bit. You'll be happy to hear that my Catholic guilt is lifting even if it is only a little. I still bless myself when I see a coffin and this morning after Colm left I couldn't help but say a silent prayer that I hadn't made a complete fool of myself last night and if I had that everyone else was drunk enough not to remember. Of course Colm remembers. He's playing a match today so he didn't want to drink too much. What did I say to him? It's really annoying me. I don't want to ask. I'm hoping it will start to come back to me.

Top 2 reasons why living on my own is horrible:

1. Missing you.
2. Missing you.

Oh and apparently he carried me from the bridge home. He said I fell asleep in his arms. I was really apologetic but he said I shouldn't worry, it was no problem, in fact I'm so small and light he managed to stop off at the chipper for a burger and chips with the lads while I slept on his shoulder. I really am so embarrassed. Thank God I was wearing jeans. I'm never drinking again. And the weird thing is I don't even feel that hung over but maybe that's because I've gone back to bed. I don't know.

You should have seen this place the night I moved in. It was disgusting. The kitchen was like a grease factory and I'm not even going to talk about the bathroom because the memory alone makes me want to gag. Now it's still a dump but it's a clean one. I nearly lost a finger cleaning the toilet but that's another story. I was thinking that I could subsidise university by getting a cleaning job. It would be really handy. I could work my own hours and it's cash in hand. Medicine is a 5-year course and we only start to get paid as interns in year 6. Neither Declan nor I have financial backing and I'm really starting to worry about how we're going to live. Maybe I was talking about that last night. I don't know.

I've been thinking a lot about our future lately. Declan is really worried he won't get medicine. It's his dream and he says if he has to he'll repeat. I'd die if I ended up in Cork alone! And I know that everyone thinks I'll just swan into a place but honestly I don't know if I will and when I think about not getting a place, instead of being upset I feel relieved. Isn't that weird? Of course I'd never say that to Declan because he's up the walls but 5 years is a long time. We'll be in our mid-twenties before we'll able to earn a single penny and then we'll have huge loans to pay back. Apparently we can only get a loan in second year and Ellen says it will depend on how well we do in our first-year exams. I haven't heard that before. Have you?

I was gutted when you weren't there the other day but it was nice to hear Clooney at the end of the phone. He told me all about his stalker – it's awful for him. He did mention that he was thinking about heading down this way so I hope he does. It is beautiful here when the sun is shining. I can't wait to show him around and he's going to love the water sports. I told him where to find me so I can feed him if he needs feeding. Oh I forgot to tell you the chef in the restaurant is showing me how to cook and I love it.

I spoke to my mother for the first time two days ago. She's going back to Lourdes again with the Legion of Mary. I eventually managed to speak to her on the phone yesterday and the first thing she asked me was if I was going to Mass. I said that I was fine and thanks for asking. It made me laugh. She didn't like that because Mass is not laughing matter. She said she was going to pray for me and canvas others in her group to pray for me too because I'm going to need all the prayers I can get. She said my plan to live in sin will secure my place in hell. I was really pissed off. I haven't spoken to her in an age and all she could do was threaten me with damnation. She thinks I should go to Trinity and live at home and let Declan go down to Cork on his own. She says I'm too young to be tying myself to one boy. She actually said I'm too young to have a clue about life and love, this coming from a woman who has no one in her life. And anyway if I'm going to hell for having sex or living with the boy I love then everyone I know is going to go to hell and heaven will be full of priests, nuns and weird spinsters who talk to themselves and smell like cat wee. I think I'd prefer to be in the fire with friends rather than in the clouds with weirdos, speaking of which I'm really happy for you and Ben. He sounds very mature and cool. I think it's a good idea to have sex with him. He sounds like he knows what he's doing which is a big bonus because it took Declan and me ages to get it right and I think it makes a lot of sense to lose it before you go to London. Plus you don't have the burden of worrying about going to hell so there's nothing stopping you.

Anyway that's about it. Maybe I'll go for a sleep, don't feel like doing anything now. I really miss you and can't wait to hear more about you and Ben.

Lily XXXOOOXXX

P.S. I wonder where we'll both be in six years. It seems so far away. Like another lifetime.

* * *

Eve saw the hulking Ginger Monster with his navy blue jumper on. He had his back to her and he was leaning over a woman on the rack. *Please, not me, please, not me.* She tried to look over his shoulder to see if it was her but he kept moving and concealing the person strapped to his contraption. She felt burning pain in her legs and her arm as though they were being pulled apart. *Oh crap, it is me*. He raised his arm high in the air and moved a little to the left so that she could see Ben's wife Fiona tied to the rack. She was wearing the little white-and-navy-striped T-shirt and the pair of white tight pretty shorts that she had worn on their last boating trip. Eve remembered the outfit from their Facebook photos. She had liked the outfit – it was cute but not too cute, with clean lines, expensive but not ridiculous. It was perfect. She had flowing brunette hair and a warm friendly pretty face. She had boobs and hips and her skin was glowing and tanned. She was relaxed, happy, and healthy. *I bet she doesn't suffer one long headache.* Eve remembered studying the photograph and feeling jealous of the happy brunette, but now in Eve's nightmare Fiona was screaming so loudly that Eve could feel herself trying to cover her ears but only with her good hand because the other three limbs were still being invisibly pulled apart. She found a button at the side of her temple and tried to press it, hoping the fire would come and engulf the pain but it didn't. The Ginger Monster plunged his fist into Fiona's chest and ripped out her heart, she watched it beat in his hand for a second or two before her eyes closed, and Eve watched him throw it into the same wicker basket that held her rotting limbs.

She woke up in a sweat. It was after 10 a.m. She was sorry that she'd insisted on Abby removing the catheter because she was desperate to pee and she couldn't face having to perch on a bedpan. She was sore and groggy and the image of Fiona wouldn't fade away. She briefly contemplated wetting herself – after all, she didn't have a shred of dignity left. Once she'd pooped into a bedpan after taking an hour to do it, bearing down and gnashing her teeth while a nurse popped her head in and out of the thin piece of fabric that separated her from three women of a certain age who although unsolicited decided to act as cheerleaders.

"How we doing, chicken? Is the poop near the shoot yet?" Anne said.

"Don't think about it, just let it happen," Lindsey said in a moment of lucidity.

"I'd love to have one," Beth said and moaned. "I'm backed up to high heaven here."

Eve pressed the call button and asked Abby for a bedpan.

"Of course," she said. "How'd you sleep?"

"Awful."

"She was screaming again," Anne said to Abby.

"The nightmares will pass," Abby said.

"Maybe," Eve said.

Lily appeared in the doorway with the detective Eve had spoken to that night and despite her trauma and shock she instantly recognised him.

"Detective Thomas," she said.

"Close," he said. "Thomas Hickey." He shook her functional hand.

Abby asked him to wait outside while Eve took a pee in a pot. Lily waited with him outside.

"She won't be long," she said. He nodded.

"She's an old friend," she said. He nodded.

"Any news on the person who did it?" she said and he nodded. *OK, I'm starting to see a pattern here.*

"Good," she said. "Have you spoken to Ben's wife?" He nodded. *Enough with the nodding just answer the question, sunshine!*

"Does she know about Eve and please do something other than nodding," she said and he looked at her and waited a moment before speaking as though he was making a decision whether to answer her or tell her to mind her own business.

"She knows he was walking along a dark road with a woman on the evening of the accident," he said.

"Has she asked about Eve?"

He nodded.

Ah, come on! "And you've said?" she pressed.

"What I know," he said.

"Which is?" Lily said and he smiled, admiring her tenacity.

"Which is . . . nothing more than they were hit by a car by a drunk driver at approximately 10:16 p.m. on the night of the 1st July and that we have located and charged the man responsible."

"So Ben's wife must have questions?"

"I'm sure she does," he said.

Abby appeared in the hallway.

"Do you have to inform Eve of Ben's condition?" Lily asked the detective.

"Is there a reason to keep the truth from her?"

Lily shook her head. "She's just been through a lot," she said.

"You can go in," Abby said and he nodded and smiled at Lily before going to sit with Eve.

Eve was raised in her bed so that she could look the detective in the eye. She was experiencing a dull throbbing pain in her limbs as though they were hollow and under a great weight, liable to snap at any second. It was bad but it wasn't bad enough to press the button and anyway she'd noticed that the amounts of painkiller had been reduced. The relief wasn't as strong but neither was the nausea and grogginess. She wanted to be alert while making her statement. She needed to make sure she did it right. *I won't let you down, Ben.* Eve knew that the likelihood of Ben's recovery was dwindling with each day that passed. She knew that if he lived he had a wife by his bedside ready and willing to love and care for her husband. She knew that if he died that woman would be the one to lead the mourners grieving for him. She knew that if his affair was discovered everything he and his wife had together would be tainted. *We didn't want to hurt anyone.* If he died Fiona would second-guess every word, deed and gesture and he wouldn't be there to fight with or explain. *If I could do it all again.* Fiona would be tortured and haunted. *I won't let that happen, Ben.* She prepared herself to lie like she'd never lied before. *I just have to stay as close to the truth as I can. Everything will be fine.* She sipped on her water because her lips and throat were dry and for some reason she felt scared she'd lose her voice. *This has to be right.*

The detective told her that they had found the man who had knocked her down. His name was Eamonn Colgan. He had fallen asleep while parked in his neighbour's driveway. Her blood was all over the car and remarkably her description of the man was a perfect match down to his Claddagh ring and his navy jumper. He claimed he remembered nothing of the accident but with his alcohol levels, her blood evidence and testimony they would get a conviction. He asked her for a follow-up statement and she was ready. She told him that she and Ben Logan were very old friends. *True.* She said that actually he had been her first love. *True.* She said that they had reconnected on Facebook a couple of years ago.

True. She said that when she came home to be with her dying father they had met for coffee. *True*. She said that his business was in trouble. *True*. He was keeping the failure of that business from his wife. *True*. And that she was trying to help with the business. *True*. She said that she had just sold her own successful and profitable business in the USA. *True*. That she had money to invest if the right opportunity came along. *True*. That on the night they were knocked down she had agreed to buy into Ben's business. *False*. And that they were on their way to have dinner and celebrate their business arrangement. *False*. In fact, he was just about to call his wife to meet with his new partner and join in on the celebration. *False*. Their relationship was strictly business. *False*. But she cared about him. *True*.

Although the detective was far more interested in confirming her recollection of what happened when the car struck her and verifying her astoundingly accurate account of the incident, he did remind her that she had described herself as Ben's girlfriend on the night in question. Eve didn't remember doing that and, although she was momentarily put on the back foot, she recovered quickly. She told him that at one point that night she had thought she was eighteen again. There were many fleeting moments of confusion. *True*. He did mention that she had originally identified him as Glen Medeiros. Eve didn't remember that either but it made her laugh and then cry.

"I used to call him that when we were teenagers," she said.

"After the singer?" he said.

She nodded.

"We were having a bit of the bet about that at the station," he said.

"He had curls and a dodgy dress sense back then," she said and her eyes leaked despite the wall she'd built to keep them at bay.

"I understand," he said.

"I can't stop reliving that night," she said. *True*. "I don't know why I'm crying," she said. *Lie*.

She gathered her thoughts together. It was important to maintain her performance. She imagined turning off a tap in her mind and her tears stopped flowing.

She asked him to make sure Ben's wife saw her statement as soon as it was appropriate. She didn't want her thinking anything untoward. Eve said she was conscious that her life must be difficult enough without having to worry about who her husband was with that night.

"I know what I'd be thinking if I was her," she said.

He nodded and agreed an affair was one possible conclusion. She didn't know if he believed her story or not. It wasn't pertinent to him making a case against a drunk driver and so maybe he didn't much mind. When he confirmed he would ensure that Fiona was given a copy of her statement, she asked as nonchalantly as she could how Ben was doing.

"I'm afraid he's not going to make it," he said.

"Excuse me?" she said and, although she'd thought his death was possible, the confirmation sent a shock through her body that reverberated long after he'd stopped talking.

"He was declared brain dead yesterday afternoon. The ventilator will be turned off tomorrow morning," he said.

She nodded slowly. "Oh," she said, fighting the urge to scream.

"I'm sorry," he said.

"Yes," she said, inhaling then exhaling. "So am I. His poor wife." *Don't lose it. Don't lose it. Don't lose it.*

He nodded and thanked her for her time. He told her he'd be back with any follow-up questions if necessary and either way he'd be in touch. He left her sitting up in her bed, staring at the thin curtain surrounding her bed. *He's gone.* Tears collected. *He's gone.* Her eyes, nose and ears burned. *He's gone.* She blinked. *He's gone.* Tears fell. *He's gone.* Her nose ran. *He's gone.* Her heart ached. *He's gone.* Her stomach turned. *He's gone.* She pulled the blanket over her head with her good arm, burying herself under it, grieving alone, in stifling darkness. She pushed the button retracting her bed until she was lying flat; she allowed her hidden tears to pour out unseen and silent. *He's gone.*

Lily watched the detective walk down the corridor. He was in the lift before she left the nurses' station and walked into Eve's ward.

She walked over to the mummy lying in the bed and when she saw the damp sheet over Eve's face and heard her muffled cries she slipped her hand under the blanket and held her friend's hand the way she had all those years ago on a sunny day in Eve's back garden. When Eve finally stopped crying, Lily took her hand out from under the blankets and walked away, giving Eve time to recover.

Lily was busy. It was one of those days where she didn't seem to stop. It was four when she finally got to eat some lunch. Declan was just out of surgery and so they grabbed something together. When she saw Ben's wife and his mother sitting staring into middle distance with two untouched cups of coffee in front of them, her heart raced and she lowered her head, afraid that if either woman focused they'd spot the nurse that used to know Ben and who called in to check on him at least twice a day. They had become acquainted with her face and they'd even spoken once or twice. Ben's mother remembered Lily's mother. She cleaned the house of a friend of hers. She asked after her. Lily replied that she was fine and that she'd moved to the UK many years ago and Mrs Logan had burst into tears.

"I think we're losing him," she'd said and she was right.

Ben Logan was all but lost. The decision to turn off the ventilator was made soon after their conversation.

Lily worried for poor Fiona. Although Eve had never said it, Lily knew she was sleeping with Ben. She couldn't bring herself to sympathise with Eve's pain the way she could have if he hadn't been married. She knew she was being judgemental, pious and puritanical but she couldn't help it. Ben's wife was about to lose her husband and, when he was in the ground, it was likely she'd discover his affair and he'd die all over again. Lily knew how that felt, wondering how and why and what she could or should have done to change something she had no control over. *Poor Fiona*. Every time she saw her weary face she felt worse for her. Eve had always done exactly what Eve wanted to do and to hell with what anyone thought and this woman was about to pay the price. Of course she pitied Eve too but mostly she wanted to avoid any conversation about Ben because it would be hard to sympathise without seeing Fiona's face. Lily kept her head down but she didn't need to worry – Fiona didn't see past the middle distance.

Declan was looking forward to the dinner party they were due to attend and that Lily had forgotten all about. She had nothing to wear, she was tired and Alice Gibson the host had made her feelings about Lily very clear from the first time they met. As far as Professor Alice Gibson was concerned Lily was beneath her. She was a pretty little thing that bounced around the hospital in pink. Alice was a serious academic. She was not an ugly woman but she was built like her blocky father, she carried a few pounds around her waist and she battled with a hairy chin. She didn't have time for small talk or jokes or raising men's egos by laughing at the stupid comments they made after a few drinks. Alice Gibson was a serious woman, highly intelligent, and although fascinating when lecturing on the subject of medicine she was a dreadful bore socially. When Lily revealed her intellect to be more than her match, Alice's indifference grew into jealousy. She was a poor host, never failing to be rude.

"I really don't want to go," Lily admitted while picking at a wilted salad.

"We can't cancel on the day – it's rude."

"That's rich," Lily said.

Declan laughed. "Alice did not spill wine on you on purpose."

"Yes, she did. She's also stood on my toe twice, and she's turned her back on me and excluded me from conversation nearly every chance she gets."

"She's just not socially graceful."

"She's a bitch."

"She's Rodney's wife and Rodney is my good friend so we're going and we're going to have a good time," he said playfully.

But Lily knew that no matter how playful the delivery he was laying down the law.

"Fudge cake," she said and he smiled.

"And you should wear that gold bangle I bought," he said.

"I hope you don't mind if that's all I wear," she said before sighing.

Alice would be dressed in something that would no doubt look dowdy and fuddy-duddy but it would be expensive. She tried to think of her limited wardrobe and what Alice hadn't seen before but she'd seen anything worth seeing. *Bugger-balls*. She didn't have the money or time to shop so she decided to wear a simple red dress she'd worn countless times before. She didn't doubt that it would make Alice's night. She'd already commented on the fact that Lily seemed too attached to the dress on a previous occasion but Lily felt comfortable in it, it suited her and most importantly it was clean.

She left Declan still eating and headed back to her ward. On the way she bumped into Adam.

"Have you been roped into this dinner tonight?" he asked.

"Yeah. You?"

He nodded. "She emailed me to tell me she's sitting me beside Tracey Barber."

"Who's Tracey Barber?"

"I've no idea but apparently she's a political analyst and I'm going to love her," he said and she laughed.

"Well, if she's anything like Alice she'll be a real keeper."

He chuckled. Adam had about as much time for Alice's pomposity as Lily did.

"I wonder what insult or injury she has lined up for me?" she said.

"We can only wait and see."

"At least we have each other," she said and when he blushed she pretended not to notice. *Whatever you're thinking, Adam, get over it. Please.*

Declan wouldn't be working over the weekend and he was looking forward to relaxing and having a few drinks and, because he had the alcohol tolerance of a teenage girl, Lily could only hope that he'd fall asleep before saying or doing anything to embarrass her.

Clooney spent the day trying to raise his sister's spirits but it wasn't an easy task. It didn't help when he'd mentioned that he'd bumped into Paul and that the gang were going to come and visit. She started to cry.

"I thought you'd be happy," he said, confused.

"I'm exhausted, in agony, my bloody legs are broken, my shoulder is a mass of metal. My head hurts, my bloody eyes burn. Ben is . . . No, Clooney, I am not happy."

"Two bloodys in one sentence. That's serious. I'm sorry."

She shook her head. "No. I'm sorry. It's nice of them."

"What can I do?"

"Bring Ben back to life."

"I wish I could."

"Not as much as I do."

Lily appeared with the meds trolley. She came to Eve last.

"Time for your heparin injection," she said.

Eve had to have one of these injections once a day – it was the only injection not administered through the cannula and it stung like a bee. Clooney looked away. He'd always hated injections. Eve made the screwed-up face she made every time. Lily rubbed the spot with an alcohol swab. "Over."

Just as she said that Fiona Logan walked through the door. Lily's heart nearly stopped. *Oh fudging fudge cake.* She looked from Fiona to Eve. She seemed relaxed. *Shit, does she know who she is?*

Fiona approached the bed.

"Eve?"

"Fiona," Eve said and she smiled.

Lily didn't know where to put herself. *What the hell . . .*

"Lily," Fiona said.

Lily waved. *Did I just wave?*

"This is my brother Clooney," Eve said and Clooney stood.

Fiona put out her hand to shake his. "Hi, I'm Fiona Logan."

"Ben's wife?" he said, suddenly catching on.

"Yes," she said.

"Oh right," he said and clearly he was as uncomfortable as Lily but Eve remained calm and cool.

Oh God, oh God, oh God, Lily thought, *Eve, be nice, be cool. I need to sit down. No, I need to get out of here. Oh God, I need to pee. Oh Christ, please don't break her.*

"Please sit down," Eve said, indicating the chair her brother had just got off.

Fiona sat. "I'm sorry it took me so long to come here," she said.

"I understand," Eve said.

Have I just walked into an alternative universe? Lily thought. Clooney was silent and watching. Lily didn't know whether to stay or leave. She put the needle into a sharps bin and fixed the blankets on Eve. She eyed the blood-pressure pump. *Maybe I should go and come back.*

"I saw your statement," Fiona said.

"Good," Eve said. "I was anxious you knew exactly what happened and how it happened."

"I appreciate that," Fiona said, tearing up. "I had wondered why he was there. I was thinking all sorts. I feel stupid now."

"Don't," Eve said.

Oh, you lying bitch, what did you say? Lily wanted to move but she couldn't – curiosity planted her feet to the floor.

"We're turning off the . . ." Fiona said but she couldn't finish the sentence.

Eve nodded. "I know," she said. "I'm so sorry."

She appeared calm and detached but not so detached as to be cold. She showed the exact amount of emotion you would for an old friend.

When did you get to be such a good liar? Lily thought.

"It's like a nightmare," Fiona said.

"I wish there was something I could do," Eve said.

"That night . . . was he really going to call me so that we could celebrate?" Fiona asked before choking up.

Eve nodded. "Yes. He had been working hard on a plan to salvage the business. I have a copy of all his accounts if you want it back."

"No," Fiona said. "Thank you."

Bloody hell, I've heard it all now, Lily thought.

Fiona stood up. "This time tomorrow I'll be a widow. You'll help me put that bastard Eamonn Colgan away?"

Eve nodded. "Oh yeah," she said.

Fiona walked out of the room.

Clooney looked at his sister and smiled. "You did the right thing."

Eve looked at Lily for a comment on her performance and Lily sighed and shook her head. "The right thing," she mumbled to herself and she walked out of the room. Clooney followed her, calling her name. She turned to face him on the corridor.

"You're judging her?" he asked.

"She had an affair with a married man and now she's lying about it. Don't get me wrong – I'm thrilled she did it for Fiona Logan's sake but Christ, Clooney, it's a long way from doing the right thing."

"I see," he said. "You're still perched on that high horse of yours."

His words were like a slap in the face. Smarting, she replied in a manner most unlike her. "Fuck you," she said and she walked away.

At eight o'clock on the dot, Gina, Gar and Paul arrived into Eve's ward laden with cards, fruit baskets, flowers and sweets. Clooney was still there. Lily had gone home. Anne, Lindsey and Beth were wide awake and looking to interfere.

Gina gasped when she saw Eve. "Jesus!"

Gar overcompensated for his wife's reaction. "You look great, way better than we expected," he said before giving his wife a filthy look.

Paul dragged some chairs over and sat down.

"Hey, Scarface. Would you like a sweet?" he said, holding up a box of Roses.

Eve shook her head to say no but smiled at him, grateful he was so understated and unflappable.

Gar and Gina sat on one side of the bed, Clooney and Paul on the other.

"It's nice to see she has people in her life," Anne said. "It looked for a while like she'd no one. Except the tall fella."

"Are they for me?" Lindsey said to Paul, pointing to his sweets.

"No," he said and Anne laughed.

"How rude," Lindsey mumbled.

"None for me, thanks," Beth said as though someone had offered her a sweet. "I still haven't been able to go." She rubbed her stomach.

Gar laughed at the old dears' conversation. Gina was too focused on Eve and what she had to say about the accident to listen or to care.

Within minutes the old ladies' own visitors came and filled up the room and, with their chatter firmly in the background, Eve told her friends that she had been with Ben for business purposes.

Gina seemed disappointed. Clooney was quiet. Paul said nothing. He wasn't about to tell Eve that he'd spilled the beans on her affair the previous evening. He respected the tack she was taking. He empathised with her decision to lie. It was for the greater good. It made sense. Eve wasn't a seasoned liar, she didn't make a habit of it and preferred the truth but not at any cost.

The story of her accident was juicy enough to take Gina's mind off Ben, that is, until Paul asked after his condition. Eve faltered. While she collected her thoughts Clooney answered on her behalf. He told them that the machine was being turned off the next day. They looked at Eve for a reaction. She gave none. She was somewhere else building another wall, one block, two blocks, three blocks, four.

"I have some news," Paul said in a timely bid to distract them from his friend who needed saving.

He went on to tell his open-mouthed pals that he was getting married and having a baby. Even Eve was momentarily pulled away from her imaginary wall. As briefly and with as little information as he could possibly get away with, he told them that he was in love with a beautiful woman called Simone.

"But you're gay," Gar said.

"I'm bisexual."

"But you said you were gay!" Gar said.

"I was wrong. I'm bisexual."

"How could you be wrong? I don't . . . All this time? I'm . . ." Gar looked at his wife who hunched her shoulders and then to Clooney and Eve. "I don't understand."

"I don't know what to say." Paul wasn't one to explain himself. He didn't have the tools nor did he feel the necessity. *It is what it is.*

"So why didn't you just say so before now?" Gar asked.

"Because he's nuts," Eve said.

"Something like that." Paul smiled at Eve. "I was with Paddy for eight years."

"And he did make a really big deal about coming out," Gina said helpfully.

"I've heard it all now!" Gar looked from his missus to Eve to Clooney and back to Paul. "You're my friend. How did I not know this?"

Gar really didn't know what to make out of what Paul had said. When they were younger Paul was the guy he looked up to. He was the one that always had girls chasing him, he was always with the prettiest girls, he was discreet and never spoke about his conquests but it was obvious that he was good with girls and he had a rock star's choice. Then when he came out as gay Gar couldn't understand it and it messed with his head for a long time. *Was Paul ever with those girls? Was he with them just to save face? And if he was and he didn't like girls, how come he was so good at being with them?* Paul was so private and Gar was so shocked at his friend's coming out that they had never really discussed it. Each preferring not to discuss Paul's sex life for their own reasons.

Gina had spent years trying to form a bond with Paul but he was a closed shop. He liked her, she was a nice woman but she was his friend's wife not his friend. Gina had initially been upset by this but after a few years she just accepted Paul and his oddities. *He is what he is.*

"I stripped my top off in front of you," Eve said and Paul nodded and smiled.

"Yes, you did," he said.

Clooney stayed silent. He didn't know Paul well enough to really care whether he was gay or bisexual. He was just glad the conversation was distracting his sister.

"Congratulations," he said when everyone fell silent.

Paul thanked him.

The others followed suit.

"I can't wait to meet her," Gina said.

"I can't believe you're going to be a father!" Gar said.

"Me neither." Tears filled Paul's eyes and his friends basked in his happiness for a moment before he became uncomfortable and changed the subject. He asked about Lily and immediately Gina was re-engaged.

"What's she like?" Gina asked.

"The same," Eve said.

"What's Declan like?" Gina asked.

"I don't know. I haven't seen him," Eve answered. *And I don't want to.*

"But he works here," Gina said.

"Yeah."

"Weird."

"Not really."

"So did she mention why they dumped us all?" Gar asked.

Eve had a good idea as to why they disappeared, at least she thought she did but then again there could have been one million reasons. It was all so long ago. *The past is the past. Let it go.* She didn't answer Gar.

"Is she here?" Paul asked.

"Her shift finished two hours ago," Clooney said, looking at his watch. They had been there over an hour. "Well, I guess we'd better go – it's been a long day for Eve."

Eve thanked them for coming and Clooney accepted a lift home.

"They're a nice bunch, chicken," Anne said after all the visitors had been cleared out.

"Thanks, Anne."

"Except of course for the freak. You know what they called people like him in my day?"

"No."

"Greedy."

"Oh."

Lindsey was asleep and Beth busy watching TV.

"Of course it takes all sorts," Anne said.

"Yeah," Eve agreed.

"Would you like a bonbon?"

"No, thanks."

"I could call a nurse to drop one over to you?"

"I'm fine."

"I'm sorry about your friend."

"Which one?" Eve asked, wondering if it was the dead man or the freak she was talking about.

"The one you call out to in your sleep," she said and when Eve started to cry Anne kindly pretended not to notice.

Alice was as rude as Lily predicted. Upon opening the door she stood back and surveyed Lily's outfit.

"Ah, looking great," she said, following with an air kiss, "in the old favourite."

Lily was in a mood and so instead of being her usually congenial self, she replied with steel in her voice. "Is that new?" she asked.

"Yes."

"Well, if you take it off now you could still get a refund," Lily said, passing her by without as much as a second glance.

Adam handed her a glass of champagne. "Nice," he said.

"Not in the mood for this tonight."

"I see that."

Declan didn't pay any attention to the words spoken between his wife and his friend's wife. He was more interested in talking to Rodney. They were discussing the surgery they had been involved in together that day.

The group gathered in the lounge, waiting to be called into the dining room. Alice stayed in the kitchen, pretending to preside over the catering company she'd hired but instead she was busy fuming and double-checking her look in the mirror.

Usually at parties or events and particularly in large rooms with new people Declan would watch Lily from a distance and, if he saw her conversing with an unknown man, he'd call her to him. When she'd come he'd say, "Lily, can you come stand by me, please?"

"What do you want?"

"My wife, if that's OK."

If she disappeared at that same party or event for longer than five minutes he would chase her down.

"Lily, where the hell have you been?"

"In the toilet."

"It doesn't take half an hour to go to the toilet. What were you up to?"

"It does if you're in a bar full of women with only two loos. For Christ sake, Declan!"

And if she spoke to a man who he could clearly see appreciated her, even if he was in the same company, he would make little of her to make a point even though it didn't always work out in his favour.

"Lily, I'm sure Greg is just being polite, nobody really finds gardening interesting."

"Greg is a gardener, Declan."

When attending Rodney's intimate gatherings, mostly he ignored her.

Lily and Adam stood together by the piano. Declan would have been jealous if he hadn't been so sure that Adam was gay. He had decided this a long time ago in spite of the many women that Adam had been with, and not just because Adam never married, because as far as Declan was concerned he had a quality. He couldn't really explain this quality, instead he simply compared it to having the X factor. Declan liked to look at a beautiful woman. Adam liked to talk to her. Declan was well groomed. Adam was dapper. Declan was an ex-rugby player, Adam spent his secondary school years ballroom-dancing. Lily knew her husband was wrong about Adam but she encouraged his misconception by never arguing his points. It was nice to have a male friend that Declan wasn't suspicious of. And over the years Adam had noticed that her husband's theory allowed him closer access to Lily and so he didn't ever care to put him right, no matter how rude or obnoxious he became when drunk.

In the car on the way over Declan had laughed at the notion of Alice lining up a date for Adam. "That's a waste of time," he'd said.

Lily stayed silent. She was busy thinking about how she'd reacted to Eve and more importantly what Clooney had said. '*Still perched on your high horse*' – *what was that supposed to mean? He doesn't know me!* Yet it bugged her and she wondered why she reacted so badly when Eve had done everything she could to minimise damage to Fiona. She felt bad. *And after all who the hell am I to come down on a lie? I spend my life lying. Who does the truth serve? No one. Eve has probably endured one of the worst days in her life and I was a stupid bitch. Damn it. What is wrong with me?* She was thinking about how sad and lost Eve was as Declan laughed it up about Adam and the poor cow Alice had set him up with.

"She just won't listen," he said. "She's determined to marry him off."

"She should mind her own business," Lily said, reminding Declan to remind Lily to play it nice.

"Lily, I need you to be nice to Alice," he said sharply.

"I will be nice."

"You're in one of your humours," he said.

This grated on her because he would often intimate that her humours were directly linked to or as a consequence of her fluctuating hormones. She ignored him. She was picturing Eve's face and the heartbreak that was written all over it.

"I don't know why they insist on asking him over anyway," Declan twittered on. "It's not like he ever stays long. Probably off to the Phoenix Park to get himself some arse." He looked over at his wife to see if a reaction was forthcoming. It wasn't. She was lost in her own thoughts.

Her mind had drifted back in time to when Eve was a teenager in love. *I think I'm falling in love, Lily. I'm scared, Lily. He makes the world feel like a better place. I wish it could always be like this.*

"What are you thinking about?" Declan asked.

"Nothing," Lily said.

"Impossible. Tell me what you're thinking?"

"I'm thinking I wish I was at home in a bath." *I'm thinking of knocking you out as soon as we get home, creeping back to the hospital and taking my old friend to say goodbye to her teenage sweetheart.*

"You have a look in your eye," he said.

"No, I don't."

"You do."

"Just drive the car, Declan."

Standing by the piano Adam and Lily talked pleasantries for a minute or two before Alice came in and introduced him to Tracey, being careful to turn her back on Lily and completely exclude her from their company. Adam grabbed Lily's hand and mentioned to Alice that she had inadvertently excluded Lily. She pretended that it was an accident, Adam and Lily pretended that they believed her story. Tracey stood there quietly, waiting to be introduced to Lily. When the introductions were over, Alice left Tracey to stand with Adam. Lily stayed put. Alice turned and with a look that suggested she wanted to punch Lily in the face suggested that Lily join her in the kitchen.

"I'm fine where I am, thanks," Lily said.

Adam smiled and Tracey, not realising the situation, told Lily that she looked stunning in her dress within Alice's earshot.

Tracey was a nice woman. She was tall and looked a little horsey around the jaw-line but she had pretty eyes, blonde hair and a good figure. She wasn't Adam's type but she had a good sense of humour and, if he had met her in a bar and Lily wasn't standing beside her reminding him of the woman he really wanted, he might have slept with her if it had become an option.

Dinner was boring. Declan was slurring after two glasses of wine and the whiskey Rodney had insisted he drank as soon as he walked through the door. Rodney didn't seem to notice because he was too busy arguing politics with Tracey.

"You can say what you want about Fianna Fáil but are the others going to do any different?" he asked. "No!" He slapped the table with his hand.

"It's important for the electorate to show their contempt for the way in which business has been done. The only way to do that is by voting out the current regime," she reasoned.

"Cut off one head and another one grows," he argued.

"They're all a bunch of thieving bastards!" Declan said. "The French revolutionaries had the right idea. Off with their heads!" And he knocked his glass of wine over with his hand.

Alice jumped up and immediately started to clean up.

Declan apologised profusely while Rodney talked over him and so the never-ending night seemed to go on.

Adam met Lily in the kitchen.

"Is it late enough to leave?" he asked.

"Yeah, get going," she said.

"What about you?"

"I'm stuck until Declan can't stand any more," she said, looking at her watch. It was eleven o'clock.

"One more whiskey and that will have been achieved," he said, pouring another large glass and walking into the sitting room where the others were seated. He handed Declan the glass.

"Oh, you're not trying to get me drunk enough to have your way with me, are you?" Declan asked him.

Rodney laughed but Alice was unimpressed.

"Don't be ridiculous, Declan," she said, looking at Tracey, "there's no need for that."

"Apologies, Adam," Declan said, clearly believing himself to be on a comedy roll, "I know it's Rodney you fancy."

Rodney laughed again. Adam nodded and in his head he swore it was the last time he would accept an invitation to eat with either of his colleagues.

"I think it's time to take my leave," he said. "Goodnight all. Tracey, it was nice to meet you."

"To meet you nice," Declan said, doing his best impression of Bruce Forsyth which was pretty bad.

Alice tutted to signal she was unhappy that the boys were acting like children.

"I'm sorry, Adam," she said at the door. "I could ask Tracey for her phone number for you?"

"I can get my own phone numbers, Alice," he said, "but thank you." He waved at Lily who had emerged from the downstairs bathroom. "Goodnight, Lily."

"See you tomorrow, Adam," she said.

Alice closed the door and turned to Lily. "You know, maybe Tracey would have had a chance if you didn't monopolise Adam's time."

"Excuse me?"

"No. I won't. You think you're better than everyone else."

"That's rich coming from you, Alice."

"I see you with Adam," Alice said. "Your husband might be blind to it but I see."

"You are an elitist, angry, arrogant bitch, Alice," Lily said and she walked into the dining room and grabbed her drunken husband by the arm. *Where the hell is this coming from? God, Declan is going to kill me.* "We're going."

"What?" he asked, confused.

"Now," she said.

"I do feel a little sick," he said as she hauled him into the car. He fell asleep on the drive home.

Lily was smarting. *How dare Alice Gibson! Who the hell did she think she is? As if. Why can't she mind her own damn business?* Lily had always known Adam wasn't gay for one reason and one reason only and it was the way he looked at her. She didn't actively encourage his favour. She never pretended to be available. She didn't behave salaciously in his presence. He was a friend and a shoulder she sought to cry on when things were difficult with Declan but lately it was becoming more and more obvious that Adam had feelings for her. She could pretend not to notice when others didn't but as soon as Alice said it out straight the game she was playing with herself was over. Damn it. *Why do you have to look at me like that, Adam? I just need a friend.* If her husband noticed she was teary-eyed, he didn't mention it.

He was so drunk that Scott helped her carry him from the car. She stripped him in a matter of minutes and he was asleep and snoring before the light was turned out.

Scott was up and watching a movie. It was one o'clock and Lily was sober and ready for action. She couldn't leave the house without Scott noticing. He'd hear the car in the driveway, plus technically she could do with his help. She went into the sitting room and reminded him that she had talked his father into allowing him to work with his grandfather in a job that was starting the following Monday.

"I know. Thanks." He shrugged.

"I need your help," she said.

"With what?"

"I need you to help me with a patient."

"OK?" he said in a tone that suggested a question followed.

"I'm asking you to help me for free but if you do I'm going to

171

buy your silence with fifty euro," she said, holding up the fifty-euro note she'd just stolen from Declan's trousers.

"Buy my silence? Why?"

"Because you can't tell your dad."

"Is it legal?"

"Of course it's legal!"

Scott looked at the money and hunched. "OK."

They made it to the hospital in fifteen minutes. Scott followed Lily up to Eve's room. He waited in the corridor while she talked to another nurse for a few minutes before the nurse nodded and turned her back. He stood at the door while she slowly and gently woke Eve.

"Eve."

Eve opened her eyes. "Lily."

"Hi," she said, smiling.

"Hi."

"I'm sorry for being a bitch earlier."

"It's allowed."

"How about we take a little trip?"

"Where?"

"To see Ben."

Eve inhaled. "I'd really like that."

Lily called Scott from the doorway. He pushed in the narrow trolley that he was going to help slid Eve onto.

"This is my son Scott," she said and Eve smiled at him.

"It's nice to meet you, Scott," she said.

"Wow, you're in bits!" he said and Eve agreed.

"You should see the car," she said.

Lily unhooked Eve from her drip. She instructed Scott on what to do. They untucked the sheet and used it to lift Eve from her bed to the trolley. "Lift on three," Lily commanded and they did and after a little negotiating they were on the way to the fourth floor. Lily had called ahead from the car, asking permission of the nurse in charge. She was waiting for them when they arrived in the corridor.

"Keep it quick," she said.

"We will."

Lily and Scott pushed Eve into Ben's room. Eve's heart beat faster as she passed through the doorway. They placed her by Ben's side. The area was small and they could barely fit the narrow trolley beside his bed. They parked her and when Lily squeezed her hand it was shaking.

"We'll be outside," she said and they left Eve alone with Ben.

She couldn't touch him because they could only fit her into the room with Ben to her left-hand side. She tried to reach with her right hand but she couldn't. He had colour in his cheeks – his skin was being oxygenated by the large tube that was coming out of his mouth that was attached to a machine that was pushing air into his lungs. His chest moved up and down. She watched it and when she closed her eyes she could feel her head resting against it.

"I met Fiona," she said. "She seems lovely which makes you a total dick for cheating on her but then you always said she was lovely which makes me a total dick for being the one you cheated with," she said and she waited as though by some miracle he'd answer. "She doesn't know. She'll never know. She is yours and you are hers and I'm just a . . ." tears stained her battered face, "I'm just a lonely woman who wanted . . ." She stopped and placed one finger on her lips as though to silence herself while she thought of the right thing to say. "I'm just someone who loved you once a long time ago." The pain in her heart sharpened as though an invisible knife was twisting inside her. It threatened to take her breath away. "I'm going to forget the past year if you don't mind. I'm going to remember you back then when you were mine. It was really such a short time but I want you to know it meant so much. You were my first real love but then you know that. What you don't know is that you were my only real love and if I had only known what I know now I would have done everything differently that night, that stupid, stupid, stupid night. And when I dream of you I'm going to dream that we're back at Paul's party and you take me to the bottom of his garden, to the bench beside the pond with his mother's dead fish in it and we'll kiss and hold each other and when you tell me that you love me and that you want to come to London with me I'll say I love you back and we'll make plans to be together and it will be perfect. In my dreams I'll be your wife and we'll never be by that wall on that night. There won't be a car coming and a drunk behind the wheel. There will be you and me and children and grandchildren and all the mushy stuff you said you wanted that night when you were only nineteen." Eve dried her eyes with her wrap. "I'm sorry I was such a fool."

She stayed silent after that, allowing her tears to flow like a river, emptying the contents of her broken heart. She had never cried for anything or anyone the way she cried that night and she wasn't sure if it was the fact that she'd almost lost her own life, or guilt, or love or the morphine but when they came to take her back to her room she had never ever felt so scared, so sad and so numb all at the same time. She couldn't touch him, she couldn't look back, all she could do was cling on to her old friend's hand and sigh and sob and beg her to turn back and let her see him one last time. *It should have been me. It should have been me. It should have been me.*

"Oh Lily, please take me back, take me back, take me back and place his hand in mine just for a minute!"

Once Eve was back in bed, Scott stood by the door and watched his mother placate the distraught woman. She caressed her hair and soothed her with whispered words as she had done with him and his sister so many times over the years. He couldn't hear what was being said but the woman quietened down. Before Lily left her, Eve clung to her hand. Lily bent down and kissed her forehead and she said something that seemed to make the woman relax. Lily covered her up to her neck and tucked her in. She turned off her light and left the woman staring at the ceiling, silent and calm.

In the car on the way home Scott asked his mother what she'd said.

"Oh nothing," she said.

"Seriously, tell me."

"I said I'd make it better," she said.

Scott laughed out loud. "You'll make it better? The guy is a fucking organ donor!"

"Don't say fucking, it really is vulgar," she said, thinking of what she'd said to Clooney and regretting it.

"Sorry – fudging – but come on!"

"Remember when you were ten and your best friend in the

whole world was moving to Kerry and you cried and cried and cried."

"What was his name again?"

"Steven Maher."

"Steven Maher, God, I must Facebook him."

"Anyway, you were a lost soul and nothing either your dad or I could promise seemed to make it better. A new football didn't work, a trip to the zoo didn't work, a –"

"OK, God, Mum, I get it."

"Well, it was only when he left and I held you in my arms and said I'd make it better that you quietened down."

"Maybe I was just tried of crying."

"Maybe or maybe you knew that no matter what it took I would do everything in my power to make it better."

"You're a mental case, Mum."

"Cheers, son."

Lily and Scott sat quietly in the car for the rest of the way home. She was lost in times gone by and he was left to contemplate why the broken woman was to be kept a secret from his dad. When Lily parked the car and they walked up to their front door, he turned to his mother.

"I'm sorry for your friend," he said.

"She's just a woman I felt sorry for," Lily tried to lie.

"She's the girl from the photos you keep in the shoebox in your wardrobe," he said and he handed her back the fifty euro, "and I don't know why you're lying or being weird but I promise I won't say a word."

Lily should have been annoyed at her son for invading her privacy but she was too alarmed to be.

"You didn't read those letters, did you, Scott?" she said, trying hard to hide her fear.

"No, a girl from the last century bleeting on about rubbish? Made it about three lines and lost the will to live."

If he noticed her sigh of relief, he didn't say anything.

She shoved the fifty euro into his shirt pocket. "Take it. It's your father's and if you ever rummage through my stuff again, I'll tell your next girlfriend that you would take you winkie out in the supermarket and ask old ladies if they thought you were a big boy."

"That never happened," he said, horrified.

"Well, she won't know that and don't you dare use this against me in future negotiations," she said.

"Mum, seriously, I don't have to negotiate any more. I'm nineteen."

"Trust me, son, that's when the negotiation starts."

Lily watched her son climb the stairs before she headed outside into her garden. A white half moon hung in the black sky. She walked to the swing-set that she insisted they buy for Daisy when she was five. It was a large metal structure with two swings featuring one red seat and one purple one. It had been carefully constructed and rooted in foundations so that it could support an adult's weight. Lily and Daisy had countless summer days swinging together but it had been abandoned by Daisy and her friends for many years. Lily still sat on the purple seat when she felt sad or playful or contemplative or simply in search of solitude. She could often be found on her daughter's swing, day or night. Often when she couldn't sleep and it wasn't too cold she'd put on a coat over her nightdress and venture out and swing for while, thinking about her days and dreams.

One morning when she woke up to snow she wrapped up warm and put her wellies on. She trudged to the back of the garden, cleared the seat off and swung as high as she could and in her head she replayed the scene of her and Eve battling as to who could touch the sky first, swinging faster and faster and higher and higher until their feet were touching the sky.

"The one who swings highest gets a wish!" Eve said.

And Lily couldn't decide on a wish but it didn't matter because Eve's long legs assured her win.

"I love you, Eve Hayes."

"I love you, Lily Brennan."

She thought about the goodbye scene she had witnessed. She thought about Eve and how sad and sorry she had been. She thought about Ben. He'd never again see a red sky, he'd never again dip his feet into a fast-flowing river or feel the touch of a loved one. He'd never again smile, or laugh or make a joke. He'd never shout or scream in joy or pain. He'd never cry or moan. No more pain or loss for Ben Logan because even as Eve poured out her heart to him he was long gone.

Lily looked up into the night sky as she swung higher and higher, attempting to tip the moon with the tops of her toes.

Where are you now, Ben? Are you reaching for the light or running from the darkness? Is Danny right? Are you simply gone or are the possibilities for you endless? Maybe you've moved on to another dimension or a parallel universe? Maybe you've shed your skin and returned to an alien ship and you're about to receive a commendation for a completed mission. If you knew you were set to leave this world so soon, would you have done it all differently?

Lily thought about the last question for a long time. *If I knew I was set to leave this earth soon, would I do it all differently?* The liar in Lily said no, she wouldn't. She loved her children, her husband and her life, but recently events had awakened the young girl in her who had been silenced a long time ago. She was the girl with the world at her feet and the one who threw it all away out of guilt, fear and the overwhelming need to be everything to everyone and that girl was whispering in Lily's ear, calling into question every choice she'd made and the kind of life she led. *Are you a wife or a glorified slave? Are you an equal or subordinate? Are you loved as a woman or a possession? Are you free? Are you happy? Are you all you can be? Do you love or pity your husband? Do you fear him? Why do you never say no? Is this it? For better or worse till death do you part? Are you lonely? Do you miss your friend? Do you understand what happened that night all those years ago? If you knew you were set to leave this earth soon, would you do it all differently?*

On the night before Ben Logan's family turned off his ventilator and he was taken to surgery to have his organs harvested so that others could live, Lily Donovan sat on a swing in her garden and admitted to herself that aside from her children she regretted every other decision she'd made. *I hate my life.*

Chapter 7

And death shall have no dominion

Sunday 22nd July 1990

Lily, Lily, Lily,

We all know what happens when you drink too much. You get maudlin and that's all that's wrong with you. Stop over-thinking everything and I know that's rich coming from me but you are just driving yourself crazy for no reason. You are the most intelligent person I know. You will sail through medical school. 6 years might seem like a long time but it will fly by. When I close my eyes I can still see us playing on the swing-set and it feels like yesterday. As for your mother we both know she is a mental case. She always has been and she always will be so anything she says has got to be taken with a pinch of salt, although having said that no one not even a mental case is wrong 100% of the time. I think she is right about not attaching yourself to one boy at your age. I'M SORRY, DON'T KILL ME. If you're really concerned about money

178

why not go to Trinity and live at home? You could see Declan at weekends and holidays. Would that really be the end of the world?

OK so my big news is that Ben and I have DONE IT and it was AMAZING. Danny was on a big golf day with his pals so I knew we wouldn't see him till the middle of the night and Clooney was in town with friends. I brought Ben into the house and he spent ages looking around. He's really nosey. He looked at all of the photos and took ages over them asking questions, of course the first being why I'm such a moody cow in pictures and how come you were in so many. He wanted to know about my mother and he asked loads of questions like what was our last conversation and did I remember the way she laughed or smelled and it was weird because I've never really had that conversation before. I didn't want to have it because it's so depressing and I didn't want the vibe to be depressing, I wanted it to be sexy but he wouldn't let it go. He kept asking so I told him about our last day out together as a family, do you remember it? You were there too. We were 6 and Clooney was 8 and we went to some park reserve. I can't remember the name of it. Can you? There was a lake and barbeques and we played in the water and Clooney and Dad fished and Mum lay out in the sun. The car boot was open and the radio was on. When she was cooking she was singing along to the songs and I remember how beautiful she looked and that I stood staring at her for such a long time, wishing I could be just like her. I haven't thought about that day in years and then suddenly it was all so clear in my head - you and me paddling and sitting in the shallow water. You had a swimsuit with a duck on it and mine had big pink polka dots. I dared you to lie straight back and let a wave wash over you and you did it and nearly coughed a lung up and then you made me do it too for revenge but the wave didn't cover my face like it did yours and you called me fathead and we both thought it was really funny and she warned us to be careful. Do you remember? You and Clooney chased each other around the picnic area and made Danny run with me on his shoulders. And then she collapsed just by the car. One minute she was walking and then she disappeared and someone passing noticed her and called to my dad. He had her in his arms in no time and he rocked her back and forth like she was a baby. Clooney started to cry. When you saw him cry you cried. I don't think I did. I just stood there needing a wee but afraid to move. That was the beginning of the end for her, that day in that place I can't remember. I told Ben about the memory and suddenly I was crying. ME CRYING???? He said that it's good to cry every now and then and maybe if I did I wouldn't be so gloomy in photos. He laughed at his little joke and then he dragged me upstairs to my room. He spent ages looking around there. I had to stand in front of my knicker-drawer in case he tried to open it but he didn't. He sat at my desk and straight away he noticed that I'd carved B.G.M.L into it. He said, I'm already inscribed on your desk, and I tried to laugh it off saying he was not. He said, well, what does B.G.M.L stand for and I was trying to think so I delayed answering by saying what do you think it stands for. He smiled and said ' Ben Glen, Medeiros Logan. He's very quick, Gar could have been looking at that for years and not got it. I said no it stands for Don't Go Morning Light. MORONIC I KNOW. He fell around the place laughing and kept repeating Don't Go Morning Light over and over and I went so red in the face I had to give up and say fine, it's you, don't let that head of yours get any bigger or it will topple off that little body. Then he lay down on my bed and he stared at me. I didn't know where to put myself so I decided just to go for it and lie down beside him as in you're not going to intimidate me, Ben Glen Medeiros Logan.

He put his arm around me and instead of kissing me he asked me to tell him another story. I didn't want to. I still wasn't the better of the first one. I asked him to tell me something and he told me that he'd been expelled from boarding school for smoking and getting drunk when he was 14! He said there were four of them who used to sneak booze into the school in shampoo bottles and they'd pay the grounds keeper to buy them cigarettes. They had a key for one of the sheds and they'd get up out of bed around 1 a.m. and go to the shed and drink and smoke till around 4 a.m. They got caught because they were being watched because they all kept falling asleep in class. He said his parents went insane and he was brought home and it was really bad for a while but then they'd just lost his sister and his mother was in an awful way anyway. He said he thinks about that time often because his mother spent most days crying, his dad was a zombie and he was so unhappy he felt sick all the time. He said that he made a promise to himself he'd never ever feel that badly again. I told him that was a stupid thing to say, that no one can make promises like that. He laughed at me and said I was right but it would have been nice if I could have just agreed to make him feel better. I said I didn't realise that was a requirement. He kissed me FINALLY and I've told you before he's way better than Gar but I mean by hundreds and thousands of miles. I took off his shirt and he took off mine and he has a really good body. Then he had my bra off and our tops were skin on skin and his chest was so warm and I could feel his heart beating and when I unbuttoned his trousers I could feel he was about to burst through them anyway and then STUPID ANNOYING Clooney arrives home shouting out my name. I couldn't believe it. Ben didn't freak out like Gar had. He asked me if Clooney normally barged into my room and I said no so he just lay there smiling and he pressed his finger to my lips and when I didn't answer Clooney the third time he called he stopped calling and disappeared somewhere. And then Ben was inside me. JUST LIKE THAT. One minute he's lying beside me then he's on top and then INSIDE!!!!! No crowbar necessary. It was unbelievable and the first time hurt and there was some blood but not enough to freak me out. Before we got going Ben made me put a towel on the bed which was good thinking although I was in such a rush to get going I picked up Clooney's football towel, it's one of his favourites. I washed it immediately but I still feel bad about it. Anyway we did it again another 2 times and we've done it about 10 times since then and every time it gets better and better. I'm blushing just thinking about it. I'm totally in love with him and I couldn't be happier I waited to be with someone like him. That first time we lay together for ages and although I did feel sticky and was longing for a shower, when we talked and he held me in his arms I thought to myself this is what it should be like. When I couldn't wait any longer he talked me into joining him in the shower. You should have seen us scurry along the landing like 2 mice trying to avoid Clooney. We got into the bathroom and locked it and got into the shower and washed one another which was again AMAZING. We were all soapy and it was all lovely and of course Clooney tried to open the door and suddenly he's calling my name and Ben is grinning and I'm having a heart attack so I just try to put him off by calling out that I'm sick. He wondered why I didn't answer him when he came in and I told him I didn't hear him and to go away I wasn't well. And then he asks me if I have the shits because Terry the Tourist had the shits and was hospitalised with dehydration the previous day. Ben was trying not to laugh. I said that I had pains and asked him to go away. Finally he left us alone. Couldn't believe I'd got away with it. Now I know how

Clooney feels when he's entertaining. NOT GOOD. Anyway the next day Ben called and I introduced Clooney to Ben and Clooney asked if we wanted coffees. I said no but Ben said yeah, that would be great! PISSED OFF. So anyway we then spent the next hour listening to Clooney go on and on about his stalker and how she's ruining his life. Ben was really interested and asked loads of questions and I just wanted to get up the stairs, then Clooney suggested that we watch a film together and Ben agreed so we ended up watching The Terminator with my stupid brother. Later when I walked Ben out he said we'd have plenty of time and we kissed at the door and I just kept thinking no we don't have plenty of time, we have one summer together. I'm going to London and as much as we want it to work out I can't afford to come home until Christmas which means we would have been together for less time than we'd been apart. So it didn't make sense to me wasting time watching the stupid Terminator. We have to take every moment we have together and make the most of it. I was going to say it to him but I didn't because I didn't want to stop kissing and I can't just make a point with Ben and move on – he always has to discuss it to the point that I'm sorry I brought it up in the first place. So Clooney left yesterday and I'm thrilled because when Dad's at work Ben and me have the place to ourselves and Dad's working on a big project so he's going to be out a lot. It's bliss. Ben wanted me to go to his house the other day but his mother would be there so I said we'd be better going to mine. He asked me if I didn't want to meet his mother and I said no not really and that seemed to hurt him which I don't understand. I told him that mothers don't really like me and that he'd probably be better off keeping me to himself. He laughed at that but I'm serious. Your mother hates me. Gar's mother thinks I'm rude and Declan's mother ignores me, then again she's so stuck up she ignores everyone. Clooney's stalker was hanging around outside the house last night. I wanted to go out to her but Ben said he'd do it. He went outside and they sat on the wall and they were there for ages and I was looking out the window wondering what the hell they were talking about and then she just walked off. He came back in and told me that he'd explained to her that she was worth more than standing by a pole looking into the house of some guy who didn't care about her. I told him he should give up marketing and become a psychiatrist. He said he reads those books all the time. He got into them after his sister died and his mother got so depressed that they had her on suicide watch for a while. I didn't know that – he hadn't mentioned it before. It's very sad and now I feel bad about not meeting her. Maybe I'll suggest going over soon. Anyway I'm not sure his little talk worked because I saw Stalker Girl again in the village today and I don't think she has any good reason to be there so we'll see.

How's Colm? Do you remember any more from that night?

Love you
Eve

P.S. Gar split up with his Bray girl. Don't know why but I'm meeting him and the lads on Tuesday night so I'll fill you in next Sunday and Paul was seen in town with a girl who looked like a supermodel and it turns out she is a model! Don't know any more than that – it was Declan who told me his sister saw them and Paul is being really coy about it. SICKENING.

P.P.S. Declan's fine. I'm being much nicer to him you'll be happy to hear. He really misses you and he's doing a lot of overtime at his dad's garage to try to get money for *college. I called down there the other night to ask him to Ben's next gig. I think I interrupted a fight with his dad but I might be wrong because his dad was really nice to me and told me I could stay for a coffee if I wanted to. I said no but then Declan insisted. He must really miss you if he wanted me to hang around!!!! So I did and it was weird. You know the way we normally only really ever slag one another off? Well, instead of doing that we actually had a real conversation. We talked about the 32 year old woman who jumped off the cliff on Tuesday because her boyfriend left her and it was deep. I finally get what you see in him (Haha at last)*

* * *

The funeral of Ben Logan was a huge affair. Family, new friends, old friends, acquaintances, neighbours, work colleagues, staff, suppliers and even some creditors and competitors turned up. The church was packed to the rafters, forcing many to stand outside. It was a bright hot July day and between the hymns, speeches and sermon, birds could be heard twittering loudly from the trees that lined the church grounds. There wasn't a person there that had a bad word to say about him. Every second story that was told brought peals of laughter or tears of joy and desperate sadness. Ben Logan had been a blessing to all who knew him. He had been kind, considerate, caring, friendly and funny. He was a good and fair boss, a friendly neighbour, the kind of friend that stays in your life forever even if you haven't seen him in a long while. The music was poignant and when a young girl by the name of Rosy Carey sang Eric Clapton's 'Tears in Heaven' there wasn't a dry eye in the house. Ben's dad spoke on the altar, he talked about the son he had cherished and lost, focusing on how Ben after an initial flirtation with being a bad boy had turned into the boy his mummy could lean on after his sister died tragically aged ten. He knew in his heart that she'd be waiting on the other side to greet him and quoting from the song he said he was confident she'd know his name when she saw him in Heaven. He spoke about Ben's determination, his love of music and travel. He spoke about his beautiful wife Fiona and the happiness she had brought into his life. He talked about how generous Ben was, even managing to make a joke about Ben's organ donations.

"There will be five lucky recipients of Ben's organs, well four – let's face it, his liver's a dud."

The crowd laughed loudly, thankful for the momentary break in bleak bitter heartbreak.

At the graveyard a friend of the family played and sang Blink 182's 'I Miss You' as they put what remained of Ben into the ground.

Lily had squeezed into the back of the church and in the graveyard she stood slightly apart from the crowd. She had no real business there. She had never spoken to Ben Logan when he was alive; he was just the boy from the bowling alley that couldn't seem to take his eyes off Eve. Their relationship had begun and ended one summer when she was down the country and so the only memories that she'd formed of him were through Eve's descriptions of him in her letters. Those letters had been Lily's long-time lifeline with her old friend; she had kept every one in the shoebox her son had stuck his nose into, along with some pictures of them together when they were young and inseparable.

Fiona spotted Lily as she was being led away from the graveyard and thanked her for coming. She asked how Eve was and Lily told her that it would be a long road but that she'd be fine. Fiona seemed happy to hear it. She had accepted Eve's story as truth and Lily was happy now to play her part in the lie. She asked Lily if she wished to join them in the hotel but Lily made her excuses and left the people that had shared in Ben's world behind her. She would later report to Eve that he was a very popular, good man who was loved and cherished and would be missed every day thereafter.

Eve knew that, despite her depth of feeling for Ben, their time together should have remained in the past. She was never much more than a fantasy figure to him and he was part of another life she had tried to cling to. Although her feelings for him were real their relationship was not. She realised in those first few days lying in a broken mess that she didn't even really know him. If she had gone to that funeral she would have been as much of a stranger to Ben as Lily was.

"Even the best people make mistakes," Eve said, referring to Ben and not herself.

"Yes, they do," Lily agreed.

"I was just so tired and lonely."

"You don't have to be lonely any more," Lily said.

And in that moment Eve realised that Lily was her friend again. She waited until Lily left the room and raised her blanket to cry in peace.

"Is she crying again, Anne?"

"She is, Beth."

"Jesus, I've never met one like her!"

"Just leave her be, chicken. There by the grace of God go I."

Ben's old band mates stayed on for the afters of his funeral. Billy had travelled from America to be there. Tom, Ben's cousin, had travelled from France. Finbarr and Mark lived close by and they had remained close all those years. Theirs was a tragic and long overdue reunion. They joined the rest of the mourners in a hotel in South Dublin where they drank and sang and told stories about a boy and man they knew, loved and would miss.

Fiona was on medication as was Ben's mother. They were both prescribed by the same woman, Ben's Aunt Celia. She was a GP and a great believer in medicating during times of stress. "After all, stress is the number one killer after road accidents," she said. Ben's dad looked at his sister as though she was insane. She didn't seem to notice that she'd said anything inappropriate, instead she just crossed her arms over her substantial chest and pursed her lips like a duck. Lots of people were inappropriate in their attempts to comfort the lead mourners who had sat for hours on end in a church shaking hands with a seemingly never-ending line of people who squeezed their swollen hands a little bit too hard in a bid to convey that they really meant what they had said.

"At least he didn't suffer," Lorna O'Loughlin said. "If he had suffered it would have been a desperate situation altogether." If Fiona wasn't so altered she might have asked how much more 'desperate' Lorna thought the situation could get. Her husband who hadn't even turned forty had been hit by a drunk driver – he was dead, his organs were gone and he was about to be buried in a fucking hole in the ground. But she didn't say any of that. Instead she nodded and Lorna went off, delighted to have helped with her words of wisdom.

"Thank God he didn't see it coming," Michael Hannon said to Ben's mother whilst leaning on the pew. *What the hell does that mean?* She nodded and hoped he'd move on quickly.

"It would have been worse if it was cancer," a random person said. *Huh.*

"At least he died when he was still living," another one said, winking as she squeezed Ben's dad's hand until he hurt. *What in Christ's name?*

At the reception it was clear that Fiona hadn't eaten or slept properly in over a week and she was fading. Ben's mother had just buried her second child and every one who knew her was acutely aware that it would be a long time before she came back from losing him, if ever. She sat there quietly holding Fiona's hand. She didn't speak or drink tea or have a sandwich or a piece of cake. She just picked a spot on the wall and stared at it until she could go home or Celia gave her another little white pill. Ben had been his mother's rock. As his father had said in the church, Ben was the one she leaned on. He was her friend and confidant. There wasn't a week that went by where Ben didn't visit his parents and, although he got on famously with his father, his mother was one of the true loves of Ben's life. She knew that, his wife knew it, as did his friends and family. It was a running joke.

"Fiona, do you take Ben and his ma to be your lawful wedded husband?"

It was one of the things that made Ben so likable. For those who weren't quite as deeply in despair, Ben's funeral was the perfect celebration of his life. The drink flowed and the musicians played and laughter followed tears followed laughter.

All the while Billy sat watching the crowd lament his old friend and band mate. Billy had left Ireland for America when he won a J1 visa in some sort of lotto. His departure put the nail in the coffin of a band that had been struggling for a long time. Initially his decision had been met with resentment but over the years his fellow band mates had all come round. He had set up his own electrician business over there and, while he might not have been Donald Trump, he employed thirty guys, lived in a nice house and could support his four kids comfortably. He had been the last band member that Ben had reconnected with and again it was via Facebook. They had only been in touch for two years and during those two years they had shared with each other the things that they didn't share with anyone else. Maybe this was because Ben and Billy always had a special connection which had made Billy's abandonment all the more terrible in those early days, or maybe it was because they weren't proximate to one another and it was easier for Ben to tell someone a million miles away that his business was going under and that he was terrified that he was falling in love with the girl who broke his heart when he was nineteen. Billy had heard the extraordinary story of the accident and who was involved and, when it was relayed that his dealings with Eve were purely professional, he remained silent. Ben had told him in a recent email that Eve had returned to Ireland but that they had agreed not to see one another. Ben wanted his marriage to work. He beat himself up about the affair the previous year. He had questioned everything about himself, his wife and life. *Why did I open this can of worms? Why did I think we could just be friends? How can I do this to Fiona? How can I do it to myself?* Billy had been there in the aftermath of Eve all those years ago. He had been the friend to pick up the pieces. Ben had mourned Eve as though she had died. She had been so cruel and careless with his heart and she had all but destroyed him. If Billy's decision to move to America was the final nail in the band's coffin, Ben's broken heart was the first. Billy couldn't bring himself to dislike Eve despite what she had done to his friend because he had kept her secret all those years and it was only when he unburdened himself and told Ben about the day that followed their break-up that Ben, after punching him in his face, decided to make contact with Eve again.

"OK, I deserved that," Billy said. "But you're happy so don't do anything stupid."

The first time Ben had sex with Eve and much later that evening when his wife was in bed and he was working on budgets on his computer, he saw that Billy was online and he messaged him.

<<Did a bad thing with Eve>>

<<Not going to pretend to be surprised>>

<<I love my wife>>

<<Apparently you love your dick more>>

<<When did you become Captain Judgement?>>

<<After I made the same mistake you did and lost my first wife, my first house and my dog>>

When Eve returned to Ireland and made contact with Ben again he had nearly suffered heart failure then and there and, even though she assured him that she did not expect them to take up from where they left off, he knew deep down that with the attraction they shared it was inevitable. He contacted Billy online.

<<She's back>>

<<If you want your marriage to work stay away>>

Ben assured him he would but over the next while he did admit that they were in contact.

<<She's just giving me business advice I swear >>

<<I'll buy that when I sustain a head injury >>

<<I'm not saying I don't want her. I haven't met up because I don't want to put temptation my way. All our dealings are via email>>

<<Keep it that way>>

That was the last session of instant messaging between the two men. Even as Billy had signed off with a warning, he knew that Ben wouldn't be able to help himself around Eve and it was just a matter of time before he'd see her again. He had considered a number of scenarios which would bring about the end of Ben's affair and/or marriage but not one of the scenarios he had thought about even came close to his death.

The bar in the hotel was stuffed with mourners. Fiona and Ben's mother, father and brother were sitting in a corner. The two women were high, the two men were talking to the never-ending stream of people that were still approaching to shake their hands. The old band members sat together in a corner reminiscing about the good old days when they dreamed of becoming rock stars. It was well into the night before one of them brought up the fact that Ben had been with Eve on the night he died.

"Of all the people to be with on that night," Finbarr said.

Billy was very confident that he was the only one in the room that Ben had confided in about his affair and so he said nothing.

"Eve Hayes," Tom said shaking his head. "She was a real beauty back in the day."

"Seriously banged up now," Mark said. "Fiona said she was in an awful way."

"Still can't believe she was going to step in and save the business," Tom said. "Still, Fiona saw the business plan Eve had sent on email and it was really impressive."

"Well, that one could smell a profit a mile away. She made a killing on her own business," Finbarr said.

Billy found it interesting that not one person seemed to question why Eve was helping Ben. Instead he listened to everyone and anyone talk about what a wonderful marriage his friend had and what a good man he was and that he landed on his feet the day he met and married Fiona.

When he walked over to Fiona to sit with her for a while she was pleasant and numb and grateful to everyone for coming and worried that it was all too much for his mother whose mind was elsewhere for most of the day.

"Did you know the woman he was with?" she asked Billy.

"Vaguely," he said. "They were together for only a very short time when they were kids."

"She was going to invest in the business but I don't know what to do with supermarkets. I'd rather pay off our creditors and close the business down. We have good insurance. It would be a clean start. Do you think that's callous?"

Billy didn't know Fiona very well – in fact he'd only met her once before when Ben and Fiona visited him and his family in Chicago while on a road trip. It was during that trip that he had unburdened himself about Eve.

191

"I don't think it's callous at all," he said.

"Do you think Eve will be disappointed?"

Billy felt uncomfortable. *Why is she asking me this? Does she suspect? Does she think I know something? Why ask me? Why would she care?*

"I think she's a businesswoman who has had many deals scuppered for lesser reasons than an old friend's death," he said.

Fiona's eyes leaked and she nodded. "I'm leaving here. I don't know where I'm going but I can't stay here."

Billy nodded. There wasn't much he could say. Ben's mother hadn't spoken once during his brief time sitting with her and even when he addressed her she looked right through him as though he was invisible. There was no escape for her. Billy needed to get away from the two women as soon as he could.

Before he made a break for it, he told Fiona he'd miss his old friend greatly.

"If someone told me I'd only have him for ten years I'd still have married him," she said.

"I know he'd feel the same," Billy said and he wasn't lying, because aside from Ben's infatuation with Eve he remembered the guy who had come to Chicago and bounced out of an RV and introduced him to his beautiful wife. He was grinning and hugging her close and when she moved his eyes followed and when she spoke he smiled. He couldn't keep his hands off her, much to Billy's second wife's annoyance. "She's a person not a Goddamn puppy!"

Billy surveyed the large room filled with people whose Ben's life had touched and sadly he accepted that day would be the true end of his friend Ben Logan. And despite Ben's feelings for a girl who broke his heart when he was a teenager and didn't know any better, in that room and where it counted she was just some forgotten footnote and, thanks to her lie and Ben's family and friends' willingness to believe it, that's where she would remain. He bore his own guilt silently. If he had never brought up Eve and if he had kept secret the day they had spent together in an A&E room after Ben had run out on her, Ben wouldn't have contacted her and he wouldn't have been on that road and hit by that drunk, but then again he deserved to know the truth and Eve deserved the truth to be told. He was twenty-one and too stupid to really know what to do for the best back then. Eve made him promise to keep their day together a secret and she made a lot of sense when she told him that her relationship with Ben wouldn't survive London and it was better to leave things as they were. She was trying to be brave and do the right thing but if he had his time again he would have told him straight away, then maybe things would have turned out so much differently. *I'm sorry old friend. RIP.*

During the second week of Eve's recovery Lily was off duty. She used many excuses to come and go from the hospital that week. Her husband found her most attentive, bringing him packed savoury lunches and dropping in to see if he needed any dry cleaning picked up as she was passing.

"You could have phoned."

"I was passing."

She'd spend twenty minutes with her husband before heading down to her ward and spending an hour with Eve. It was a different dynamic when she came as a visitor. They talked about everything and anything, filling one another in on the years that they had missed. Clooney would show up most days and the three of them would talk about their happy childhood spent together. It felt like Lily the missing Hayes had come home. *Danny would have loved to see her again. If only I'd got knocked down last year,* Eve thought. A silent unspoken pact between the girls meant that they would never speak of the night that cemented the end of their friendship but other than that everything was on the table.

Lily told Eve about the birth of her kids.

"Horrifying. Hence only two kids and Daisy was a mistake. I cried for the first month."

Lily told Eve about her house and her need to have everything in its place.

"Scott thinks I have OCD."

"He's right. When you were a kid you used to line up the towels on the rack like the psychopath in *Sleeping With The Enemy*."

Lily told Eve about her job.

"I realised that Mrs Moriarty wanted me to be a doctor more than I did."

"Who was Mrs Moriarty?"

"Our Guidance Counsellor."

"I don't remember her."

"That's because you knew exactly what you wanted to do and wouldn't take any guidance from anyone."

"Oh, right. Well, you're an excellent nurse, probably the best nurse in the world." She smiled when Lily raised her arms in the air and bowed. "And you seem to really like it. Do you?"

"Yeah," Lily said. "Nursing has been my escape." As soon as she said it she knew she'd said the wrong thing. *Damn it.*

"Escape?"

"From the house, the kids and the neighbours who use me when they want something but never remember to invite me to their coffee mornings – the usual," she said, careful not to include her husband in the mix.

"Ah," Eve said, "that's just because they're jealous bitches."

Lily laughed again, pleased that she'd sufficiently dealt with her slip, but also because that was something the old Eve would have said. "I hardly think that's the case," she said.

"It's exactly the case," Eve said. "In most rooms, you're probably the best-looking woman in there by a mile with your tiny little frame, your coffee-cream skin, big saucer-brown eyes and that silk hair of yours. You heading for forty and you look fourteen. You're funny, sweet, kind, warm, intelligent and basically every middle-aged-woman-battling-the-bulge-and-trying-to-hold-on-to-her-husband's nightmare.

"If that's the case, you're a middle-aged woman – how come I don't get on your nerves?"

"Because even with a face full of stiches I'm better-looking than you. I do have the personality of a storm trooper so you'd have me there but then again I have no man for you to rob plus I know something they don't."

"What's that?"

"You're loyal to the point of self-sacrifice."

Lily felt sad. They were both silent for a minute or two before Eve resurrected the question about nursing.

"So aside from escape and your sheer brilliance, is nursing where you want to be?"

"You know I always liked beauty. Hair and make-up, maybe for fashion shows and photography – that was the real dream if I hadn't been so dumb as not to follow it."

"I remember that *Girls' World*," Eve said. "And you insisted on doing my hair all the time."

"You had such beautiful hair."

"And it's not beautiful now?" Eve laughed.

"It's short."

"So are you."

Lily laughed. "I used to do Daisy's all the time but she won't let me near her now."

"God, now that I think about it, when we were younger that's all you used talk about. In fact, when my mother got sick you used to come over and insist on brushing her hair once a week and I used to talk about designing clothes and you'd talk about doing hair and make-up! Then it all changed. Why?"

"I got the best Intercert exam results the school had ever seen and Mrs Moriarty told me a girl with my intelligence should do more with my life, like for instance medicine."

"You were always open to suggestion."

"And you certainly benefited from that," Lily said, remembering the many times Eve had easily talked her into acts of insanity all in the name of fun.

"You never wanted to be a doctor – that was Declan's dream. You wanted to be a wife and mother and nursing was a good option – it kept you close to him and you could breeze through it and earn more quickly."

"Exactly."

"It used to make sense but now your kids are nearly grown up."

"Daisy's only twelve."

"All I'm saying is, if it's still the dream why not go for it?"

"Because life's not that simple, Eve."

"No one is saying it is. The right decisions are usually the hardest. I'm only suggesting a beauty course, not exiling yourself on an island."

Lily was silent for a while, thinking about what Eve had said. *I could do it. I know I could. If I knew I was set to leave this earth soon, would I do it all differently?*

On another day Eve told Lily about her time in London, Paris and New York.

"Amazing?" Lily asked.

"Sometimes."

"You must have met incredible people."

"Ah, people are people."

"Come on, tell me one fabulous thing."

Eve thought about it for a minute and sighed. "I had sex with a few movie stars, a rock star and a politician. He was a kinky one."

"You are joking."

"His wife videotaped it."

"Ah, come on!"

"We watched it back afterwards over pizza and wine. They were a lovely couple and it was a great night but when they were drunk enough I recorded some talk show over it because my ass looked huge and nobody wants that."

"Are you joking?" Lily asked very seriously.

"No. I swear."

"Who was it?" Lily was nearly falling out of her chair she was leaning forward so much.

"Can't say."

"Ah, come on!"

"Lean in."

Lily leaned in.

Eve whispered a name.

Lily leaned out with her mouth open. "No fudging way!"

Eve nodded.

"I've heard it all now," Lily said.

Eve laughed. *No, you haven't even heard the half of it.*

Clooney would tell the girls stories about his time spent in exotic and troubled locations.

"Do you ever get tired of it?" Lily asked.

"All the time," he admitted.

"Tell her about the time you were in a plane crash," Eve said.

"Ah. Now. What?" Lily said, bracing herself in the chair.

"We were flying in a 6-seater turboprop plane and about to land just outside New Orleans. The plane came up short of the runway, we hit an embankment, lost the right wing and propeller but luckily everyone survived. The worst injury was a broken leg."

"Clooney came out without a scratch and that's having helped three people out before the plane burst into flames," Eve said.

"Of course you were the hero of the piece!" Lily said, smiling.

Clooney just hunched. "Like Eve said, I wasn't injured so if I had stood around it would have made me a really big dick."

"What's he saying about a big dick?" Beth shouted at Anne.

"Nothing. None of your business. Let him talk," Anne said and waved over at Lily, Eve and Clooney who nodded and waved back.

"Any news on my private room?" Eve whispered to Lily.

"I'm working on it," she said.

Over those first three days of Eve's second week in hospital the trio talked about their past, their present and their hopes for the future. Clooney and Eve were both obviously on the cusp of life-changing decisions, although while Clooney talked about what he would do and where he would go, Eve was strangely vague which just wasn't like her. Lily listened, staying quiet while fantasising about making a drastic change in her own life. But when Eve was feeling really blue Lily could walk through the door and cheer her up.

"Take your head out of your arse! Isn't that what you Americans say?"

"We both know that I'm not American."

"Really? Then what's with the twang."

"I don't have a twang!" Eve said with disgust.

"Oh yes, you do!" Clooney agreed.

Then he went on to slag off his sister for having some kind of half-bred cockney accent when she was in London and a serious French lilt when she lived in Paris. Lily joined in, remembering how Eve talked like she'd swallowed a bucket of spit the one summer they spent learning Irish on a small island off the coast of Cork.

No matter how sad or bad Eve felt, together Clooney and Lily could make her laugh and, most importantly, laugh at herself.

In the middle of that second week Lindsey was moved into a care home.

"Goodbye to you all, tell the blonde she's invited to my party, the others can stay at home," she said to the nurse who was helping her into her wheelchair.

"Ah, blow it out your arse!" Anne said as Lindsey waved from bed to bed as though she was the Queen and those around her were commoners standing behind barricades waving flags and hoping for a smile or glance their way.

Anne went home a day later. She insisted on being wheeled up to Eve. She took her hand. "You'll be alright, chicken," she said. "You have your brother and your friend, you're not alone any more."

"Thanks, Anne."

"And, chicken, don't make a habit of sleeping with married men – even if they don't die on you it leads to nothing but heartbreak."

"OK."

"And, chicken . . ."

"Yes, Anne?"

"Tell that bisexual that I'm glad he picked the right team."

"No intention of it, Anne," she said.

Anne laughed and waved and then she was gone, leaving Eve with Beth who appeared to be stoned must of the time and two new women she didn't have time to get to know because as soon as a private room became available she was moved into it.

"Bye, Beth!" Eve said as a nurse wheeled her away.

"Are you going home, love?" Beth asked.

"No, moving into a private room."

"Oh good, it would be a crime to let you go, you're still in an awful way."

Eve was hospitalised six days when the physio on her shoulder started and it would go on for her entire nine-week stay. It was agonising. Every day for forty minutes, simple stretching and resistance exercises became torture. Eve would count down the hours and minutes until the physiotherapist Mica came to her room. She'd take a deep breath and they'd begin. The pain was immense but after some coaching and cajoling she'd push through, often crying during the session. Mica was nice but stern and took no prisoners.

"I know it hurts but if you want your shoulder to work again you've got to do this."

"I don't, it's fine, one good arm will do."

"Don't be ridiculous – now push against me."

After physio was concluded Eve received two painkilling pills, the dread lifted and her day would begin. She'd read books, stare at daytime TV, sleep when she could, read more books, and watch more TV. Visitors broke the monotony. Gina would come most days when the kids were in school. She brought little food gifts of cheesecake, homemade banana bread and colourful cup cakes. Eve didn't eat cheesecake, banana bread or cupcakes when she wasn't confined to bed and feeling like a beached whale, never mind when she was. The nurses appreciated them and looked forward to Gina's arrival. She talked about the kids, the price of things, general news and every now and then she'd bring up Paul and his impending nuptials. Gar had taken the news of Paul's bisexuality badly. He couldn't understand why his friend had been so deceitful. He couldn't comprehend why Paul spent so much time lying to himself and others. Gar felt let down. He looked at Paul and saw a stranger. *All these years*. He thought about the things he told Paul about himself and Gina and the things they got up to the bedroom. He would never have done that if he didn't think that Paul was on another bus. *Jesus Christ, he might have been imagining her and me and him. Ah, for fuck . . .* Gina was worried because Gar had been avoiding Paul and, aside from a few work mates that liked to play rugby on a weekly basis in the summer, Gar didn't really have friends.

"He'll come around," Eve had said one particularly nice day when the sun was beating in through the window and she was sweating like a pig.

Eve's headaches were getting worse. *Nothing like being stuck in an overheated stuffy hospital to give a girl a headache.*

Lily ran in having had lunch with her husband and Gina nearly fell over in a bid to get up and hug her. Lily was happy to see Gina but she did feel a little awkward that there was an elephant in the room and Gina wasn't as good at avoiding it as she and Eve had been.

"Where the hell did you go?" Gina asked.

"Ah, you know."

"No, I don't know."

"Cork, then here."

"Why have you never come home?"

"Oh, we settled in Dalkey."

"Yes, very posh, but only down the road so why have we not seen you?"

"Down the road might as well be America when you've got two kids," Eve said helpfully.

Gina nodded and laughed. "I hear that. I've got two as well, they're younger than yours. You must have had Scott straight away."

Eve had told Gina all about Lily's children which Lily spoke about a lot. Eve usually didn't like people's stories about kids – as fascinating as they thought they were, they usually weren't – but Lily could always tell a good story and her kids seemed funny if not a little spoilt but Lily would admit that herself. Lily agreed that she did get pregnant very early on, in fact she conceived on the honeymoon but that had always been her plan so it was a very welcome development.

Gina wasn't letting go. "I still don't understand why you never came home."

"My mother preferred to visit us."

"But it's your hometown."

"Look, Inspector Clouseau, some people move and keep on moving," Lily said and Eve laughed.

"OK, OK," Gina said with her hands up. "We just missed you, that's all."

Lily had missed them too. She nipped in on the Friday evening when Declan was away at a conference in London and Paul and Clooney, Gina and Gar were there. Gar was subdued, having been made visit by his wife. He didn't want to see Paul and he couldn't care less about his friend who'd abandoned him the first chance she got. Paul wasn't one for making a fuss. He pretended he didn't notice Gar's mood which he figured he'd get over soon enough and he'd never really minded about Lily and Declan's defection. *People do what they do.* He just got Lily a chair and told her it was good to see her.

"How's Declan?" he asked.

"Fine thanks," she said and that was the end of that.

When she got up to leave, Clooney stood up with her.

When she left he waited a moment or two before he made his excuses, leaving Paul and Eve to fight over the remote control, and Gina and Gar to glower at one another. He caught up with Lily in the corridor. They walked to the lift together.

"Going down," he said, pushing the lift button.

"You wish!" she joked and he laughed.

They walked to the car park together and just as they were about to part he stopped in his tracks and asked her if she wouldn't mind getting something to eat with him. Clooney knew that Declan was away and he knew that Daisy and her friend were fed and that Scott was working late in his grandfather's garage and all she was going home to were heated-up leftovers followed by washing and ironing.

"I'm sick of eating on my own," he said.

"I don't know," she said.

"Two old friends grabbing a bite to eat . . . please," he said and pouted. "I'm so lonely."

Lily had always been a sucker for a sad story. "OK. I'm giving you an hour."

"Is that an hour from now or from the time I order?"

She thought about it for a minute before concluding that she'd take note of the time and she'd decide depending on whether or not he was boring.

"I'm never boring," he said.

"I'll be the judge of that," she said and he followed her to her car like a playful puppy. Clooney was bored and he hated being bored. Paul was busy planning a wedding and moving his fiancé to Ireland. Gar wasn't available to anyone and of the friends Clooney once had in Ireland not one remained. Val Kilpatrick lived in London, his school friends had all moved abroad and his college friends lived around the country and, because he'd never stayed in

Ireland longer than a week or two before his dad was diagnosed with cancer, he had never bothered staying in touch. When he'd returned last time, he was busy with his dad, busy with Eve and with Eve came Gar, Gina and Paul. Now he was busy doing nothing most of the time but sitting on his sister's balcony and thinking. Clooney was more of an action guy than a profound thinker. He didn't like being alone too long. He wasn't a reader and so getting lost in another man or woman's world wasn't something that appealed to him. He had finished his contract in Afghanistan. He had broken ties with Stephanie. He wasn't going back there and he wasn't sure where he would go next. Time would tell and until then he would sit alone in an empty, modern, cold, unfamiliar apartment waiting on the appropriate times to visit his bored, moody, frustrated sister. *Tick tock tick tock tick tock tick tock.*

Lily pulled up outside a restaurant that she was unfamiliar with but it was on a main road and there seemed to be a lot of parking. They got out and she followed him inside. The place was quaint, old-style Italian, with gingham tablecloths, candles in red glassware and wood counters and benches. The smell of ripe tomato sauce and pizza cooking in the big pizza oven hit them both and, for the first time in a few days, Lily actually felt hungry. Since that night on the swing Lily had been deprived of sleep and off her food. Her mind was constantly racing. She'd been questioning everything about herself and her life and things that she hadn't seemed to notice for years started to become huge problems. Like earlier in the week at breakfast time.

"Mum, I'm thinking I'll have the spinach omelette. Dad, I'm working on a vintage BMW today," Scott said.

"Year?" Declan said.

"It's an early V8."

"Mum, I'm in the mood for pancakes but only if we have the proper syrup," Daisy said.

"A 501?" Declan said to Scott before looking toward his wife. "Make mine a grill, easy on the pig though. I have a morning meeting and I don't want to have bacon breath."

"A 502," Scott replied.

"Nice," Declan said. "I'll bet it's belonging to one of the Browne's.

They made a ton of money in exporting butter in the 50's through to the 70's. The father was a huge vintage car enthusiastic I'm sure his sons have followed suit. I worked on some of those beauties myself back in the day. Oh, and Lily, can you made sure the egg doesn't break – it was broken yesterday."

No 'please'. No 'thank-you'. When the hell did I become a bloody dogsbody?

"I'm making a grill," she'd said. "You are all either in or out."

And her family stopped what they were doing or saying around the table and looked up at her.

"You're joking. Right?" Scott said.

"Seriously not funny," Daisy said.

"What's this?" Declan said.

"I'm not a chef. This is not a restaurant. Do you want a grill or not?"

The two kids looked at one another and then at their father. He mumbled something to them about her hormones, making little of her, as he so often did and they laughed together.

For such a long time Lily would have either let it go or made a joke so as to regain her ground but that morning she had taken the pan that was in her hand and thrown it across the kitchen. It hit the wall and gouged out a piece of plaster. Declan and the kids sat in their chairs, stunned.

"Kitchen's closed," she said and walked out of the room.

When her week's nursing was over and her week off begun, she had faced a dilemma. She wanted to visit with Eve and Clooney and Gar, Gina and even Paul who she hadn't clicked with as well as Eve had in the past. She always thought he was too quiet, aloof and she sometimes found him cold but it was nice to be close to the people she'd grown up with and had been apart from for so many years. She couldn't tell Declan, not just because of his hatred of Eve, but because he didn't like Lily to have friends of her own. He didn't like her to stray off her daily routine. He had to know where she was at all times. Every day was the same if slightly different, there was a day planner on the fridge that was to be adhered to and it left little room for personal time. Lily hadn't really noticed that her life had been eaten up with responsibility and, although it used to bug her that her mobile phone was used as a tagging device by her husband, she had never really felt truly trapped before. If she left it ring more than five rings, he questioned her.

"Where are you?"

"In the supermarket."

"What took so long to answer?"

"For God's sake, Declan, I had to fish the phone out of my pocket."

"Who are you with?"

"Buffy the Vampire Slayer. Would you like a word?"

"Don't get smart. You know I worry."

Every time Declan questioned her or harassed her about where she was or where she was going, what she was doing or who she was with, he told her it was because he worried and for so long she'd accepted his harassment as a symbol of his love albeit an annoying one. But something was changing in Lily, for the first time in a long time her eyes were really open and she was looking at her life though a different lens, one not so rosy. *If I knew I was set to leave this earth soon, would I do it all differently?* Over the years she had helped Declan build her own prison. She became a wife and mother in the same year. When all her peers were out drinking and carousing and expanding their minds with drugs or books she was breast-feeding, sleep-deprived, and the woman behind the man who would someday become a heart surgeon. In her determination to excel in everything she did and, to fulfil Declan's dream of marrying a dedicated housewife, she became the best housewife she could be and that took time. Lily Donovan made Nigella Lawson look like a slacker. From early on she cooked different meals for her husband and kids. It had made sense when Scott was a baby and a fussy eater and Declan was a resident and working every hour God sent. Then Daisy came along she was another fussy eater who happened to have polar opposite tastes to her brother and at that stage it was easier to feed her kids different foods but at the same time. So at five every evening Lily's children ate their meals and then their plates were cleaned away and the table reset so that Declan could call or text her when he was leaving the hospital so that she could prepare a fresh meal for him. Declan liked two courses during the weekdays and three at weekends. For a long time Lily and Declan couldn't afford a cleaner and that was when the kids were younger and arguably there was more work. When they could afford one Declan did offer to pay but by that stage Lily had a perfect routine, everything was in its place, her home was hers to control, and she didn't like the idea of having someone pick up after her or her husband or children. She'd heard terrible stories from the neighbours about cleaners who had stolen from them or worse commented on a child's dirty underpants left on the floor. She didn't like the notion of anyone commenting on her children's underwear and so between cooking breakfasts, packing lunches that other kids would dribble over, and presiding over two seatings for dinner, she'd clean the house top to bottom, she'd garden according to the requirements of each season. She'd run her kids to and from school, rugby, ballet, football, piano, friends' houses, parties, discos, bars, nightclubs and the pony club. Before she even really realised it, every moment of every day was accounted for and there was no room for her deviating from that schedule. In the early days and up until the mid-noughties, Lily worked the night shift which meant she always worked one week on and one off. On the weeks that she worked, she'd be home for eight in the morning and she'd meet Declan in the doorway on his way out. She'd rustle up breakfast and lunch for her kids and pack their bags and when they were gone she'd sleep for five hours. When she woke she'd clean, shop, garden and then pick up the kids, ferry them around before feeding them at five, and then prepare dinner for Declan depending on the time he was due home. Lily's nightshifts affected Declan's breakfast for two weeks out of every month. When her shifts changed to twelve-hour day shifts, he was utterly horrified but in a bid to keep her husband happy Lily had made bits of herself to ensure his life was not affected much. She had set the bar so high he couldn't see why she would let the perfect little world she'd created slide on account of nursing ungrateful strangers. Declan got used to being able to read the planner on the fridge on any given day and know where his wife would be each and every moment and what she was doing. Over the years he'd slowly become more and more clingy and more demanding of her time. Any deviation from her daily schedule caused him a kind of angst that would leave little room for rationality.

Lily had filled up her days with so much work and responsibility and she'd spent so many years making excuses for her husband's controlling nature and paranoia that she hadn't allowed herself to really look at her life for what it was. *A fudging prison sentence.* This became so apparent to her when she was forced to plan her daily escape from her home and duties just so she could go to a funeral or visit her old friend and spend some time with her. And because she was undergoing an inner crisis and behaving erratically one minute, throwing pans across the kitchen and the next arriving in her husband's office with gourmet picnic baskets, Declan was confused. He didn't know that she was simply using him as an excuse to be in the hospital but he did sense something was up. He briefly considered early menopause but, just in case her madness wasn't medical, he decided to keep a closer eye on his wife. His phone calls increased which meant she often had to leave Eve's room to answer her phone and make up a plausible lie and with each day that passed it got harder. *Why can't you just give me five minutes' peace?* When he was forced to go to London for a weekend conference Lily was delighted as she was badly in need of respite. He had tried to talk her into going with him the evening before but she was steadfast in her refusal. He behaved like a spoilt child and she ignored him. When he realised he wasn't going to get his way, he demanded she come upstairs and perform her duty as his wife. He sometimes used sex as a weapon but only when he was really pissed off or angsty. If Lily was being dogmatic and/or defiant he would unzip his pants and tell her to suck him off. *Nothing like a woman on her knees sucking cock to put her in her place.*

Lily went up the stairs and sucked him off. He grabbed her by the back of her head and pushed her into him.

"Deeper."

How about I bite it off?

"Harder."

Halfway up or at the neck or base?

"Come on, swallow it!"

I mean, what's the point in biting the tip off or even half of it off

*when I could chow down on the whole lot. I'll swallow it alright –
they'll have to cut me open to get it out.*

When he was just about to come, he pulled her by the hair off
him and then he threw her on the bed and pounded into her as
though he was drilling a hole into the earth's crust. When he was
finished he rolled over and turned on the TV. She got up and
showered and before she left the room he told her that sometimes
she was such a disappointment in bed it literally left a bad taste in
his mouth. *You don't leave such a great taste yourself, Dicknose.*

Lily didn't care; she had freedom from him for three whole days.
The conferences on Friday and Saturday were intense, the evenings
involved scheduled group fun and Sunday was a golf day. Declan
couldn't make calls during the conferences and previous years
dictated that if he tried to make calls to his wife in the evening or
while on the golf course he would be forced to do so in front of a
crowd and there was always one who would later make jokes about
it. Lily may have been treated like an unpaid prostitute by her own
husband but he was leaving for three days and so when she left him
sulking in their bedroom she skipped down the corridor with a song
in her heart. *Free Nelson Mandela, Mandela will be free, Oh
Nelson Mandela!*

In the restaurant with Clooney, she placed her phone on the table
in front of her. *Just in case.* She looked around the room for
somewhere quiet where she could take a call after no more than five
rings if she needed to. She saw an area that was quiet and cornered
off. *That will do in a pinch.*

"Are you scoping the place out?" Clooney asked, amused.

"Something like that."

They looked at the menus. Clooney wanted pizza. "It just smells
so good."

Lily favoured a pasta dish, something spicy with lots of chicken.
Her body craved protein.

"When is the last time you had a meal?" Clooney asked as he
watched her inhale her dish.

"A few days, maybe a week," she said as a matter of fact.

"You've lost weight," he said, "You're skin and bone." He picked up her hand and put his finger and thumb around her wrist. There was room for two other wrists in the circle his fingers created.

"Is that why you asked me to dinner? To feed me up?"

"No," he said, "my intentions were purely selfish." He gently rested her hand back on the table. "Are you OK?"

She could see he wasn't asking to be polite or because he couldn't think of anything else to say. She could see that he was concerned for her and had a genuine interest in how she was. Those steely eyes of his were looking straight through her lovely happy Lily façade and right into her soul. She was either going to avert her eyes and break contact long enough to form a lie or she was going to hold his stare and admit that she wasn't OK.

"I'm great," she said, looking over his shoulder and towards the window.

"Liar," he said before he changed the subject and they began talking politics.

She noticed that when she spoke he actually listened, and even when they didn't agree, which they often didn't, he didn't dismiss her or worse again patronise her. They debated American foreign policy. She argued for pulling out of Iraq and Afghanistan and much as it pained him he argued against just upping and leaving.

"If you saw the damage done."

When he argued it was with passion, but without inflated ego or pride, and if he didn't agree a point he wasn't vitriolic. It made a nice change. He was gentle and happy just to be hanging out, exchanging ideas.

Lily made him laugh, genuine belly laughs.

He liked her turn of phase.

"I made a buggery balls of it to be honest."

He liked her sunny disposition.

"There's always something to be grateful for. Like shoes and the Stereophonics."

He was especially enamoured with her penchant for innuendo or a good dirty joke.

"Did you hear the one about the horny pilot?"

"No."

"As the plane began to descend towards the airport, the captain announced: 'Ladies and gentlemen, this is your captain speaking, we are now arriving at Dublin airport. On behalf of the staff and crew, I'd like to thank all of you for flying with Aer Lingus. We hope you had a pleasant flight.' The captain forgets to turn off the intercom. He turns to his co-pilot and says 'Christ, Bernard, I really shouldn't have eaten that curry before we took off. When we land I'm going to go to the hotel, take the biggest shit of my life and get a blowjob from Jenny the new airhostess.' The pilots then laugh. Jenny, who is seeing to the passengers, darts towards the cockpit, trips over an old lady's walking stick and lands on her back. The old lady looks down at her and says, 'No need to rush, dear . . . he said he's going to have a shit first.'"

Clooney laughed and Lily bit her lip the way she always did when she was pleased with herself. While talking and laughing Lily managed to finish her meal. It was the first meal that she hadn't just chased around with her fork in days. She marvelled at her empty plate.

"Want some dessert?" he asked and she was about to agree to it when her phone rang. He saw the fear register in her eyes and the look of panic that crossed her face when she saw her husband's name on caller ID and she realised the area that had been quiet and closed off when they entered the room was now open and bustling with people. One ring and Lily registered the caller. Two rings and Lily realised the restaurant was too busy to pick up in. Three rings and she was standing and looking around herself like a wild woman. Four rings and she was running to the front door. Five rings and she picked up in the car park.

"Hello?" Just as she said hello a large truck passed her by on the main road. *Oh God, why did I choose a restaurant on a main road, what kind of fool am I?*

"Where the hell are you?"

I could say I'm in the garden and a truck passed the wall, no, no. He'll ring the house to check up on me if he hasn't already.

"Can you hear me?"

Oh fudge, cake, bugger-balls, think, think, think . . . OK, OK, OK, go old school, Lily.

"Hello?" Lily said loudly.

"Yes, hello, can you hear me?" he said.

"Declan?" she said as though she was straining to hear.

"I can hear you perfectly. Where are you?" He was clearly annoyed. Someone in the background was talking to him. "Just give me a second, will you?" he said to whoever dared to address him while he was on detective duty.

"Declan? Declan?" Lily said. "Oh, for God's sake!" She sighed and hung up. Then she turned off her phone and exhaled loudly. Her hands were shaking. *Don't be ridiculous, Lily, just calm down. You are not doing anything illegal. You are just having dinner with an old friend. Relax.*

She went back into the restaurant and sat down. She was still flushed and despite her little pep talk she was still trembling slightly.

"Does Declan normally have that effect or is it just that you're with me?" he asked.

Lily shook her head from side to side. "We were having such a nice time, Clooney."

He knew she wanted him to let it go so he nodded and pretended to let it pass. *What the hell is going on?*

After surveying the menu they agreed that two coffees would be a healthier option than dessert. Lily felt a little sick having eaten more food than she had in days and possibly because of the phone call she had handled so badly. *He's going to lose his mind.* Clooney knew that she was itching to go and the easygoing energy had changed as soon as Lily saw Declan's name light up on her phone. He had noticed that when she came to visit Eve she was constantly looking at her watch and she practically jumped every time a staff member walked into the room and made a reference to her being there, most especially when they mentioned her husband's name in the same breath. Like the time when Marion came in to take Eve's pulse.

"Hey, Lily, you here again? Declan must be taking advantage of this."

"We're both way too busy to be fraternising here . . . besides, I'm going. I have to go."

"You've just got here."

"Busy busy. I'll see you soon."

Or the time when Abby came in to give Eve her heparin shot and noticed Lily sitting there.

"Lily, fantastic, I was going to mention the Heart Foundation Ball to Declan but I know you deal with the diary in the house – can we put you down for two tickets?"

"Absolutely."

"OK, great, I'll mention it to him when I see him later."

"Oh, no, no, don't, it's fine. I'll just check our diary and get back to you."

"Oh. OK."

"OK, I've got to go."

And she was gone.

Clooney wasn't the only one who had noticed it. Eve did too.

"Just leave it, Clooney, it's none of our business," she'd warned.

He agreed but there was something about the way Lily was reacting that bugged him. *Is that fear?* he had asked himself many times.

That question had been answered in the restaurant.

Clooney had ordered a taxi to pick him up during their coffee and as soon as it came they paid the bill. Clooney tried to pay but she insisted on going Dutch. They paid and walked outside together. He leaned in to kiss her cheek and she backed away slightly, alarmed.

"I'm sorry, I was just saying goodbye," he said, embarrassed that she had thought he was leaning in to kiss her mouth.

"I know. I'm sorry. I think I'm just tired," she said. She hugged him and, as much as she wanted to stay in his arms, she pulled away quickly. "I can't go into the hospital tomorrow or Saturday so I'll see Eve when I'm back on days on Monday."

"OK," he said. "I'll tell her."

Lily watched him get in the taxi and the taxi drive away before she got into her car. She took her phone out of her pocket and put it on the seat beside her. It remained off. She exhaled and gripped the steering wheel and she cried.

Chapter 8

One day one month one year one life

Wednesday 25th July 1990
09:00 am

Dear Eve,

When you walked in on Declan and his dad arguing did you hear shouting or what? Was Declan acting weird? What did he say? I can't seem to get him on the phone the past few days. His father told me he was out but I know he was there because he always waits on my calls. Tell him I'll keep trying but please ask him to write to me if there's something wrong. OK? Thanks for being good to him. I knew if you gave him a chance (it only took 2 years) you'd like him. He is very deep and emotional. Please let him know I love him and miss him. I hope he's OK and I can't wait to see him when I get home.

    I can't believe I've been here nearly one month already. Only another month to go and I'll be coming home and we'll all be preparing to go off to college. I know your course starts in early September but at least we'll have a few days together before you go. If it's sunny we should go up onto the cliff together and bring a blanket and a picnic and we'll walk to the gap in the fence and head down the grassy slope that takes us to our special place. We can lie on our blanket looking out toward Wales and daydream about your life in London and mine in Cork. We can reminisce about all the good and bad days we had as kids.

Me getting my nose broken in basketball – Bad

Me getting to know Declan as a result of that broken nose – Good

You stuck in bed for two months with glandular fever – Bad

Getting your first sewing machine and discovering your love of design – Good

So much has happened to us in the past 18 years and most of it has been shared experiences. It's amazing really when you think about it. I remember it all, don't you? All that time we spent on those two swings in your back garden daring each other to touch the sun. The time you picked up Sarah Potter's dog Franko's dog-doo and wrapped it in a Cadbury's wrapper and left it on Terry the Tourist's gatepost and he picked it up and when he realised what it was he wiped his hand on his jacket and screamed like a girl. I wee'd myself laughing. When we snuck out of our bedrooms in the middle of the night and met Gar and Declan in the golf club and we stayed out most of the night. The first time we ever drank together and you kept repeating the word 'Follow' and bursting out laughing as though it was hilarious. These are the memories that will keep us close when we are far away from each other, these are the memories that keep you close to me now.

Well, I might as well admit it you were right about Colm. He tried to kiss me on Monday night so give yourself a big round of applause. I'm really pissed off. I told him time and time again that I only liked him as a friend and after our conversation last week I really thought he got me but he hadn't. There was a bonfire in the woods at midnight so we left from work together and walked through the woods and as we were walking he started acting weird. One minute we're happily talking about a funny incident in the restaurant and the next minute he's telling me that I'm making a mistake with Declan and I'm too young to be thinking about settling down. I couldn't believe it, firstly I've never said anything about settling down (that I can remember and it's incredibly uncool to bring up something disclosed by a drunk person who has admitted time and time again to memory loss) and secondly who is a 16 year old to tell an 18 year old what's what? And please don't side with him. I know your views about life and love but you spend another two years with Ben and then talk to me about moving on. Anyway I told him it was none of his business and he said it was because he was really into me and then he kissed me. I couldn't believe it, one minute we are talking and the next his tongue is down my throat. I pushed him off and I was hopping mad. He apologised because he could see I was steaming but I really wasn't in the mood to hear it. He told me he'd never try it again and that he just thought that if we kissed that I'd see that we could be good together. I kept telling him over and over since I arrived that I only saw him as a friend and that I had a boyfriend so how stupid does he have to be? And I know you saw it coming and you'll say well that's boys for you but come on. I was nice to him, I liked him, he was my friend, does that mean I led him on? Because seriously, as we were getting close to the bonfire that's what he said, can you believe it? He walked off in a huff and I just didn't have the heart to go to the party so I came back here. My head was bursting with our argument, I kept thinking about it over and over and what I should have said and where it had all gone wrong. He hasn't really spoken to me since. Work is weird. He's being polite but he won't make eye contact and there's no laughing and messing around any more. Ellen noticed but she's staying out of it besides she's really wrapped up in Orfeo. They spend most of their time together in his hotel accommodation when we're off and when we're working the restaurant has got so busy that she's run off her feet as head waitress. So in one week our little gang seems to have fallen to pieces. It's sad and I'm sad. I wish I was home with you and Declan but it's only another month. I can do another month.

On the bright side Clooney arrived and he came to the restaurant yesterday. He's in great form and looking great. He must be lying out by the tent all day because he's the colour of Danny's old mahogany desk. His friends seem nice, Marty and Vince, but Vince's girlfriend Pauline seems a bit snobby. I met them for drinks after work last night and I was having a laugh with the boys and she was giving me daggers all night. She looks at me like I'm dog-doo on her shoe and she definitely doesn't share my sense of humour. It's really timely that Clooney is here, seeing as Colm isn't talking to me and Ellen is so busy shagging that she doesn't have time for anyone else. The minute her relationship gets serious she drops her friends.

I have a day off tomorrow so Clooney has asked me to go boating with them. I said I wouldn't go because of Pauline but Clooney said not to mind her, she wasn't going because she hated the water, then he announced to the lads that I was going with them and suddenly she wasn't afraid of the water at all and she's now going which is painful because it's bad enough being in her company in a large bar never mind a small boat. Clooney thinks it's hilarious and made that cat meowing sound which I hate and it drives me mad. I only met her yesterday and in one day she decided she hated me. What a bitch.

I phoned my mother on Sunday. She's seeing someone!!!! Can you believe it? I can't really. I think she might be hallucinating. She says he's from the UK and he's over in Ireland for six months working on a thesis on (you've guessed it) religious devotion but here's the kicker, he's not a Catholic, it's a broad paper on all religions and their followers. He sounds like a smart guy and she says that what started off as a fight on the church grounds turned into lunch, then dinner and she's seeing him again. She sounded really giddy on the phone and it was really nice to hear her in such good form. His name is Albert. I hope he sticks around for a while, it would be nice to see her happy.

OK that's it. I'm off to see the wizard.

I love you and miss you and wish everyone was as easy to read as you and everyone just said it like it is like you do.

Lily,
XXXXOOOOXXXX

P.S. I showed Colm a picture of you (before the fight) and he said you were a bang which is country-speak for beautiful.

P.P.S. I've learned how to make quiche so I'll make it for our picnic on the cliff. Remember that time we got stoned up there with Paul and Gar and you ran around singing The Hills Are Alive With the Sound of Music? Still laugh at that.

One last thing. Rate these horror films in order of preference: Friday The 13th , Fright Night, The Lost Boys, Nightmare On Elm Street.

Mine are as follows:

1. The Lost Boys (Because Corey Haim is so cute singing in the bath and I love the granddad. "One thing about living in Santa Carla I never could stomach, all the damn vampires.")

2. Friday The 13th (Because it was my first horror, I was staying over, your dad made sausage rolls and let us stay up watching it until after midnight)

3. Fright Night (I love vampires)

4. Nightmare on Elm Street (Because it was amazing but it gave me nightmares for a whole month afterwards)

XXXOOOXXX

* * *

Every morning started at five. Eve's dreams were often interrupted by the sound of buffing. The steady hum of the machine gliding over and back across the floor on the corridor outside her door would invade whatever reality she had created in her head. The first time it was during a particularly weird and vivid dream. The Ginger Monster's appearances weren't as spectacular as they had once been. Once in a while he was reduced to just a drunk. When he appeared that morning it was only to dance on her grave. It was a jig of some sort and he was wearing Michael Flatley type attire which made her smile even as he hornpiped his way around her headstone and back in time for his big finish. What Eve found more disconcerting than the dancing drunk was the writing on her headstone which read:

HERE LIES EVE HAYES
SPINSTER, BUSINESSWOMAN AND TOTAL BITCH.
THE WORLD IS A BETTER PLACE WITHOUT HER.

Spinster? Really? Ah, come on. It would appear that even in REM sleep Eve identified herself as a businesswoman and bitch and she concurred the world would be better off without her and a few billion others due to overpopulation, but the word *spinster* really stuck in her craw. *I don't want to die single.* She was contemplating the words on her headstone when the Ginger Monster seemed to reboot. He faced forward, his arms tight by his side and his legs began to hop wildly. *Alright, alright, I've seen the show.* It was then that she heard the steady hum in the background and turned to time to see a swarm of bees approaching. They moved through the blue sky and as they did they seemed to swallow it whole so that light became darkness. She pictured really outlandishly large heads on tiny bee bodies with large open mouths that held nothing but two sharp teeth, darkness and death. *Huh,* she thought, *well, I'm already dead so . . .* She looked around to the Ginger Monster who was too busy attempting a two-hand reel by himself to notice the sky had disappeared down the gullets of the killer bees and they were heading straight for him. The hum grew louder and louder until eventually he looked up and screamed so loudly that Eve had to cover her ears. She was waiting for him to disappear but instead she woke to look at the face of the woman who had been buffing the floor.

"You were screaming, darling," she said.

"Sorry."

"Would you like me to get a nurse?"

"No, thanks."

The woman nodded and left her to return to sleep. The woman buffing the floors had become some sort of alarm clock. The sound would infiltrate her dreams. Sometimes her brain allowed her to recognise it and it signalled a time to wake and recalibrate. *Oh, I'm not in the chocolate factory licking cherry wallpaper, I'm in a hospital bed and that noise isn't the revving of the Wonka's wondrous boat it's that damned buffer. Oh no, it's five o'clock!* One eye would open then two, revealing the small boxed room, the white wall that she stared at most days and the tattered poster which she knew by heart.

The Message Is The Same In Any Language!
Operite Ruke
Lavarsi le Mani
Lavese las Manos
Xin Hay Rura Tay
WASH YOUR HANDS

To her left was a large window with a window-sill wide enough to sit on comfortably. It looked out onto the staff car park. The habit had formed in the first few days: Eve would open one eye followed by her second eye, she'd glance at the poster and read it despite herself, then she'd look toward the window to see if any doctors or nurses were coming or going. If there was nothing to see she'd close her eyes and it was only at that point that she'd consider whether or not her body felt better or worse than the day before. Some days her body didn't wake up for a minute or two after her brain. The first time she woke and couldn't feel a thing from the neck down, she panicked, but she quickly got used to the numbness and was grateful for it in lieu of the torturous pain endured those first few days. Other days her body seemed to be waiting for the buffer lady to wake her because, as soon as she opened one eye, the skin on her right casted leg began to crawl and by the time her second eye was open the itch was so bad that she tore at the plaster hoping by some miracle that her fingers would break through just so she could scratch the healing wounds that lay beneath its solid surface. Sometimes her shoulder would ache so badly that she considered what life would be like without her left arm. Can you amputate a shoulder? The dull pain in her left leg was bothersome but once it was wrapped in blankets and nobody leaned heavily on the bed or made any attempt to put anything near it she felt comfortable enough. One of her recurring dreams was of men lining up to place concrete slab after concrete slab on her shin-bone. The men would have to climb a ladder to place the top ones and when the weight seemed completely unbearable the Ginger Monster would be placed on top and there he'd snooze in the foetal position with his thumb in his mouth, reminding her of an Anne Geddes baby picture. She was incredibly grateful for the buffer lady on those mornings. When Eve woke at five she tried to return to sleep quickly. Her movements were limited and so she shuffled slightly after reading the poster and looking out the window and when she knew that she'd been awake long enough so as not to slip back into the dream she'd escaped from, she'd close her eyes, inhale and exhale, and she'd go back to sleep until six thirty when a nurse would wake her up to take her temperature, blood pressure and to ask her a series of questions about how she felt and if she needed any medication. On the rare occasions that the buffer lady intruded on a good dream, when she was on the cliff sitting on green grass and gossiping while Lily styled her hair or when she was watching Ben rocking the stage in a small venue in Dublin. *I'm Ben Fucking Logan and we are Gulliver Stood On My Son!* The crowd went mental and in the background she could hear the hum. *Not now, not now, not know.* Sometimes it would work – she'd close her ears to the sound of the buffer lady and the dream would continue and take her from Ben's stage to the park to that wall. *OK, I'd like to wake up now.*

On the weeks that Lily was working she'd wake up to her and a thermometer.

"Good morning, sunshine," Lily'd say, pressing it against her forehead.

"Morning, Lil."

"How you feeling?"

"Bored, frustrated, sore, decrepit and insanely itchy."

"Did Clooney bring you that cast-scratcher?"

"He found it on-line. They say because of its nylon plastic combination you can bend it as much as you want and it won't break."

"And he broke it?"

"Didn't even get to scratch once."

They'd talk while Lily worked and then all too soon she'd have to move on to another patient.

"You're all good. I'll see you for your bed bath later."

Then she'd be gone and Eve would be truly awake. She'd read that stupid poster and look out the window and turn on the TV and watch some morning show where people were unreasonably happy about cheap badly made clothes and she'd ponder the long day that stretched ahead. She wouldn't be able to relax until physio was over. The dread would kick in as soon as she'd been served breakfast because once that was over it would be less than an hour until Mica or that other physio Norman would come through the door and forty minutes of torment would begin. Mica was no nonsense but at least she had a sense of humour.

"Come on, four more and you can punch me in the arm," she'd say.

"Five more and I can punch you in the face."

"Sorry, the face is too pretty."

"I'll be the judge of that!"

Norman was serious and although he was kinder he wasn't any fun. Also when he moved her he'd insist on doing so after counting down in Irish – *a h-aon, a dó, a trí* – before each lift.

"Are you ready? *A h-aon, a dó, a trí!*"

Oh, just do it already.

"OK, here we go. *A h-aon, a dó, a trí!*"

"That's very annoying," she said one day. "Do you know that?"

"I do now," he said but it didn't deter him later when he moved her back into bed. "Are you right? *A h-aon, a dó, a trí!*"

"Annoying bastard," she mumbled.

He chose to ignore her.

Physiotherapy was over by eleven thirty every morning. After that came lunch at twelve and once lunch was over Eve would watch the TV, wall or window until Clooney came in around two. He'd stay till about four and then, if Gina couldn't get in or if Lily was too busy to call in or not working, she'd revert to watching the TV, window or wall. She read the fashion magazines but even they became boring and there weren't enough in print to keep her occupied more than one day a week.

Adam would check on Eve's progress most days.

"Can you move your arm for me?"

"No."

"Excuse me?"

"If you wanted to see my arm move then you should have been here when *A h-aon, a dó, a trí* was here because that's torture time and you're two hours too late."

"*A h-aon, a dó, a trí?*" he said, laughing.

"You know who I mean," she said.

"I do. Come on, no resistance, just show me a little movement, please," he said sweetly.

"God Almighty," she said but she moved her arm and he was pleased.

"I don't think we're going to have to go back in. It was touch and go but because I'm a genius, *A h-aon, a dó, a trí* is persistent and you're a fighter, things are looking good."

She had come to enjoy his little visits. Sometimes Lily was there too and the three of them played off one another like they were old friends.

"Is she still demanding to be taken to the toilet?" he asked Lily one day.

"She won't drop it but it's just too early."

"I'm right here," Eve said.

"How are her stools?" he asked with a grin.

"Jesus Christ. Right, that's it, both of you out!" Eve said and Lily and Adam laughed, pleased with themselves and their childish toilet humour.

Not so funny when you're sitting on a bedpan and supporting your entire body weight with one arm, bastards!

"How long more do I have in here?" Eve asked them one fine day.

"At least another month," Adam said.

"No," Eve said.

Adam looked at Lily and they grinned at one another.

"Yes," Adam said.

"Look, here's the deal, I'm giving you three more weeks to get me mobile. After that I'm leaving."

"That's not a deal, that's an ultimatum," Lily said.

"Really, Lily?"

"A deal suggests that we get something back," Adam said, nodding in agreement with Lily.

"OK, you make me better in three weeks and I'll buy you a new car, Lil, and I'll help you pick out a more suitable one, Adam."

"What's wrong with my car?" Adam said.

"Nothing wrong with it, it's just not you."

"Oh, and you know me?"

"I know that you're tall and awkward and no matter how far you shove the seat back you look like Sideshow Bob driving around in his little clown car."

"Oh, it's so good to have her back!" Lily said and laughed.

Adam thought about what she'd said. "Caroline talked me into buying that car," he said. *I really hate that car.*

"The ex you wouldn't marry?" Eve said.

Adam looked over at Lily who shrugged.

"She asked," she said.

"Yes, the ex I wouldn't marry."

"Are you holding on to it because you think she'll come back?"

"No."

"So get rid of it and buy something you fit into," she said. "And more importantly get me out of here."

"Let's get you sitting on a toilet first and we'll see how we go from there," he said.

As the days passed and her face wounds were healing, she became more conscious of the way she looked and smelled. Clooney had been instructed to bring in her creams and perfumes but she still couldn't wear any clothes approaching normal. Clooney added to her collection of shawls, all of which he bought in a light silk under instruction because Eve thought that if the Ginger Monster hadn't killed her, the heat in the hospital would. Her hair was a mess and needed cutting. She had Clooney contact her hairdresser and he came into the hospital and washed and cut her hair. It was an ordeal but Nick was a total pro. Lily helped lift her into a wheelchair which she wheeled in the bathroom and Eve leaned as far as she could over the bath while guarding her damaged arm and praying it wouldn't knock against anything. Nick used the showerhead and gently washed her hair and because she really couldn't get too far over the bath he ended up washing most of her and himself as well. With her hair washed and both of them drowned rats, she sat in the chair in her room while he cut and styled her hair. It was a sharp cut, she had lost weight and her face appeared even sharper again.

"You could have been a model," he said.

"You mean before I was aged or ravaged?" she said with a smile to let him know his answer didn't matter.

"So you've a scar on your face. Harrison Ford has a scar and *hello?*"

The stitches were gone and her lip was back to its normal shape and that scar was on the inside so it couldn't be seen. The area around her eye was back to normal aside from some light yellow bruising and all that remained was a pink angry line that measured three centimetres across her left cheek.

"Do you think I should wear make-up?" she asked, pissed off that she faced the possibility of having to put on make-up every day for the rest of her life. *Just when I've retired. What a pain . . .*

"Not yet, you're still healing," he said.

"I know but."

"But what?" he said.

"Nothing," she said.

"Are you interested in someone in here?"

"Oh, don't be ridiculous, Nick!"

"Oh my God. You are!"

"I am not."

"You're going red."

"That's anger, frustration and the damned heat in this place."

Nick had known Eve, years before, when they were both training in London. He had done the hair and make-up for a lot of her shoots. They were both equally ambitious, both Irish, and both workers. They had got on from the start and he was one of the few people that she missed when she left for Paris. When she had returned to Dublin the previous year she'd looked him up. In the years between he had become very successful in the UK before returning home to set up a high-end salon in Dublin. When he wasn't on photo shoots, fashion shows or working on ad campaigns, he was in the salon. He was an old and good friend but his time was limited as Eve's had once been. They didn't socialise but Nick knew her well enough to know she was hiding something now.

"OK, whatever you say," he said.

"I just don't want to look like damaged goods."

"You are not damaged goods."

"I'm the definition of damaged goods," she said.

It was during Eve's second week that the window became a little more fascinating. She started to identify the faces and cars, timings and rituals of the hospital staff. There was nurse she called Patty because she could never ever seem to get out of her car, lock it and walk inside. She'd get out, pat her handbag, lock the door, walk about two metres then pat her bag again and turn around and either re-open the car and get something or go back and check the door of the car to ensure it was locked. Patty was a great source of distraction on the days she was working. Eve could almost do a commentary on the woman's movements and it was better than watching a fly walk in circles on the wall.

She'd watch Adam come and go. He always parked his silly car in the same spot. Doctors had designated parking – she had to pay closer attention to the nurses because they parked where they could and there were a few spots out of sight. Adam would get out of the car and lock it. He'd never check himself or fix his hair or double-check to see if the car was locked. He was just in and out except on the days that he'd meet someone coming the other way which was most days. He seemed to know more people in the hospital than anyone else – either that or he was just friendlier or on more boards. He'd stop and talk and Eve would wonder who they were and what they were talking about. Sometimes the conversations were short, sometimes a little longer. Eve saw him with Lily a couple of times. Lily was always harassed and on the run. She seemed to leap from her car and there were a couple of days that it appeared that she hadn't taken the time to lock the door. Lily was a runner. She'd run from the car to the hospital and back, the only time she stopped was when she met Adam the saunterer. He'd stop her and they'd talk for a minute or two before harassed Lily would run in or outside.

There was a doctor that always sat in his car for five minutes before getting out or driving away. He was close to the window so Eve could see that he wasn't on the phone. He just sat there. *Praying? Meditating? Sleeping?* He always took off his suit jacket and put on his white coat before leaving the car. He carried his suit jacket over his arm as he walked in and she never saw him speak to anyone.

Eve was casually glancing outside on the first day of the third week when she saw Declan Donovan for the first time in twenty years. She noticed him parking his car – the top was down and she recognised him at once but initially she didn't trust her eyes. The car was a Mercedes of some sort – she wasn't sure what class as she had never been too interested in cars. Adam drove a sports thing in red. She didn't know why but it didn't suit his personality. Lily drove a Volkswagen Polo that was five years old and had a dent in its rear bumper – as a result of Scott driving into a post on his first and last lesson with his mother, Lily told her. The Merc was new and eye-catching. Even from a distance she could see the cream interior before Declan put up the top and got out. *Is that you?* He put his suit jacket on before he closed the door of the car. He brushed it down and looked at himself to ensure he wasn't wrinkled. *That is you, isn't it?* He strode confidently toward her. The closer he came to the doorway three floors under her, the surer she became. *Oh God, yes, it is you!* Her heart-rate increased, her pulse shot up. Anxiety made her stomach flip and not in a good way. *I feel sick. I feel sick. Oh, Eve, seriously? Puking is a tad overdramatic, don't you think?* Apparently not because Eve puked on herself and it was Lily who took care of her.

"What brought this on? Has Clooney been feeding you on the sly? You know you can only have hospital-sanctioned food."

"No," Eve said absentmindedly but then, when she focused on Lily's question, she reconsidered. "Well, yes, of course he has. I can't be expected to live on the slop I get in here – but I'm not sick, I'm fine."

"You pulse is elevated. Are you in pain?"

"No. I'm fine."

"Headache?"

"I always have a headache."

"That's not right. I'm going to call Adam."

"Don't, don't, please don't call Adam."

"I'm calling Adam."

"Crap."

Lily had confided in Eve that Adam was the only real friend she had in many a long year and she was worried he had developed feelings for her. She didn't want to lose him but she wasn't interested in him sexually and wouldn't have been even if she wasn't married. Eve knew the minute she saw him that he wasn't to Lily's taste – she knew this because, even in her fragile state, he was most definitely to her own. He was tall and lean, not particularly broad but muscular. He had the body of a long-distance runner. He had a head of floppy brown hair that seemed to do its own thing. She wondered if he even had to brush it. Some days his eyes looked brown and other days they appeared to be green. She wondered if it had something to do with the light, the weather or his mood. He had a wide smile and good teeth. He dressed with flair, his suits were always a little different and stood out from the pinstripe, grey, black and navy brigade. He liked linen and wore it well, his shirts were always coloured or patterned, never white and never boring. He had fashion sense, which could be seen by those who didn't as him being odd or chichi or, as in Declan's case, dandy, but Eve approved. *Damn, I look like hell.*

Adam came about an hour later. Eve's pulse had regulated and she was no longer nauseous. He looked at her chart and sat. Since she moved into her room he had begun sitting whenever he visited her and as the time passed the visits increased and so did the time he spent sitting by her bedside. Initially he gave Eve extra attention because she was Lily's mystery friend. He was loyal to Lily and he liked that Eve was the secret he helped her keep from Declan. Adam couldn't stand Declan and not just because he was rude and his sense of humour was up his arse but because he didn't like the way he treated Lily. *If I had a woman like that I'd treat her like a goddess.* After those first five or six days, when Eve had been so out of it that she was simply a set of healing bones as opposed to a person, he began to like her. She was a smart mouth. She didn't suffer fools gladly. She wouldn't be talked down to. *No wonder she and Declan don't get on.*

"I don't like these headaches," he said.

"So turn down the heat in this place," she said.

"It's not that hot."

"I could grow marijuana in here."

He laughed. "Tell me about the headaches."

"Well," she said, "they are basically pains in my head."

Adam laughed. "I can see why you and Lily are such good friends."

"Does it affect one or both sides of your head?"

"Both sides."

"Is the pain pulsating or a pressure or tightening pain?"

"Pressure."

"Would you describe it as moderate or severe?"

"Moderate."

"On a scale of one to ten assign numbers to moderate and severe."

"Oh, for God's sake!"

"Just do it."

"Moderate is about a four or five and severe is nine or ten. My arm is usually around a nine, my right leg zero, my left leg four to a six and my head is a three to a seven depending on the moment, minute or hour."

"Do you feel nauseous?"

"Sometimes." *A lot and especially when I see that prick Declan.*

"Are you sensitive to light and sound?"

"Sometimes." *Like now.*

"Any stiff neck, confusion, double vision, weakness or numbness?"

"No."

He asked another hundred questions and she answered no to all of them.

"Any changes in personality recently?"

"I curse more."

"You curse more," he said, nodding and smiling.

"Yeah, I'm not sure if it's because I'm back in Ireland or if it's because I'm crippled but the word *fuck* sounds so much better to me now than it did when I lived in the States."

"The word *fuck* aside," Adam said, "I think you're suffering from chronic tension or daily persistent headaches. I could send you for some neurological testing to be sure. "

"No need. I got the all-clear recently and the headaches haven't changed since then."

"I'm going to prescribe you something for the headaches and then I'm going to open the window."

"No."

"Why."

"There's a weird smell."

He opened the window and put his face outside. He pulled back. "There's no smell," he said.

"It comes and goes."

He leaned out the window. "Well, there is a vent just below and to the left of you. It could be coming from that. I'll have maintenance take a look."

"OK."

"And," he said, "I've been looking at a new car."

"Good for you."

"I'm thinking a BMW."

"As long as you can fit in it, buy it," she said.

He smiled. "OK," he said and left her alone to stare out into the carpark and admit to herself that she was attracted to Adam. Adam, who was not only her doctor. *Eve, the bloody great cliché!* He was Lily's friend and he clearly had a crush on her. Not to mention the fact that Ben Logan wasn't even cold in the ground. *I don't love him or anything, Ben. I just like him. He's nice and you're dead and besides life is short. I don't want to die alone and you were never even mine. I miss you though. I hope that if you are conscious somewhere in the universe or beyond it's a good place full of love, light and happiness and not a fucking hothouse where you spend day after day hovering on bedpans and looking at morning TV, walls and a car park.*

It was just after six and she watched Declan make his way to his car. She watched for about twenty minutes before getting bored and turning to the wall.

The Message Is The Same In Any Language!
Operite Ruke
Lavarsi le Mani
Lavese las Manos
Xin Hay Rura Tay
WASH YOUR HANDS

She turned on the TV. The news was on. Clooney would return at seven thirty with a new perfume. She had worn Chanel No. 5 all of her adult life but she couldn't stand the smell of it any more. She sent him to find something new so that she could wear it when Paul came with his fiancé Simone. It would be Eve's first introduction and she wasn't that enthused. She didn't like meeting new people, her head hurt, she was pissed off that she liked Adam and Lily's week off was starting and she'd made it clear she couldn't visit as much. Eve hadn't asked but she knew it was because of Declan. He had been playing on her mind, going so far as to take the Ginger Monster's place in some of her more disquieting dreams.

Days blended with little defining one from the other. Eve's car-park watch now revolved around Declan. Once she witnessed Lily and Declan collide. It was at an odd time. Lily had forgotten something in her car and was heading toward it, Declan had just parked. It was after midday. Sometimes on a Tuesday or a Wednesday Declan didn't arrive to the hospital until after midday. Eve surmised he had rooms elsewhere. Lily never really went to the car-park in the middle of the day and it was unusual for her to forget something. When they met, Eve watched as they stood talking to one another. They seemed distant but polite – that is, until Declan seemed to grab Lily's arm aggressively. Lily pulled away easily so he couldn't have hurt her but it upset Eve. She wanted to jump out of bed and yell out the window. *Keep your hands off her!* But she couldn't jump never mind walk and it wasn't her business anyway. She did ask Lily about it and Lily brushed her off.

"Oh nothing, he was just being playful. I wasn't in the mood."

Eve knew she was lying and Lily knew that Eve knew she was lying and they left it at that.

When Clooney came later that evening it was the first thing she said to him.

"Do you think Declan is a wife-beater?" she asked.

"You mean, do I think Lily is a battered wife?"

"Same thing," she said.

"No, it's not. I don't know Declan, I know Lily, and there's no way she'd put up with getting beaten."

"Yeah. I suppose you're right," she said, "but then again I know Declan better than you do and I think he has it in him."

After Eve said that, Clooney did confide in her about Lily's reaction to her husband's phone call the night they were having dinner.

"You had dinner together?" Eve said.

"Didn't Lily tell you?"

"No, she did not."

"Probably too small a detail."

Bullshit, she thought. *Now Clooney is exactly Lily's type. If of course she wasn't a happily married woman.*

Eve became stronger. The first time she went to the toilet she was wheeled in and although a nurse had to hold her she pulled her own pants down and insisted on being left alone to do her business. It was only when she screamed, "Oh no, shit on my hand, shit on my hand!" that the nurse appeared and washed her hand thoroughly with a bacterial soup.

The Message Is The Same In Any Language!
Operite Ruke
Lavarsi le Mani
Lavese las Manos
Xin Hay Rura Tay
WASH YOUR HANDS

When the sun was at its hottest Clooney began to take her into the hospital gardens and there they'd sit for hours people-watching and enjoying the sun, the flowers, the smell of grass and each other's company. Eve was getting stronger by the day. She was becoming more fluid and she was finding inventive ways to make her one good arm work for her. Adam admitted she was recovering extremely well. He was still concerned about her headaches but her shoulder was making a remarkable recovery and after the first two weeks of resistance she had come to an understanding with her two physiotherapists. She worked tirelessly on her shoulder and her left leg. She spent more time out of bed and in her electric wheelchair. She zipped around the corridors, stopping to chat with Marion, Abby and all the other nurses she'd come to know. She steered clear of the canteen because Lily had mentioned once she was meeting Declan there and Eve was terrified of bumping into him. Clooney would bring in picnic supplies from her favourite deli and, when she wasn't feeling nauseous from the smell coming from the vent that nobody seemed to be able to do anything about, they'd eat on the grounds on fine days and in the conservatory on others. Her friends came and went, less and less as the time went on but even having slacked off she saw most of them twice a week.

Simone had been a revelation. She had never met Paddy but Gina had maintained he was very like Paul – quiet, closed off and sometimes even cold. Gina suspected that Paddy didn't like her and Gar and she was right. Paddy had nothing against them – they just had nothing in common. Eve knew this because in a rare candid moment Paul had admitted as much. "He would have liked you though," he'd said.

However, Simone was an open book. She sparked with Gina so much so that Gina was utterly charmed. Simone was beautiful to look at but she had softness to her features that Eve hadn't seen in other models of her kind. She was extremely excited to meet Paul's friends if not a little disappointed that Gar couldn't make it. Gina made up a dreadful excuse and turned red. It was clear she was lying to all. Gina was a horrendous liar. She always overcomplicated her lies, turning them into tall tales that seemed to have no beginning, middle or end. She'd start strong but end up getting lost and mumbling, hoping someone would intervene and stop her. Paul did so by complimenting her on her dress. She blushed again, aware she had made a bollocks of the excuse, and Simone noticed and felt sorry for her. She hugged her and told her she was really pleased to meet her and that Paul had spoken really highly of her which really shocked Gina but Simone was either a much better liar or genuine and Gina chose to believe the latter to be the case. Simone did seem to know an awful lot about Paul's friends. Even Clooney was shocked when she talked to him about the places he'd been and the work he did. Either she was a politician in a model's body with an photographic memory or Paul had opened up to her in the time they were together more than he ever had with any of his friends over the many years he had known them. He seemed more relaxed around her – he touched her and leaned on her, he laughed more easily and spoke more and in longer sentences. It was interesting to watch. Gina and Simone got on like a house on fire. They were like two peas in a pod and destined to be friends for life. *Funny old world*.

Gar sometimes visited Eve at lunch-time on his own. He'd sit and eat a panini or ciabatta roll and sip on a takeaway coffee while she picked at her hospital food.

"It's not that bad," he'd say.

"It's not that good either."

"Want half my panini?"

"No, but thanks."

Gar noticed the smallest improvements in Eve and he was very encouraging. He always made her feel better, reminding her that there was light at the end of the tunnel.

That's a light I'm not ready to see yet, buddy.

When she got bored she'd bring up Paul.

"Have you spoken to him yet?"

"Nothing to say."

"That's a bit childish."

"You think."

"Yip."

"I'm not even angry any more," he said one day, "I'm just disappointed."

"I understand. He's your friend, you thought you knew him."

"Exactly. Gina thinks I'm making a big deal out of it."

"I think he didn't know who he was for so long that, when he finally realised or accepted it, he felt silly. That, combined with the personality of a guy who is so private he doesn't tell himself his own secrets. It has nothing to do with how he sees you as a friend."

Gar laughed. "He was always like that even as a kid. I'd ask him how he did on a test and he'd say bad or good – he'd never give the actual mark. When we were teenagers he'd disappear and we'd never know where he was, until he'd just turn up. We all decided he had this amazing sex life and all, with girls from different towns and villages, but we all made it up in our own minds because he never said a word."

"I know," she laughed. "Lily and I used to call him the virgin-taker."

"I mean did he even have sex with any of those girls?"

"I've no idea." Eve said and laughed. "Probably not. Can you imagine if Paddy was the first person he had sex with?"

"Oh, that makes perfect sense, no wonder he fell in love."

"You see, we're doing it again."

They talked about Simone and how she seemed nice and he was happy and comfortable and different around her. Gar worried that Gina was getting too close.

"After all, they're not married yet and the way things are going he could run off with the priest next."

Gar felt better when he was laughing about his friend, not because he enjoyed being cruel, but because it was a release from feeling like a fool. He couldn't help but focus on all the time he and Paul had spent together over the years and, although he had confided in Paul completely, Paul had locked him out like an unwanted visitor. He also wondered why he hadn't noticed this before. *Was it because I thought he was having sex with men and I just didn't want to know? What does that say about me? And why does it matter so much?* Also it really bothered Gar that Paul knew he was pissed off and avoiding him but he had made absolutely no effort to approach or appease him in any way.

"You know what he's like," Eve echoed Gina's mantra.

"It's not good enough," Gar said.

"He's not going to apologise for not telling you his business until he was ready to tell you his business, so get over it and be friends or get over it and don't," she said one day while looking over his shoulder to see who was coming and going in the car park. She saw Declan pull into his spot and pointed. "There's Declan."

Gar nearly broke his neck looking around. When the car was parked and Declan was getting out, Gar got out of his seat and stood by the window staring down. Eve warned him not to get caught. They were both a little excited, like two kids doing something they shouldn't be doing. When he looked up and stared straight at the window as though he felt someone looking at him, Gar spun around to face Eve.

"He's looking, he's looking, he's looking!"

He quickly sat down and they laughed at their foolishness, sure that he hadn't really seen Gar and aware that Lily hadn't told him that Eve was in the hospital.

Gar had stopped wondering why Declan had walked away from his life and friends a long time before and even seeing him in the flesh didn't stir up any feelings of loss.

"Another one I didn't know," he said.

That's for sure, Eve thought.

Lily met Gar a few times while she was working. She'd stop in and say hello. Gar had always liked Lily – she had a calming effect on Declan who was highly strung and competitive, which made him a great rugby player but a bit of a hothead off the pitch. Lily could make Declan laugh at himself. He relaxed when she walked into any room. They were a good couple. Gar had been jealous of him back then. Declan and Paul were the stars on the pitch, Gar always lagging behind. Paul had any girl he wanted or didn't want as the case may have been and Declan had Lily.

When Gar had gone out with Eve first, he thought he had finally matched up to the two boys, but Eve wasn't interested and, because Gar had an issue in confidence back then, when Eve supposed the problem was all him he mentally agreed that it must have been. They made good friends but they had zero chemistry, despite the fact that she was beautiful and they had good fun as long as they weren't touching and kissing, because kissing Eve was like kissing a wall. He had really made an effort too but the greater his efforts the worse the results. It was only when he and Eve parted and he kissed other girls and went on a little spree he realised that it wasn't him and it wasn't her – the problem was simply them. Eve and Gar were never going to work. He was with her to compete with the lads and she was with him because he was one of the few boys who wasn't afraid to ask her out. Poor Gar had never felt quite good enough and, if he was honest with himself, that was why Declan's desertion had caused so much pain in the early days. *The first chance he had to get away from me, he does.* And why Paul's lie of omission hurt so much was for the very same reason. *I'm a fill-in for Declan and clearly a pretty poor one.* Gina had spotted Gar's poor-me tendencies early on and done her best to rid him of his insecurities but, as hard as she worked at pointing out how great and good he was, there was always something in the back of his mind that told him that he wasn't. Nothing he ever achieved was good enough. He always looked at other people, what they had achieved and what they owned, and compared himself unfavourably. To all who knew him, he seemed so at ease with himself and content with his lot, and he was for the most part. Which was one of the reasons he and Gina hadn't gone crazy in the boom years and racked up ridiculous debt. When others were buying holiday homes abroad and bigger and better homes in Ireland, he was happy with his house. He didn't need a new car and he never liked to go to one place on holiday more than once. *What's the point in that?* But it didn't stop him from placing greater worth in others than in himself because, despite the love of a good woman, two beautiful kids and a lovely home by the sea, there was a little part of Gar that always hoped that his life would be a little larger than it turned out to be. "Just be content to be content," Gina had counselled many times. He'd never allow anyone else to see that side of him – it was a side he didn't like. He knew it was petty and silly and over the years he'd become better at ignoring the voice that told him he wasn't good enough but it got louder when the people he cared about let him down.

"What are you thinking about?" Eve asked when he had slipped into silence for an awfully long time.

"You can't change people," he said.

"No, you can't."

"We are what we are," he said.

"That's right."

They had a few lunches together where they did very little talking and instead they just watched TV together. He'd bring Eve a takeaway coffee and sometimes a slice of cake even though she told him not to. Clooney enjoyed it with afternoon tea.

Clooney and Lily became closer that month too. They'd find a place in the hall or a space in an old TV room or disused smoking room to have a chat. They never discussed Declan or even the kids. They'd talk about this and that, everyday things over a coffee or a shared slice of cake that Gar had brought Eve or a muffin that Clooney would pick up in the coffee shop one street away. Chocolate-chip muffins were her favourites. Eve often slept for an hour in the afternoons and it was during that time that he and Lily would catch up. They were both very relaxed in one another's company – they had grown up together, and they didn't have any expectations of one another. They knew and cared about one another.

Clooney had forgotten how well she knew him.

"The sale of the house fell through," he said one day.

"Oh no! I thought it was it done deal."

"The guy lost his job just as they were about to draw down the loan."

"Oh, the poor man!"

"I suppose so. To be honest, I was thinking 'screw him, now I have to deal with that stupid house'."

"I love that stupid house."

"Great, do you want to buy it?"

"You and Eve are lucky, you find it easy to let go."

"So do you," he said. "After all, you let us go."

She nodded sadly. "I didn't feel like I had a choice. It's not something I'm proud of." *If I knew I was set to leave this earth soon, would I do it all differently?*

He didn't push it. He hated to see her sad and so he changed the subject.

"Maybe we'll keep it. I might move back here some day," he said.

"You're just saying that to avoid doing anything that involves money or solicitors – you wouldn't last a year here," she said and smiled.

"Now how do you know that?"

"You used to give me your pocket money because thinking about what to spend it on would stress you out," she said, smiling.

"Nah, I just wanted you to have it," he said and smiled.

"Don't worry," she said, getting up, "Eve will be back on her feet sooner than anyone thinks and she'll take over."

"I'm counting on it," he said and she squeezed his hand and left him, to go back to work. Clooney watched her walk away. *If I had you, Lily, would I ever let you go?* Deep down he knew he would but she'd make it hard.

In the month that passed after Declan returned from London things in the Donovan household began to change dramatically. Initially he had sulked because of the phone incident even though Lily had made a decent effort at lying. She told him she had gone for a walk and her phone ran out of juice. It was simple but plausible. It shouldn't have led to any further questions or drama but of course it did.

"You never walk."

"Because I never have time to walk."

"Oh, so I take up so much of your time that you can't go for a simple walk, is that what you're saying?"

"No, Declan, that's what *you're* saying. I'm saying I went for a walk."

"I don't believe you."

"I don't care," she said.

"Excuse me?" he said.

"You heard me, Declan. I don't give a shit. I'm a grown woman and if I want to leave my house and have a walk, I will, and you won't dictate to me what I can and can't do or where I can and can't go. Those days are over."

She had never said anything like that to her husband before, primarily because she'd never admitted to herself that he had taken total control of her life.

Bugger balls, bugger balls, bugger balls. What have I done? OK, just be calm, it's OK, it's fine. Everything is great, everything is lovely, and everything is fantastic. What am I doing? If I knew I was set to leave this earth soon, would I do it all differently? Jesus, Lily, stop saying that!

Declan had been with Lily since he was sixteen years old. He knew her inside and out, he had been party to every smile, laugh, cry, moan, whinge, every grimace, every lie and every truth for twenty-two years. He knew Lily better than she knew herself. He had started to spot the changes in her in the days and weeks preceding his trip to London. She always had a smart mouth but she was getting more cutting by the day. She wasn't as tolerant of his idiosyncrasies. He was a worrier, she knew that. He liked things in order. He liked routine. He liked to know where his wife was and who she was with. *Why the hell is that suddenly a crime?* Not to mention the fact that she liked routine, things in order, and she was the one who had instigated her own routines. It was Lily's planner on the fridge, not Declan's. He wasn't some sort of keeper but he deserved to know her location at any given time. He was her husband. She was his wife. She had her duties and he had his. Lily may have sometimes tired of him because sometimes he even annoyed himself but lately she had been remiss most of the time. She appeared bored when he talked and she didn't seem to notice when he was down. The last good chat they had together was when she was exhausted in the bath and he had presented her with a gold bangle. *What the hell does she want from me?* The night in Rodney's had been alarming. She would normally have made an effort to be pleasant but she had gone into that house looking for a fight. Alice had nearly died of mortification when Lily told her to send her dress back. She wasn't used to Lily's sharp tongue and Rodney confided in him later that she had been so upset by Lily's remarks that she had vowed never to have Lily in her house again. Rodney was Declan's only real friend and he had been disgusted that Lily had caused a rift. When he said it to her she was gleeful.

"Good. I'm thrilled. She can give it out but she can't take it."

He was hurt that she was so pleased to have caused difficulty between him and Rodney. Of course they could see each other on the golf course or in any number of situations but warring wives would no doubt cause problems. She couldn't see how upset it made him or if she did she didn't care. *She's jealous, Lily. Why couldn't you just suck it up?*

Then there was the incident when she threw the pan at the wall and told her family the kitchen was closed and since then she had put on one breakfast every day and not even asked him what it should be. One morning he woke to a bowl of porridge. The kids didn't even bother attempting to eat it. He at least had taken a spoon before signalling his disgust but again his wife didn't seem to care.

"Eat it or leave it," she said then she walked out of the room, leaving her kids and husband sitting there liked stunned mullets.

"Is Mum having a breakdown?" Daisy had asked.

"No," he'd said, "she's just tired."

"I'll grab something with Grandad," Scott said, getting up. "We usually take a break for a natter and a roll around ten anyway."

Every time Declan's son mentioned something trivial that clearly suggested his relationship with his grandad was a world away from the pain and torture his father had endured, it was like a knife in Declan's chest. He put on a happy face for Scott but Lily knew how much it hurt that his son was enjoying a relationship with his father that he never had, but again she didn't bring it up. She didn't care. She had divested him of her interest, care or consideration. Their sex life was worse then ever. Lily just lay there like a cold fish. He hadn't tied her up because of her shoulder injury and even if he had she'd just have made him feel skeevy not sexy. She was looking at him differently and she was pulling away. She wouldn't answer a straight question and, although she kept denying there was a problem, Declan wasn't a fool.

The first time he saw Clooney was when he was in the canteen eating lunch with Rodney. He noticed him a few times before he actually recognised him. He was sitting alone in a chair directly opposite, staring straight out the window onto the gardens. He was lost in his own world and Declan admired his physique – he was strong, broad, built for rugby. He wondered if he played the game. When he crossed the floor to refill his coffee he noticed him more, he was familiar somehow. Declan wasn't sure if it was his eyes, face or gait that resonated but, as Rodney was talking he found himself losing concentration, and by the time he put a name to the face he had no idea what Rodney was talking about. When Clooney left the canteen Declan made his excuses and left Rodney to finish his lunch alone and then, like a creeping child, a spy or stalker he followed Clooney at a distance until he reached Lily's ward. Lily was off that week and so he wasn't risking his mission being scuppered by an unwelcome encounter with his wife. Clooney disappeared into Room 8. He waited for the nurse to move away from her station before taking a look at the room list. Seeing Eve's name written in black and white wasn't as shocking as he would have thought, as seeing Clooney had softened the blow. Having said that, he felt decidedly uneasy, his tie felt tight and his hands a little clammy. The hospital was suddenly too hot and stuffy. He needed air and space to breathe. He was grateful for a cool breeze. He sat on a bench in the hospital gardens for a few minutes, thinking through the meaning of Eve's presence on his wife's ward. It certainly explained her behaviour, her disappearances and her inability to explain where she was or who she was with. The gourmet packed lunches every second week suddenly made sense. *She wasn't coming here for me, she was coming here for her.* The lies of omission and outright deceit was breathtaking. Lily hadn't seen Eve in twenty years but she was back and Lily was hiding her from him. *Is it because you don't want to hurt me? Is it because I said I never wanted to see her again or hear her name spoken? Is it because you love me and you don't want to open that old can of worms again? Or is it that you don't trust me? You want her back in your life. You remember that you love her. Some friendships are forever. Isn't that what you said to me when we were sixteen and your best friend did everything to break us up and you wouldn't chose? But eventually you did choose, Lily. You chose me. You should have told me.* He had to work out what to do and he couldn't make a decision. *Say something or say nothing?* He decided to say nothing and just let it play out but while doing so he'd tighten his grip on Lily. He wasn't going to let her slip away, not because of things that bitch Eve might be saying or doing. If he confronted her directly on the subject it could lead to an ugly discussion or fight that he didn't want or need, so he decided the best course of action was to make his wife as busy as possible on her days off and to keep as close an eye as he could on her when she was working.

Declan was unable to handle complex emotion. When sad, confused or troubled, these feelings usually snowballed into one all-consuming anger and this anger is what drove him to make his wife suck him off in such a disrespectful and brutal way the night before he left for London. Like a dog marking its territory or a spiteful, vengeful man or like his dad, Declan lashed out when he was hurt. *You did this to us, Lily.* But afterwards lying alone in their bed he felt sick, sad, worried and sorry. *I'll make it up to you. I'll bring back something nice, Lily.* He tossed and turned all night because Eve was back and Lily was pulling away. *Oh God, don't take her from me!*

When he returned home from London he rang her more and when she was back in work he made more visits to her ward. He watched her try to hide her panic. *Just tell me, Lily.* He stood smiling as she squirmed, pretending he was innocent and had no idea how his impromptu visits affected her. *This is killing you so just tell me, Lily.* On two occasions he watched her sit in some cosy corner sharing cake with Clooney. He was far enough to remain unseen but close enough to bear witness to the tenderness between them. That's when the anger and bitterness resurfaced. *You fucking slut.* When Declan was angry he became unreasonable and mean.

"You're getting fat," he said later that evening.

"No, I'm not," she said, aware that she was underweight if anything.

He looked her up and down and sighed before walking out of the room, leaving her to wonder what he was playing at.

On the weeks that she was home he'd fill every moment of every day with important jobs he needed doing and when he ran out of jobs he'd offer her assistance to neighbours like Rachel Lennon when she needed someone to look after Nancy who was still recuperating from her eye surgery. *I'll just keep her busy until that bitch and her brother are out of our lives.*

"You told her what?" Lily had screamed.

"I told her you'd take Nancy Monday to Wednesday while she helps settle her mother into a care home," he said calmly.

"You had no right."

"Don't be ridiculous, the kid needs to be minded, you're home and Rachel was desperate."

"Rachel hasn't bothered her arse speaking to me since the day I checked on Nancy in the hospital," Lily said, seething.

Declan dismissed her, delighted that his encounter with Rachel Lennon over the recycling bins had paid off. *Let's see you go for your walks now.*

When he had time off, he'd return home even if it was only for an hour. He'd check her phone for calls. He'd read her texts. He even went through the dirty clothes hamper and checked her knickers to find traces of sexual excitement. He was single-minded in his mission. He would determine if Lily was cheating with her new best friend Clooney and if she was he'd destroy her.

That day when Eve had seen Lily bump into Declan in the car park, he had seen her flirt with Clooney outside Eve's door. She had been too busy laughing to see him standing so near by.

"Where are you going?"

"My car."

"Where are you going in your car?"

"I'm getting my lunch which I forgot in the boot if that's OK with you."

"You're pushing it and since when do you bring in your own lunch?"

"Since my account is running low and I married a mean bastard."

Lily went to walk away and that's when Declan grabbed her arm.

"What do you mean you've run out of money? Who did you spent it on?" he said.

She had spent it on Eve and now she was sorry she'd mentioned it. She pulled her arm away.

"I don't ask you what you do with your millions and you've no business asking me what I do with my pittance," she said and she walked to her car.

He had stood frozen in place for a second, not sure whether he should follow her and throttle her or take deep breaths and move away. He chose the latter option. He fixed himself, checked for wrinkles in his suit and walked inside, unaware that he too was being watched.

Lily was suffering a personal crisis. While on the one hand she was enjoying every moment she spent with Eve and Clooney, on the other hand something inside her had snapped and she was no longer content to live the life she had been living. She was in flux. Unable to see a way forward but sure that there was no way back. The more crazily her husband was behaving, the easier he was making it for her to disengage. Every day that passed, every job he gave her, every cruel word he spoke, all served to chip away at the pity and understanding that had kept her by his side all those years. She looked at her kids. Scott was a young adult and at twelve Daisy was old enough to understand. *Wasn't she?* If she and Declan split up it would be hard on them but if she stayed she might actually lose her mind. *What's worse, divorced sane parents or married crazy parents?* Before what she referred to in her own head as 'the snap' she had been the rational to her husband's irrational. She had been the reasonable to his unreasonable. She was the one that had held everything together and glossed over it so that her children could live happy normal lives but she did so at her own expense. She wished that she could have carried on until Daisy turned eighteen but she couldn't. It was all too much. She couldn't stand playing her part in the charade any more. She was living on her last nerve. She suffered severe anxiety, so much so that Adam had prescribed her medication. She made him promise not to tell anyone.

"What's going on?" he'd asked.

"Nothing," she said.

"Don't tell me nothing and then ask me to prescribe."

She had refused to sit, preferring to stand, but when she knew he wasn't going to be as pliable as she'd hoped she sat and fidgeted instead.

"I'm going through some things with Declan," she said.

"I see."

"I can't sleep . . ."

"And you're not eating." He looked at her thin frail body.

"Scraps here and there. It's hard to eat when your heart feels like it might explode."

"Is there anything I can do?"

"Yes, you can prescribe and not say anything."

He wrote on his notepad and Lily took the paper and read it. He'd prescribed a week's supply of pills and then he had written the name of a counsellor.

"She's very good," he said.

"Thanks," she said and when the prescription was filled she binned the name and didn't think about the counsellor again. *It would take one hell of a counsellor to sort my problems out.*

When she was away from work it was almost harder to keep going. She missed her daily chats with Eve, even if she did push Lily to the limit.

Eve would look her up and down.

"Something's wrong," Eve said.

"Nothings wrong."

"Not stupid."

"Not wise either."

Or

"You look tired," Eve said.

"I am tired."

"Is the fact that you're unhappy keeping you awake?"

"Mind your own business."

Eve would try to coax her to relax and eat with her and prod for information.

"Share my sandwich with me," Eve said.

"No, thanks."

"So what? You'll only eat cake with Clooney?" Eve raised her eyebrow and grinned.

"It's not like that," Lily said.

"Something's going on with you."

"Eve. Please."

"OK, OK," Eve said, holding up her one good hand, "always in your own time, Lily B."

"I'm Lily D."

"Not to me."

The days when she was home and without Eve pushing her buttons and without Clooney's calmness and kindness, she veered between snapping at Daisy and trying to make it up to her.

"Mum, can you find my black coat?"

"You are big and bold enough to look for it yourself," she said while cleaning the toilet.

"Mum, will you listen to me play?" she said as Lily made her way out the door to the dry cleaner.

"Not now, Daisy."

"Mum, when you've stopped vomiting can you make my breakfast?" she said, standing over her mother who was leaning on the toilet bowl.

"*Leave me alone!*" Lily screamed before she returned to vomiting the meagre contents of her stomach in the toilet.

There were days when the child didn't even get a sentence out before she was dismissed.

"Mum."

"Go away, Daisy."

"But, Mum!"

"I mean it, whatever it is, deal with it."

The once attentive, patient, loving mother of the year was turning into someone Daisy didn't recognise or even like very much. *Where's my mum gone?* Daisy didn't cry but her confused face was heartbreaking and a remorseful Lily would attempt to make it up to her with gifts of her favourite sugary doughnuts, unwanted hugs and apologies. *I'm turning into Declan.*

Running around taking care of the various jobs kept her busy and minding Nancy was an added complication to already stressful and busy days. Nancy was a dote but she liked to talk and rarely took a breath. It was hard to cope with her constant rabbiting on while washing, drying, shopping, scrubbing and even vacuuming.

"Lily, ma wha na ma wha na na."

"*What?*" Lily shouted over the vacuum.

"Lily, ma wha na ma wha na na."

"*What?*"

"Ma, wha, na ma wha na na."

Lily turned off the vacuum. "What?"

"I've seen *Pirates of the Caribbean: Dead Man's Chest* three times."

"OK." She turned the vacuum back on.

"Mah, Lily, it's man na na na."

"*What?*"

"It's man man na na na."

She turned off the vacumm cleaner.

"What?"

"It's not scary."

"Nancy."

"Yes, Lily?"

"Can you leave Lily alone for approximately ten minutes?" she asked through gritted teeth.

"OK," Nancy said, "and then we can do my eye drops."

"Fine."

It was after she had taken care of Nancy for three days and somehow managed to do the laundry list of new jobs her husband had heaped upon her, that Nancy appeared when Lily was out in her garden one morning.

"Hi, Lily."

"Hi , Nancy, how's your eye?"

"Good."

"It looks good. I bet it's nice to have the patch off."

"It's nice. I miss it sometimes. What are you doing?"

"Gardening."

"Why don't you come to my house for coffee, cakes and a chat?" Nancy said.

"I'm really busy, but thanks, Nancy."

"But all the women are there."

"What women?"

"The neighbours. Mum has made lots of cakes."

Lily was stopped in her tracks. Rachel Lennon had used her to mind her daughter for three days and then invited the entire neighbourhood to a coffee morning and excluded her. In the past she would have been hurt but she would have put on a happy face and said nothing, but not any more. In her mind she pictured a scene straight out of *Desperate Housewives*. She'd rip off the dusty green apron she wore gardening and she'd march over to the Lennons' like a woman possessed. She'd make a grand entrance and say something smart, cutting and witty before telling Rachel to shine up her bloody buttons with brasso. She'd embarrass Rachel Lennon in front of all the neighbours before making a grand exit.

"Yes, Nancy, I'd love to come. Thank you," she said, dropping her shovel and walking toward the Lennons' house with Nancy behind her talking about the Dolans' dog who was some sort of Youtube star.

"He wears a hat and makes a bumping sound. It's very funny."

The door was on the latch. Lily walked inside and entered the kitchen leading to the garden where most of the women were sitting, including Rachel. They were chatting and laughing, then they saw her and stopped. Rachel stood up and sheepishly greeted her.

"Lily? How are you?"

They weren't drinking coffee although there was some made – they were quaffing wine before twelve noon. They looked at her as though she was some sort of alien.

She looked around the room at all the women, most of whom she had helped in one way or another over the years, all there enjoying themselves, having deliberately excluded her, and she didn't feel smart or pithy any more. The hurt was overwhelming. *I bent over backwards to be friends with you people.* She tried to speak but words wouldn't come. *What have I ever done to any of you?* Instead of a witty line came tears. Her eyes filled too quickly to stop their flow and so she stood there in the middle of the Lennons' garden crying while the neighbours silently watched her.

Amy Fitzpatrick, a bleached-blonde-haired, botox-riddled woman was pressing her glass up against her lips as though it was the only thing preventing her from commenting or maybe even laughing. She was forty-five years old, skinny and haggard, despite her doctor and beautician's attempts to make her look otherwise. She looked like she hadn't eaten since the mid-eighties and Lily had long suspected she was a bulimic who starved herself by day and binged and purged at night. She dressed in the same clothes as her twenty-year-old daughter and the years of overdoing it on the tanning bed had left her with dark spotted crepe-textured skin. She was mean as a snake and had argued or battled with every one in the room at one point or other and yet she was invited.

Naomi Smith, a woman in her mid-thirties who had once been extremely svelte and glamorous, still knew how to dress but she'd let herself go as soon as she'd become pregnant with the first of her five children. She had a face full of cake. She didn't know whether to chew or swallow so instead she just let it melt in her mouth. She was still a beautiful woman but her size, her investment in her children, and her husband's haunted look suggested her lady garden was closed for business. When she wasn't eating, cooking or baking she was talking about her kids. She would drone on and on with the most boring stories about what Patrick said or what Veronica did and Shane is such a hoot and Davey's so sweet and did I tell you about the colour of Michael's poo last week? She was the woman that everyone avoided on a day like this where they just wanted to get pissed in the early morning/afternoon and yet she was still invited.

Sofia Harris was wearing sunglasses, looking at the floor and wrapping a napkin around her fingers tightly. She was a tense nervous individual at the best of times, in her late forties and the mother of IVF twins that she found hard to manage. One of the babies was born with a heart problem and she had spent the first two years of her little girl's life in and out of hospital. The twins were five and her little one was fine but needed to be monitored and as a result she was hyper-vigilant. She often leaned on Lily when things were tough and, as the only one actually drinking coffee at the coffee morning, she had the good grace to be embarrassed. Sofia liked Lily and had often gone to bat for her with the other ladies but they all agreed Lily wasn't a girl's girl and she probably wouldn't bother coming even if she was invited.

There were others that stood, some smirking, some grimacing, some just staring in a kind of mild shock, some faces Lily didn't know. She looked at Rachel whose facial expression had changed from registering surprise to discomfort.

"I think you should go," Rachel said and she was right.

Lily had no business there; she was an intruder and a crying one at that. *Eve was right. You are jealous bitches*. She found her feet and started to walk away but before she did she managed two words.

"No more."

She left the women speechless. There wasn't a word said or a sound made as she made her way through the Lennons' house and toward their front door. It was as though she'd left the women frozen in that very uncomfortable painful moment. She met Nancy coming out of the toilet.

"Bye, Nancy."

"Bye, Lily."

Lily ruffled her hair. "Be nice to your brother."

"OK," she said and in her head Lily said goodbye to the little girl.

Not sleeping was the worst part of 'the snap', watching every moment and minute go by, watching darkness turn to light, hearing the alarm go off and putting her two feet on the floor with that dreadful burning sensation in her eyes, a heavy head and a palpitating heart. Some days the only thing she ate was half a slice of cake or muffin with Clooney but she could live on little and when she was back to work and when she took time to sit with him she felt better. He had a calming, relaxing effect on her – he was like the human equivalent of lavender. He noticed her weight loss and the circles around her eyes as did Eve. She challenged her numerous times but Lily tried to sidestep her questions.

"Are you trying to make me look fat?" Eve had said jokingly, the first time she noticed Lily's rail-thin physique.

"Haha."

"What's going on?"

"Same ol' same ol'," Lily said in that sing-songy voice she used when she was trying to avoid confrontation.

"You don't eat when you're stressed," Eve said. "You lost over a stone before the Intercert exams and Mrs Connolly thought you were anorexic. Turns out you were just a big fat worry-wart swat."

"You've caught me out. Mrs Connolly was right."

"It's him, isn't it?"

"No," Lily said firmly.

"You're a liar," Eve said and Lily walked out the door.

Clooney attempted to approach her in a gentler fashion. They were sitting together in the conservatory. Lily was so tired and so suffocated by her husband's tightening of the reins that she had become a little careless or maybe just more carefree about being seen sharing coffee and cake with him. He broke the slice in two and handed her a piece. She smiled, looked at it and sighed. She ate it slowly and tried not to gag. She was so tired and constantly on the verge of tears. Her happy façade was crumbling. Clooney watched her hand shake and, instead of questioning her, he simply leaned over and pulled her gently into his arms. He kissed the top of her head and he told her to go to sleep. She laid her head on his lap and there she slept for twenty minutes and for the first time in weeks.

Chapter 9

The rocky path to freedom

Sunday July 29th 1990

Lil,

Hate to say I told you so but Colm was always going to try it on with you, no matter what you said or did he was after you from the start. I could smell it from the page. Just read that back and it looks weird but you know what I mean. As for Ellen and her Spanish cookie, I hate girls like that. The minute they get serious with a boy they disappear. How sad is she? Gina's older sister Helen is like that – she not only ditches her friends, she ditches her family. Gina told me on the QT so don't say anything but Helen's last boyfriend beat her up really badly and locked her in the house and when her dad went over to sort him out she took the boyfriend's side. WHAT A MENTAL CASE. Anyway he ended up leaving her and now she's at home but Gina says she's like a ghost. She doesn't really do or say much, she just lies around the house. I said she should be checked for a brain injury because I read something about it in a magazine. She said she was checked again and again. Don't say anything but she spent some time in the nuthouse when she tried to kill herself after he left. The poor girl she must be a sado-masochist.

Well, at least you have Clooney and his friends and Colm will get over it so don't worry about it. Tell my brother I said hi and the house is quiet without him. It's amazing to have the bathroom pretty much to myself. Dad is gone so early in the morning and it means I can relax in the shower and I can't wait to live on my own. Having said that I'm going to be in college accommodation sharing with a bunch of God knows who's for a couple of years which will probably be worse than sharing a bathroom with Dad and Clooney - at least they are both really clean. London is getting closer and I'm really nervous. I've been sewing up a storm. Gina asked me to make her a dress for her sister's (not the nutter, can't remember her name, the one who is ancient) kid's Confirmation. She bought some beautiful material. I made her a cream mid-length dress and she loves it and it really does suit her. I'm really happy with it but other than that I'm in pretty bad humour really. Ben's stupid grandmother had a stupid stroke and she lives in stupid Cavan. He's been there since Monday evening. She's 92 and apparently she's on the way out so the family have to stay there until she pops her clogs. She's been breathing her last for 7 days now and I wish she'd just hurry up and die already. I know it sounds harsh but she managed 92 years on this planet and I'm with her grandson one month and she decided to die and worse than that die slowly in CAVAN. Even if she was doing it down the road at least I could still see him. I really miss him. I mean I miss him so much my bones hurt and I feel like crying all the time. I know. SAP. I keep thinking about the way he looks, smells and feels. I have a T-shirt of his that he left here last week. He was wearing it under a jumper and he forgot to put it on after we had the most amazing sex (more on that when I see you) anyway I put it away in a drawer and every now and then I take it out and sniff it. Next thing I'll be put into a nuthouse like Helen. Anyway every day that goes by and she doesn't die is another day I don't get to see Ben and the worst of it is even if she does die today right at this minute I still won't see him until at least Wednesday because of the stupid funeral. He phoned me last night and I asked him if he could say goodbye and come home and then go down when she dies which I think is a very reasonable request but he said absolutely no way was he leaving his mother. We had a bit of a fight then because I'm not sensitive enough. I told him he knows who I am and I am what I am. I'm not going to pretend that the death of a 92 year old woman he doesn't even really know is sad news especially as she's been demented for years which means even if she did once know him she wouldn't remember him and probably doesn't even know or care that he's there. ARRRGGHHHH!!!! It's so frustrating. He said his mother is really upset and when I asked why he hung up the phone. He did call me back later but he was really pissed off with me even though I apologised. He said I could be very cold. I said I prefer the word practical. He said I can call it what I want but it worried him. I said there was no need to worry – I'm not going to turn into a psycho and kill his family – although I could see myself putting a pillow over his granny's face. Does that make me evil or expedient? Anyway it was our first fight and afterwards when he rang back for the third time he said he was sorry and he knew I was odd when he fell for me and he loved me and I told him I loved him too on the stupid phone. God I miss him so much it actually makes me want to vomit and it makes me feel really bad for being so mean to you all this time about Declan. Finally I know what you mean and every stupid love song I ever hated has meaning and makes me ache. I actually started to cry in the café the other morning when The Smiths' There is a Light that Never Goes Out' came on the radio. Remember how I used to think that was fatalistic bullshit? Well, suddenly the image of being hit by a bus or a truck with Ben by my side seemed plausibly heavenly and when I say I cried, I bawled, big fat tears. Terry the Tourist's mother was in having tea and scones with some English pal of hers, a very proper lady called Vera, and they both came over and comforted me thinking someone had died which is ironic because if Ben's' old bat' granny would actually die then I'd get Ben back and I wouldn't have to be crying at stupid songs on the stupid radio.

Declan is fine. I don't really remember how he was that day after the fight with his dad, maybe a bit quiet but then we had that conversation and he seemed fine. Why are you freaking out about it? I fight with Danny all the time and God knows you fight with your mother. It's what teenagers and parents do, Lily!

I haven't really got a lot of news. Paul is never around and Gar is seeing another new girl again from Bray and Declan told me it's the other girl's friend and that's why they broke up. He decided he preferred her friend and her friend went off with him happily. Can you believe it? Gar's a big stud in Bray. It's weird, he seems way more confident and happier. We're getting on really well when he's around. He called into the coffee shop the other day and he was in great form. He says his new girlfriend is amazing in bed and I said EXCUSE ME as if he was trying to intimate that I wasn't but he apologised and said he didn't mean it like that and he was just happy that things were working out for us both which I thought was really nice. I'll miss Gar when I'm in London. He's a good friend. He said he's going to help me move some of my designs from my bedroom to the garage. I can't even get into my wardrobe there's so much stuff there and Clooney's not here and Danny mumbles about a sore back every time I mention it. I told him I'd make dinner. I hope he likes beans on toast. I've been spending a lot of time with Declan in the past few days. I have my lunch hour at 3 in the coffee shop and he has his at 3 too so we sit on the side of the street and eat sandwiches together. He said he hasn't heard from you and he's really worried. I told him you were probably really busy but when I mentioned that Clooney was down there he got a bit shirty. I told him to relax, you'd swear he had headed down there to ravage you the way Declan was acting. I explained just in case he was thinking anything weird that Clooney might as well be your older brother and I told him that you loved him and would never do anything to hurt him and I even mentioned that I had tried to get you to leave him a number of times and you wouldn't. First he got really annoyed and then he laughed saying I was weird. I prefer the word honest. WHATEVER. Anyway he seemed to calm down. Jesus, Lily, you really need to call him because he's up to 90 about it. Other than that he's fine, he's not as uptight about his results as he was. He said he's just going to hope for the best and if he doesn't get in he's going to freak out then which is a much better plan than freaking out now. It's weird that Declan and I are working two shops away from one another and spending time together. I really didn't know him before, Lily, and I still think he's arrogant, has a pole up his arse and he's way too intense but for the first time I see what you see in him. He's kind. I mentioned I thought a certain bolt looked brilliant and I could use it in my designs and since then he's been collecting odd-looking scrap metals for me and he has a really good eye. He gave me so many bits and pieces that I ended up made a necklace with some of them and some wire and a woman stopped me on the street and asked me where I bought it. He's going to keep giving me bits he thinks might work in clothes or jewellery. I swear there is a bolt that I know would make a cool ring I just have to think about what to do with it. And he's funny, he's very dry, it's like he talks and you either think 'what a dick' or you realise he's joking and laugh. The other day he said I'd be a great seamstress! I nearly punched him in the face until I realised he wasn't trying to put me down, he just didn't really know what a designer is. I explained and he was nice about it although I'm not sure he gets it. If it's not medicine or law he seems a little lost. His dad passed us on the street the other day when we were sitting there and he was drunk as a skunk - he dragged me up off the pavement and started dancing around with me. He was just messing but Declan got really annoyed. He pushed his dad off me and his dad pushed him back and then pointed at him and laughed. There was some big match on so his dad went off with a friend to do a little more celebrating and gave Declan the rest of the day off but when he left Declan kept working. He's hilarious. What a swat!

Anyway I've no more real news. It's been a really quiet week,, boring to be honest. I really miss you. Gina says hi. She's hasn't really been around, she's working late nights and spending most of her time in bed which is a pain. Tell Clooney that Danny and me miss his spag bol and don't worry about Colm, it'll blow over soon - look at me and Gar, two months ago we weren't even talking.

Love
A very bored Eve

Oh and my top 4 are as follows:

1. Friday The 13th (For the same reason as you. Remember halfway through it Clooney jumped up behind you and said boo and you lifted out of the seat and started crying. Priceless.)

2. *Nightmare On Elm Street (Because I'm not a baby)*

3. *Fright Night (If it had been my choice it wouldn't be in my top 4, I'd pick Psycho or When A Stranger Calls. Vampires are retarded.)*

4. *The Lost Boys (I love it but it's a comedy not a horror)*

* * *

The more complex Declan's emotions, the more irritable and irrational he became. His wife was cheating on him with her old best friend and her brother. They were the two people who had nearly destroyed their relationship in 1990 and she was hiding her relationship with them from him. He should have said something. He should have told her he knew about Eve and sat her down and asked why she would keep Eve's presence a secret or maybe acknowledge why she had handled the situation as she had. He should have been kind and understanding and spoken to her about how and what she felt on seeing her old friends again. He should have sympathised and emphasised. After all, twenty years had passed and twenty years is a long time. He had built a life with her and they had two children together and that counted for something. He should have gone to see Eve and made it right with her. He should have shook Clooney's hand and let bygones be bygones. *We all make mistakes.* Of course his stubbornness, vanity and paranoia prevented him from doing any of the above. There was a time in Declan's life when he trusted Lily with every thought in his head, every hidden secret, every fear and shame when he was a deeply traumatised lonely boy desperate to escape a life of misery. When his father tortured him and his mother ignored him he gained strength from Lily's love and he believed in her and trusted her completely. She had broken that trust only once and that was enough to ensure he never fully trusted her again. He had sworn he'd forgiven her and had begged her forgiveness but he was a liar. Not only did he not forgive her sins, he blamed her for any sins he'd committed as a result of her breaking his trust because if she hadn't . . . he wouldn't have . . . *It could have all been so different. Fucking Eve and Clooney Hayes! If I thought I could get away with it I'd have them both killed.*

If Declan had been another kind of man he would have taken his wife in his arms and told her that he loved her and asked if she was happy and if she wasn't what could he do to make a difference. It might have worked. Lily might have opened up and told him she needed space to breathe, she was sick of feeling like a slave to him and the kids. She wanted their sex life to be more about love than service. She wanted him to consider her feelings and to stop treating her and the rest of the world like his enemy. But then you can't change just because a person asks you too. Maybe that's why Declan didn't confront his wife. Maybe he knew that she would use his confrontation as an excuse to try to change him and the way they lived and he liked life as it was. He didn't want anything to change. He didn't know how to change. It wasn't possible and anyway who was Lily to tell him he needed to change? She had spent eighteen years calling him paranoid and maybe sometimes she had been right but this time he wasn't paranoid, he was right. Declan didn't say anything to his wife because even though a tiny part of him was whispering '*You'll lose her*', the bigger part of him, the egotistical, arrogant, paranoid and angry part was screaming to him '*She's making a fool of you so sort the bitch out and end this!*'. Every day that passed, every look between them, every word unspoken, every lie he elicited from her lips cemented his fury and fuelled his thirst for justice. Declan Donovan was bubbling and it was only a matter of time before he'd reach boiling point and all hell would break lose and Lily would suffer his wrath but then it would be over. Never once, as paranoid as Declan Donovan was, did he think his wife would walk away. *I won't let her.*

When the cast on Eve's right leg came off, it was a cause for a mini-celebration. Lily brought a little cake with a candle which she made Eve blow out before she wrapped it up so that she and Clooney could eat it later. Eve's shoulder was improving every day and it meant that she could start to walk with the use of crutches. Her shoulder ached but she was determined and her first attempt at walking, while aborted after six steps and a dizzy spell, was considered a resounding success. The first day she didn't have to be lifted in and out of bed brought about tears of joy, not least because she wouldn't have to listen to Norman say the words, *a h-aon, a dó, a trí. It's the little things.* Her first real bath felt as though she was submerged in what the religious would call Heaven. Her first shower, although she was forced to sit down and was accompanied by a nurse called Monica who spent her time talking about her lactose-intolerant niece, was truly blissful. The water tumbled down on her and she closed her eyes and it felt like she was in a tropical storm. *Remember, Ben, when I told you about my time in Kenya with Clooney. This is what it felt like.* She often talked to Ben even though she knew he wasn't listening. It didn't matter, she just liked to say his name. Sometimes she'd give out to him like when her bowel refused to cooperate and she was stuck on the loo for an hour looking at the poster on the door that had a picture of a brown sack with the word biohazard written on it and two injections. It read: **Reminder: Dispose of Hazards properly.** *I'm trying Ben. I am trying. I feel like I'm pushing out a baby here. By the way, I'm sorry you never got to be a dad. I think you would have been a good one.* Sometimes she'd tell him about Adam. *He's nice, Ben, he's kind and he laughs when I talk. Sometimes when I'm attempting humour, sometimes when I'm deadly serious. I entertain him. I like it.* When she had been worked hard by her physiotherapist and she was sweating, hurting and exhausted, she'd fall into her clean white hard bed and close her eyes and talk to him about what could have been. *I should have offered to bail you out. I should have invested in you instead of screwing you so I guess I screwed you twice. You could have saved your business and your and Fiona's life would return to normal. Where are you now, Ben? Are you somewhere or nowhere? Was being unplugged your full stop? Did you know it was happening? Did you hear them cry? Did you call out in your head for more time or were you happy to let go? Are you gone? It should have been me, it should have been me, it should have been me. I'm sorry, Ben. I'm sorry for being weak and stupid and selfish and I know you are too.*

When she'd open her eyes after an hour or two of sleep she'd focus on the poster.

The Message Is The Same In Any Language!

Operite Ruke

Lavarsi le Mani

Lavese las Manos

Xin Hay Rura Tay

WASH YOUR HANDS

Then she'd turn to the window. *Ah, there you are, Patty.* She'd check the time and she'd turn on the TV. *It's two o'clock and that's* Ellen *time. Ben, did you ever watch Ellen? She rocks.* For someone who never watched TV, Eve had a new-found respect for the medium. She watched shows she'd never seen before like American cop shows, *Bones – funny,* and *Criminal Minds – freaky.* She liked hospital shows like *Grey's Anatomy* and *House,* mostly because she could identify with the people in the beds, but her absolute favourite were the chat shows. They were a revelation and even though she didn't know some of the guests, the hosts themselves were the stars of the show. People like Ellen, Graham Norton, Piers Morgan and Conan O'Brien became Eve's new old friends.

Adam called in most days to sit and chat and, even though she threatened not to speak to him when he refused to let her out after her original deadline, she had forgiven him and in their own way they had become close.

"What are you doing later?" she asked one day after *Ellen* and before *Coronation Street.*

"I'm going on a date," he said.

"Blind or with someone you actually know and like?"

"Blind."

"What do you know about her?"

"She's forty-five, divorced, two kids and owns her own bakery."

"OK so she's older, has children who will no doubt hate you, and she sells fatty food. Sounds like a dream come true. What does she look like?"

"I told you it's a blind date."

"So you haven't even seen a picture?"

"No."

"Then don't bother going," she said.

"Why not?" he asked before laughing.

"Attraction is based on looks and if you don't like the way she looks, no matter how nice she is, an hour spent making small talk won't make a difference."

"That's sounds shallow," he said.

"I prefer the term *accurate* and, besides, I know you like them pretty."

"What's that supposed to mean?"

"Lily," she said and she smiled at him. "You have a thing for Lily. Don't worry, most men do."

Adam blushed and stuttered, "I – I – I –" before giving up.

"Here's the thing, even if Lily wasn't unhappily married and we both know she is, you are not her type."

Adam inhaled, shocked that Eve could be so blunt.

"How do you know that?" he said, attempting to sound merely interested as opposed to concerned.

"Because you're my type and we always had opposite tastes in men and still do."

He shook his head and smiled. "I'm your type?"

"Most definitely. You see, Lily likes her men square and broad, she likes the V-neck-jumper-and-deckshoe-wearing guy with a stripy shirt for good measure. She likes the average bear and you are not the average bear and I like that about you"

"I'm touched."

"No, you're not – you're sad because you know I'm right about Lily. She's never looked at you that way, there's no sexual tension between you, and even though you could look at her all day she doesn't see you as anything more than her friend."

"You're right," he admitted.

"Do you like the way I look?" Eve asked. "Don't be afraid to tell the truth. If I'm not your type I can take it."

"I'm your doctor," he said, suddenly feeling a mixture of sadness and discomfort.

"You won't be forever, so answer me."

"I think you're beautiful," he said.

"So when I get out of here, take me on a date."

"I can't, Eve," he said and she smiled.

"You could if you wanted to. Life's too short, Adam, and we could have some fun," she shrugged, "so you can't blame a girl for asking."

"I'm your doctor," he repeated and he moved to leave.

"Adam," Eve said, "whatever happens or doesn't happen with us, be Lily's friend. She doesn't have many and she counts on you. Don't hang in there hoping that it will turn into something else because it won't. She's never going to love you like that because if it were possible she'd love you now. Don't hold it against her."

He nodded and thanked her and he didn't come to see her again for three days.

Hey, Ben, did I tell you, I really messed up with Adam.

Lily spent the month of August avoiding her husband as much as possible. He was making life extremely difficult, turning up at any and all places at the most inopportune moments. It had got so bad that the only time she felt safe from him was when he was in surgery and so she did a little spying of her own, keeping tabs on when it was safe to share her coffee or lunch break with Clooney. Lily knew what she was doing. She knew she was falling in love with Clooney. She knew that, even though they weren't having sex, she was cheating on her husband and with every look, glance, touch and tender moment shared she moved further away from him. She tried to pretend to herself that it was simply friendship and that Clooney was like family but she knew and he knew that there was something between them. They were playing a dangerous game and it was exciting and fun and Lily hadn't felt so alive in a very long time. But she was a wife and a mother of two and Clooney was the kind of man who came into a woman's life, made her feel special for a while and then left. He had never promised to be anything else. He wasn't a liar – like his sister he shot from the hip. He never made promises he couldn't keep. They talked about what he would do and where he would go after Eve made a full recovery and he never once said he'd stay and Lily never once even intimated that she'd like him to. Every day they could, they would sit together and drink each other in, both living on those tiny touches and brushes that seem to mean so much when you're falling hopelessly in love. They lived in the moment the way Eve and Ben had once done because in the moment there was no husband or kids or guilt or faraway countries calling – there was only Lily and Clooney, electrically charged and fizzing around one another.

Eve would have had to be blind or emotionally stupid not to see what was happening but she said nothing. She would not interfere. She had done that once before and it had cost her dearly.

August was passing by quickly and Eve was getting stronger every day. Lily worried about a future that didn't include her caring for Eve and spending time with Clooney. She couldn't imagine life returning to the way it was. *I was so unhappy for so long*. When Lily wasn't lost in Clooney, when she returned to the real world, the guilt she felt was so immense it threatened to choke her. She was down to a ridiculously low weight; she suffered from stress headaches and a kidney infection that wouldn't go away. Although she was sleeping thanks to the tablets, she was suffering from dizzy spells and she knew that she couldn't go on and it was just a matter of time. She spent days and nights thinking about the effect a break-up would have on the kids. Her whole adult life had been about her kids, she had dedicated herself to them, she had lost her youth to taking care of them and despite being taken for granted and allowing herself to be treated as a second-class citizen in her own house, she had few regrets because being a mother was her greatest pleasure and achievement. But she was suffocating, she had been dying slowly for many years and she was so miserable it hadn't seemed to matter but suddenly she saw light and hope and the possibility of a better future. She knew that Clooney was not the answer – she knew he'd never stay – but the way he made her feel had ignited in her the spirit to fight for a better life. *I deserve better*.

One afternoon in the gardens she joined Eve and Clooney. Eve was in her wheelchair but determined to use her crutches so she and Clooney walked with Eve wobbling and cursing between them.

Declan was involved in a long surgery so Lily didn't feel the need to be careful. She was just enjoying an August day with some old friends. It was innocent and she was happy. She had an hour for lunch. They spent half of it walking Eve around and when she was exhausted but determined to make her own way up to her room in her wheelchair with her crutches lying across her lap they conceded she was able to use an electronically powered wheelchair and they stayed behind on the grass under a hot sun. Lily hadn't been feeling well all day. She was used to getting on with things no matter how poorly she felt but her back was killing her, the antibiotics she was taking for her kidney infection weren't working and she was battling waves of nausea even though there was little or nothing for her stomach to expel. Clooney placed his jacket on his lap and she lay there while he gently brushed her hair with his hand and they talked about the past and reminisced about Danny. She had loved him so much she filled up and he wiped away her tears.

"He loved you too," he said.

When the hour was over she stood up quickly and a little too quickly because she fainted. Clooney caught her mid-swoon and she woke up in his arms.

"You need to see a doctor," he said.

"Handy that I'm here then," she said, smiling.

"You need to take care of yourself," he said.

"I will," she lied.

He hugged her tightly and she held on as long as she could.

"You can't go on like this," he whispered in her ear. "We can't go on like this."

When he was sure she was OK and she was steady on her feet and she promised to take care of herself, she smiled and told him that she'd see him later and she left him sitting on the grass to think about what they were playing at.

He didn't see the guy with the camera photographing their every move. He hadn't noticed him on any day over the previous month – he was used to seeing the same faces every day, they tended to blur into the background. He stayed sitting in the garden for another few minutes before returning to Eve. When he passed the guy on a bench taking a picture of the fountain, he mentioned the guy had a nice camera. The guy smiled at him and nodded and Clooney walked on, unaware he was being watched and evidence was being gathered and Lily was in danger.

When Adam returned to Eve's room after a three-day sabbatical, he did so rather sheepishly.

"Well?" she said.

"Well what?"

"How did your date go?" she asked and he relaxed and sat and sighed and told her.

"You were right," he said.

"She was ugly."

"No," he said, "just not my type."

"When can I get out of here?"

"Well, you're doing really well and all going well maybe next week."

"And then you'll ask me out."

He shook his head but he was smiling and she knew he was considering her proposal. They remained silent for a minute or so, both quite content to be still in one another's company.

Eve looked at Adam. He was so busy thinking she could almost see the mouse run on the wheel.

"What are you thinking?" she asked.

"I'm thinking that Lily is falling for your brother."

"Oh, you spotted that."

"Hard to miss."

"It is when you are interested," she said.

"I can't just switch it off."

"I know."

"Do you think she'll leave Declan?" he said.

"I don't know."

"Does he love her?"

"Clooney?" she asked.

He nodded.

"I think he's always loved her," she answered, "but Clooney's a rolling stone. He might be what Lily wants but he'll never be what she needs."

"Why do you like me, Eve?"

"You're kind, gentle, you have a great laugh, a good sense of humour, you're accomplished but you aren't defined by what you do. You're sexy, athletic, warm and I think you'd be really good in the sack. Speaking of which, when do you think I'll be match fit?"

He laughed. "You're a very interesting woman," he said.

"OK, well, that's a start."

"I had a dream about you the other night," he said.

"Good or bad?"

"Good, very good," he said and she grinned.

"Now you're talking!"

It was a Friday night. Clooney met Gar and Paul for a drink in the local pub. Gar had forgiven Paul after a month of snubbing him and following the realisation that people don't change and after Paul called up to his house and asked him to be his best man. Paul didn't acknowledge his friend's anger, disappointment and frustration; he brushed it under the carpet along with everything else uncomfortable in his life. He simply told him that he wanted him to be his best man and promised that he had no more secrets.

"What you see is what you get," he said.

"Finally."

Paul smirked. "It was a long time coming."

"All you had to do was be honest about who you are."

"It's easy when you know but it took a long time to work it out."

"You were always a bit slow," Gar said and Paul nodded his agreement.

"So will you be my best man?"

Gar nodded and sniffed. "Yeah," he said, "of course I will."

Paul pulled him into a hug and they slapped each other on the backs and their world was restored to rights. No more conversation necessary.

It was seven weeks to the wedding and Paul had spent the day picking out menus and registering for gifts. He was in the humour for a quick drink and he wasn't in the mood to talk. He switched into listening mode, allowing Clooney and Gar to entertain him with their argument on whether or not Brian O'Driscoll was the greatest rugby player in the world or whether he was just a good rugby player from Ireland. That argument lasted a good half an hour. Every now and again they would look to him to add his comment but he remained silent and pensive. They talked about soccer and the matches that would be played the following day. They made a bet as to who would win in a game between Manchester United and Liverpool. They talked about weapons of mass destruction, the fall of communism, ethnic cleansing, Kim Kardashian and wave energy. Paul remained quiet throughout.

Eventually Clooney remarked on Paul's silence.

"You haven't said two words."

"Tired of talking, been talking all day, can't talk any more," he said.

"He does this," Gar said.

"If you're so tired, why did you come out?" Clooney asked.

"Because if I stay home Simone will want to keep talking," he said.

Gar burst out laughing. "Welcome to living with a woman!"

"You can't help who you fall in love with," Paul said, shaking his head, "but if I could it would be a man."

Paul was going through a transitionary period in his life and he was happy but also fearful. Everything was changing so fast and he hoped he was fit for the challenge. *What kind of husband will I be? What kind of father? Will this woman be enough for me? More importantly, will I be enough for her?* Introducing her to his family was scary. Predictably, his mother reacted with joy and praised God for putting her son back on the path toward heaven. It sickened him. She fawned over Simone as though she had been sent directly from God in an answer to his mother's prayers. Simone told the story of how they met over dinner. His father ate quietly as she spoke, Paul's brother and his wife sat gobsmacked and not quite sure what to think, and his mother interrupted every second sentence to thank God.

"It was a coffee shop in town," she said.

"The power of prayer," Paul's mother said.

"We just started talking and I don't know – something clicked."

"And that's the power of prayer!" she said again, slapping the table.

"I knew straight away," Simone said and she smiled at him.

But Paul wasn't in the mood for smiling. He was in the mood for fighting. He wanted to hurt his mother the way she hurt him every time she insisted he needed to be saved. *How fucking dare you? You're the reason I hated myself till I was twenty-six. You're the reason I thought about killing myself every day I lived in your house. You're the reason I've spent so many years hiding I don't know how to stop. The power of prayer! If prayer had any power you would have been hit by a bus.*

Simone could see him smarting and she could feel his pain. She turned to his mother and smiled sweetly.

"You know, we're going to aim to be faithful but at the end of the day he's always going to yearn for a bit of cock but sure that's only natural," she said.

Paul's mother's mouth fell open. She dropped her fork and looked around her as though she was hearing things. Paul's brother Alan burst out laughing and his wife joined in. They were like two kids hunched over, trying not to laugh but it just made them worse. Paul sat grinning like a Cheshire cat.

"I love you," he said to Simone.

"I love you too," she said and kissed him, "exactly as you are," and she looked at his mother who was rendered dumb.

Paul's father said nothing. He had reacted badly to Paul's coming out but over the years he had educated himself and he didn't have the same religious concerns as his wife. He had grown used to having a gay son, now he was a bisexual and getting married and having a baby. It was all a bit much. He had read a few pamphlets but they raised more questions than gave answers. *Christ, I'd need to do a degree in this bloody thing.* He didn't know how to feel or what to say so he stayed quiet. Paul was like his dad in that respect, when in doubt he'd say nothing and hope it would all work out.

"Do you think Eve will be able to dance at my wedding?" Paul asked Clooney over his fourth pint and a little happier to chat.

"Maybe."

"Why, do you want to make sure there's someone worse than you on the dance floor?" Gar asked.

"Something like that," Paul said but it was more than that.

Paul may not have been one to talk about his feelings but it didn't mean that he didn't feel things intensely. He had been rocked by Eve's accident. Having just got her back, to nearly lose her in such a sudden and dramatic way hit him hard. Eve was the one he could quietly be himself around. She accepted him as he presented himself, heterosexual, gay, bisexual, quiet, secretive, she never seemed to care. Eve allowed people to be who they were and she either liked them or didn't. She was the polar opposite of him and he found her open nature, strength and confidence a comfort. Her searing honesty and her devil-may-care attitude inspired him. He was a sentimental old sod behind his calm cold demeanour. Eve's near-miss reminded Paul that for the first time in a long time, in Simone and the baby, he had love and security and he was terrified it would all go away. *What if I don't deserve this? What if they are taken from me? What if I fail them?* He had sleepless nights after Eve's accident, seeing her dying on the ground, seeing Simone beside her and the baby in her arms covered in blood. He had woken up screaming. Simone was beside him to soothe him and talk him down.

He told Eve about his nightmares one afternoon when they were alone together. It was the first time he'd really opened up to her about anything really personal and, if she realised it was a major step forward in their relationship, she didn't make a fuss about it.

"Perfectly normal to be anxious," she said.

"I'm scared I'll let them down," he said.

"Why?"

"Because . . ."

"Because what?"

"You know why."

"Can I be honest?" she said.

"You're always honest."

"I know but I'm asking permission because what I have to say is harsh."

"OK," he said tentatively.

269

"You don't think you're good enough because you were raised by an ignorant phobic woman who told you every day of your life that because you liked men there was something wrong with you. You need to realise that you are a better and stronger person than her and you need to stop torturing yourself."

"OK," he said, smiling. "That wasn't so harsh."

"I'm not finished. You're like me – we're selfish, restless people. We do what we want to do when we want to do it, we bore easily and we put ourselves first. Let's face it, we're both adult baby assholes and in your case it's time to put others before yourself and that's scary."

He laughed. "I can do that. Simone makes that easy," he said.

"Good," she said and she smiled, "then you'll be fine."

"What about you? Are you going to grow out of being an adult baby asshole?"

"No," she said.

"Fair enough."

Gar and Paul were watching snooker on the TV over the bar and Clooney was lost in his own world, thinking about Lily. He was worried for her. She was fading away in front of his eyes. She spent her life running around after people and taking care of everyone but herself. He wanted to wrap her up in cottonwool. He wanted to feed her and bathe her and care for her. He couldn't stop thinking about her and every time he did he battled the urge to run to her house and save her from the man she should never have married. Clooney didn't know Declan and he certainly didn't know what he was capable of but he knew Eve hated him, he knew that he was the reason the girls didn't speak for twenty years and he knew that Lily was at a crossroads. She would either choose Declan or she'd choose herself. Clooney was there the last time she faced that decision and she chose Declan. *Who's it going to be, Lily?*

It was while Clooney sat in a pub with Gar and Paul lost in his own thoughts while they drank, watched a snooker match and commented or grunted at one another every few minutes, that Lily's crisis came to a head.

Scott's car had broken down and his grandfather was keeping it in the garage until they had time to look at it. Lily said she'd pick him up and it was after seven when she got there. Scott and his granddad were happy, both under separate cars with the radio on. Lily felt strange walking inside the garage. She hadn't been there since she was a young girl. The place was exactly the same but the vibe had changed utterly. Scott rolled out from under his car as did his granddad. They were two peas in a pod, happily covered in grease, sharing a rag to wipe their hands, both smiling and talking with one another easily. It was another world from the bleak place she remembered. She said no to a coffee and she was anxious to leave.

Scott's grandfather smiled at her.

"It's nice to see you back in here," he said.

"Thank you, Mr Donovan," she said.

"How many times? It's Jack."

Lily would never be comfortable using her husband's father's first name because for so long he was Mr Donovan, the ogre she dared not speak to.

"He'd make a serious mechanic," he said of Scott and Scott grinned. "But I suppose his dad wouldn't like that."

"I'm sure he'll be happy with whatever Scott chooses," she said.

"Doubtful," Scott said and he and his granddad grinned at one another. "Dad's too much of a snob."

"Your father is what your grandfather made him!" Lily snapped. She was suddenly uncomfortable with her son and grandfather making fun of Declan. *How dare you? You destroyed him. It's your fault he's broken. It's your fault I've been trying to fix him since I was sixteen years of age. It's your fault he never had a real chance.* Suddenly Lily was crying.

Scott and Jack looked at one another and neither knew what to say. She dried her eyes quickly and ordered her son into the car. He said goodbye to his granddad and he waved them off.

Lily was quiet in the car.

"Is everything alright with you and Dad, Mum?"

"Why do you ask?"

"Because you're both acting like freaks."

"No," she said. "It's not."

"Well, whatever's going on I think he's going to try to make it up to you tonight," he said.

"What makes you think that?"

"He's given me fifty euro to go to the movies and Daisy's staying with Tess."

"Oh," Lily said, half-happy they would finally have the space to talk and half panic-stricken by what needed to be said. "I'll drop you at Josh's then?"

"Yeah."

"Mum?"

"Yeah."

"How's your friend?"

"She's good," she said, smiling. "She's good and cranky which means she's getting back to herself."

"I'm glad," he said.

She pulled up outside Josh's house and he got out.

"Good luck with Dad," he said and he ran into the house.

He'd seen his parents fight and sulk a lot over the years and there was no reason for him to think that this time around the result would be any different. *There's been weeks of sulking, tonight there will be a big row, then Mum will give in and by the following weekend she'll have some nice new jewellery.* Scott didn't expect his life to change forever that night but more often than not the biggest changes come unexpectedly.

Declan had met with his PI as soon as his surgery was over. The guy had been waiting for him in his office. The pictures of Lily and Clooney were on his desk. He opened the folder and saw his wife with her head on another man's lap. He gritted his teeth and flicked through the other pictures. They were smiling at one another, hugging, touching, sharing food, looking at one another the way lovers do. He sat at his desk, looking at large colour pictures of Lily and Clooney falling in love.

"Have they slept together?" he asked in a calm detached manner which suggested to the man he hired he didn't care either way.

"Not on my watch," the guy said. "Your wife is a very busy woman. The only time I see her sit and take a breath is with him."

"I didn't ask you if she sat."

He flicked back to the picture of Lily with her head on Clooney's lap. He had his hands in her hair.

He wrote a cheque and told the guy to go. He left and Declan sat in his office, swallowing hard, battling the urge to get up and tear the place apart. He practised breathing in and out and focusing on being calm but he couldn't contain himself. His blood rushed to his head, his ears burned, and his heart rate was through the roof, he felt like he was on fire. Awash with adrenaline, he physically needed to fight. He stood up and turned the table over, smashing his computer screen. He took the chair and he flung it against the wall, smashing the glass frame that held his doctorate. He kicked the brains of the computer around the room and when there was nothing left to break he kicked a hole in his door. When the place was wrecked he picked up his folder of photos and exited, only turning to calmly tell his stunned and terrified secretary to have someone clean up the mess.

Lily got home a little after eight. The house was in darkness, Declan's car was in the drive but when she called his name he didn't respond. She took off her coat and hung it up. She walked up the stairs and turned on the landing light. She walked into the bedroom, took a shower and when she was dry and in a comfortable pair of trousers and a soft wool top she went downstairs. She thought he might still be sulking somewhere, maybe the sitting room or his office but they were in darkness too. The kitchen was empty. She wondered if he was canvassing the neighbourhood to see if any ungrateful neighbours needed her services or maybe he had gone for a run. He had been running a lot in the recent past. She didn't care, she wanted everything to be over but she had no idea how to begin the conversation that would lead to the end of the marriage. *I just can't do it any more.* She was scared too, that he'd throw her against a wall or worse he'd throw himself off a cliff. He had manipulated her with that threat on many different occasions in subtle and not so subtle ways. *I would die without you. I swear to God, Lily, if you walk out that door I'll cut my damn wrists.* She was going to ask him to leave and he would lose it, he'd scream and shout and cry and roar and then maybe he'd beg and threaten but she intended to hold firm. *Please just go. Let me breathe. Let me be. I'm so tired.* He'd ask her what had changed and the answer would be nothing and that was the problem. But of course that was a lie. Everything had changed. She'd reconnected with her old friend, she'd realised how short life was and she was falling in love with another man. She felt silly and bad and wrong and selfish and doing anything for herself felt so alien she wasn't sure if she could go through with it. *What if he does cry and beg and wail and plead? Could I really let him go, knowing what he's been through? What do I say when he brings up the kids? What if they hate me for breaking up their family? What if he says no? Do I leave? Where do the kids go? Do they come with me? Do we even have a place to go? No. He'll have to go. God knows he can afford it. What if he falls apart? I'm so tired of feeling sick with guilt and wishing every hour and day away. Why doesn't he come home so we can end this? Where the hell are you, Declan?*

When it was clear he wasn't coming home, she undressed and put on her nightdress and got into bed. *I don't understand.*

She didn't hear him come in. She woke with his hand clamped on her mouth and nose and he was moving inside her. Her arms were ripped up over her head and he was holding her wrists in place with one hand. She heard her shoulder pop and felt a nauseating pain. It was sometime in the early morning. She could smell the booze. Her head was rammed into the bed-board, her neck was strained, she couldn't breathe and her insides felt like they were tearing. She tried to scream but it came out muffled. He was vicious and violent and as he attacked he warned her to shut her dirty mouth. She struggled to breathe and there was a moment before she managed to bite his stubby fingers that were jammed into her lips so that she thought she might suffocate. She managed a quick breath before he repositioned his hand and it bore down on her face so heavily she thought her nose and cheekbones might snap. He flipped her over on her stomach and pushed her face into the pillow so hard she thought she'd smother for sure, then she felt the pain like a knife cutting through her back passage.

"Do you like that, you fucking whore?" he said as he penetrated her over and over until she passed out. When she woke up her lip was cut and bleeding, she had a severe headache, her shoulder was dislocated and her anus was torn and bleeding. She got up slowly to the sounds of him taking a shower. She looked on the bed and saw the folder open and the pictures of her and Clooney talking, eating, smiling were strewn across the bed. Some of them had spunk on them, others had her blood. She realised her husband was going nowhere and there would be no talking or negotiation. She knew if she didn't get out, she'd either walk down to the kitchen and pick out the sharpest carving knife and plunge it deep into his heart or she'd end up being raped and tortured again, so she put on her flip-flops and a pair of fresh knickers lined with a panty pad to absorb the blood and she walked out of her bedroom and down the stairs. She picked up her coat from the hanger in the hallway and with her good arm she slung it over her shoulders to conceal the blood on her nightie. She picked up her handbag and she opened the front door and walked outside. She got into her car slowly and carefully. She drove to Eve's place. She'd never been there before but she knew the apartment block. She had never taken Clooney's phone number because there was no reason she could think of to ask for it and anyway she was scared that Declan would find it on her phone. She saw the building on the cliff and in the distance as she turned up the narrow dirt road that Ben Logan had been killed on two months before. She drove up to the block and parked. She slowly and painfully got out and, once she'd rehung the coat over her shoulders, she held it together tightly with her fist and walked to the main door. She looked on the panel and every name was there bar Eve's but she knew Eve well enough to know that if she was going to live in an apartment it would be the penthouse so she pressed the button and when nobody answered she pressed it again and this time she held it down.

Clooney sounded sleepy when he answered but he woke up as soon as he heard her cries. The door buzzed open and he waited for the lift, bouncing up and down and resting his hands on the door, willing it to open. When it did he saw her bruised and bleeding and her arm clearly dislocated.

"He raped me," she said. "He called me a whore and then he raped me."

Clooney brought her inside. He was silent and he led her by the hand. She was guarding her other arm. She didn't know whether she wanted to sit or stand or move or lie down. Clooney knelt down so that she was looking down at him. He held her hand and he smiled at her.

"You're safe now," he said and her burning eyes leaked tears of acid on a sore and tender face. She sobbed, her fat lip opened and bled again and he stood up slowly and held her cheek against his and whispered in her ear that he had her, she was safe and there was no going back. When she was calm he asked her if he could look at her arm.

"It's dislocated," she said.

"I know. We're going to need to pop it back in."

"You know how?" she asked and he nodded.

"I've dislocated this baby four times," he said, pointing to his left shoulder.

He took her arm and he very slowly rotated it until it hit a 35-degree angle. The pain was immense and she couldn't help but scream as the joint slid back into place. She felt immediate relief. She sighed and rotated it slowly.

"It's OK?" he said.

She nodded and plonked on the floor. She bent her knees and hugged them tight He sat beside her and when she held out her hand to him he took her in his arms and he held her tight and she cried and he rocked her there on the floor. When she fell asleep he carried her into bed. It was when he placed her under the covers that he saw the blood on the back of her nightdress. Clooney lay in bed watching her sleep and he thought about all the things he wanted to do to Declan. He wanted to drive to his house and burn it down with him in it or to pull him into the street and beat him to within an inch of his life or strip him naked and whip him, or run him over with his car or just punch him in his face. He wanted the world to know what he had done, to walk around the hospital and his neighbourhood with a bullhorn shouting it out and to see him stand in front of a judge and be sent down. He was angry and raw and sick to his stomach and then a question occurred to him. *Has he done this before?*

The next morning Lily woke to a running bath and breakfast being cooked. Eve's robe was on the bed and Lily put it on quickly so as to hide the blood. She walked into the kitchen and Clooney smiled at her and pointed to the sofa. When she was settled with a rug over her, he placed a tray with a small plate of scrambled eggs on her lap.

"Eat."

"Can't."

"Three bites, not all at once, take your time," he said, "but please, three bites."

She nodded.

He served himself and he sat down opposite her. She was playing with her food, moving it around the way she did when they were kids. He took the fork and put the smallest piece of egg on it and fed it to her. He watched her swallow and smiled.

"There's a bath in there ready for you but we have to talk about whether or not you want to press charges before you get into it."

She looked at him and shook her head. "He's the father of my children," she said.

"And last night he violently raped you."

"I can't."

"You know I won't make you do anything you don't want to but, Lily, this should be recorded."

She was crying again – silent fat tears just kept coming, burning tracks into her face, creeping down her neck and soaking the collar of her nightdress. Clooney stood up and hugged her close.

"I'm sorry," she said.

"Don't be sorry," he soothed, "you don't have anything to be sorry about."

"I can't," she said.

"OK, OK," he said.

After that he asked her if it would be alright to take some photos of her face. She agreed. He brought her into the bathroom and when she wanted to undress he gave her privacy and got some of Eve's things and walked in with his back to her and put them on the chair next to the bath.

"We'll buy something that fits when you feel a little better," he said.

Then he picked up her nightdress and took it out of the room. When he walked into the kitchen, he looked at the blood and semen stains, then carefully folded it, wrapped it in clingfilm and put it in a bag.

When she was washed and dressed in clothes that were too long and too wide for her, he insisted she had her shoulder properly looked at. When she finally agreed he rang Adam, told him what had happened and asked him to come to Eve's place. Adam came straight from home and arrived within an hour. He examined her shoulder and her face. She wouldn't let anyone near her below and he didn't press on the condition that she saw a gynaecologist later. He was a bone man and she'd been through enough. She found walking hard, she was in such bad shape, and it shook him to his core. He put her back into bed and gave her something to help her sleep.

"You can't say anything," she said as he was leaving the room.

"Everything will be OK," he said and he closed the door.

He joined Clooney in the kitchen. Clooney poured him a coffee and the two men sat in silence, neither knowing what to say or do.

After a while Adam scratched his head.

"We should report it," he said.

"We can't."

"We have to change her mind."

"I've kept the nightdress. It's got his semen and her blood on it."

"Jesus Christ," Adam said. "I always knew that Declan was an asshole but this is something else."

The two men fell silent again, both of their minds busy running through macho scenarios where they'd slay the demon and save the damsel in distress but the damage had been done and they were powerless to act without her consent. Even if either of them had been the types to go to his house or place of work and punch him or kick him or hit him with a baseball bat until he needed to be hospitalised, who would that serve? It would only cause Lily more pain and her children distress. If they said something and Lily didn't back their story, Declan would be the kind of prick who would sue for defamation and both men knew, regardless of the evidence kept by Clooney, Lily would never file a report. She had said it herself – Declan was the father of her children, she would never allow them to think that their father was capable of such a disgusting treacherous act. She wouldn't do it to them. They were two decent men not capable of plumbing the depths necessary to scare Declan. They both felt frustrated and impotent. Lily had told Clooney about the photos which meant that Declan was building a case against her for infidelity if necessary.

"But you haven't been together?" Adam said Clooney.

"No."

"But you want to be?"

Clooney sighed. "I fell in love with Lily when I was fourteen and she was only twelve."

"And you were never together?" Adam said.

"One summer a long time ago," Clooney said, "and I ended up driving her back to him."

"I'm sorry."

"We always wanted different things. She wanted a family. I wanted adventure. She wanted a home. I prefer on a tent on a beach. All she ever wanted was some stability. I couldn't give that to her."

"And now?"

"I think I'm always going to be the guy who leaves," Clooney said. "Can't help loving her though."

They resumed musing quietly, each man working out a separate strategy to get Lily back into her home and get Declan out but both concluded it was impossible with one hand tied behind their back. If Lily didn't threaten to charge him he'd have no reason to leave. In fact Adam was absolutely sure he'd revel in his small victory. If Lily was going to leave him he'd make damn sure she left with nothing.

"We could bluff?" Adam said.

Clooney perked up.

"We could say that she was going to press charges if he didn't get out," Adam went on as Lily walked into the room.

Clooney wondered how long she had been listening. She didn't pretend she hadn't been. She sat on the sofa with Eve's robe tied tight. She hugged a pillow. "He won't believe you. He knows I'll put the kids first. He'll play with you and then he'll raise the stakes, he'll call me names and tell you I like it rough and he'll hope that one of you punches him so he can call the guards and if you don't he'll tell you to get out of his office because, you see, Declan doesn't think he's done anything wrong. You can't scare someone who believes they have justice on their side." She was calm and eventoned. She knew the man she had married well. "Thank you for trying to help me though," she said and she smiled. "I'm going to be fine," she said. "I always am."

Clooney didn't make it in to the hospital to see Eve that day, instead he lay in her large bed with Lily in his arms.

Early that evening Lily remembered Daisy was waiting to be picked up. She phoned Tess's mother and confirmed that it was OK for Daisy to stay another night. The woman offered to put Daisy on the phone but Lily said no and it was OK because she wasn't able to lie and she wasn't ready to attempt to explain herself to a twelve-year-old.

Afterwards she talked to Scott and made sure he was alright.

"The old man had a serious hangover this morning," Scott said.

"Scott, I'm leaving your father," she said.

"What?"

"I'm going to ask a solicitor to send him a letter asking him to leave the house but if he refuses I can't go back. I have no money. I don't know where I'll be staying so you and Daisy might have to stay with him for a while until I get settled."

"You sound like you're crying. Are you crying, Mum?"

"I'm fine," she lied. "I'm sorry."

"It will blow over," he said.

"No, Scott, it won't."

"You can't leave him," he said as though her previous words had just sunken in.

"I have to."

"You need to come home," he said in a voice that reminded her of Declan.

"Don't speak to me like that," she said.

"Why are you doing this?"

"Because I have to."

He called her a bitch and told her she was ruining everyone's lives and he hung up.

She bit down on her already cut lip and Clooney presented her with more food he wanted her to eat.

"Kids," he said, putting a small piece of fish, baby potatoes and some steamed veg in front of her. "Selfish little bastards, aren't they?"

It was her first real smile. She nodded her head, picked up the fork and lifted some food, put it in her mouth, chewed and swallowed.

Later that night, back to facing Clooney in bed, aching all over and consumed by exhaustion but battling to stay awake, she smiled a little.

"I'm almost free," she whispered.

He leaned over and kissed the top of her head before cupping her beautiful fragile face in his hands.

"Yes, you are," he said. "Now go to sleep."

Chapter 10

The blame game

Lil?

Hello?

Where are you? It's been two weeks and not a word.
Have you forgotten all about us? Declan is freaking out.
I've never seen him so upset. He says you haven't called
and when I told him you hadn't written he lost it. He had
a massive row with his dad because he won't give him time
off to go down there after you. I was there! I went into
the garage to have lunch and collect my odds and ends to
make some jewellery (I've even sold a few pieces in the
café!) and he asked me if I'd heard anything and I said no
and he said you hadn't called and then he started to bite at
his fingers the way he does when he looks like he wants
to start crying and then his dad came in and said something
shitty about me being there but he did it in a mumble so
I couldn't actually hear what it was but just loud enough

so I knew he was unimpressed with me being there. Declan said to him he needed time off to go away and his dad just laughed him off and Declan walked right up to him and I swear it looked like Declan was going to punch his father in the face and then his father squared up to Declan and it looked like he was going to punch Declan in the face and I was thinking holy shit but anyway I think they remembered they weren't animals or that I was there or something but they both backed away from one another. I told Declan I'd come back for lunch later but didn't return. I thought it best to give him some room to cool down. He was really angry and it wasn't pleasant to be around. Anyway I went back the next day to see how he was and I was running really low on those small fiddley bolts that make such lovely bracelets. Can't wait for you to see the stuff! I'm using Gina's dad's old kiln now too. I've a few pieces put by for you but meantime Barry Douglas wants a necklace for his girlfriend - as if he has one but imaginary girlfriend or not he's a paying customer - and Rebecca Kelly is looking for a pair of earrings. I don't charge much which is probably part of the charm but still, between me making the stuff and Declan sourcing it, we could have a nice little business going. Oh and don't worry, I haven't forgotten about that dress you wanted made for the Debs Ball. I picked up the pattern last week while I was in town and the material is my present to you. I hope you like it when it's finished. I can't wait to see you in it. Anyway back to the story. So I went back to the garage to see Declan and pick up my bits. I waited until I saw his father pass the coffee shop, he never really tends to work past four. Anyway I brought in some leftover cake that would have gone off or into the bin and a sandwich for him but he was too agitated to eat. He said that his dad wouldn't let him go down the country and he was holding his wages. I couldn't believe it. Can you?

Anyway Declan was kicking things around and acting like a caged animal, one minute calm the next throwing such a tantrum that if I wasn't so busy ducking from a box of screws hitting the wall it would have been laughable. I mean I understand his frustration but he is so dramatic. Anyway I managed to calm him down. I told him if he needed to borrow money I'd give it to him it's the least I could do bearing in mind I've earned about 200 quid selling jewellery made from scraps he sourced. His humour changed completely, he picked me up and twirled me around and told me I was the best friend in the world. It was nice to see him so happy. I told him I should get Terry the Tourist to take a photo just so that we could all have a record of it. Anyway his mother's birthday is late next week and it's a big one she's 40 so he has to stay here for that but afterwards he's on the way down to you. He says he'll leave his dad a note. I can only imagine what it will say. Anyway you're welcome but seriously please write. I know it's probably got really busy in the restaurant and the weather's good and you're probably friends with Colm again and Clooney's there with his pals but I'm up here all alone - well not all alone but it feels like that. I was so bored the last Wednesday I went to see Ghost with Danny. It was brilliant. You should see it if there is a cinema down there. Is there a cinema down there? Anyway finally Ben's granny died last Friday. She had been anointed 4 times which is weird considering that if you believe in that stuff surely once should do the trick. Anyway the funeral was on Monday so Ben didn't get back until Tuesday. It was so great to see him. He looked tired and he needed to cut his hair but other than that he is so handsome. I'd forgotten how handsome he is. He walked into the coffee shop and I swear my heart skipped a beat and my insides fizzed a little. I love that feeling, don't you? Although it plays havoc with my appetite and you know I love my food. Anyway we had the best night ever on Friday night. Ben rented a hotel room in town. I told Danny I was going in to a gig and we stayed there from 5 o'clock in the evening until last bus. It was a small hotel that had the worst wallpaper I've ever seen and it smelt of smoke but the sheets were clean and the bed was big. We had such a good time. He really makes me laugh when I'm with him and I know it's stupid to say but I really feel beautiful and when he touches me Arrrghhhhhh! But it got me thinking and suddenly I felt really sad. I didn't tell him because I didn't want him to feel sad too but I've only got 3 weeks left before I leave for London. He forgets my course starts a whole month before everyone else's. I remind him but I don't think he wants to remember that. I think he wants to pretend and that's OK. I understand that. I wish I could pretend but I have to get ready, I have to focus, this is my lifelong dream. He fell asleep for a while and I lay there looking at him and I cried because even though I was inches away I missed him already. I thought my heart was going to split down the middle. I felt genuine pain so I went into the bathroom and I cried there. When he woke up I was in the bath and he joined me and I felt better but still it's constantly on my mind. 3 weeks, Lil, that's all we have left. It makes me want to puke just thinking about it. Do you remember when we were sitting in Paul's dad's car and Roy Orbison came on the radio singing 'Love Hurts' and I said it was the worst song in the world? Well, it's still in the Top 10 shit songs of all time but finally I get it when I think about getting on that plane and leaving home, my dad, Clooney, you, the lads. I think it'll be OK, we'll write and see each other at Christmas and I won't be in London forever and I'm sad and lonely but I know I'll be fine. When I think about leaving Ben I think I actually might die. It's so stupid and dramatic and pathetic because I've known him for such a *short time but the thought of losing him takes my breath away. I don't like it. This is not where I wanted to be this summer but even so (the last two weeks aside and Ben's stupid gran R.I.P.) this is the best summer I've ever had. 3 weeks left. Are you even going to be home in time to say goodbye? Please write to me. I miss you.*

Eve

CAN YOU BELIEVE OUR RESULTS ARE OUT TOMORROW!!!!!!!!!

* * *

When Lily went to collect Daisy she was gone. Declan had picked her up. When she went to Jack Donovan's garage she found him there alone. Declan had asked Scott to stay home to mind his sister.

"He's been busy," Lily said.

"Is Scott right? Are you leaving Declan?" he asked.

"Yes."

"For another man?" His question was without malice or judgement.

"For myself," she said.

"Is he like I was?" he asked and he looked at her straight in the face. His eyes felt like a tractor beam locked on to hers and she couldn't escape his look.

"No and yes probably. He's never touched the kids."

"You?"

"Once or twice," she said, breaking away from his stare.

"I never touched his mother," he said in almost a whisper while wiping grease from his hands with an old tea towel.

He pointed to two old battered chairs that he and Scott sat on to share their lunch. She sat and he sat opposite her.

"You said the other night that he is what I made him," he said. She nodded. She remembered saying it.

"I put my hands up. I was a terrible father and I did terrible things but at some point Declan has to take responsibility for who he is and for what he has done."

"Suddenly you're the Dali Lama," she said, shaking her head. "I remember the various states he was in when you'd finished with him. I remember the marks and the bruises and the crying. I've listened to him scream your name in his dreams and, yeah, you're right we are more than our past and it's not a good enough excuse. But sometimes when he's at his most vicious, paranoid and bullish, I look at him and I see you as clear as if you were standing in front of me. He's your son, Mr Donovan. He is what you made him genetically and socially. Maybe you're not the narcissist or the bully you used to be or maybe you're just a different kind and even if you've changed utterly through the AA or finding God or peace or purpose, I'm glad for you, but don't think we'll ever be allies because we won't."

She stood up and brushed herself off.

He stood up. "I understand," he said and he went back to work as she walked out the door.

Clooney was waiting in the coffee shop a few doors down. It had changed a lot since the days that she grew up in the village and Eve had worked there. He had a coffee waiting. She told him that Scott had been called home.

"What's he playing at?" Clooney said.

"He's rounding up his troops," she said.

Adam had called to tell them that Declan had requested a few days off. Lily needed to go to the house and get her clothes and, although she knew bringing Clooney would give her husband more ammunition to use in front of the kids, she was too terrified to go by herself.

They pulled up outside the door. They sat in the car for a moment while she braced herself. She opened the door and got out and walked up the path and he followed closely. She put her key in the door and it turned easily. The door swung open and she stepped inside. She could hear him in the kitchen, the radio was on and he was talking to Daisy. When she walked in they were both at the island and Daisy was showing him how to make muffins. There were baking utensils everywhere and they were both covered in flour. Declan was licking icing off his fork and Daisy was doing the same. They both stared at her as though she was an unwanted intruder. Scott came in through the back door from the garden. He stood staring too. In the thirty-plus hours since the rape, her husband had managed to turn her kids against her. *Always the victim, Declan.*

"What are you doing here, Mum?" Scott asked. He was angry but when he looked from his mother to his father his expression changed to concern. *What have you said, Declan?*

Clooney appeared behind her and put his hand on her shoulder.

"What is *he* doing here?" Daisy demanded.

"He's my friend."

"We know who he is. Dad showed us the pictures," Scott said.

She looked at Declan and she wanted to scream, '*Did you show them the photos with my blood on them or another copy?*' Instead she just shook her head.

"You're a scumbag," she said.

"You have a nerve," he said, "bringing him into our children's home." He was standing behind Daisy holding on to her shoulder, mirroring Clooney because as ever he was the master manipulator. If he hadn't positioned his twelve-year-old in front of him Clooney might have jumped the counter and beaten him to a pulp. Declan knew exactly what he was doing. Scott backed up and fell into line with his dad and sister and the battle lines had been drawn.

"You said you had to go the other night, Mum, so you should go," Scott said, "but wherever you end up we're fine here with our dad."

Lily looked into her husband's eyes and they were cold, betraying no feeling at all, but his lip curled slightly to signal his smug satisfaction.

Even if she couldn't bear to tell her children their father was a rapist, she could have said that their father was a liar and that she was leaving because he was a bully, manipulator, a paranoid control freak who had mentally abused her for years but she didn't. They had already been led to believe that she was some kind of whore who chose to run off with another man. Showing them the pictures that although innocent were no doubt incriminating, was only a small example of what he was capable of and, although her children looked at her with anger and hate in their eyes in that moment, she refused to fight or plead her case. She would not sink to his level. She would not damage her kids any more than he would choose to damage them. This was only the start. He would use the kids, tell them whatever damaging tales he needed to ensure they stayed by his side. He'd focus all his energy on guaranteeing they felt his pain and pitied him for it as she had done for so many years. He would try to make it impossible to leave him but she couldn't stay. She was leaving her children with a wolf in pain and there was nothing she could do but wait, bide her time, let them know how much she loved them and that she was sorry for being selfish and putting herself first but she had to before it was too late. She decided in that moment she would get them back and they had been raised by her to recognise what real love was and even if she'd spoilt them a little they were good kids who would forgive her and she'd get them back.

"OK," she said, "I understand. I just want you to know that I love you both and I will always be there for you."

Maybe believing that was the only way she could go up the stairs and clean out her wardrobe. Clooney stood on guard while she filled three cases with everything she owned. She didn't take the jewellery; she left it all there except for a few strings of beads that Daisy had made for her in art class. One case was filled with photo albums and the old shoebox with Eve's letters and photos. She was packed and ready to go within twenty minutes of arriving. The kids stayed in the kitchen with their father and she left without saying goodbye.

She didn't see Declan smashing his cup in the sink and storming upstairs to his room when she'd gone. She didn't see Daisy's tears and Scott reaching for his little sister's hand. She didn't witness her son growing up in the matter of one night, instinctively realising he was his mother's obvious replacement and stepping up to the role she'd vacated, relying on all the rainy afternoons she'd sat him on the counter and taught him to cook when he was young and curious and liked to spend time with his mother. She didn't see him get his sister up in the mornings and make sure his dad's dry-cleaning was dropped and collected on the way to and from his granddad's shop. She didn't hear Declan venting at his kids when he was feeling so sorry for himself that the only way to unburden himself was to share the pain he felt inside. She didn't hear the ugly things he said, blaming them for their mother leaving with another man.

"If you were better kids, smarter, brighter."

"If you weren't such smart mouths."

"If you didn't play that stupid piano every night, noon and morning."

"If you weren't such a bloody disappointment."

She lay awake alone in Eve's bedroom those first few nights wondering what their lives would be like without her and how long it would be before they'd allow her to try to make it all better. *I've got to make it all better.*

After that first day and night when she and Clooney lay together and he held her and whispered encouragement and kissed her head and stroked her hair, they separated. He allowed her space to heal mentally and physically. The last thing he wanted to do was hurt, pressure or to frighten her. She was experiencing a special kind of anguish reserved for mothers separated from their children. He'd seen it many times before and for many different reasons but the look was always the same. There was a resignation and guilt in her eyes that he tried to talk away even though he knew that there was nothing he could say. Those first few days she kept to herself save for mealtimes when he made sure she sat down at a table and ate, regardless how much or little food she managed to get through. She needed to fight her demons and he stood back, allowing her time to battle patiently, waiting till she'd won.

Eve was not so patient. She had been hospitalised for nine weeks and she was more than ready to leave. She was bored and restless and, although she was still weak, the physiotherapists had done a good job at getting her semi-mobile. She walked with great difficulty, her shoulder was still painful, and she suffered muscle wastage on both legs and her left arm but she could afford to have a physio attend to her in the house every day. The second operation Adam suspected she might need on her shoulder was finally deemed unnecessary and she had two people waiting to care for her when she got home.

Adam was the one who broke the news to her that Lily had left Declan. He had waited until the last day of her nursing week before the attack. She was not due in for another week and so Eve had not suspected anything was wrong even when Clooney didn't turn up. She just thought he was taking a day off and maybe helping Paul who was overwhelmed with the list of wedding duties that Simone had assigned to him before she returned to London for an early hen party with her model friends. They had decided on having a small non-religious ceremony in the function room of a hotel in Westport. The Atlantic Coast Hotel & Spa would be the venue, there would be a female officiant for the wedding service and then dinner would be served in the Blue Wave restaurant followed by drinks and dancing in the Fishworks Bar & Café, and for the hardened drinkers and partiers there would be a bus to take them to Matt Molloy's Bar for a late-night traditional Irish session.

"Why Westport?" Eve had asked him.

"It will annoy my mother."

"The non-religious ceremony?"

"The same reason."

She had laughed at the notion and was happy he was pleased to piss his mother off. She had never warmed to the woman. When she asked why he'd picked the hotel, he told her that it was because they had spent a weekend there when he first started seeing Simone and they had gone every couple of months since.

The spa was run by an Indian Ayurvedic doctor, Dr Thomas. He could diagnose and treat conditions with hot oils, massage and provide individual dietary and everyday living recommendations to promote healing and ensure balance and health.

"It's about what you eat and when you eat it," Paul said. "It's all about the vata, pitta and kapha."

"The what, the what and the what?" she asked.

"We're all made up of either vata – air and ether, pitta – fire and water, and kapha – water and earth."

"Oh, sounds amazing," she said shaking her head, pursing her lips and raising her eyes to signal her sarcasm.

"It's the mother of all medicine," he said. "Give it a go. If anyone needs to rebalance you do."

She was sitting in a hospital bed at the time and sick of doctors, nursing, prodding and poking. She assured him that she had her fill of medicine.

"Trust me, the massages are sublime and they will help you repair."

She laughed. "You should work for the tourist board," she said, before admitting that she was horrified by the notion of anyone massaging her – physiotherapy was still torturous and the notion of an Indian woman walking on her was terrifying.

"Remember the summer we did our Leaving Cert?" he said.

How could she forget? That summer had come sharply back in focus in recent times.

"That rugby game we played in August?" he went on. "A friendly with the Dun Laoghaire lads?"

"I remember. You dislocated your knee."

"Well, actually, it was a guy called David Sweeney who dislocated my knee. He did it because I had met him in a gay club and we kissed and I wanted to kiss again but he was deeper in the closet than I was if that is even possible. We had words before the game."

"You went to gay clubs back then? I thought your first gay experience was in college?"

"Not the point of the story."

"Don't care."

"He was angry and when he attacked he really attacked. He really did some damage."

"OK."

"And I've suffered pain ever since."

"Is that why you're rubbish at tennis?" she said with a grin.

"I have arthritis in the knee," he said. "And after one session with Dr Thomas, I kid you not, I felt no pain and it's been years since I've felt no pain. You have to be careful, Eve. Things could go badly for you if you don't take your long-term recovery seriously. He can help. I mean it."

"So the wedding is all about me," she said.

"No, it's all about us but you should capitalise."

"This new, open, sharing you is unnerving."

"Don't get used to it," he said.

She shrugged. "Whatever."

When Adam arrived into her room that afternoon, after he had left Clooney to nurse Lily, he sat by Eve's bed and she was happy and looking forward to hearing the plans that were being laid down to bring her home. He was quiet and white in the face and he didn't smile the way he always smiled when he saw her.

"What?" she asked and for a moment she thought they had discovered a reason she couldn't be released sooner rather than later.

"It's Lily," he said.

"What about Lily?"

Her heart beat faster because she had heard that tone of voice before when her mother was sick and her father was sick and Ben was an organ donor. *Tell me!* her mind screamed but she didn't say a word, she just waited for the worst. Adam was uncomfortable and unsure. He didn't know if he should tell Lily's old friend Lily's personal news but then again she was staying in her house and obviously attached to her brother. Also he felt bound to Eve, not just as her doctor but as her friend. If he was honest, he was attracted to her and maybe even a little besotted. He owed her the truth and the people living in her sterile, beautiful, sea-view penthouse owed her the same, plus he wanted her perspective. She was always so clear-headed about everything. He just didn't know how to report it. It actually caused him physical discomfort. The words seemed to get caught in his throat and his shoulders tensed and he could read the impatience on her face.

"He . . ."

"He what?" she asked, knowing immediately it was Declan who had done something.

"He . . ."

"Have you got some sort of speech impediment all of a sudden? What?"

"He raped her."

Eve blanched, the colour literally draining from her face.

"How do you know?" She was a little hoarse and her voice

shook a little, not so much that someone who didn't know her would notice, but in the nine intense weeks they had spent together Adam felt he knew her well.

"He dislocated her shoulder, her lip and face was swollen, he ripped her apart down . . ." He was a doctor but he didn't want to say it because Lily was his friend. Even though she was married, possibly in love with Eve's brother and although he had developed feelings for Eve, he still cared deeply for Lily. Thinking about her in pain made him heartsick.

"Where is she now?" Eve said, slipping into business mode.

"Your place."

"Where are the kids?"

"At home."

"They can't all stay in the apartment," she said. "Where's Clooney?"

"Taking care of her."

"OK," she said, nodding. "I'll take care of the rest."

"Aren't you surprised? Aren't you disgusted?"

"Not surprised," she said, "and Declan Donovan disgusted me a long time ago. How is she?"

"She says she's OK."

"She'll be fine. She'll be back to herself in no time. If this is what had to happen to get her away from him, fine."

"The kids are with him. He's going to fight her all the way and she won't use the rape to fight back."

"I understand. He'll be dealt with," she said.

When Adam established that she didn't intend on hiring a hit man, he left her to make calls and take control. That was Eve's gift. Getting knocked down meant that it had been taken from her and nine weeks was far too long. The bitch was back.

Watch out, Declan, here I come, you fucking prick.

Eve was finally discharged four days after Lily's attack. The neurologist came back and repeated question after question before Adam would finally sign her out. Mostly she spoke the truth but in some cases she lied. She wanted out.

"Do you ever feel dizzy?"

"No."

"Any double vision?"

"No."

"Muscle-jerking?"

"No."

"Changes in sense of smell?"

"No."

"What about the headaches?"

"Always had the headaches," she said, fully aware the entire file was full of her stupid headaches. "Just let me go."

She was wheeled to the door by Abby and Adam walked by her side. Clooney was on the other side and she knew that Lily was waiting at home. She was excited. *We're all back together, Clooney. Just like old times.* She was also sad and angry and ready for war. Eve and Clooney were so different in so many ways and he and Lily were so similar. *Always taking the high road.* Eve had become a multi-billionaire by being the exact opposite. Money didn't interest her, the game did, and she never lost the game. Her jewellery was worn by every credible personality and star in the spotlight, her high-end couture stuff was on every catwalk in Milan, Paris, New York and London, and that doesn't just happen by accident. It had taken years of hard work and a cut-throat attitude. When the economy started to downturn she spotted it before anyone and created a line to be distributed by a major supermarket in the USA. The board fought her every step of the way but she held firm and fought them all and they went from a high-end million-dollar enterprise to a high-and-low-end billion-dollar enterprise. Eve loved and was passionate about her art but she was also a cold and calculating businesswoman at heart, and those kind don't lose because nothing gets in the way of their win. Declan Donovan had won way back in the summer of 1990 and only because she was naïve and she wouldn't hurt Lily any more than necessary. Still the plan fermenting was sweet in that she would finally get one over on him, all the while helping her friend. *Patience pays.*

The day Abby rolled her out of the hospital with Clooney at one side and Adam at the other was a glorious one. The glass doors opened and, under a blue sky and a hot yellow sun, she rolled out onto the car park she'd spent so much time looking at. There was a part of her that panicked a little, she was leaving the place where Ben had last lived and finally died. She was leaving the place where she had said her goodbyes to him. *I'm getting out, Ben. I promise when the time comes I'll make sure the Ginger Monster is jailed. It's not much but it's all I can do.* Lily would be waiting back at the apartment, she wanted to see her, and she hadn't seen her since the rape. She missed her, she wanted to mind her and make it all go away. When she got as far as the edge of the pavement she insisted on using the crutches that lay across her lap. She shambled from the path to the waiting car and getting inside and belting up was a little more awkward than she had expected. When she was finally settled she opened the window to take a last look at her home for the past two months.

Adam leaned in.

"Don't bully your physiotherapist," he warned.

"Don't be late for dinner," she said.

"What dinner?"

"The dinner to welcome me home," she said, before looking at Clooney. "You promised me a dinner?"

Clooney smiled. "Of course there's a dinner. Tomorrow night, everyone's coming and yes Adam's invited."

Adam smiled. "Looking forward to it."

"By the way, you're not my doctor any more."

"There are follow-ups," he said.

"Screw you, I'm going private," she said and waved as Clooney drove off.

He stood there laughing and, as he waved her goodbye, he thought about what it would be like to sleep with her when she was less fragile and was more comfortable in her own skin. How long that would take he couldn't say. Everyone heals, both mentally and physically, in their own time but he hoped she wouldn't get bored of him in the meantime. *I think we could really be something.*

When Eve finally made it home, Lily was waiting. She had the place full of flowers to add colour. Eve didn't really like flowers but she understood her pal's need to make the place less industrially clean and more homely. To Eve the cool blue sea, the green grass, the warm yellow sun, the streaming rain or grey cloudy sky were the features of the high-pitched-ceiling glass-filled apartment but Lily favoured sentimental warmth. She liked coloured walls, flowers, fridge magnets, pictures, photos and just enough clutter to suggest a family lived there but not so much to appear messy or mentally unwell. Eve liked clean lines, bare surfaces and strong architecture. There were some new cushions on the sofa and a small, wooden, brown-framed, faded picture of her, Lily and Clooney on the mantelpiece of the fireplace that separated the kitchen from sitting room. *That's got to go*, she thought before taking a moment to consider why and where Lily had kept it all this time and, when she picked it up and looked at the two of them swinging on the old swing-set, it make her want to cry.

"The one who swings highest gets a wish!" Eve would call out.

"I can't think, I can't think!" Lily would say frantically as they climbed and climbed and when they couldn't swing any higher, Lily would scream out at the top of her lungs.

"I love you, Eve Hayes!"

"I love you, Lily Brennan!"

When she looked closer she saw a faded Clooney behind Lily, pushing her. Lily and Clooney had their usual cheesy grins but she was sitting with her arms folded and a face like thunder. Clooney was about seven, she and Lily were about five. She remembered the day. Her mother was behind the camera saying encouraging words and her dad was jumping up and down, waving and acting the fool. Clooney and Lily thought it was funny, Eve didn't. *Poor Dad*. The memory of him pulling faces and jumping on one leg made her smile but only for a moment and then she wanted the picture gone again. *Sentimental but hideous*. She purposely hadn't made a fuss when the lift opened and she and Lily had greeted one another – she just hugged her and told her she was happy they were together again. Lily was sad and still struggling with her new reality. Eve reacted to complex emotions she didn't understand by being practical. She dropped onto her hard white leather sofa and hugged one of Lily's purple furry cushions only because her limbs ached and her sofa although a work of art seemed somewhat uncomfortable and unwelcoming.

Lily handed her a cup of freshly brewed coffee and Clooney hovered.

"I love you, Lily Brennan," Eve said out of nowhere.

Lily was caught off guard and tears filled her eyes.

"And you're going to be OK," Eve said. "I'll make sure of it."

Lily nodded. "You always took care of me," she said, remembering the bullies who taunted her for her sallow Mediterranean skin and soft brown lips. "But I'm a big girl now."

"Don't be silly, you're tiny," Eve said and she grinned.

Lily thanked her for her hospitality and she went to bed early, leaving Eve and Clooney alone. They went to the balcony and over a bottle of wine, under an outdoor heater and looking onto a black sea, he told her in great detail what Declan had done.

"Is the house still up for sale?" she asked.

"As soon as the buyers pulled out, the sign went back up a few weeks ago."

"We need to take it down for a while," she said.

"Lily?" he said.

"Lily and the kids."

"They think she's the devil," he said, shaking his head. "He has completely manipulated them."

"They'll get sense," she said in a tone that suggested that if they didn't get there on their own she'd do something about it.

"Eve," he said, warning her.

"He'll get sense."

"Eve."

"Leave it with me."

"Don't do anything Lily will regret," he warned.

"I promise I won't," she said.

They sat together in the cool night air under a blow-heater watching the black water lap and fold and, when the bottle of wine was finished and Eve was drunk enough to allow Clooney to carry her, they went inside.

"I can walk. It's not sore, it's not sore, wish I'd got pissed earlier," she said, shambling around on crutches and pulling a fresh nightdress out of a drawer. She smelled it. "Mmmmmm, it doesn't spell of hospital but it does smell of cedarwood."

She headed to her dressing table with Clooney following to make sure she didn't fall and smash herself. She didn't, she waved him off.

"Goodnight, go to bed, I'm fine."

He left her alone.

"It's good to have you home," he said before closing the door and allowing her the first real uninterrupted private time she'd had in over two months.

Clooney made his bed on a pull-out sofa in Eve's office. He thought about why his sister felt she needed a pull-out sofa for an office that was a staircase away from her own bedroom but then he knew his sister had spent many years sleeping in her office and old habits die hard. Before he went to sleep he turned on her computer and checked his Facebook. There were a few messages from people he worked with and friends he had made over the years. He made some comments and looked at a few photos that had been recently posted. Mark Grey, a guy he'd worked with on and off over the years, had taken an office job in Geneva after marrying Barbara Cashin one of his ex-girlfriends. He had posted photos of their brand-new baby boy Laurence. There was one of Barbara holding her son and beaming into the camera, another one in which they were all huddled together, father, mother and baby. Mark had aged a little but he was proud and grinning wildly. Clooney hadn't worked with either Mark or Barbara in years. He and Mark had shared a place together in Kenya and at the time Barbara was Clooney's girlfriend but, when it became apparent that she was looking for more than just a fling, he ended it. She took it badly and they hadn't spoken for a while. He left Kenya and Mark and Barbara behind and the next time he met them in January 2005, when every seasoned, hardened and able NGO made their way to Indonesia in the aftermath of the tsunami, he met them again in Aceh. By that time they were living together and engaged. Barbara had softened toward Clooney and Mark was happy to see his old pal again and they'd been keeping in touch on and off since. They looked happy and settled and it was nice to see but also a little unsettling. Over the years the majority of the people he had started out with had settled down and either gone back to work within the aid organisations in their own country or in major cities across Europe and America. Very few were still in the field, travelling from country to country and job to job. He would be forty in December and he was tired but not tired enough to envy Mark and his new sedentary suburban, nine to five, picket-fence life. *Good luck but it's just not for me, man.*

He checked his main email account and saw three messages. Two were from Stephanie, the first dated the 20th August. The subject read: Sad news. She told him that a British journalist they both knew had been diagnosed with cancer and flown home to London to deal with his health issues. The second was dated 27th August. The subject read: Hello from Paris. She told him that the final day of her last period was the 18th June and she had remembered the date because she had ran out of tampons in the desert and the only thing that was clean and usable was her favourite silk scarf which she had to kiss goodbye to before shoving it down her knickers and hoping for the best. She had returned to the hotel on the 2nd July. They had sex that night and for some reason the coil chose not to work and it meant that she was ten weeks pregnant. She was in France. She had travelled there for an abortion and a break. She told him that abortion was only legal up until the 12th week in pregnancy and she had to be there for a week before the procedure for mandatory reflection so as soon as she realised how far gone she was she had jumped on a plane. She had been there two days. She was having the procedure done in five. She asked him if he was free for a weekend in Paris, saying her procedure had been scheduled for the following Wednesday and, if he arrived on the Friday, they could spend a long leisurely weekend together in The Ritz before she returned to Afghanistan. The email was three days old.

He sat in Eve's swivel-chair, resting his head on his knuckles reading the email over and over again. It was so blasé. *An abortion and a break?* The email was short, matter of fact and didn't give away any emotion. It was typical of Stephanie. She probably had a harder time deciding whether to shove her favourite silk scarf down her knickers than to abort their child. He didn't want to be a father and he wasn't judging her, he was just emotional. This was a baby, his and hers. Not wanted but there, and even if she did get rid of it in two days' time, it was there now, growing inside her. His mind was racing. He wasn't made for fatherhood. She wasn't maternal.

They were rolling stones. They had been careful not to conceive. She had the coil and he'd only stopped using condoms when they'd both got clean blood tests. They were really fond of one another but they weren't in love. She was also a soldier in her heart, a fighter, a warrior. She would have been a good and fierce mother but war is no place for a child and war was the only thing Stephanie understood. She didn't belong on an American base any more than he belonged in a United Nations city office.

She's ten weeks pregnant. He googled what a ten-week-old foetus would look like.

Week 10: Embryo is now a foetus

The foetus is now the size of a strawberry.
The feet are 2mm long (one tenth of an inch)
The neck is beginning to take shape.
The body muscles are almost developed. Baby has begun movement.
While still too small for you to feel, your little one is wriggling and shifting.
The jaws are in place. The mouth cavity and the nose are joined.
The ears and nose can now be seen clearly.
Fingerprints are already evident on the skin.
Nipples and hair follicles begin to form.
She'll be eleven weeks pregnant at time of termination.
He was almost scared to look but he couldn't help himself.

Week 11: Neurons multiply

The fingers and toes have completely separated.
The taste buds are starting to develop.
Baby has tooth buds, the beginning of the complete set of twenty milk teeth.
Baby can swallow and stick out his or her tongue.
Whole body except tongue is sensitive to touch.
Cartilage is now calcifying to become bone.
If it is a boy, the testicles are starting to produce the testosterone hormone.

He read and re-read it. *The whole body except the tongue is sensitive to touch. Will it feel anything?* He found a yahoo answer site in which pro and anti women basically tore lumps out of each other and called each other names. He looked at medical sites and saw the same arguments although without the name-calling. Most in the medical field agreed that pain was more likely to occur in the third trimester. It was too soon for the baby to be aware and feel pain. *Whole body except tongue is sensitive to touch.*

He started his reply on email. She hadn't even left a phone number and she hadn't sent another email since. He had stopped looking at email when Lily arrived on his doorstep. He had focused on her and nothing else. He wondered if Stephanie was even that bothered. Three days had passed since she told him that she was pregnant. The subject heading was interesting. Hello from Paris. *Was she having a good time?* He hoped so. *Did she feel heartsick like he did?* It was unlikely.

Hi Stephanie

He deleted it.

Stephanie

He deleted it.

Oh Steph

He deleted it.

I'm so sorry.

He deleted it.

I just picked this email up.

He deleted it.

He sat over the computer, tapping the J key lightly with his finger. *We could spend a long leisurely weekend in The Ritz before I head back to Afghanistan.* Was she in The Ritz? He googled the website and got the phone number. It was just after 2 a.m. in Ireland which made it 3 a.m. in Paris.

He phoned the hotel. The receptionist picked up after four rings. She sounded bright and breezy as though it was the middle of the day. In broken French Clooney apologised for calling so late and asked to be connected to Stephanie Banks' room. She took a minute and advised that Stephanie had requested not to be disturbed after 10 p.m. He explained it was very important. She considered for a moment and rang the room. She put him through after a few moments. Stephanie sounded sleepy.

"Hello?"

He could hear her fumble for the light.

"I just picked up your email," he said.

"I was wondering why you were so quiet," she said and yawned.

"Are you alright?"

"I'm fine," she said and he could hear that she was relaxed and stretching in the bed the way she always did when she was half-awake half-asleep.

"Are you sure this is what you want?"

"It's what we both want," she said.

"Thanks for telling me."

"I hoped to see you."

"Eve just got out of hospital today."

"Wow, she must have been in a bad way."

"She was."

"And now?"

"She'll be OK," he said. "Are you scared?"

"They're going to put me out," she said.

"When and where?"

"Thursday 1 p.m., 10, rue Vivienne."

"I'll fly in that morning," he said.

"You don't have to."

"I want to."

"I'm really tired," she said.

"Go back to sleep."

"And Clooney . . ."

"Yes."

"Thanks."

He hung up and looked for flights that would get him to Paris as early as possible on Thursday morning. He went on-line and found a flight leaving at 7 a.m. and arriving at 9:45 a.m. He booked it and emailed her the time he'd arrive. He asked her if he should meet her in the hotel or if he should go straight to the clinic.

Then before he closed the computer he read the last email. It was a job offer to head up a food programme in Peru. It had been up and running for four years and headed up by a man he was aware of but had never crossed paths with. He was leaving with no reason given. There was an attached file explaining the WFP activities, the areas covered and the strategies. The guy was leaving in November but the hope was that he would be in Peru as soon as the 1st October to work with him before he left. He didn't open the attached file. He did answer the email, asking for one week to think about it. He closed his computer and fell onto the pull-out sofa. He lay there in the dark with his eyes wide open and his mind and heart racing.

Stephanie needs me but only briefly. I want Lily but she is a mother going through a nasty separation. She is bound to Ireland. What about Peru? No more war. I couldn't be a stepdad to those kids no more than I could be a father to Stephanie's child even if either of them had wanted me to, but then why not? What if Stephanie changes her mind? Could I step up to the plate if I had to? Of course I'd do my best. What about Peru? I could do something in Peru. A fucking baby. If it is a boy, the testicles are starting to produce the testosterone hormone. Eleven weeks. What if Lily and I do get together? Would I end up hurting her like last time? Would she want now what she wanted then? What if Stephanie wants me to ask her not to have an abortion? Women change when they get pregnant. There's a child growing inside her. My baby is growing inside her. Do I want to ask her not to have an abortion? No. What would it mean for both of us? A completely different life? I don't want a different life. What does that make me? Eve needs me here now but for how long more? Would I even consider staying in Ireland and settling down? No. Even for Lily? I just can't stay here. What about Peru? It would be a fresh start on a project that's actually working and supported by local government. How the hell did we get pregnant? Damn it, Stephanie, if you're so sure and so cool about it why did you even tell me? Lily, you make me so happy – if only I could be what you need me to be. What about Peru?

The next morning Clooney was tired and quiet. Eve slept late. It was the first time in a long time she didn't have someone prodding or poking her at ridiculous hours of the morning. Clooney sat at the kitchen counter drinking coffee and watching the waves curl and splash against the rocks and the edge of the country.

Lily appeared in a pair of cute cotton striped blue-and-white pyjamas. The legs were too long on her, the string was knotted tightly and they were away too big around the waist and it bunched. The boxy shirt was a little long and she held it with both fists. Although she'd just woken it didn't have one crease in it and when she passed him she smelled of roses. She looked at him from under her thick chestnut-brown fringe, full of concern.

"You didn't sleep," she said.

He nodded. "A lot on my mind."

"Can I help?"

"No," he said.

"Please, try me," she said, pouring coffee from the pot into his mug and into one of her own. She sat opposite him and he looked into her big brown eyes and wondered how much she had been through over the past twenty years. *I'm so sorry, Lily.*

"I have to go to Paris tomorrow," he said.

"Oh." She looked disappointed. "For how long?"

"A few days."

"Is that all?"

"I'll be back."

"But not for long," she said and she smiled but her smile was just a mask.

"Never here for long."

"I'll miss you," she said and she lifted her coffee up to her soft mouth and drank as she stood and walked back into Eve's spare room.

It was after eight and Paul and Simone were the first to arrive to Eve's welcome-home dinner with four bottles of wine and a twenty-four pack of beer.

"Think you have enough booze there, pal?" Clooney said, laughing.

"Better to be safe than sorry," Paul said, breaking out a beer and handing it to Clooney before taking one for himself and putting the others in the fridge. He'd been buying wedding suits with his father who'd read a book on bisexuality called *Bi Any Other Name: Bisexual People Speak Out* and he'd been answering questions for most of the day.

"If you were stuck on an island would you rather be with a man or woman?"

"I'd rather be with the one I love."

"So say Simone drowned, would you rather be with a man or woman?"

"I don't know, it depends on whether the person is attractive, fun, intelligent, sexy, if we have a spark or not."

"OK say you have all that, which one?"

"Oh for God's sake, Dad, I don't know."

"If I was bisexual I'd pick the man – just in that setting mind," he said and Paul stopped in his tracks.

"Really."

"Oh yeah. Given the choice with just two of us on a remote island with no telly, I wouldn't have to tell him what I'm thinking every five minutes and I love your mother but it would be a lovely break not to have to beg to get my end away."

Paul had laughed and put his arm around his dad. He wanted to tell him he loved him and appreciated him but he stopped short of that and instead he just smiled. His dad was happy enough and gave him a nudge.

"Best of both worlds, son," he said.

"She's the one, Dad."

"I know," he said, "but if you're ever stuck on an island," he said and he winked and they walked on down Grafton Street and toward the place where Gar would meet them to try on suits.

It had been a long day and Paul opened his can and took a large slug before saying hello to Lily who was busy cooking up a storm.

"Good to see you, Lily," he said.

She was wearing a black V-neck dress and although she was too thin she looked beautiful. She smiled at him. "You too, Paul," she said.

"Sorry to hear about your marriage trouble," he said. Clooney had told everyone bar Adam and Eve that Lily and Declan had split up because they'd grown apart.

"Thanks, congratulations on your wedding," she said.

Lily had missed out on Paul's gay years. The last time she'd seen him he was with a beautiful girl and as far as she was concerned, bisexual or not, nothing had changed.

Simone was standing in the middle of the long kitchen-cum-dining-room-cum-sitting-room staring at the view out of the two-story glass wall. Balcony lights shone down on the water, highlighting a ship that was passing in the distance. She turned from the window to look at the mezzanine office with its inbuilt bookshelves and beautiful wooden spiral staircase that Eve couldn't get up.

"This place is amazing," she said.

"It's very Eve," Clooney said.

"Speaking of . . . where is she?" Paul asked.

Lily said she'd go and get her. When she was gone Paul looked at Clooney.

"So are you sleeping together yet?" he asked.

Clooney looked at him with wonder. How the hell . . . He didn't answer and Paul didn't need him to.

Adam arrived before Eve appeared. He brought more wine and a bottle of expensive whiskey but was happy to share in the beer. He loved the place too.

"It's very Eve," he said.

Clooney smiled. He liked Adam and hoped his sister wouldn't chew him up and spit him out like she had done with everyone bar Ben Logan.

Gar and Gina arrived late and hassled; the baby-sitter had told them that she couldn't stay past midnight because she had a test she was studying for. They'd tossed a coin as to who got to stay late. Gina lost.

"Studying my hole!" Gina said. "She's probably meeting some young fella. I get out one night in a blue effing moon!"

They arrived with more booze to add to the huge stockpile. Gar poured himself a glass of red wine and Gina and Simone sat together on Eve's uncomfortable white sofa talking about how amazing the place was.

"But a deathtrap for young kids," Gina said, looking from the spiral staircase out over the balcony with a low wall four stories up, to the grounds that seemed to fall off the cliff.

"I mean a view is all very well but you'd think they'd put up some kind of fence in the gardens. Our youngest would just run off the end of that just because he could," she said and Simone rubbed her stomach, hoping her kid wouldn't be as simple as Gina's sounded.

In her bedroom Eve was having a meltdown because she had nothing to wear. Lily looked in her vast wardrobe.

"You do seem to have a thing for jeans and vest tops," she said.

"I had a black dress that I liked but I wore it the night of the accident with Ben. Clooney had it dry-cleaned but I can't wear it again. And anyway you're wearing black."

"What about the red one?" Lily asked, pulling one of the only three dresses she could see, one of them being the black dress in a dry-cleaner's see-through bag.

"It's too low-cut."

"OK, the white."

"I'm too white for white."

"So how about jeans and one of your beautiful cashmere V-neck jumpers?"

"Adam will think I haven't made any effort."

"Adam will think you're beautiful."

Eve considered Lily's comment for a moment before making an admission. "I know he likes you but I told him you'd never go for him," she said.

"I know, he told me," Lily said and smiled.

"Interesting."

"He said you were a good friend."

"Yeah, well, he doesn't know me."

"He's right," Lily said. "You are the best of friends."

Neither of the women wanted to get into the past.

Eve hovered on one crutch and pulled down a pair of jeans and a cashmere jumper. "These will do, it's probably a lost cause anyway if he's still mooning over you."

"Oh, I think you've given him something else to think about! He talks about you all the time." Lily took the jumper and jeans from Eve before following her wobbling her way over to the bed on her crutches.

Eve took off her robe and sat in a silk bra and knickers set that Lily imagined cost more than her own entire wardrobe. The scars on her shoulder and legs were still red and angry.

"What does he say?" Eve asked, looking down at the scars and wishing they'd fade and go away. *I don't have forever for you to disappear, you know.*

Lily made a mental note to buy some bio-oil for her friend while helping Eve put on her jumper. She still had trouble raising her left arm. Lily worked around the problem easily.

"Well, he asks lots of questions about when we were kids, what you were like and when he talks about you he grins like stupid teenager. He repeats the things you say and laughs to himself. He's falling for you."

"You don't know that!" Eve snorted.

Lily pulled her jeans up and dragged her off the bed into standing position and Eve held on to Lily's waist while she zipped and buttoned them.

"Yes, I do, because he looks at you the way he used to look at me," she said, relieved for herself and happy for her friend.

"I don't even know if I can fall in love with someone other than Ben Logan."

"Only one way to find out. Now put some make-up on and come outside. I've got to check on the dinner."

When Eve finally emerged everyone was sitting at the dining table drinking, talking and laughing. Lily was being the perfect hostess with Clooney by her side. Music was playing. Gar was taking the piss out of Gina much to everyone's entertainment. She was blushing and saying stop it and Paul was holding Simone's hand and laughing hard. Eve stood back, leaning on her crutches, and watched her friends and even though Ben wasn't there he was never hers anyway and so everything felt right. The room seemed different filled with people and sound. She realised she wasn't alone any more. *I'm home. Finally I'm home.*

Adam turned to see her. He stood up and walked over to her.

"You look stunning," he said and he kissed her on the mouth and when he pulled away she grinned.

"You're fast," she said.

"Not really, I've wanted to do that for a while now."

She leaned in and kissed him again and only stopped when her legs felt like they were going to go from under her and Clooney shouted at her to get a room.

"This *is* my room," she said.

The rest of the night they spent eating Lily's gourmet food, drinking wine, telling stories and laughing. Even Paul opened up once or twice with a few stories of his own.

When it turned midnight and a drunk and emotional Gina had to go home to relieve the baby-sitter, Eve struggled to the door to say goodbye, together with Lily and Simone.

She hugged Lily and told her she had missed her. "Don't ever go away again," she said.

Lily laughed and promised she wouldn't.

"It's good to have you back," she said to Eve. "I was getting a real pain in my ass sitting in that hospital."

Down the hallway, she leant out of the lift and shouted back, "Simone, don't go changing!" She waved as the lift doors were closing.

Lily helped Eve back to the sitting room where she sat with Adam, Clooney, Gar and Paul talking about the old days. Adam and Paul realised they had dated two of the same girls from Mount Anville School and they reminisced about them before Clooney asked if Donald Blair was gay. He wasn't but it led to a conversation about who was gay in the rugby teams they had played against.

"Martin Walsh," Clooney said.

"No way!" Gar said.

"Had him," Paul said.

"Didn't you go out with his sister at one point?" Gar said.

"Yeah."

"Christ!" Gar said. "To think I used to wish I was you." He shook his head. "Now don't get me wrong I wouldn't throw her out of bed for eating peanuts but Martin Walsh!"

"Wasn't he the guy with the cauliflower ears and the smashed nose?" Eve asked, getting up to join Lily in the kitchen area.

"When we actually got together in college he had two missing teeth as well, but there was something about him."

"Christ," Gar said, shaking his head.

Simone laughed. She was sitting on the floor in a yoga position and although she was the only one not drinking she was enjoying herself immensely. "I think I'm really going to like it here," she said, before getting up to pee for the eighth time that night. Paul marvelled at how chilled she was about his past. It was as though she was a miracle sent from heaven but not to save him from damnation as his mother believed but to finally allow him to be comfortable in his own skin. *Thanks, Simone. God, thank you. I love you.*

Adam followed Eve in the kitchen area. Eve was settling herself at the counter and Lily was cleaning it.

"Hellva better night than dinner in Rodney's," he said to Lily.

"It's a better life," she said and she wondered how her kids were and when they'd start picking up their phones when she called. *Give them time, Lily.*

Adam kissed Eve and told her he was going to leave. She wanted him to stay but he was working the next day.

"I'll call you tomorrow," he promised.

There was a taxi waiting for him downstairs. He said goodbye to the boys and stopped to say goodbye to Simone when he met her coming back from the bathroom.

When he was gone Eve grinned at Lily who was making coffee in the hope that the boys would at least pretend to drink it.

"Good kisser," she said, before making a tick sign with her hand.

Simone joined them at the counter. Lily handed her a peppermint tea. She hugged it with her hands. "I've eaten so much I could burst," she said before taking a drink and focusing on Eve. "So are you taking Adam to the wedding?"

"Hadn't thought about the wedding," Eve said.

"Well, start thinking about it."

"Do you think he'd come?"

"With bells on," Lily said.

Simone nodded. "He's a smitten kitten," she said.

"I wonder what sex will be like," Eve said, looking down on herself.

"Like it was before except you won't be as bendy," Lily said.

"Dr Thomas will sort you out in the spa," Simone said. "One Padaghata massage and you'll be circus bendy."

When the night was over and everyone had gone home, Eve was exhausted. Lily helped her to bed and, when she'd turned off the light and closed the door, Eve lay in her bed alone talking to Ben about the night. *Paul and Martin Pigging Walsh. I've heard it all now.*

Clooney helped Lily finish tidying up.

"The next dinner party we have we'll get a caterer in," he said, not liking the idea of Lily doing so much work.

"Over my dead body," she said, happy that he was thinking of staying around at least long enough to have another dinner party. *Live in the moment, Lily, just enjoy the moment.*

When the dishes were done and the counter was cleaned, they parted. He said goodnight and told her he'd be gone before she woke. She nodded and wished him good luck on his trip. He thanked her and they both hovered but it was only for a second before they turned and walked their separate ways.

The next day, two weeks and twenty-four unanswered messages later, Lily turned up in Jack Donovan's garage. Scott was alone as his granddad was out buying parts. He came out of the office, smiling, when the bell that signalled a customer rang but his expression changed when he saw his mother.

He asked her what she wanted.

"World peace," she said.

"Very funny," he said.

"I have more."

He was angry and understandably so. She trod gently.

"How are you?" she asked.

"I've been better."

"And Daisy?"

"She's devastated."

"Things will get better," she said. "I've taken a month's leave from the hospital. I'm going to find a place and when I do you can come live with me."

"We're going nowhere," he said.

"You can think about it."

"You might have left Dad but we're not going to," he said and she could hear Declan's voice again.

"I did leave your dad but I will never leave you," she said.

"Really? Because that's what it looks like, feels like and smells like so you must be talking shit."

"I told you when I find a place –"

"Are you moving in with him?"

"No."

"He's that woman's brother, isn't he?"

"Yes," she said and she wondered how much Declan had said about Eve.

"How long have you been sneaking around behind Dad's back?"

"I couldn't tell your father that Eve was in the hospital because I knew he would try to stop me from seeing her –"

"And *him*."

"And him, yes, his name is Clooney."

"Stupid name."

"What I've done has nothing to do with Clooney," she said.

"Then what?"

"Remember the summer when you were thirteen and you broke your leg on the second day of a month-long stay in France? All the other kids would play all day in the pool and you couldn't so you sat far enough way so as not to be splashed but close enough so that you could hear the kids playing. You were so near to all that fun and freedom but you might as well have been a world away. You were lonely and ignored and you were miserable."

"What's your point?"

"I've been living that summer for twenty years."

"You're saying that you hated life with us?"

"I'm saying I hated my life with your father."

"Are you sorry you had us?"

"No. You kids are the one good thing –"

"He's a mess without you."

"It will get better."

"You've broken his heart," he said and he wasn't accusing her so much as stating a fact.

"It will get better." *You have to have a heart to break it.*

They stood staring at one another for a few moments.

"I should go," she said. "I'll be in touch." She moved to walk away.

"Mum!" he called and she turned around.

"Daisy misses you," he said.

"So tell her to answer her phone," she said and he nodded. "And, Scott, don't let your dad tear you down. When he's in pain he does that so just remember it's not you, it's him."

He said nothing he just pursed his lips tight. He wasn't going to say anything bad about his dad. He might have softened toward his mother momentarily but he was still angry with her and he still blamed her for breaking up his family and destroying his world. *Why do you have to be so selfish? Why can't you just be happy? Why don't you love us enough to stay? How could you leave us?*

Lily walked out the door and when she got to the car she felt like she needed to keep going so she put her bag in the boot and walked to the back of the harbour and up onto the cliff and there she found the spot where she and Eve spent so much of their youth and she sat looking out toward Wales and thought about what she was going to do. *I'm so sorry. I made such a mess of everything. It's all my fault. Please forgive me.*

Chapter 11

From Paris to Peru

Monday 20th August 1990
11:15am

Eve,

I'm so, so, so sorry for not writing before now. I just didn't know what to say. I've started so many letters and they've all ended up either completely crossed out or blank and crumpled in the bin. A lot has happened in the past few weeks and I'm not sure how to tell you or what you'll think of me. I'm not even sure what I think about myself. I'm so confused. I can't stop crying. You probably know that I aced my Leaving Cert (I know Clooney phoned Danny) and it's great news it really is but there's a part of me, and I don't know why, that wishes I'd failed. If I had I'd have to repeat and it would give me more time to think about what I really want. Does that make sense? As you know Declan did well enough and he'll definitely get Medicine in Cork. I haven't spoken to him but he's left lots of messages in the restaurant. The owner is beginning to get really annoyed. I know you did well. Danny told

Clooney. I'm thrilled. I know it doesn't mean anything to you because you're creative and you are going to St Martin's based on your portfolio but it's a great result. How did Paul do? And Gar? I know I should have rung you and I know you think I don't care but I do. It's just all been so weird here.

I wish you were here and then I think it's probably best you're not because you'll kill me. You and Clooney are like my family. There isn't a memory that I have that doesn't include you and him and Danny. Your dad has been the closest thing I've ever had to a father. I love you all. You are the family my mom couldn't ever give me. You know that. You know I love you and you know I love Clooney. I've always loved him and not like a brother, like a boy, like a man, but he was always older and it was never right because he should have been like a brother. I didn't think he felt the same way. I always thought he saw me as the little annoyance that made him laugh or smile every now and again but mostly got under his feet when he was trying to be cool with all the beautiful girls that flocked around him. I never for a moment thought he'd ever think of me like that.

We started spending a lot of time together. At first it was just us messing around together and the only thing missing and out of the ordinary was that you weren't there and then one night he came back to my place and I made him some quiche and we shared some beers. The stupid electricity went because I'd forgotten to get 50p pieces to feed the meter so I lit some candles and we just sat together and talked and when it got cold because that flat is so damp it's a wonder mushrooms don't grow on the walls we got under a blanket together on the sofa and I don't know what happened because one minute we were laughing and then we were kissing and I know this is freaking you out but it was amazing and I was screaming what the hell in my head and I couldn't stop and we slept together and I won't go into it because I know you'll lose it if I do but I think I'm in love with him. For the whole time I didn't even think of Declan once. It was only when he left the next morning that I remembered I had a boyfriend that I loved and I do love Declan. I'm so confused and I feel so bad. I actually feel sick all the time. I can't talk to Declan. I keep ringing and leaving messages with his mother when I know he won't be there and I know he's probably losing it but I just don't know what to say and I can't lie to him.

Clooney and I have been together every day since. He's left the tent and he's staying here with me. I've had some of the best times of my life with him and there are moments when I think I've died and gone to heaven but then the guilt comes and I want to die because I can't turn my back on Declan and I do love him.

I really do and besides Clooney and I are just a fantasy. I'm never going to be his girlfriend. He told me he's leaving. He hasn't told Danny yet so please don't say anything. He's bored with his course and as much as he loves his radio show he's feels he's done all he can do on it. V Kill P is moving to London to be with her girlfriend and he said it just won't work without her. He did an interview in Dublin last month to volunteer building houses in Africa. He's going in a few weeks. He's always been into that stuff and I know he will love it and it will be the adventure he has always craved but when he told me I actually felt my heart breaking in two. He said it like I should be happy for him and I am of course but I can't stop crying because maybe he'll miss me but he won't miss me like I'll miss him. Our family is breaking apart, you're going to London and he's going to Africa and I'm supposed to go to Cork with Declan and if I don't and I will and I do love him but even if I didn't where would I go? What would I do? I have no passion, no scratch that I do, my passion is Clooney but he's leaving me and so he should. I'm not really even his anyway, I'm with Declan who needs me. He would never walk away. I do love him. I'm so confused and scared because I don't know what I want to do or where I want to go. Am I going to study Medicine just because I can? Am I moving to Cork because that's where Declan wants to be? All I know is I'm losing my family, the people I love and without you what am I going to be? I can't believe I've done this to Declan. He can never know. It would destroy him. Please never ever tell him. Tell no one. It's just our secret.

Clooney is coming over tonight and I think I'm going to end it. I keep saying that but then I see him and he's only going to be here for another week so . . . I don't know. I've never been so confused. Please write back to me, please don't be annoyed or let down. I love you. Clooney and I being together doesn't change the fact that you are my best friend. Nothing can change that.

Please tell me what to do. I need your clear thinking.

I'm so sorry,
Lily XXXOOOXXX

* * *

The plane landed in Charles De Gaulle Airport on time. Clooney hadn't drunk much the night before despite the quantity of booze. He was clear-headed and focused on getting to Stephanie. She had emailed him back and told him to meet her in the clinic as she would be there from nine o'clock. He got into a taxi and gave the guy the address and then he sat back and watched Paris whiz by. Neither man spoke. '*Je Realise*' featuring James Blunt was on the radio. James Blunt was one of Stephanie's favourite artists and Clooney didn't know if it was to do with his music or his background as a soldier. It spilled into the music, the pain and anguish, the loss, the immorality and the focus and importance. Death and destruction, however lamentable, was bigger and more important than an ordinary day spent pottering in your local city picking up the latest fashion or talking about a film you want to see. She identified. He listened to the song and lost himself in the streets, the blue street signs, the bridges and the majestic corner buildings. When they reached 10, rue Vivienne he paid in euros and he got out. It was twelve thirty.

He walked inside and asked for Stephanie Banks. He was directed to a room. Stephanie was genuinely glad to see him. She beamed as though they were meeting in a coffee shop or on a sun-soaked beach. Instead she had a hospital gown on and she was lying in a bed and the same yellow toggle stuck in her hand that Eve had for so long. They hugged and she was grateful he came.

"Of course I'd be here," he said, conscious they only had twenty minutes before she'd be taken into theatre.

She smiled and kissed his hand as tears built in her eyes. She would not let them fall. She was made of sterner stuff.

"It's for the best," she said, knowing he was softer than she was.

"I know," he said.

"I just wanted to see you, nothing more," she said.

"You know me so well."

"Well, you are me without the balls," she said and she laughed. It was a hollow laugh. The situation didn't allow her to feel true joy. She sighed and took him in.

It had been a long nine weeks since he'd left. She'd been working solidly since. She'd got into some scrapes while he was away but that was nothing unusual. She'd also come upon a story that might make her career if she played it right. If she didn't she would be sunk, she'd be disgraced and maybe even jailed on some trumped-up charge but she felt she was smart enough to combat whatever was thrown at her and she'd either succeed and she'd make a change or fail and become a victim of the man. Either way the message would get out and although she'd prefer the former, Stephanie Banks didn't care much either way. *That's why I can't be a mother*.

"Tell me your story," she said, ever the journalist.

"I've been offered a job in Peru."

"And?"

"And my sister nearly died, her lover died."

"And?"

"And the girl I loved and walked away from when I was twenty was just raped by her husband."

"And you think you can save her."

"No," he said because he knew only Lily could save Lily.

"Do you still love her?"

"I think I do but then . . ." he said and he put his hand on her stomach.

"We're not bad people," she said and she battled tears again. They were never going to win. Her eyes dried and she tilted her head and smiled.

"We just want different things," he said and took his hand away from her stomach.

"Exactly," she said, "and I choose me."

"And I do the same."

"We're not bad people," she repeated and yet they silently mourned the thickness of her belly and wondered what could have been if they were different people who wanted different things in a different time and place. When she was taken away he smiled and waved and he waited in a corridor watching French TV. She wasn't gone too long, less than an hour. She was asleep for another two. She woke up with him by her side. She was groggy and had cramps. He stayed for an hour and long enough for a chat and to feed her a little toast. When she was sleepy and visiting hours were over, he made his way back to her room in the hotel. She had let them know he was joining her. The receptionist gave him a cardkey to the room that they would share the next evening. He fell on the bed and phoned Eve's. Lily answered. He asked how she was and Lily said she was fine and then they talked for half an hour but in all that time he never told her why he was in Paris and she never asked. *I wish you were here with me now, Lily. I'm such an asshole.*

On the day that her brother went to Paris Eve woke up to a breakfast made by her best friend Lily. They sat together and it was just like old times. They didn't speak, they just enjoyed the silence that comes with knowing someone well enough to shut up. When they were finished Eve picked up her phone and booked a taxi to the hospital. Lily was confused.

"Are you OK?" she asked.

"Fine."

"What are you going back there for?"

"I have a meeting."

"With who?" Lily asked.

"Does it matter?"

Lily didn't know how to answer but she knew Eve well enough to know that she was up to something.

"Do you want me to come with you?"

"No, thanks."

"OK," Lily said. "I'm not going to ask."

"Best not to."

After that Eve received a phone call from the storage facility that was holding her family's furniture. She asked them to return it to the house that they'd picked it up from. When she'd finished the conversation she called Lily.

"It's sorted," she said.

"What's sorted?" Lily asked, coming in from the den where she'd spent twenty minutes cleaning the skirting boards which she complained were a disgrace when Eve had begged her to stop. Lily couldn't relax in the presence of dirt and she needed distraction.

What in hell is the cleaner doing? Eve wondered.

"The house is off the market, the furniture will be back by the end of the week and it's not bad. Dad refurbished in the late nineties and it's yours for as long as you need it."

"Your house?" Lily said, mouth agape.

"The house we grew up in."

"Your house."

"Our house."

"And Clooney?"

"He watched two parents die in that house, you know that. He doesn't want the money from it and I don't need it and you are a part of all that was good in it. I think that Danny would be happy and proud."

Lily cried. "I was never happier than when I was in that house."

"I know."

"Are you sure? I'll pay rent as soon as I get back to work."

Eve didn't care about rent and neither did Clooney but she knew that Lily needed to feel that she was contributing because that's the way Lily was.

"Consider it a trial. If you're happy there and you think you could live happily in the house, buy it."

"It will be a long time before I can afford a house like that," Lily said.

"We'll do you a good deal and anyway the divorce settlement

will more than cover the cost."

"That could take years, especially if Declan fights it which he will."

"Maybe he will and maybe he won't," Eve said. "Either way we can wait."

"It's charity."

"It's friendship."

"It's too much."

"Bullshit, it's just enough."

Eve's taxi man was a Londoner who had left London because he'd fallen in love with a Dublin girl. The money wasn't as good but he maintained it was a better life. He lived close to town and despite the amount of taxis on the road he made a good living because he told her he had the ability to think outside the box. She didn't ask him what that meant, she just accepted his statement as fact because she didn't care enough to talk deeply on the subject. They pulled up to the hospital and he was a gentleman and helped her out of the car. When she was upright, had paid him and was facing the doors, she leaned on her crutches for a moment looking at the hospital name before making her way in.

She stopped at reception and asked for Dr Declan Donovan's office. When asked why she was there, she told the woman that she was there to quote for redecoration. Adam had told her the news of Declan wrecking his office. The gossip had spread across all staff in the hospital. Redecorating made sense. The woman grinned at her and gave her directions. She sat in the waiting area in front of his PA who told her that without an appointment she had no hope of seeing him. Eve was smug.

"I disagree," she said.

"OK, he's in surgery so you'll be waiting."

"That's fine," she said.

She had brought at book and had emptied her bladder before she arrived. He appeared two and a half hours later. He strode in and picked up post from his in-tray and barely acknowledged his PA.

Eve struggled into standing. He turned and saw her and his face turned from shock to stone in one second. She was prepared. She grinned fiendishly, just enough to put him on edge without verging into panto villain.

"Declan," she said.

"Eve," he said and his complexion paled in front of her eyes.

"Do you have a minute for an old friend?" She appeared cool but internally she was a mess. *Keep it together Eve. Focus and get this done.*

He smiled at his PA. "Of course," he said through gritted teeth.

Eve made her way slowly into Declan's office. He closed the door behind her as she sat down. He sat behind his desk and folded his hands under his chin.

"What can I do for you?" he asked.

She laughed. "I think this meeting is more about what I can do to you," she said.

Outside Declan's PA typed up medical notes, oblivious to the fact that her boss was being blackmailed.

Clooney picked up Stephanie the next morning. She was sore but not so much that she didn't want to stop for coffee in Montmarte. She made him sit for an artist who drew caricatures of both of them. They spent a fun and frivolous morning. They enjoyed coffee and croissants and laughed at their keepsake drawings which were destined for a bin. They represented a moment in time and a sad moment at that in cartoon form. It was a distraction and nothing more. When they got back to the hotel it was late enough to eat and they did so in the restaurant. Stephanie was bleeding into a pad. She was raw and uncomfortable. They had something light and then they made their way up to the room. She stripped off and he ran a bath because Stephanie loved her baths. When it was ready she stepped in and he sat outside and held her hand.

"Are you coming in?" she asked.

"No," he said. "I'll mind you from here."

"Bullshit," she said.

He moved around to the top of the bath and he massaged her

head. She rested against his hands.

"My dad says God will judge us if we're wicked as opposed to righteous."

"You know I don't believe in God."

"I do."

"And it's all relative. Your dad killed countless men and possibly women and children in the name of his country. You just report on it. You let go of a baby not born. Which one of you is wicked?"

"He believes in what he's done."

"And you don't."

"I acted selfishly, he didn't."

"He killed living, breathing, terrified people in the name of war. Our baby was eleven weeks old, it didn't know day or night, a touch or love, a smile, she or he had never cried, never experienced grief or sadness. That little one didn't battle and wasn't afraid. The people that die every day in war know what it is to breathe, to pray, to beg, to suffer, to lose, to die and to grieve. If our baby suffered it was for one second. Those people your father has affected are intimate with suffering – they are fighters who clung to life. If anyone knows what I mean, you do." And she did.

"We are not bad people," she said.

"No, we're not."

She didn't cry because she couldn't bring herself to but she let him stroke her hair and lull her into comfort. When he helped her out of the bath and covered her in a large towel and brought her into the room, she lay on the bed and he presented her with a silk scarf that he'd managed to pick up when she was asleep. It wasn't exactly like the one she shoved down her knickers but it was close and expensive enough. She lay in the bed and hugged it.

"Sometimes I wish I was different," she said.

"I know how you feel," he said.

He got into bed with her and held her tight and they slept together and the next day they lay together and when she cramped and battled with bleeding, he was there to ferry her from toilet to bath to bed. They ate good food, talked and laughed, and in their own way mourned a life that never was.

Clooney waited until Stephanie left on her flight to Afghanistan.

The procedure had taken more out of her than she'd expected, both physically and emotionally. When they said goodbye it was final and worthy of their relationship. They hugged one another tightly and they both accepted they wouldn't see one another again. It was the parting of two kindred spirits destined not to love one another for whatever reason.

I will miss you, Stephanie Banks.

I will miss you, Clooney Hayes.

When he waved her goodbye and she disappeared behind airport security, the load he carried started to lighten and he moved toward his gate and toward home and Lily.

When Eve returned home she sat on her high bar stool at the counter and Lily made some coffee.

"I saw Scott on the street today. I called to him but he refused to stop," Lily said.

"He'll get over it."

"I just want to know how he did in his college exams."

"I'm sure he did very well and when he stops acting like a selfish dick he'll tell you."

"He's just torn. His father has made it clear to the children it's him or me. He's scared, that's all."

"You'll get them back," Eve said, savouring the memory of the recent conversation she'd just had with Declan. *And sooner than you think.*

"He's always got one over me."

"Those days are gone."

"Not while he's got my kids."

"Everything will be fine," Eve said and just as she spoke Lily's phone rang and she saw Daisy's name flash on the screen.

"It's Daisy," she said, beaming. "It's Daisy." She answered the phone as she walked toward Eve's spare bedroom. "Daisy," she said in a voice full with tears and thanks. She closed the door behind her and when she returned she was happy and confused and also a little upset.

"Daisy is coming to live with me as soon as I get into the house."

Happy.

"How did she know I was moving into a house?" *Confused.*

"Declan phoned her and told her he was too busy to take care of her. She's devastated." *Upset.*

"Why would he do that?" she asked.

"He's a selfish, hurtful sociopath," Eve said.

"He is a sociopath," Lily admitted to herself out loud and for the first time. "Still, I don't understand. He wouldn't give up his power like this. It's not like him."

"Maybe he's seen the light," Eve said and inside she was dancing.

"There's something going on."

"Who cares?" Eve said. "You're getting your baby back. He's out of your life."

"Do you think Scott will forgive me?" Lily asked.

"Of course."

"He's old enough to decide where he wants to live."

"So let him."

"She could barely speak, she was crying so hard," Lily said. "I think I hate him."

"Good, that's healthy. I'm proud of you."

Daisy had done exactly as she was told in the aftermath of her mother's departure. She had refused to speak to her and studiously avoided all her calls just as her father had instructed. She had done all the jobs her father asked of her. She had been on her best behaviour. She was quiet and not at all demanding. She wondered what she had done to make him suddenly call her up in the middle of the day and tell her he didn't want her living with him any more.

"Call your mother. Tell her to pick you up."

"But, Dad?"

"Start packing. You'll be moving out as soon as she moves into that house."

"But, Dad."

"*Daisy!*" he roared. "Just do what I tell you! Phone that slut you have for a mother and tell her that you'll be moving in with her and do it now."

She was stunned; it was like she had been punched in the stomach. She was shaking when she made the call. She hated her mother for leaving but she also missed that joy and lightness she had brought to their house. It was dark and empty without her. Even when Declan wasn't shouting and screaming and when he was trying to be what dads are supposed to be, it was difficult and hard work for him. Daisy felt sorry for her dad. It didn't stop her from fantasising about leaving him but when he ordered her to leave she was bereft. He had told the kids he needed and loved them desperately and now he was making her leave. *What did I do to change your mind?* Daisy's mother had abandoned her and now her father was kicking her out. Lily had tried to soothe her but she couldn't hear her mother over her own sobs and how could she believe anything she said anyway? She lay on her bed and cried herself to sleep. It was only five o'clock when she closed her eyes and drifted off, she didn't wake at seven when her father came home and heated up an M&S dinner in the microwave or when Scott ran up stairs and changed before running out to get drunk with Josh, Cedric and Ethan. Neither of them checked on her but it didn't matter. She slept until hunger woke her the next morning at eight and when both men had left for work, leaving her with another long day alone and waiting to be thrown out of her own house.

Lily was like a cat on a hot tin roof. She just wanted to get into the house and get her daughter back. On the day that the estate agent handed Eve the keys back, Lily insisted on driving back to her old house to pick Daisy up to show her their new place. Eve went with her. She parked the car in the driveway.

"It's nice," said Eve.

Lily wouldn't get out of the car.

"What if he's there?" she said.

"He's never there during the day. Besides, you have me."

"No offence but you are currently a cripple."

"I could beat him to death with my crutches."

Lily smiled. "Declan might not be the only sociopath in my life."

Eve shrugged – even shrugging hurt her shoulder. The physiotherapist that came to her house was some kind of Nazi hell-bent on making some kind of name for herself by having Eve recover in record time. The idea appealed but the reality was most uncomfortable. Eve was particularly sore. *I could still take him.*

Lily decided to ring Daisy and hope that'd she pick up. She did after she let it ring out twice. When Lily said they were outside the house in the car she came to her window and Eve could see Lily's twelve-year-old daughter peering out. Lily asked her to go with them to see the house. She said no and that she was busy with Tess and besides her dad had told her not to leave the house. Lily told her she would love to show the new house to both of them, after all that's where Tess would be visiting her. Then there was an intense whispered debate between the girls. Daisy hung up and Lily grinned at Eve when the two girls appeared in the doorway and walked down the path.

Tess actually bounded up to Lily where she stood beside the car and hugged her tightly.

"I really missed you, Lily."

"I missed you too, Tess."

Daisy took an age to walk down the path. She had no hugs for her mother. She stared at Eve.

"Is that her?" she asked.

"I'm Eve."

"She's my friend," Lily said.

"She's a bitch," Daisy said.

"And your father is still as charming as ever," Eve said, knowing exactly where the child's attitude was coming from. "Now get in the car, we haven't got all day."

Lily tried to hug her daughter but she pulled away and got into the back seat beside her friend. She was silent on the journey. In contrast, Tess spoke all the way.

"You're the jewellery-maker," she said to Eve.

"Designer," Eve said.

"My mum says you're loaded and went out with loads of famous people."

"You're mum's right."

"Is it true you went out with Robert Downey Junior before he went mental on drugs?"

"Which one is he again?" Eve asked.

"*Chaplin,*" Lily said, immediately engaged. She didn't know a lot of celebrities because she wasn't much interested in magazines but she knew him. *I love him.* Lily would see magazines lying around the hospital but every cover looked the same and all the banner headlines read the same. They were filled with faces she didn't know and with things she couldn't afford. It was depressing. Meanwhile her best pal possible shagged Robert Downey Junior.

"*Iron Man,*" Tess said.

"Oh, I saw that on the plane," Eve said. "No." She shook her head. "Not my type."

Tess laughed. "You're cool," she said.

Daisy gave Tess a dirty look. Tess didn't care.

"So is he on drugs?" Eve asked.

"No. That was ages ago. He was in prison and everything. He's much better now."

"I wouldn't fancy his chances in prison," Eve said.

"Eve!" Lily said.

"It's true," Tess said. "Some people are just too pretty."

"OK, change the subject," Lily ordered.

Tess complied. "So do you live in a mansion?"

"No."

"Do you have servants?"

"I have a cleaner but Lily is better than her so I might have to fire her."

"Was the guy who died in the car accident your boyfriend?"

"How did you know about that?"

"It was in the paper."

"Was it?"

"Duh," Tess said. "You're famous."

Lily shrugged. "There were a few journalists hanging around the hospital in the early days. You were out of it and we got rid of them."

"Was he your boyfriend?"

"Is that what it said?" Eve said, clearly panicked.

Lily put her hand on her knee. "No. It wasn't," she said. "It said you were business partners and that you were going to sell your jewellery in his supermarkets. It said you'd gone from high end to

329

low end to no end."

Eve laughed. She was relieved that the local papers still showed as little concern about the facts as they had when she was last home. When her father died, some red-top journalists had come to the funeral to get a photograph of her in black and a comment. She told them to go to hell. The line under the photograph had read: '*Eve Hayes' Father's Hell.*' Eve rarely suffered from press intrusion. When she was in America she was one of many uber-successful people who didn't court the press and when she was home she lived under the radar, never attending the many press events or parties filled with very important strangers that she'd been invited to in the early days. With every no-show or rejection the invites petered out until there were none. She had no interest in forging some sort of name for herself as a minor celebrity in Ireland. She had retired. She was looking for peace and as a result something relatively newsworthy had to happen to gain media attention but she wasn't famous enough for them to dig for stories. *Thankfully. I'm so sorry, Ben. Where are you today? Here? There? Nowhere?*

They arrived at the house and Lily stopped the car. She smiled a big wide smile. Her eyes sparkled. Eve handed her the key and she squeezed it tight. It was a beautiful blue-sky day, the tree lined driveway led to the large white house with a pink-flowered creeper which covered most of the walls. The door was still a beautiful dark blue. The wooden bench still sat under the big oak tree in the centre of the front garden. Lily's heart raced. She looked at Eve.

"I feel like I'm home," she said.

"You are," Eve said, looking at her friend so happy and moved by the place she grew up in. She wished she could feel the same about it but, like Clooney, Eve had lost too much in that house for her to ever feel about it the way Lily did.

They got out of the car.

Tess loved the house. "It's amazing and you're only a few stops away on the DART!" she said to Daisy who was subdued and standoffish.

Lily opened the door and that led to the big wide hallway. She held the big old mahogany banister that curled at the end and looked at the freshly painted walls that Eve had insisted on getting done when the furniture had been taken out. There was no evidence of the family pictures that had hung there but in her mind Lily saw them all. The old wooden floors were varnished and gleamed. They took Lily to the large open kitchen which led to the patio and garden that she and Eve had spent so much time in. She looked out the large glass patio doors to see the swing-set she and Eve had spent most of their childhood on and she clapped her hands together.

"I loved that old swing-set!" she said before biting her lip.

"I know, I know," Eve said.

Lily surveyed the kitchen. It was very different, all mod cons with an Aga cooker and a separate wall oven and microwave.

"Your dad did this?" Lily asked with wonder.

"He had a girlfriend who liked to cook," Eve said and she wondered how Jean McCormack was doing. In that moment she decided to call her. She was a lovely woman. She had made her father's final years very happy. She wondered why it hadn't occurred to her before but not for long as Lily's hand-clapping and sighing distracted her.

She followed Lily out into the garden with Tess and Daisy in tow. Tess sat on the swing and Daisy sat on the one next to her.

"It's just like yours," Tess said.

"No, it isn't," Daisy said.

Lily looked at the trees that had grown so tall that she could only barely make out Terry the Tourist's old place. She walked inside and headed down the hall into the sitting room with its big old window that looked out onto the front lawn featuring the bench and old oak tree. She traced her hand around the fireplace. She opened the big white wooden doors that separated it from the dining room. She'd forgotten how big it was, it was the room used least in the house. She found Eve sitting on the stairs.

"Can I go up?" she said.

"It's your house."

Lily took the stairs two by two and Tess ran in and followed her. "Wait for me, Lily!"

Daisy appeared in the doorway. Eve looked at her.

"So are you always this miserable and annoying or is this just because your life has been turned upside down?"

Daisy leaned on the doorway. "Is my mum having an affair with your brother?"

"No." Eve said. "But they do care about one another. They always have. Your mother practically grew up in this house. She was loved here."

"She was loved at home."

"No, she wasn't. Daisy, you don't see that now because you're a kid and kids are selfish assholes who think the world revolves around them. You were happy so she must have been, right?"

Daisy blinked but said nothing.

Eve nodded to herself. "Your mother put your dad, Scott and you before herself for nineteen years. She worked, cleaned the house, baked cakes, told stories, cooked all day and night. She had no friends, no spare time and no life. She was on edge, and busy protecting you from your dad's frustrations, paranoia and temper. She was lonely and miserable and she couldn't do it any more."

"You're making my dad sound like he's evil or something."

"Your dad's a dick, Daisy, but your mother won't say that because she doesn't want to hurt you."

"But you don't mind hurting me?"

"I'm a stranger to you and I'll bet what I've said about him is nothing in comparison to what he's said to you about your mother. Does he mind hurting you? Think about it," she said and she got up slowly and stood with her crutches.

"He's my dad."

"And she's your mum so if you're going to stand up for him and his imperfections, the very least you could do is the same for your mum."

"You think you know it all."

"No, I don't," Eve said. "But I know more than you. Tell your mother I'll be in the car."

She hobbled outside, leaving Daisy to stare up the stairs after her mother and Tess.

Lily dropped Eve off at the apartment and took the girls for something to eat in Eddie Rocket's. They had ordered and were sitting in the booth with Lily facing both the girls.

"You didn't say what you thought about the house?" she said.

"It's nice," Daisy said.

"What about your room? Do you like it?"

"It's nice."

"I love it," Tess said.

"What about Scott?" Daisy said.

"He'll be in the room on the left."

"Does he know about the house?" Daisy asked.

"I haven't shown it to him yet."

"So that's it, we're all just going to leave my dad?" Daisy said and her eyes filled up.

Lily tried to take her hand but she pulled away. "You'll still see him. You can visit and stay at weekends if you want. He's still your dad."

"Are you going to move *him* in?"

"Who?"

"The man with the stupid name."

"No."

"But you will at some point. After all, it is his house."

"No. He doesn't live in Ireland. He'll be going soon."

"When?"

"Soon."

"Do you love him?"

Lily blushed and stammered and she really didn't handle the question very well at all. Of course she loved Clooney but they weren't going to be a couple as much as she would have liked that. They were never meant to be anything more than they already were. *He was my family first, Daisy.* Daisy picked at her food. She was like her mother – when she was stressed or sad she found it hard to swallow. She had lost weight just as Lily had gained weight. Clooney had insisted on feeding her up and she had filled out – she was still tiny but her bones no longer stuck out. *I'll do the same for you when you're home with me, Daisy.*

Tess was just happy that nothing had to really change. Daisy would still be going to the same secondary school with her in September and Lily was back in her life. She had really missed her kindness and warmth. She had enough distance to see what Daisy couldn't or wouldn't. *You're so lucky, Daisy. Sometimes I close my eyes and I wish I was you.*

Lily dropped Tess off at her home. Her mother appeared out of nowhere and practically ran to the car to get the gossip.

"I heard," she said.

"Everything's fine," Lily said.

"Tess was devastated and poor Daisy – are you alright, Daisy?"

"I'm fine."

"I hear you're living with that designer, Eve Hayes. I can only imagine what the place is like," she said.

"I'll be moving into my own place soon," Lily said. "Tess will always be welcome."

"That's good of you," she said.

"I should go," Lily said and she put her foot down and left the woman standing on the street.

"How many years have I dropped that child off and it's the first time she's ever bothered to come to speak to me," she said. "Bloody people!"

She dropped Daisy off outside the house.

"Are you coming in?" Daisy said.

"No."

"Fine," Daisy said and she tramped up the path.

Lily called her. "Daisy!"

She turned.

"I love you and I will make it up to you."

"How can you?"

"By being happy," Lily said.

"At least someone is," Daisy said and she put the key in the door and closed it behind her.

Adam arrived in Eve's with a picnic basket. It was still early enough to eat outside. He insisted that they go down to the grounds and sit on a blanket on the grass looking out at the sea. He helped Eve down onto the blanket and he propped her up with cushions he took out of the car.

"You think of everything," she said.

He opened a bottle of wine but neither of them was in the mood for drinking. Instead they just lay on the blanket, looking up at the darkening blue sky and talking. Eve told him about Lily moving into the house and that Declan was letting go of the kids. He propped up on his arm and gazed at her.

"Doesn't sound like him," he said.

"No, it isn't like him."

"Does his decision have anything to do with the medical records you had me pull the other day?"

"Yes," she said.

"Are you ever going to tell me what happened?"

"Some day," she said and he nodded and leaned over and kissed her. They kissed for a long time, so long in fact it reminded her of Ben and being a teenager when kissing was king and it made the world spin faster. Adam made the world spin faster or maybe it was only because of her dizzy spells, she wasn't quite sure.

They talked about his job and how stressful it was. He was fascinated that she had retired and asked her all about her plans.

"I have none."

"Are you scared?"

"No."

"So you can just walk away from your life's work and your whole identity?"

"Yeah."

"And you don't miss it?"

"Not one bit," she said and they fell silent. "I told you I'm retired."

"You'll get bored," he said.

"Maybe," she said.

"What about marriage?"

"What about it?"

"Is that something you want?"

"Lily told me you don't do marriage. Is that why you're asking?"

"Partly that and partly I just want to know what you think."

"I think it's a nice day out but a piece of paper doesn't guarantee anything and that makes it redundant."

He nodded and smiled. "Always so clear-headed."

"Some people see that as me being cold."

"I'm not one of them."

"So why are you so against marriage?"

He lay back down and faced the sky. He told her that when he was seven his father left his mother for another woman. The woman became pregnant and she wanted to be married. Divorce wasn't allowed and so he sought an annulment and, despite being married for seven years and having a seven-year-old son together and despite having no grounds, he was granted one on the basis that he had been coerced into marriage because of pregnancy. He went on to marry the other woman and they had four children. Adam's mother never really recovered. She never allowed herself to get close to another man and she died alone of a massive heart attack at the age of sixty.

"Did you ever see him?" Eve asked.

"No."

"Did you care?"

"Yes."

"You shouldn't have. It's better to have no dad than a bad one."

"How would you know? I hear yours was the greatest dad in the world."

"It just doesn't make sense to waste time on someone who doesn't want you," she said, "especially when there are so many people who do." She grinned and he leaned over and kissed her again. "When are we going to have sex?"

He laughed and shook his head. "When you're feeling stronger."

"I feel strong now," she said.

"OK, well then, soon."

"You're fobbing me off," she said.

"No. I'm giving you some time."

"It's time I don't want."

"When is the wedding?"

"Two weeks," she said.

"OK," he said, "we'll do it then."

"I haven't even asked you to the wedding."

"But you're going to."

"I'm not waiting two more weeks."

"Yes, you are."

"For God's sake!"

"You know, for an atheist you call out to God's name a lot."

"You should hear me in the sack," she said and smiled.

"And Jesus Christ and –"

"And I say holy shit too but it doesn't mean that I think there is a blessed turd sitting at the right hand side of the Lord," she said and he laughed.

"Good point."

They lay together until it got chilly and when it did he helped her inside. When he was leaving she asked him if she was really going to have to wait another two weeks and he said yes but he'd make it worth the wait.

"Well, you better be wearing bells then!" she shouted as the lift closed.

Eve was in bed when Clooney got home. Lily was sitting in the lounge area with her feet up, drinking a glass of wine and enjoying one of the many books from Eve's library. She jumped up when he arrived, clearly glad to see him. He looked jaded. He was quiet. She poured him a glass of wine and asked if he was hungry. He was. He sat on one of the barstools at the island and watched her survey the fridge and pull things from the pantry, chop and cook. She was relaxing to watch, she made preparing a meal out of thin air look easy. She sat with him while he ate the most delicious pasta dish he had ever tasted.

"You should have been chef."

"I should have been a lot of things," she said.

He lifted the fork up to her mouth and she opened and swallowed.

"Did you eat today?"

"Yes," she said.

"Good."

"I was in the house," she said and she grinned. "Thank you."

337

"Don't thank me. I'm just happy you are happy."

"I am," she said. "Declan isn't fighting me for the kids. It's so unlike him."

Clooney didn't say anything. Instead he just insisted she take another bite of food.

"How was Paris?"

"Sad," he said.

"Should I ask why?"

"I'd prefer if you didn't."

"OK."

They talked for a while after dinner and when it was past midnight Lily said goodnight and she made her way into Eve's spare room. Clooney pulled out the sofa in Eve's office. When he went to the hot press to get clean sheets and pillows, he stood briefly outside Lily's room. He leaned on her door and wondered if she was awake or asleep and if she wanted him like he wanted her. She opened the door and he fell forward. She laughed.

"Are you alright?" she asked as he righted himself.

"I missed you," he said.

"I missed you too."

And she lifted onto her tip-toes and she kissed him and when her soft lips hit his he melted into her and after that there was no parting them. He lifted her up onto his hips and he carried her across the room and he was ever so careful to gently place her onto the bed. He found his place between her legs and he was careful to make sure she was comfortable and she wanted him. He was gentle and sensual and when they touched there was heat and she wanted him like she'd never wanted anyone before. When they were sated they lay together fizzing, relaxed and at the same time mentally energised, and she opened her heart.

"I shouldn't have pushed you away all those years ago," she said.

He traced his finger on her chin. "You didn't."

"I was so scared," she said.

"I never understood that, till now."

"I did love him."

"He needed you," he said, knowing that Lily always yearned to be needed.

"You didn't," she said with eyes leaking.

"I'm sorry."

"My fault. We are what we are."

He brushed away her tears and they lay together in one another's arms and even though she was still scared about her future and that of her kids, she was happy and she realised she hadn't been happy in a really long time. *I remember now,* she thought and Clooney asked her why she was smiling.

"I'm happy." She admitted. "I'm actually happy."

"Good. I'm happy too."

"Where will you go to next?"

"Let's not talk about that now."

"Why not? You're the man who leaves," she said, acknowledging that she had overheard him talking to Adam days before. "It's OK. I'm not eighteen any more. The life I wanted I got and I didn't like it."

"I've been offered a job in Peru."

"I've never been to Peru."

He grinned. "Are you thinking of coming to visit me?"

"I think I might."

"I'd really like that," he said and he kissed her before they fell into a deep and peaceful sleep in one another's arms.

Chapter 12

Where Croagh Patrick meets
the shores of Clew Bay

Thursday 23rd August 1990

Lily,

I don't know what to say. Your letter finally arrived yesterday. It's, as you say, been a long confusing few weeks. When the results came out and you didn't write or call, Declan and I were really worried. Then Clooney told Danny you did so well and he told me and I told Declan and we really didn't know what to think when we didn't hear from you. Declan kept asking me why you weren't in touch. I felt sorry for him. He was so sad and lonely and I couldn't understand what was keeping you from us. Of course now I know. It was a shock. I knew you and Clooney were close but I never for a moment thought that you'd be together. I suppose that's because I'm emotionally stunted, at least that's probably what you and Clooney are saying. As far as I was concerned he was like your older brother. It was a shock. I think it was mean

of you not to write and to leave me hanging. I was worried
and thinking all sorts. By leaving me and Declan alone up
here worrying about you, I felt like I was put in a spot
and I had to be there for him or something, I don't know.
It was all so frustrating. You just dumped us and I don't
want to talk about you and Clooney because it's just
stupid. How could you be so mean and stupid? You talk
about love and what it means but when it comes down to
it you're as clueless as I am. Ben and I are over. We broke
up last night. Paul's parents were away so he held a party
at his house and Ben brought Billy along and they were
drunk because they'd played an afternoon gig and they'd
been drinking since. Ben kept pestering me about London. He
told me he didn't want me to go and asked if I could find
a college closer to home, he'd even done some research and
gave me a list of places that are nowhere near as cool as
St Martin's and said that I'd have to apply for next year.
It's an argument we've been having on and off since the
results came out. He thinks my results are good enough
to get me into the National College of Art & Design but I
don't want to go there, I want to go to St Martin's in
London. Last night he told me that if I wouldn't apply to
NCAD he'd leave his course and come to London with me.
Just like that. He was drunk and Billy was pissed off
because he didn't even consider the band and he said he
loved me and if I really loved him I'd stay or at least talk
about him coming with me. It was so stupid. He was
messy and argumentative and I was already on edge having
just read your letter. He pushed all the wrong buttons, he
called me insensitive and cold and I said he was a stupid
boy and said I wasn't willing to give up my dream to be
with him after just one summer and he was a fool if he
was willing to give up his band. Billy was on my side - he
threw a beer at Ben and called him names. They got into a
fight and I left and went inside. I met Declan on the

stairs. He had a black eye. I asked him what happened and he burst into tears. He was drunk too. We were all drunk. I brought him into the bathroom and cleaned the cut over his eye. It was really deep and I told him he needed stitches but he said it would be fine. It had stopped bleeding but it was a hole in his face. He kept drinking from a bottle of vodka. I asked him how it happened and he said he was mugged. He wasn't because his wallet was in his pocket but he wasn't going to tell me so I didn't push. We went into Paul's room just to talk. Declan was devastated he hadn't heard from you and I was feeling really guilty because I knew you were with my brother. We drank some more and bitched. I told him about Ben just to change the subject from you and suddenly he knew what was what and he put Ben and me down saying we were only a silly summer fling and Ben was an idiot and basically all the things that I'd said to Ben but hearing them from Declan really annoyed me. I told you I was drunk. He said that I'd forget about Ben because as much as I thought I loved him I hadn't a clue what real love was. Of course he meant that he knew which was annoying bearing in mind he hadn't heard from you in weeks and you were sleeping with my brother. I flipped. I told him. I said you were probably sleeping with Clooney as we spoke. He got very quiet and the second I said it I regretted it. I tried to talk to him and tell him it meant nothing and that Clooney was going away in September. He looked like I'd ripped his heart out. Even as drunk as I was, I could see the damage I'd done. I didn't mean it, I was just too angry and frustrated and he has a way of lording it over everyone like he knows best and I just wanted to hurt him but not that much. He started to shake and to sob and I'd never heard sobs like that before. I sat beside him and hugged him and he hugged me back and cried on my shoulder and then he kissed me and I don't know why but I kissed him back.

I've been trying to work out why I did that all day but I can't tell you why because I don't know and I'm not going to blame being drunk because I knew what was happening. He started to take off my top and I let him and then I realised what we were doing and I tried to stop but he didn't listen and he's so strong. He pulled up my skirt and he was kissing me so that I couldn't say stop it. I tried to hold him off but it was like I wasn't even there and then we were actually having sex. That's when Ben came in. He just looked at us and Declan stopped for a moment then told him to close the door on his way out and I was just shocked. I couldn't speak. I tried but I just couldn't work out what was happening. Ben just ran and I wanted to go after him but I couldn't move. He left the door open but Declan didn't even notice - he just kept going and going, digging into me and I can't describe the pain. You probably think I deserved it, maybe I did. I couldn't swallow, my ears were ringing and I kept thinking this was a bad dream. Afterwards Declan cried and cried and said that we did to you what you did to him but I didn't want to do anything to you. He hugged me and thanked me for being there for him. I just sat there numb and I didn't know what to say. I was angry at you, yes, of course I was angry but I didn't want to do that to you or Clooney or to Ben. I feel sick and today Billy came by and he was shouting, saying I had ruined Ben's life. I reminded him that the last time I saw them they were fighting. He told me that I was a cold bitch and if I didn't want to be with Ben I should have just said something as opposed to fucking the first guy who looked at me. I didn't do that, I swear, Lily, I had no intention of having sex with Declan. I never wanted him and I wouldn't do that to you. I don't know what happened. I know you hate me by now. You don't care that I've spent my whole day in hospital. When Billy stopped shouting he realised that I was bleeding.

Something is wrong, I said. He brought me to A&E. They are keeping me in. I'm writing to you from a temporary bed in A&E. You probably think I deserve that and maybe I do. Dad's away on a junket so don't worry, he won't find out. I know I have a nerve asking you but please don't tell Clooney. If I could take it back I wouldn't have said anything. I was just so angry at you and Clooney and Ben and Declan and I know it's no excuse. Billy said he'd post this for me. I told him it was important that it goes today because if I don't send it today I never will and you deserve the truth. I want you to know I'm really sorry. I've never felt worse in my life. Ben is gone. He won't talk to me and I don't blame him. Billy has promised he won't say a word about today, probably for Ben's sake as much as mine or maybe more for his sake. He's still really angry with me but he's here and that's something. I keep thinking if it was the other way around would I forgive you and the answer is I don't know. I hope I would but I can't say. Life is confusing at the best of times and I don't know what I can say except that I'm so sorry. Please forgive me, Lily. I don't know what my life would be like without you. I love you and miss you and you can marry my brother if you want.

Love,
Eve

* * *

Lily was desperately upset when Scott refused to leave his father to move in with her. He told her in no uncertain terms on the street outside his grandfather's garage that he was old enough to decide where he wanted to live and he chose his dad. He wanted nothing to do with her, her new house, man and life, and sadly Lily had no option but to accept his stance. *Please forgive me, Scott. I miss you.*

Eve had not been so accepting. *Cheeky little bastard.* She watched Lily tear herself apart and even Clooney couldn't make the pain go away.

"The house will be empty and cold, what will he live on, doesn't he realise his father is never there? And when he's frustrated who does Scott think will be on the receiving end of his anger? He'll twist him up and spit him out, he'll spread his poison and he'll make my son hate me. I might lose him forever."

Clooney was soothing and sympathetic, Eve not so much as she was bored listening to Lily whine.

"Put a sock in it, Lil, he'll come around."

"You don't know that."

"Of course I do," Eve said as though she was the oracle and was programmed to explicate the human psyche.

Lily argued that business wasn't as complex as people and although Eve always got it right in business she was out of her depth when it came to understanding the needs of her children. Eve disagreed, believing that she was perfectly situated to see the world through her children's eyes.

"They're self-centred and self-righteous," she said, pointing to herself, "I'm self-centred and self-righteous so I think I'm the perfect person."

Eve went to the garage to try to talk to Scott despite promising Lily that she wouldn't interfere. Jack offered her tea and she politely declined, asking for just a few moments of Scott's time. Jack was happy to let his grandson go for a coffee with Eve, asking only that he brought one back when he returned.

They sat together in a coffee shop, staring at one another sullenly.

"You look more like your mum," she said.

"So they say."

"Lucky for you," she said.

"What do you want?"

"Did your dad ask you to stay with him?"

"No, and none of your business anyway."

"You're right, it's not. I just want to make sure that staying in that house is your idea."

"Why do you care?"

"Because when I was your age I thought I had it all figured out and so did your mother but here's the thing: we didn't have a clue. We hadn't even begun to understand the world and the people around us."

"Well, I'm not you and this isn't the 1800's."

She laughed a little. "Funny," she said.

"I'm staying because he's my dad, it's my home and I'm not leaving."

"I feel like I should say something to shine a light but I don't know where to shine it."

"You sound like the nut-job that passes the garage every morning holding a placard with the picture of a foetus on it and shouting about its hands and feet."

"She gave me the finger yesterday," Eve said and Scott smiled.

He liked her he couldn't help it. He noticed how beautiful she was and, even though she was on crutches, she still had a certain grace.

Eve sighed; she hadn't really thought it through. She hated Declan but his son loved him and she wasn't the heartless bitch she pretended to be. She needed to make sure that Declan hadn't broken the terms of their agreement and it was clear he hadn't. Scott wanted to stay with him for his own reasons.

"So what's this about shining a light?" he said.

"I did something that really hurt your mother years ago and I lost her and it was incredibly painful and . . ."

"And?"

"And picture your life without her because if you think that stamping your feet and hiding in a corner is going to change the way things are you're wrong. She's left your dad, there's no going back. So decide whether you love and respect her enough to support her or you don't."

"She just walked out on him and us."

"I understand you love your father," she said, "but that's not what happened."

"She's destroyed him," he said and he was quiet and his eyes filled.

"She saved herself."

"You don't understand."

"I promise I do and I can see why you'd want to help and protect your father. It's a good thing, but punishing your mother is wrong and you know it. The battle lines that were drawn are gone. You don't need to pick one parent over the other. It's time to move on."

He sat silently for a moment or two. She wasn't sure if he was going to get up and walk away or if he was actually considering his mother's point of view.

"I'll come once a week for dinner," he said.

"And two Sundays a month."

"One Sunday a month."

She smiled and put out her hand and he shook it. "That's a good start," she said and handed him fifty euro to pay for three coffees and a sandwich.

"Keep the change," she said and left him to stand there and watch her make her way to the taxi cab she had waiting outside. Eve normally didn't interfere in other people's lives, she simply didn't care enough, but Lily had always brought out the lioness in Eve.

She felt elated and even a little smug as she sat in the back of that car. Lily felt too much guilt and loyalty to her children and their father regardless of his actions to really fight for herself but Eve wouldn't rest until she had her children back on side and he was as alone and powerless as he deserved to be.

The week before the wedding was a busy one. Lily spent most days cleaning the house that Eve had paid a team of cleaners to clean less than three months before. When she was alone she'd walk around the house listening to the faint echoes of her childhood. Her heart was so full she felt at times it would burst. Clooney helped her hang curtains and paint walls and when the furniture finally arrived he helped her move it in while Eve sat on the sofa and pointed her crutches toward walls and spaces. When the furniture was in, Lily and Clooney spent a day in IKEA. They came home with two cars filled with vases, pots, pans, cups, plates, saucers, duvet sets, pictures, picture frames, rugs and plants.

Clooney seemed a little haunted, having lost all sense of time in the shop. "It's just like Vegas but not fun."

When the house was pretty as a picture and her daughter's room was ready and waiting, Lily drove up to her house alone. She insisted that Clooney or Eve didn't come. Although she was nervous of Declan she felt stronger and she needed to show her daughter that from now on they were a team, she was her mother and Daisy would come first. Clooney and Eve understood and although they were both privately nervous about Lily being in Declan's presence without them, they supported her decision. She rang the doorbell and her hand shook a little. Adrenaline rushed through her body, she was filled with trepidation and excitement.

Declan opened the door, Daisy was sitting on the stairs and beside her was a large suitcase. Lily said hello and Declan glowered at her. She looked past him and toward Daisy whose eyes were red and face swollen.

"It's time to go, Daisy," she said.

Daisy stayed on the stairs.

"Daisy, it's OK, you can see your dad whenever you want," Lily said but Daisy stayed on the stairs.

It was as though she was glued there, unable to move a muscle.

Declan slowly turned to his daughter, he swallowed hard and when he spoke his voice was fragile and threatened to break.

"Daisy, do what your mother says."

She looked up at him with red-rimmed eyes and met with his cold stare and they locked.

"Do you really want me to go, Dad?" she said and he bit the inside of his cheek and nodded once.

Her eyes filled again and chubby tears fell and the sounds she made were of pure pain. She looked at her mother, silently begging her to make everything right. Lily wanted to run to her and hold her in her arms but Declan was between them and she felt that there was an invisible wall preventing her from entering. She was an uninvited vampire sucking the life out of her family. She was forced to observe the pain she had caused by leaving from a distance. Daisy stood up and when she tried to pick her case up, it was too heavy. Declan picked it up and shoved it roughly at Lily. Daisy moved to walk past her dad and as she did he grabbed her and held her tight.

"I love you," he said before pushing her away and closing the door, leaving her outside in tears and staring at the door.

Inside Declan sank to the floor, curled up into the foetal position and wept like a baby.

Back in their new house Daisy lay on her new bed in her bright new room, looking out the window and toward the big tree, the old swing-set and the big rock wall that separated the back garden from Terry the Tourist's old place.

Lily had placed Eve's old desk back in the room. She'd spent hours painting the room and putting up pictures of Daisy and her brother, Daisy and her dad, Daisy and her friends and Daisy and her mum. She'd covered the bed in a duvet with big bright beautiful flowers on it and big furry purple cushions because purple was Daisy's favourite colour, she'd hung a large framed photograph of Justin Bieber over the bed and Clooney had spent an afternoon putting up a wall of bookshelves which Lily had filled with all the second-hand copies she could find of books suitable for Daisy's age group and little odds and ends she'd bought in IKEA that brought colour and warmth to the room.

Daisy lay frozen despite all Lily's attempts to warm up the place. She was worried about her dad and Scott and she would miss her room, her piano, her house, her road, her world. She didn't know how to be with her mother, what to say or do. She was still so angry and sad and scared and no matter what Eve or anyone said it was her mother who had walked out and left them. *How could she just leave us?*

Downstairs Lily spoke in whispers to Clooney on the phone while she cooked up a storm, hoping the smell of fresh bread and Daisy's favourite Shepherd's Pie would coax her down the stairs and back into Lily's life. Clooney counselled patience and at the same time waited impatiently for the time when they could be alone together again.

Daisy did come down the stairs that evening and she picked at the food her mother made for her. She grunted at Eve when she called in to say hello.

"And here was I thinking we were past grunting. Oh well!" Eve said and Lily saw her daughter fight to stop the corners of her mouth lifting.

Over the next week it was sometimes easier and sometimes it was harder. When Daisy spoke to her father on the phone she would become silent and distant afterwards and on one occasion, when Lily answered Daisy's phone when Daisy was in the shower and Declan had rung three times in a row, she quickly realised he was drunk and wondered how many other calls he'd made in that state. She told him she'd appreciate if he wouldn't call their daughter drunk and hoped he'd make an effort to stay sober when she returned to stay with him the following weekend. He called her a whore.

"Change the record, Declan."

"What was that you said, whore?"

"Sober up."

"Don't tell me what to do, bitch," he said. "I've had enough of that from your precious Eve."

"Excuse me?" Lily said.

"Don't pretend you're not in on it, you twisted bitch," he said and he hung up.

Lily sat on her daughter's bed, dumbfounded. Suddenly the change in his behaviour made sense. He hadn't given Daisy up because it was the right thing to do, he'd given her up because he had to. He hadn't aborted his war plan, he had simply lost the battle. She sat on the bed, wondering what Eve could have possibly said to make her husband do something he didn't want to do and it didn't take long before she guessed what had happened.

Eve was getting stronger and steadier by the day, the expensive and intensive physiotherapy and pilates classes were paying off. By week eleven she was off her crutches and using a walking stick. Adam was very pleased with her recovery and one evening two nights before the wedding, when Clooney had finally grabbed some time with Lily whilst Daisy was spending the night with Tess, he came to her apartment with a bottle of wine, a bunch of flowers and a takeaway. It was their first time actually getting the place to themselves and despite his previous stance regarding sex they didn't eat their take-away, they didn't drink their wine and the bunch of flowers wilted on the counter as they enjoyed uninhibited and playful sex. They laughed and the talked and they pushed and prodded and they came and they came again. They showered and changed the sheets because they both had a weird thing about clean sheets and they had sex again and sometime between four and five in the morning they heated up a spicy Indian dish and ate that before going back to bed and enjoying another roll in the hay.

"That's the most sex I've had in a very long time," she said.

"You're not alone."

"How sad are we?"

"*Watership Down* sad," he said and she smiled.

He had remembered she and Lily had watched *Watership Down* eight times.

"That is sad," she said.

Adam was quirky and funny and kind and interesting and she liked that he was also a little lost like her. He was dispassionate about his career. He tired of the same old same old and needed a break or a new focus.

"You can focus on me for a while," she said.

"Only a while," he said and laughed.

"And you could go to hot countries and fix poor broken kids or you could invent a surgical tool that revolutionises surgery or help discover a cure for bone cancer."

"All totally doable," he said and he laughed a little.

She kissed him. "You can be and do anything you want, Adam. You are an amazing surgeon. You're just a little bored right now."

He exhaled and raised his hands in the air. "I am so bored. If I have to replace one more hip!" He shook his fist at the ceiling in mock anger. She laughed at him and he turned back to face her. "What about you? Are you going to take up knitting or painting or bridge? I hear water aerobics is popular with the retired community."

"Nah, I'm just going to lie here with you."

"John and Yoko style."

"I'd like to think we have better hair," she said.

Eve had realised that she needed to make life changes two weeks after she'd returned from Ireland and her father's funeral to her home and work in New York. She felt homesick, agitated and restless but a mild collision she'd had with a New York taxi led to her decision to sell up and go home. She had driven straight into the back of the cab. She had been working ridiculous hours, trying to make up for so much time away. She was exhausted, her head was pounding and when she was standing at the side of the road and the Irish-Italian taxi driver called Patrick Alberti was screaming and yelling at her, she remained silent, just trying to work out what had happened. She hadn't fallen asleep. She wasn't talking on the phone and because she was tired she was being extra careful to maintain alertness and watch the road. He had seemed so far ahead. She thought that there was at least another two car lengths between them. She heard the crash and felt the jolt before she saw the back of the car. His yelling faded into the background.

Oh no. Not yet. I haven't lived yet.

That evening she made the decision to stop and look around her, to be present and part of the real world, to engage with people, family and friends and now that she was doing just that each moment carried a certain beauty and resonance and it was good enough for her. Eve Hayes was finally fulfilled and content.

"What would you like to do most tomorrow?" Adam asked.

"It's five a.m. – it is tomorrow."

"OK, what would you like to do most when we wake up?"

"I'll like to take out my dad's old boat and his old water-skis . . ."

"Out of the question. Next."

"OK. Forget the water-skis."

"Let's do it," he said and he kissed her and they fell asleep together sometime after six.

They didn't hear Clooney return just before eight. He'd had a long night himself. He and Lily didn't sleep a wink. They didn't have time for sleeping, their time together was so limited and they couldn't afford to miss one thing. Up to that night they had grabbed a coffee here and there and they'd had a drink together while Daisy was in the cinema one Tuesday evening. They phoned and texted one another a lot but she missed his touch and he had missed hers. He was growing restless. Eve didn't need him any more and Lily was starting a new life and one that he couldn't be a part of, at least for a while. He accepted the job in Peru and had two weeks left before he was due to fly out. The contract was for six months.

"Six months is no time," he said when they were lying together facing one another and gazing into one another's eyes the way that new lovers do.

"It will fly by and besides I told you I just might come and see you," she said.

"A lot will have changed in six months," he said.

"Daisy will be settled and Scott, well, hopefully he'll have forgiven me a little."

"And you might have met someone else."

"No." She shook her head. "I could really do with time off for good behaviour."

"I don't mind if you do. I just want you to be happy."

"I know that," she said.

The next morning he left early so that he could avoid any collision with Daisy. He kissed her and told her he loved her and he would always love her. There was no promise accompanying his words. It was simply a statement of fact.

"I love you too," she said and she winked at him and grinned. "Now get out."

They were both big and bold enough to know that their relationship was not the stuff of legends. He would find an exotic lover and she could fall for one of the many men that would pursue her in his absence. They weren't foolish but they were hopeful that some day and somehow they would find their way back to one another. *If it's meant to be it's meant to be.*

Scott promised to stay home the weekend Daisy returned to her dad's house. He told his mother that she didn't have to worry. He and his dad would take good care of Daisy.

"We've had plenty of practice," he said because although he was thawing toward her he was still angry, especially when he witnessed his father's suffering and since she'd left his father seemed to suffer a lot.

Adam insisted on driving to Westport in his brand new BWM and even though there was a perfectly good train service. Eve needed a lot of leg-room up front and so Clooney and Lily felt captive in the back, especially when he got lost and it added another hour onto their four-hour journey. Eve had to get out to stretch her legs every now and then and Lily's small bladder wasn't the better of the two pints that she and Clooney consumed over a pub lunch on route.

It was dark by the time they arrived into Westport. Lily was asleep in Clooney's arms. He gently woke her in time for her to see the light fade from pink to navy blue over the mountains. The Atlantic Coast Hotel was a beautiful building that seemed to be cut out of rock. They walked into the reception and were greeted with warm smiles, a roaring fire, a small library, big cosy chairs and the Fishworks Cafè Bar from which there wafted mouth-watering smells promising good food, and the sounds of chatter and clinking hinting at good cheer.

Paul emerged followed by Simone as they were signing in. He was blissed out and wearing white towelling slippers which poked out under his jeans. He raised his hands in the air.

"You're here," he said and he hugged each and every one of them warmly, prompting Eve to ask if he was drunk already. Simone explained he had spent the last two days having every ayurvedic treatment he could fit into his schedule.

"He's just had psychic enema," she said.

"Sounds painful!" Clooney said.

"It's sublime," he said and he hugged Eve again until Eve threatened to kick him.

He didn't care a jot. He was on cloud nine.

"What's the name of that treatment?" Clooney asked.

"Don't worry about names," he said. "I have you all booked in with Dr Thomas tomorrow."

"You can shove that," Eve mumbled just as Paul's mother came out of the lift.

She ignored Paul's friends. "You do know they have an actual function room on the fourth floor?" she said.

Paul just smiled at her.

"Yes, he does," Simone said.

"So why aren't we using that?"

"Because the wedding party is small enough to use The Blue Wave Restaurant which is also on the fourth floor and we love it," said Simone, smiling sweetly. "We've very fond memories of it, it's beautiful and warm and everything I've ever dreamed of."

"If you'd used the function room we could actually invite some people to this thing," his mother said.

"And by people she means neighbours and by neighbours she means the people from her church who think I'm a homo."

"My advice, Mrs Doyle, is have a psychic enema and get over it," Eve said

Paul laughed and the others stayed quiet.

Paul's mother scratched her nose and then her ear. "You were always a cheeky bitch, Eve Hayes – good to see some things don't change." She looked up and down at her son. "At least *some* things don't change," she said, barely concealing her grin before she walked into The Fishworks Café Bar.

"Oh my God, she can smile!" Simone said. "It's a miracle."

Later when they were all stuffed with the best fish pie ever made and the girls were on their second bottle of wine and the boys on their third creamy pint of Guinness, Gar and Gina floated in. They too were in a trace-like state. Gina ordered a salmon dish and proceeded to tell the girls about a procedure Dr Thomas had recommended.

"He's amazing," she said. "Seriously, he's given me dietary advice, he's made me think about how I live and how I feel and recently it has not been good, he's told me the best times to sleep and to wake according to my body type – and the treatments, my God, I haven't felt this relaxed in years!"

"And as soon as we've eaten we're going upstairs to make the most of it," Gar said.

"Yes, we are," Gina agreed.

"The man's a genius," Gar said and clinked his pint glass with the lads.

Lily had suffered tension headaches and backache for years and she couldn't wait for her consultation. Eve was quiet – the only doctor she wanted in her life was Adam. They stayed up late drinking and listening to the local musicians play. All but Eve danced jigs with the locals and she was involved in the last dance when four locals insisted on lifting her up in her chair and carrying and swaying her around the room much to Adam's horror.

"Easy, easy, easy," he repeated over and over, trying to keep up with the locals and steady the chair.

Eve was too merry to feel fear. "Alright, that's enough, drop the nice lady with the brand-new shoulder!"

Around two o'clock they all disappeared into their respective rooms and, consumed by exhaustion, Clooney and Lily fell asleep quickly in one another's arms.

Adam came out of the shower to find Eve looking out at the harbour. She seemed at peace, looking out at the view of sea and mountains.

"Are you alright?" he asked, resting his hand on the shoulder he had recently reconstructed.

"I'm good," she said. "It's beautiful here."

He agreed and they went to bed.

Lily was first in with Dr Thomas, followed by an eager and fascinated Adam. Both came away from their consultation with a little more insight into themselves and their bodies. Adam was especially impressed and keen to read as much as he could on the subject. Dr Thomas gave him a book which he read in bed after a massage treatment that left him feeling relaxed and with an enormous sense of wellbeing.

"You've got to go to him," he said to Eve who was reading *Marie Claire* in the bath.

"No."

"He'll make you feel better."

"You make me feel better."

He read from the various pamphlets. "Ayurveda revives the memory of our immune system which allows our body to rekindle our intrinsic ability to heal ourselves through treatment and/ or prescriptive ayurvedic herbs and oils."

"Not interested."

"It can help with post-surgery convalescence."

"Don't care."

"Headaches."

"Really, Adam."

"It's profoundly relaxing and your body has been through a huge trauma, it's doing a great job healing but this is an opportunity to help it along. What's the worst that could happen? You have an hour-long massage and come out covered in oil? Boo hoo. I'm asking you to do this for me."

"Right, fine, Jesus, I thought all western doctors were supposed to be anti-alternative medicine."

"I'm not all western doctors and Ayruveda is the mother of all modern medicine so stop whining."

She walked into Dr Thomas' small office with her heart beating fast and she couldn't understand why she was so nervous but she was and it was uncomfortable. Dr Thomas was an Indian man with a young face and a big smile. There was nothing to fear and Eve was not the fearful type and still her heart raced and when he took her hand in his she couldn't control its tremble. Very much like her experience in hospital, he asked her question after question but this time instead of him simply adhering to a list, one question led to another more specific one depending on her answer and in some cases it was a question she'd never been asked before and despite herself she found that she was opening up and engaging. He examined her tongue, he looked into her eyes and he took her pulse. He explained pulse diagnosis at great length as he held her wrist between his fingers and thumb and suddenly she felt the desire to pull away and then she saw the look in his eye and it was too late to pull away.

"You told me that you suffer from headaches but they are not too bad," he said.

She nodded and her heart raced again. *Here we go*.

"They are bad," he said.

"I went for tests a few months ago and got the all clear," she said.

"It's time for a second opinion," he said.

"I'm fine."

"Today I'm going to get rid of the headache you pretend you're not having and when you go home you need to go for a CT and/or an MRI."

She sat silently because when the staff of St Martin's hospital questioned her about her headaches she wasn't entirely honest with them. She didn't mention the balance problems and vision problems that she was experiencing before the crash. The balance problem wasn't an issue when she was lying in a bed twenty-four hours a day and seven days a week. *I was given the all clear.* When her vision became blurred after reading for hours on end she told herself that it was because she needed glasses. *I was given the all clear.* She didn't mention the changes she experienced in her sense of smell because everything smelled funky in that hospital. Shit smelt like roses and Chanel No. 5 smelt like baby puke. *I was given the all clear.* She had reasoned that she was on a lot of drugs and locked in that tiny room for so long that it was possible all she needed was fresh air and a fresh perspective. *I was given the all clear.* If she told those endless interns who asked endless questions that one of the reasons she stopped working and sold her shares in her company was because she found it hard to concentrate, her memory was spotty, her spatial awareness was completely out of whack and the smell of cat pee made her crave bacon they would have kept her in that tiny room and she couldn't bear it.

"It's time to get to the bottom of it," he said and he looked at her sympathetically as though he could read her mind somehow. He went on to prescribe a Talam treatment to alleviate migraine and a Kizchi massage to ease her body's tension and promote healing.

Even though Dr Thomas had basically told her what she already guessed back in New York, she enjoyed the two treatments and felt decidedly better and more relaxed after them. She wasn't sure if it was the magic of Ayurveda or that finally she didn't have to pretend that there wasn't a problem but Eve felt calm and ready.

I got the all clear but they were wrong.

Adam was like a happy bunny when she returned. He'd spent the afternoon reading a few more of Dr Thomas' books.

"How would you feel about a trip to India?" he said.

"Great," she said.

That night they all had an early dinner and everyone disappeared afterwards to be with the ones they loved and to rest for the busy wedding day ahead. They woke up early and had a leisurely breakfast. Adam stayed in bed reading. Clooney swam lengths of the beautiful azure-blue pool. Lily and Eve sat in the hot tub watching him glide by under the water.

"He was always like a fish," Eve said and Lily nodded.

"Are you going to tell me what's on your mind?" Lily said.

Eve laughed and said that there was nothing.

"Are you going to tell me what you threatened to do to Declan?" Lily asked then.

Eve's smile faded. Lily was looking at her with a mixture of bewilderment and awe.

"I just reasoned with him," she said.

"Nobody reasons with Declan."

Eve just shook her head and that meant she didn't want to talk about it.

"We'll have to talk about it someday," Lily said.

"I know. Just not today."

Lily smiled at her friend and hugged her even though she knew it would make Eve uncomfortable and she pulled away quickly just as Clooney appeared, hanging on the side of the pool. He slipped into the tub beside Lily. Eve made her excuses and left them to it. One day in the very near future Eve would tell her friend about the day that she had gone into Declan's office and sat in front of him for the first time in nearly twenty years. She'd tell Lily that at first Declan had been his usual sneering self but she put a stop to it quickly. She'd tell her that Declan had told her she was a very silly woman if she thought that pleading on Lily's behalf would do any good.

"When have I ever pleaded for anything, Declan?" she'd said.

He looked at her and his eyes narrowed. "What is it that I can do for you, Eve?"

"You can give Lily her kids back, sell the house with a view to giving her half the proceeds without delay and before the divorce which you'll agree to as soon as possible."

He threw his head back and laughed.

You were always theatrical, Declan.

"That bitch is not getting my kids or my money or a divorce. She can live in a rat-infested pit for all I care. She made her flea-bitten bed and now she can rot in it."

"Or you can do what I say," Eve said.

Declan leaned forward. "And why would I do that?"

"Because if you don't, I'll go the press and I'll tell that when I was eighteen years old my best friend's boyfriend raped me at a party. I'll go on record telling them that the boy is now a very important cardiac surgeon here in Dublin. It will take them approximately two minutes to work out who the boy was."

"You're lying."

"Try me."

"It didn't happen like that."

"It happened exactly like that."

"No. We kissed and —"

"And you raped me and you hurt me." She took out the copy of the hospital records that Adam had copied for her and threw them on his desk. "And I have the proof."

He opened the file and he looked through it and then at her and he wasn't so smug any more.

"It didn't happen like that. I was drunk. You were into it."

"I don't care if you believe you're innocent of my rape or justified in raping your wife. I don't care what you think or how you feel and your employers, patients and the rest of the country won't care either."

"You'll destroy me," he said.

"You say that like I should care."

"You'll destroy my kids," he said and she laughed.

That old chestnut, you son of a bitch.

"I don't give a crap about your kids," she said and he believed her. "By five o'clock this evening I want to see Lily dancing around the kitchen celebrating that fact that you've finally decided to do something decent and you're sharing custody. In two months' time I want the house to go on the market and you will accept the first realistic price offered and I will be involved in the sale. You will be judicially separated as soon as possible and the sale of the house will be divided evenly at that stage and when the time comes you will give her an uncontested quick divorce."

"You think you have it all worked out," he said.

She got up. "Don't cross me, Declan, because I've been waiting twenty years to fuck you up."

She left him alone to stare at the report on his desk.

Thank you for taking me to the hospital all those years ago, Billy. Wherever you are.

The wedding was beautiful, it was a dream day. Gar was a handsome best man and his speech started a little rough but in the end it was both funny and touching.

"I wanted to start off light so I went on-line and checked out bi-sexual jokes but there aren't any. I suppose bi-sexuals are too busy riding all around them to be thinking up jokes."

Paul's mother's face fell and the room became deathly silent which meant that everyone could hear her when she muttered. "For God's sake, do we have to listen to that today of all days?"

Simone broke into a huge grin. She laughed a real, genuine laugh and Paul followed and like a Mexican wave that laugh rippled through the crowd. Gar sighed and wiped the sweat from his forehead. He spoke about growing up with Paul and how intimating it was to be a friend of someone who was a brilliant sportsman, intelligent and of course so handsome that every girl in Ireland wanted to be with him. Eve and Lily both made coughing and choking sounds.

"Yes, alright, *nearly* every girl including my wife."

Gina raised her glass. "Yeah, you betcha!" she said and the crowd laughed. Paul's mother seemed happier with that portion of the speech.

He talked about how private Paul had been and that although he understood it and accepted it, that privacy had created a distance over the years and that sometimes he missed his best pal even when he was in the room. When it looked like he might cry he turned to Simone and smiled widely. "But then you came along and you took him out of the dark room he'd locked himself into and you brought him out and into the light. I've never seen him happier or more content, never freer or more open."

Simone smiled and tears filled her eyes.

"You complete him," he said and he turned and winked at the crowd and they groaned at his faux sentimentality.

Paul's dad spoke warmly about his son. He didn't mention his sexuality because there was more to Paul than that and although he agreed his son was private he was a great man to keep a secret. He was honourable and patient. When he called his son patient he glanced over at his wife. It wasn't conscious but the crowd laughed and when he realised what he'd done he laughed too.

Paul's mother raised her glass and smiled. *Fine, I'll be the punchline today but when I'm in heaven and you're all screaming in a fiery hell pit then we'll see who's laughing.*

Simone's father wasn't as happy with his daughter's choice of husband as he tried to pretend. He was valiant in his attempt to celebrate but he was no actor. His speech was short and he mostly spoke about how fantastic she was and how open and vulnerable and how he'd do jail time if anyone ever hurt her. He didn't welcome Paul to the family as Paul's father had Simone, he simply wished them luck and told his daughter that no matter what he would always be there for her. Simone didn't seem to notice her father's thinly-veiled threats to her new husband and if she did she was a much better actor than her dad. She gave him a big hug and told him she loved him. Paul's mother looked like she was ready to stand up and punch him because although she felt entitled to judge her son, no one else bar God was eligible to do so. Paul was a gentleman and put out his hand to shake with Simone's dad. When they shook hands the crowd clapped.

Simone made an excited breathless speech full of thank-you's and warmth as usual. Paul remained silent.

The meal was delicious and far superior to the usual fare provided at weddings. The room looked onto the Croagh Patrick Mountain which swept down into Clew Bay and as the hours passed the light changed and the window from ceiling to floor revealed a series of beautiful landscapes.

Clooney, Lily, Eve, Adam and Gina shared a table and afterwards and when the music kicked off Eve and Adam danced slowly around the room while everyone else danced at a faster tempo. The other dancers were a distant blur. She put her arms around Adam's neck.

"Thanks for fixing me," she said.

"Well, I did tell you I'm the best in the business."

"I didn't mean that."

It was a perfect day and one that Eve Hayes would remember fondly for the rest of her life.

Eve's benign meningioma tumour was diagnosed in a private clinic. It was a Wednesday afternoon and she was alone. The tumour, although benign and believed to be developing slowly, was inoperable due to its size and location. It was damaging cells and placing pressure within her skull.

"You said your mother had a brain tumour," the doctor said.

"Hers was cancerous," she said.

"We'll be keeping a close eye on it."

She didn't ask any questions. She didn't want the answers, not while alone and not on a bloody Wednesday. She smiled and shook his hand. *Friday is a much better day for that kind of news.*

"Thanks, Doctor," she said.

"I'm sorry," he said.

"Don't be, it was a long time coming," she said and she smiled and walked out the door, leaving him to stand in his office and mentally comment that it takes all sorts.

It was a bright September morning. Daisy was back in school and had made friends with a girl called Willie which was short for Wilhelmina. They were the same age and her family lived in Terry the Tourist's old place across the wall. She, Tess and Willie had become the local IT girls. Daisy smiled more and, although the mother and daughter relationship had altered irrevocably, it had more to do with her growing up and opening her eyes to the world than it had to do with any real residual anger. If Daisy was truly honest with herself and it would be years before she was, she would admit life was better with her funny, kind, pretty, happy, playful, caring, loving mother and in her absence and after his initial breakdown her dad seemed more content without her. *Some people bring out the worst in one another, Daisy. Your dad and I are some of those people.*

Scott had come to dinner twice and even brought dessert the second time. When he told her he was enjoying the bachelor lifestyle and sharing a house with his dad he was telling the truth. They lived on M&S microwave food, the cleaner came three times a week, they came and went like ships in the night and when they did spend time together they actually talked. If his dad was in bad humour Scott just left and if Scott was entertaining a girl or friends his dad went out with Rodney or worked late. "We're fine, Mum," he said.

Of course there would be hard times to come and her kids would throw her defection in her face every time they were hurt or wounded but, extraordinarily quickly after she left home and with the support of the people she loved and who loved her, Lily's life improved 1000%. So when she asked herself the question *If I knew I was set to leave this earth soon, would I do it all differently?* the honest answer was no. *If it brought me here, I'd do it the same way every time.*

After Lily dropped her daughter to school, she picked up Clooney and his suitcase. They said goodbye in the airport. Clooney held her tight and kissed the top of her head and she fought tears and beamed him a wide and genuine smile.

"Thank you," she said.

"I love you, Lily Brennan," he said like his sister used to screech from a swing all those years ago.

"I love you, Clooney Hayes," she said and she let him go.

He walked through the gate and disappeared from view. She stood for a minute or two and collected herself.

Time for a new chapter, Lily.

Eve waited until she was strong enough to walk the cliff with Lily before she told her about the tumour. They walked up the hill together until they got to their favourite old soft, rich, green, grassy patch. They lay out under a still and warm late September sky talking the way they did as teenagers with Lily resting her head on her arm and Eve staring up at the sun.

She told her that she'd noticed she was impaired cognitively when she returned to New York and work after her father's death. She was forgetful and numbers and details that had never confused her before had become difficult to grasp. She was suffering headaches and had problems with spatial awareness. She came home because she was tired, bored and wanted a different life but she also came home because deep down she knew that time was running out. Lily rested on her arm, still and silent for the longest time, processing the information, but it was hard. She was deeply shocked.

"But you survived being hit by a car," she said.

"Funny old world."

Lily shook her head from side to side as though it would somehow change Eve's fate.

"Benign tumours are removable, they rarely lead to death," she said.

"Not this time."

"How long?" Lily said, sitting up and injecting anger into her voice as though Eve was dying slowly just to spite her.

Eve stayed lying on her side. "It's progressing slowly, my symptoms are still relatively minor, it could stall, speed up or it could slow down further. They don't know."

"So you could be here forever?" Lily said, battling tears.

"Yeah," Eve said, "forever and ever."

On the way back from the cliff they walked slowly and hand in hand until Eve decided that it was too sticky and she let go and wiped her hand on her jacket. The baby-pink sky was turning red over the harbour.

"Can we finally talk about what happened?" Lily asked out of nowhere but Eve knew exactly what she meant.

"Yeah," she said.

"Declan raped you."

"Yeah."

"I must have read that letter one hundred times when I received it and not once did I think of it that way. I thought you were jealous and mean and you wanted to hurt me because I'd crossed the line with Clooney."

"Is that why you didn't write back?" Eve asked.

"I wrote a lot of letters. Most of them were horrible and I binned them all. Declan had beaten the post, Eve. He arrived on my doorstep the day after, telling me he knew about Clooney and how you'd slept together, he begged my forgiveness and asked for a fresh start."

"I understand."

"I don't." Lily said. "I was so stupid."

"We both were very, very, stupid," Eve said and she smiled.

"I've kept your letters all these years."

"I've kept yours too," Eve said, "but let's make a pact to never read them. I tried to go back. It didn't work. Let's just stay in the present."

Lily nodded her agreement. "I want you to know that I began to understand what had really happened after we were married. I should have contacted you but I was married to him."

"You don't need to explain. I love you, Lily." She shrugged her newly-built shoulder. They walked on for a while in silence.

"A brain tumour?" Lily said. "*Really, a fudging brain tumour?*" she shouted at the red sky. "*Well, you'll have to do better than that, do you hear me?*"

Eve laughed at her friend. "Yeah, screw you, sky, universe, gods, aliens, nothingness, screw you all!" she said, shaking her fist.

Then Lily turned to her friend and tears rained down her face.

"Fuck you, Eve Hayes," she said.

"Fuck you too, Lily Brennan," she said and she took her friend in her arms and kissed her on the head the way she'd seen her brother do.

"Think about it this way, whatever happens we found our way back to one another to right our wrongs and that's worth something," Eve said.

Lily agreed and held her friend tightly. "And we'll fight it to the end."

"Yes, we will."

Eve told Adam next. He was angry and shouted at her for lying and hiding the truth. He pointed his finger at her and walked across the floor and then back again and when he finally stopped shouting, he stormed out red-faced only to return an hour later to hold her in his arms on her ridiculously uncomfortable sofa. She explained that she had come home to die and it took a car crash to make her want to live. She apologised because deep down she'd always known the all clear was a mistake. She asked him for forgiveness and wondered if he could fall in love with a woman on death row.

"I only ask because if the situation was reversed, I'd still fall in love with you," she said, "and *I'm* selfish, self-centred and truly believe the world revolves around me."

He kissed her and looked into her face sighing. "Don't forget that you're a bitch."

She grinned. "To the very end."

He insisted on more and more tests and she obliged him because it was the least she could do, having made him a part of her life when she should have known better. The Hayes family just weren't long for this world. *Good luck, Clooney, you'll be the last of us.* The results didn't change no matter how much Adam wanted them to. The outlook was uncertain. Eve could live one year or ten depending on whether her tumour stalled or continued to grow. Adam moved in two days after she told him of her diagnosis. He arrived with two cases.

"What's this?"

"I'm moving in."

"Who asked you?"

"Life's too short to wait to be asked," he said and he put his suitcases in Eve's room and after that it was their room and their apartment and the first thing Adam did when he settled in was order a new sofa. Every night he'd sit reading alternative medicines into the early hours. He kept coming back to Ayruveda.

He woke her late one night.

"What?"

"Remember when I asked you to go to India?"

"Hmmm."

"You said yes."

"Hmmm."

"So we're going to Kerala, OK?"

"Hmmm."

"Say yes."

"Yes."

He leaned over and kissed her on the lips. "I'll book it tomorrow," he said and she turned over and fell back to sleep.

She told Clooney via Skype because she wanted him to see that she was well and happy and, despite the brain tumour, healthy as she could be. He was the hardest to tell because he had received this kind of news too many times. She was bright and breezy and told him that the outlook was not as bad as he might think. She warned him not to come home.

"I'm coming home."

"So that you can sit around for the next ten or twenty years and wait for me to die? Because that's how long I intend to live," she said.

"Eve," he said.

"Live your life, Clooney, because I'm living mine. OK?"

"If you get any sicker?" he warned.

"If I get any sicker, Lily will be on to you before I even think about lifting the phone."

The rest were easy. Gina cried every time she saw her for the first few weeks but after that she settled down and realised Eve was going nowhere fast. Gar told her she was a trooper and Paul shook his head, sat down and put his head in his hands. When his face reappeared he told her he and Simone and their little one would be there for her and she wasn't to go anywhere till the kid was born because they wanted her to be godmother.

"Is that because I'm rich and dying?" she asked.

"It was because you are rich – the dying bit is a bonus," he said and she laughed.

"I'd be honoured."

"Good," he said.

The evening before she and Adam flew to India for a month's stay in Kerala, Eve waited for Lily in the kitchen she grew up in. Lily had run down the road to get coffee and she was alone and without really thinking about it she started to roam around. She went up the stairs and passed the wall that once held the pictures of her and her family which now had been replaced with a painting of a sunset. Daisy and Scott's faces greeted her on the wall at the top of the stairs. She walked into the room her mother and father had both died in. One wall was painted pale lavender and it smelled of fresh linen and Lily. In Daisy's room she sat at her old desk and traced the carving of BGML and smiled to herself. *Where are you now, Ben? Will I see you again? Are you waiting for me? Unlikely but it's a nice dream.*

She made her way downstairs and went outside to the back garden and sat on the swing that she and Lily had spent their childhoods playing on.

Daisy appeared with her schoolbag on her back. She dropped it and sat on the swing beside Eve.

"Mom told me," she said.

"Oh," Eve said.

"Are you scared?"

"No."

"Why not?"

"What's to be scared of?"

Daisy thought about it for a long time.

"I don't know," she said.

"I bought you a piano," Eve said. "They'll deliver it any day now."

"Really?" Daisy said and she was genuinely pleased and surprised. "I thought you didn't like me?"

"I like you as much as you like me."

"Well, then, that's a lot," Daisy said, grinning.

"It is, now that I've bought you a baby grand."

"A *baby grand*, holy crap!" she shouted and jumped off the swing.

"Where are you going?"

She pointed to Terry the Tourist's. "I'm going to tell Willie."

"You're welcome!" Eve shouted to Daisy's back.

Daisy stopped and turned and walked over to Eve. Eve stopped swinging and Daisy hugged her.

"Thanks, Eve. I mean it," she said and she ran off, leaving Eve alone again on the swing.

"You're welcome, Miss Daisy," she said and for a moment she welled up, wondering if she'd live to see the little girl grow up, follow her dreams and fall in love.

When Lily returned with coffee she found her contemplative friend swinging so she joined her on the other swing and they started swinging, slowly at first and then faster and faster and higher and higher until their feet were touching the sky.

"The one who swings highest gets a wish," Eve said.

"I know what my wish is," Lily said.

"I love you, Eve Hayes."

"I love you, Lily Brennan."

They screamed at one another just like they did when they were girls. When they both felt a little sick and the swing-set jerked a little ominously they slowed down to a stop. They walked back inside and they got busy living after that.

* * *

Eve's Bucket List

One month with Adam in Kerla at an ayurvedic spa. FANTASTIC I feel amazing.

Be there for the birth of Paul's baby. Ahhhh, it's a little girl called Lisa.

Oversee the sale of Lily's house and oversee the transfer of Lily's half. No gloating – time to let go.

Be at Lisa's christening. Priest didn't even ask if I was a Catholic. What an odd ceremony.

Take Adam, Lily and Daisy to Peru for two weeks. I miss Clooney.

Buy the apartment. Finally I'm home.

Get to know Scott. Ongoing.

Live unwedded and happily ever after with Adam. Ongoing.

Sell the house to Lily for €100.

Lodge €50 into Clooney's account.

See the Ginger Monster go to prison.

Be there for Lisa's first steps.

Be there for Scott's graduation.

For Daisy's wedding.

Live long enough to see Clooney and Lily reunited.

Screw it, hang on till I'm seventy.

Eve's Funeral Plan

Lily,

Make sure they don't lay me out for people to look at and touch me. The amount of neighbours and strangers that touched Danny's face was outrageous.

Regarding the (closed) casket, I'd prefer a dark one to light. Light wood just looks cheaper. And unvarnished if possible.

I've no problem with flowers as long as they are not carnations or lilies (No offence).

Obviously it won't be a religious ceremony, it will simply be a gathering to remember me and send me on my way to a full stop or a new beginning wherever that may be. I'd like you to speak and Clooney and Adam of course. I've got quite close to Daisy in the recent months and if she wanted to say something that would be cool, if not I understand. Paul won't speak but Gar and Gina might and that's fine too.

NB: I do not want the speeches to be sappy and/ or boring. Please let nobody talk about me like I was something special and the best person they ever knew (Well, maybe you can but no-one else). I hate watching the news when someone is killed and their friends and family say that they were the most amazing person that ever lived and there has never been or never will be a person like them. I've yet to hear someone say: 'Ah, he was alright, a bit of a dick with drink on him but to be fair he didn't deserve to be stabbed.' I want people to be real and say how they feel. I'm not perfect. I want that reflected.

Music: Is very important. Make sure wherever you hold the memorial service it is wired for sound. Keanan's was dreadful so don't lay me out there. I'd like 'Tower Of Song' by Leonard Cohen and I want the full song played – don't turn it off halfway. That's all eight verses. After that I'd like 'Grapefruit Moon' by Tom Waits and just for fun and for Adam, Ray LeMontagne's 'Trouble'. I'd love Daisy to play keyboard if she wants, she's such a beautiful player. The piece she does from 'The Piano' soundtrack is amazing but again I don't want to push her. Having said that, if I live till she's over twenty I'll be really pissed off if she doesn't.

There will be a large fund put aside for the after party and I want it to be a party. Leave me in the box in the funeral home and head to The Killiney Hotel. They will put on a four-course meal and I want you all to drink and dance till dawn. When I'm ashes and no matter what time of the year it is, wait until it's a sunny day, then take Danny's old boat out: you, Clooney, Adam, Daisy, and Scott if he wants to come. Gar, Gina, Paul, Simone and my goddaughter are also welcome. Bring a picnic and throw me into the sea with the fishes and Danny and don't be sad, be happy we found one another again and we were lucky enough to live the lives we've lived and when Adam is sad and lonely remind him that he was loved and will love again even if he makes his annoyed face.

I love you, Lily Brennan.

P.S. Very important, make sure to check the direction of the wind before you pour me into the sea. Wind direction is key.

Eve XXX

To whom it may concern
As of today Eve Hayes still lives.

Love
Lily

∽∾∽

If you enjoyed
The Space Between Us by Anna McPartlin
why not try
So What if I'm Broken? also published by Poolbeg?
Here's a sneak preview of Chapter One

So what if
I'm broken

Anna McPartlin

POOLBEG

1

Universe

Oh nothing lasts forever,
you can cry a million rivers,
you can rage it ain't no sin
but it won't change a thing,
cos nothing lasts forever.

Jack L, *Universe*

Alexandra
21st June 2007

Tom,

When you are shopping can you pick up the following:

    Bread
    Milk x 2
    Water x 4
    Spaghetti
    Mince (lean! Make sure it's lean and not the stuff they call lean and
charge half price because it's not lean. I want lean cut right in front of
you and I don't care how much it costs)
    Tin of tomatoes
    Basil
    A clove of garlic
    Wine, if you don't still have a case or two in the office and make
sure it's not Shiraz. I'm really sick of Shiraz.
    If you want dessert pick something up.
    I'm meeting Sherri in Dalkey for a quick drink at 5:00. She has the
Jack Lukeman tickets so I took money from the kitty to pay for them.

I'm taking a ticket for you so if you don't want to go text me. I'll be home around 7:30. Your aunt called, she's thinking about coming to Dublin next weekend. Try and talk her out of it. I'm exhausted and can't handle running around after her for 48 hours straight. Your aunt is on cocaine. I'm not messing. An intervention is needed.

Oh and washing-up liquid. We badly need washing-up liquid and will you please call someone to get the dishwasher fixed?

OK see you later,

Love you,

Alexandra

PS. When somebody close to you dies, move seats.
God, I love Jimmy Carr.

Alexandra laughed to herself and put her note up on the fridge and held it in position with her favourite magnet which was a fat grinning pig rubbing his tummy. She was damp and sweaty having run five miles which was a record and she was extremely pleased. She unclipped her iPod from her tracksuit, placed it on the counter and headed upstairs to the shower. There she sang Rihanna's "Umbrella", and did a little dance move before washing shampoo out of her hair. Forty-five minutes later she walked down the stairs with her shoulder-length glossy chestnut hair perfectly coiffed. She was wearing her favourite black trousers and black fitted blouse complete with a large bow. She stopped at the hall mirror and applied lipstick and then rooted some lip gloss out of her handbag and applied that too. She stared at herself in the mirror for a moment or two, sighed and mumbled something about Angelina Jolie crapping her pants. She smiled at her own joke whilst putting on her jacket. She picked up her handbag and walked out the door.

Alexandra walked along her own street and waved at Mrs Murphy from No 14. Mrs Murphy was busy sweeping her step but she waved and called out that it was a lovely day. Alexandra smiled and told her it was perfect. She waited for the DART and listened to a man talk about cruelty to animals to Joe Duffy on Joe's radio show Liveline. It was too sad so she switched from her radio to her music collection and only stopped humming along to James Morrison's 'The Last Goodbye' when she realised that three spotty teenagers were laughing and pointing at her. She stuck out her tongue and grinned at them and they laughed again. She sat on the train next to a man in his fifties. He asked her to wake him at Tara Street station if he fell asleep, explaining that there was something about moving trains that always made him sleep. She assured him she would wake him and true to his word he was snoring less than five minutes later. Coming up to Tara Street station she tapped his arm gently, nevertheless he woke with a start. He thanked her once he regained his senses and made his way off the train. He forgot his bag and so she ran after him and handed it to him and he was grateful but she was in a hurry to get back on the train so she just waved and ran.

The woman sitting opposite her grinned and nodded. "My own dad would forget his head," she said.

Alexandra smiled at her. "He was sweet."

The woman nodded again. Alexandra got off the train in Dalkey. The woman got off at the same station but neither made eye contact.

Alexandra made her way through the station and out into the sunshine. She continued straight onto the main street and took the left at the end of the street, after that she took a right and then another left and after that Alexandra was gone.

Elle
Sunday 31st December 1989

Dear Universe,
Please don't send a fiery ball of hellfire comet thing to kill us all. I'm only eight so if I die now I won't get to do anything that I really want to. Miss Sullivan thinks that I could be an artist. If I'm dead I can't paint and I love painting and living. Margaret Nolan says that everyone thinks that we're going to be nuked in 1999 but the real truth is that a flaming ball of death is going to crash into earth at the stroke of midnight tonight. She sits next to me in class and sometimes smells like a hospital. Her dad's a scientist and he told her so she has a good chance of being right. She's already given her pocket money to the poor

and says I should do the same so that when our time comes God will think we're decent enough sorts and let us into heaven. I forgot to go to the church to put money in the poor box because I got carried away working on a painting of my family dying in dancing fire. Jane says I'm a depressing little cow. She's always in a bad mood lately. Mum says it's because she's a teenager, she's fighting with her boyfriend and she's got fat. She's thinks being eight is the same as being slow but I know Jane is pregnant because they shout about it all the time. I'm not slow and I'm not deaf either. I feel sorry for the baby because if we all die tonight it will never have known life but then again maybe that's for the best.

OK, here are my promises to you if we make it past midnight.

1. I'll be good.
2. I'll do what my mum tells me to.
3. I won't swear.
4. I won't tell any lies unless my mum asks me to (see promise 2).
5. I'll be nicer to Jane.
6. I'll paint every day.
7. I'll help Jane take care of Mum a bit more. (I can't help all the time – see promise 6)
8. I'll give my pocket money to the poor tomorrow morning.
9. I'll be nice to Jane's baby because I've a feeling I might be the only one.
10. I won't listen to anything Margaret Nolan has to say again.

And, Universe, if we do all die in fire tonight thanks for nothing.
Yours,
Elle Moore
XXX

That was the first letter Elle Moore wrote to the Universe and once written she folded it and put it into an old shortbread tin. After her supper she tied her long brown hair in a knot and dressed in her brand-new Christmas coat, hat, gloves and her sister Jane's favourite tie-dyed fringed scarf. She made her way down toward the right-hand side of the long garden where she dug a hole between her mother's roses and the graves of four dead gerbils: Jimmy, Jessica, Judy and Jeffrey. Once the tin was placed in the hole and its earth returned she made a promise to herself that if she did live past midnight on that thirty-first of December in 1989, the following year she'd retrieve her letter and replace it with another. Little did she know back then but Elle Moore would continue to write letters to the Universe every New Year's Eve for the next eighteen years.

Jane

5th May 1990

Dear Mrs Moore,

I am writing to you today about my concerns regarding your daughter Jane. I have attempted to reach out to Jane on a number of occasions in recent times but to no avail. As you are well aware I have also attempted to communicate with your good self but that too has proved difficult/nigh on impossible. Therefore I am now left with no choice but to write this letter.

It is clear to the teaching staff and to the student body that Jane is in the latter stages of pregnancy and so it is now urgent that we speak. Jane's schoolwork and attendance suffered immeasurably last term and as a Leaving Cert student she now faces her mock examinations unprepared and with motherhood imminent. Jane seems to be incapable of coming to terms with her condition as it would appear are you but we in St Peter's cannot simply stand by and act like nothing is happening to this seventeen-year-old girl.

I urge you, Mrs Moore, to phone me or to come into the school and meet with me at any time convenient for you. I cannot allow this silence to continue any longer and so if we do not hear from you within the next week we will be forced to ask your daughter not to return to school until such time as communication has been re-established.

Over the years Jane and I have had our disagreements. Her flagrant disregard for our rules regarding smoking on school premises and the Irish stew incident that led to a fire in the Home Economics room are only two of the episodes I could mention. As you are aware we've butted heads on many more occasions, especially when she came to school with purple hair or indeed during her thankfully short-lived Cure-inspired Gothic phase. This school has a zero-tolerance policy when it comes to the presentation of its students but I must admit, though exasperated by her opposition and having to endure debate on many occasions, she conveyed her points ably and with admirable passion. The reason I mention this is that although our relationship as principal and student is chequered I feel it necessary to make it clear that Jane is a very clever girl, bright and articulate, and I have often thought that this girl could do anything she set her mind to and in twenty years I have only thought that a handful of times. I am worried for her, Mrs Moore. She has lost her sparkle and her fight. The girl I knew and, despite our differences, have a great fondness for, has all but disappeared.

Teenage pregnancy is terrible and absolutely not to be encouraged but support is not the same as encouragement and with support Jane could continue her studies and fulfil her ambitions. Surely it is not the end for a girl such as Jane?

Please come and speak to me for Jane's sake. Don't leave me with no option but to expel such a talented young girl from our school.

Kindest regards,

Amanda Reynolds

Principal Amanda Reynolds

Jane finished reading the letter aloud and blew her blonde fringe out of her eyes while waiting on her best friend's response. Alexandra twirled her chestnut hair around her finger and stared at it in silence.

After a few seconds she shrugged. "Jesus, who knew Reynolds had a heart?"

Jane felt like crying because her principal had responded to her crisis pregnancy with far more kindness and understanding than her own mother who had one tantrum after another since Jane's condition was revealed months previously. During her latest tantrum she took the time to mention how much money she had pissed into the wind by sending Jane to private school and told Jane in no uncertain terms that her education was over because only a bloody childless spinster like Amanda Reynolds could possibly think that having a baby at seventeen didn't mean an end to an academic career. She slammed the door on exiting the room, not once but twice for effect.

On that afternoon and for the first time Jane truly acknowledged the predicament she was in and how badly wrong her life had gone. She realised that she would miss her principal and she would miss school and the opportunity to go to college. She'd miss her friends who except for Alexandra had drifted away during her pregnancy and she'd miss Dominic even though he was avoiding her and was completely ignoring the fact that she was carrying his child. She could see through his school yard bravado and recognised his pained expression and haunted look and she loved him.

Following an argument with Dominic's parents who had dared to imply that Jane was a little whore, her mother had made it clear that if she saw him anywhere near their property she'd attack him with a shovel and Jane's mother did not make threats of violence lightly. Once when Jane was seven a man came to their door. He was buying and selling antiques. Her mother said she wasn't interested but he spied an antique table in the hall. He put his foot in the door and attempted to change her mind about doing business. She reiterated she had no interest and told him if he didn't remove his foot from her door she would hurt him. He laughed at her. "No can do," he said and his foot remained in the door. She counted down aloud from five to zero. He continued to push his foot further into her hallway, all the while grinning at her stupidly. It was clear to Jane's mother that this man believed her to be a stupid incapable woman and that she would not or could not keep her promise. When she reached the number zero she calmly reached for an umbrella which she kept by the door and, releasing the door, she shoved the umbrella with full force into his stomach. Startled, he bent forward clutching his midriff. She then bopped him on the head not once or twice but three times. He fell backwards, she smiled politely, said good day to him and left him winded and slightly dazed on her doorstep. Jane remembered the incident well because she had stood at the window watching the man sit on the step for what seemed like a long time before he was capable of getting up. Her mother had joined her just as he was leaving. "Good riddance," she'd said with a genuine smile. "You know, Janey, there is nothing quite like giving a smug arrogant cock like him a good dig to cheer up an otherwise grey day." Jane knew that if her mother had enjoyed giving that cock a dig because he put his foot in her doorway she would definitely enjoy slapping Dominic in the face with a shovel for putting his cock in her daughter.

After Alexandra had read the letter a few more times and lamented with Jane over her mother being a bigger bitch than Alexis on Dynasty, she opened the first of six cans of Ritz. Later when Jane was drunk on one can and Alexandra was on her third Jane compared her and Dominic's plight to that of Romeo and Juliet. Within seconds Alexandra expunged Jane's fanciful theory in an instant.

"It's like this, Janey," she said. "Romeo didn't get Juliet up the pole and then dump her at a disco."

"I know but his parents made him give me up and – "

"And anyway," Alexandra said with drunken authority, "as bad as your situation is with Dominic you don't want to be anything like Romeo and Juliet because Romeo and Juliet is a shit love story. Romeo was a shallow slut, Juliet pathetic and needy, their families were killing each other and they were in love one stupid day before they were married and then dead. Romeo and Juliet weren't star-crossed lovers, they were knackers."

"When you put it that way," Jane said sadly.

"Can you believe Miss Hobbs only gave me a C in English? I may not be able to spell apothecary but I have insight. That woman doesn't know her arse from her elbow."

Then Alexandra threw up in Jane's bin.

After that they talked about how Jane could win Dominic back but neither came up with a workable solution and so they agreed that Jane should just wait it out.

"As far as I'm concerned he's just a cock-artist but I know you love him so it will work out," said Alexandra.

"He's more than a cock-artist," said Jane.

"I disagree," Alexandra said, burping Ritz.

"He's the one," said Jane.

Alexandra sighed and tapped her can. "He'll come back, Janey.

He'll see you in school every day and he'll miss you, just give it some time." She stopped in time to throw up again, wiped her mouth and sighed. "That's better. What I was I saying?"

"'Just give it some time'," said Jane.

"Exactly. And anyway you still have me."

"I know."

"You will always have me."

"I know."

"Even if I get Science in Cork because, let's face it, I'm not going to get into UCD, you still have me."

"I'll miss you," Jane said.

"You won't have to," Alexandra promised. "I'll be home every other weekend and you can come and stay with me."

"I'll have a baby."

"Leave it with your mum."

"She's made it clear she's not a baby-sitter."

"She's such a cow."

"Yeah, she is."

"I love you, Jane."

"I love you too, Alex."

They were interrupted by Jane's mother who was even drunker than Alexandra and determined to fight.

"Go home, Alexandra."

"I'm going home."

"So go!"

"I'm going."

"So get out!"

"Jesus, what's wrong with you, woman? Can't you see I'm trying to get up?"

Jane helped her friend into a standing position.

"See," Alexandra said with arms outstretched, "I'm off!" She weaved through the corridor and walked out the front door. She turned to say goodbye but Jane's mother slammed the door in her face.

Jane's mother turned to her. "She's not welcome here any more."

"She's my best friend."

"Yeah, well, kiss your best friend goodbye."

That was the last time Alexandra was in Jane's house. Jane gave birth to a son two weeks later and, although they maintained a friendship for four months after that, when Jane became a mother and Alexandra went to college in Cork they lost contact. Over the next seventeen years Jane often thought of her friend and she missed her.

Leslie
5th June 1996

Dear Jim,

It's time to talk about Leslie. We both know she's stubborn and cut off and we both know why. When I'm gone you'll be all she has left in this world and I know it's a big ask but please look out for her.

We've talked about you remarrying and you know I want you to find someone to love and to love you. I want you to have a great new life that doesn't include overcrowded hospitals, dismissive doctors, overworked nurses and cancer. I want you to find someone strong and healthy, someone you can go on an adventure with, someone you can make love to, someone who doesn't cause you anguish and pain. Every time I see your face it hurts because for the first time I see that in loving you I've been selfish and I understand why Leslie is the way she is.

Leslie is a better person than me. I know you're probably guffawing at that as you read but it's true. She's watched her entire family die of cancer and when we were both diagnosed with the dodgy gene after Nora's death she made the decision not to cause pain to others the way Nora caused pain to John and Sarah and I'm causing pain to you. Before cancer she was smart and funny, kind and caring and she still is to me. Without her care I wouldn't have coped. I know sometimes she calls you names but trust me she knows you're not a monkey so when she calls you an arse-picker, ignore it and be kind.

I thought she was being defeatist. I thought that we'd suffered enough as a family and that we'd both survive. So I made plans and fell in love and for a while we had a great life but then that dodgy gene kicked in. Now I see you look almost as ill as I feel and I realise that my sister Leslie knew exactly what she was doing when she broke up with Simon and all but closed off. I watched her disappear from her own life. I thought she was insane back then but it makes sense now.

She put the pain of others before her own. She watched John and Sarah suffer after Nora and she'll watch you suffering after me and, although she pretends not to like you, she does and it will hurt her and it will also confirm for her that she is right to remain alone waiting for a diagnosis that may never come.

I'm her last family and friend. She hasn't even let herself get to know her niece and so when I'm gone she'll have no one and that haunts me. Please go and live your life but all that I ask is that every now and again, no matter how rude or uninviting she may seem, call to her, talk to her, be her friend even if she fails to be yours, because she has been there for me, for Mum, for Dad and Nora and I can't stand the idea that after everything she's been through she should live or die alone.

I know I say it all the time and in all my little notes and letters about this and that but time is running out and I need you to know that it's been a privilege to be your wife and, although I feel selfish for all the pain I've caused you, I know I've brought happiness too so hang on to that and forgive me because even knowing what I know now I'd love and marry you again. I suppose Leslie would say I was a selfish truffle-sniffler but I can die with that.

Yours,
Imelda

Imelda Sheehan died at eight o'clock on the morning of the twelfth of July 1996. She was twenty-five years old. Her husband Jim was by her side and holding her right hand, and sitting on the opposite side of the bed and holding her left hand was her sister Leslie. They both felt her slip away at exactly the same time. For Leslie it was familiar: the ocean of grief inside her swelled and rose but she knew what to do and so she remained still and allowed the pain to wash over her. For Jim it was so shocking: one second his wife was alive and battling to breathe, the next dead and silent. He let Imelda's hand go and stood up quickly, so quickly that he nearly fell. He steadied and hugged himself. He stood in the corner of the room as the doctor and nurses approached to confirm time of death. Leslie sat with her dead sister Imelda, holding her hand for as long as they would allow her. Jim cried and his parents, brothers and friends made a fuss of him. Leslie sat alone and frozen. She knew the physical pain that made her heart feel like it was about to explode and her ears ring until she feared they'd bleed would dissipate in time, just as the tide would turn and with it Imelda would drift further and further away until she was a distant memory and it only served to make her loss greater. Leslie had just turned twenty-seven.

Jim asked Leslie to read at the funeral but she refused. He asked her to sit beside him in the first pew when she'd attempted to sit at the back of the church. She told him she didn't want to shake hands with the people whose hands she had shook so many times before but Jim was not taking no for an answer and so she found herself sitting beside her brother-in-law with a heavy heart and an all-too-familiar swollen hand from those whose earnest sympathy ensured they squeezed too tight.

When the priest asked if anyone would like to speak, Leslie stood up. This surprised her and those around her, especially Jim who couldn't even get her to agree to a reading. She found herself standing without reason. The priest asked her to come forward but her legs refused to comply with his request and so he waited and the congregation waited and Jim nudged her and asked if she was all right. What the hell am I doing, she asked herself as she started to move toward the altar but once on the altar and standing in front of a microphone the words came easily.

"I am the last of the five Sheehans," she said. "Four days ago there were two of us, me the middle child, and Imelda the baby of the family. I should have been next, and not just because I was older but because Imelda was the strong one, the one who embraced life regardless and without fear. Over the years she's run five marathons in aid of cancer. I didn't even walk for cancer, not even once – mostly I'll avoid even standing if I can." She stopped to take a breath. There was a hint of a titter from the crowd. "She fell in love and married Jim and she always planned to have kids. Imelda always made plans and that's what I admired about her most because even when she was diagnosed with the same cancer that had killed our grandmother, her mother, father and sister she still made plans. She froze her eggs and they bought a house and when she wasn't in chemo she travelled. Even when she knew her life was coming to the end she still made plans. Little plans that don't mean much to most like 'Tonight we'll reminisce about the summer we spent in Kerry' or 'Tomorrow when the sun comes out we'll sit in the hospital grounds and watch the people come and go and make up stories about who and what they are'. She even planned her own funeral. She knew exactly what she wanted, the kind of casket, the flowers, the priest, the prayers, the attendees. She asked me once if I would speak at her funeral and I said no. I'm sorry, Imelda, of course I'll speak for you. I just was scared that I wouldn't know what to say and I didn't want to let you down. So I'll just end by saying this: I miss my dad, my mum, my sister Nora and now I miss my Imelda and I'm so sorry because it should have been me but I will see you all again and soon."

Leslie's voice was cracking, eyes streaming and her nose was running. She walked toward her seat and once she'd accepted a tissue from Jim she sat with her head in her hands, attempting to regain composure but finding it almost impossible to do so. Back then her hair was still jet-black, she was slim and although not a natural beauty she was striking. The people sitting in pews behind her felt nothing but pity for this young woman who was merely waiting for her turn to die. Later, by the side of the grave, she watched Jim grieve and if there was something she could have said to make him feel better she would have said it but there wasn't so she stood in silence waiting for the day to end so that she could disappear behind her closed door and wait for the inevitable. It never occurred to her that she'd be still waiting for the inevitable eleven years later.

Tom
25th September 2007

Transcript of Liveline radio show with Joe Duffy

"I have a Tom Kavanagh on the line. Tom, are you there?"

"I am, Joe. "

"Tom, you are trying to find your lovely wife Alexandra."

"Yes, Joe."

"She went missing on the twenty-first of June this year?"

"It was Thursday, the twenty-first of June."

"Tell us about it, Tom."

"I don't know where to start. She was last seen in Dalkey and now she's gone."

"Okay, okay, all right. How about you tell us a little about her?"

"She's funny, she's giddy, she's kind, she's friendly, she's fussy, she's lovely, Joe." Caller becomes emotional.

"The police have managed to retrace her steps as far as Dalkey. Can you tell us about that?"

"She left the house in Clontarf around two p.m. She said hello to a neighbour who verified the time. She walked to the train station and three teenagers who were there came forward to say that they witnessed her getting on the train. She's also captured on CCTV footage on the platform at Tara Street at three thirty but she got back onto the train. After the train stations were canvassed a woman came forward and identified her as getting off the train in Dalkey. She was captured on CCTV footage again there but after that . . ." Caller becomes emotional.

"And after that?"

"She was gone. She's just gone."

"Ah God, that's desperate. What time was that?"

"It was approximately four p.m."

"And where were you?"

"I was working. We were finishing a project in Blackrock."

"It says here you're a builder."

"I am."

"So when did you realise that she was missing?"

"I was supposed to be home by four. I had promised to make dinner because Alexandra was meeting her friend Sherri to collect tickets for a gig from her. She had left a note saying she'd be home by seven thirty. But I was delayed on site. I didn't get in until nine p.m."

"When did you raise the alarm, Tom?"

"The next morning, Joe." Caller becomes emotional. "I thought she'd stayed out with Sherri or maybe that she was pissed off that I didn't get home in time to make the dinner so went out again. I was exhausted so I fell asleep."

"That's understandable. What age is Alexandra?"

"She's thirty-six. She has chestnut-brown hair, shoulder length. She was wearing black trousers and a black blouse with a bow on it. She had a black fitted jacket on. She's very attractive, the kind of person you'd remember if you'd seen her." Caller becomes emotional.

"And she went missing on . . ."

"Thursday the twenty-first of June this year."

"And did she have any mental issues, Tom?"

"No, Joe. She was a very happy, well-adjusted, normal woman. She was normal, Joe, ordinary."

"Okay, okay." Joe sighs. "I'm going to ask the obvious, Tom, so forgive me. Is there any chance she took herself into the water?"

"No. No. She wasn't suicidal and the coast guard searched it and the police divers and there were plenty of people on the beach that day and no one saw her."

"Okay, I had to ask. I'm sorry for your trouble, Tom. I hope that maybe someone listening remembers something."

"And, Joe?"

"Yes, Tom?"

"I'll be at Dalkey train station handing out flyers later this evening and I'll be doing the same at a Jack Lukeman gig on Dame Street next Friday."

"Why there, Tom?"

"She was a big fan, Joe. She never missed a show." Caller becomes emotional.

"And he's very popular; lots of people from all counties will be there."

"It's as good a place as any to get the word out, Joe."

"God love you, Tom. I sympathise. Good luck to you. We'll put Alexandra's details on the website and if you could send in a photo we'll post it."

"I will and thanks for taking the call."

"And if anyone has information on Alexandra Kavanagh who went missing on the twenty-first of June 2007 would they contact Clontarf Garda Station and the inspector in charge of the investigation is Des Martin. Right, we'll be back after these ads."

End transcript.

Tom put down the phone and turned to Breda his mother-in-law. She was sitting at the kitchen table looking frail and small. She smiled at him through tears.

"You did very well, love," she said.

"You should have left this phone number," Eamonn said while pacing. Eamonn was Alexandra's older brother and he and Tom had never really been close. Alexandra's disappearance had served to widen the divide between them. "And you should have said that she was upset about not getting pregnant."

"Nothing to do with anything," Tom said. "She was fine, happy."

"You just didn't want to see it!" Eamonn shouted. "It was tearing her apart and you didn't see it!"

"Take that back, Eamonn," Tom said, walking toward Eamonn.

Eamonn in his mind was begging him to punch him. Take a swing, I dare you!

Breda called out to the two boys: "Stop it, both of you!"

Alexandra's father stood up from the chair he'd been sitting in outside on the patio. He put his cigarette out and came inside.

"Go home now," he said to Eamonn and Tom. "Go home before you both say and do things you'll regret."

Eamonn and Tom both nodded and apologised. Breda was crying again. She looked at Tom who had aged ten years in ten weeks. His black hair was almost entirely grey; his once-sparkly blue eyes were tired and circled by shadowed skin. He had been so pernickety about the way he looked that Alexandra's family, especially Eamonn, had often joked about her marrying a metro sexual. His suits were always the best of suits, dry-cleaned after one wear and cut precisely. His hair perfectly cut, and his face perfectly clean. Off-site Tom didn't look like a builder, he looked like a banker. He was wealthy and although he wasn't extravagant he left those around him in no doubt about his standing. Breda noticed his suit was now too big, his hair was a mess and he hadn't shaved in weeks. He was a shadow of the man he used to be as she was a shadow of the woman and mother she once was. She recognised his suffering as it mirrored her own and she wanted her son whose anger was more intense than his pain to stop hurting her already mortally wounded son-in-law. She promised herself she would talk to Eamonn when she found the strength to deal with his quarrel-some nature.

When Tom was leaving she hugged him and he could feel every bone in her back. She whispered into his ear. "She's still with us – I can feel it. God will take care of her – she's not alone because God is there beside her."

Tom nodded. "Try and eat, Breda."

He left and got into his car. He sat there for a minute or two and was still there when Eamonn came out of the house. Eamonn walked over to the car window and knocked on it. Tom rolled it down.

"I don't care what the police say," Eamonn said, "I don't care what my mother says. It's your fault. I blame you." He turned and walked to his own car, got in and drove away, leaving Tom sitting in Alexandra's parents' driveway crying like a baby.

Oh God, please, please, where is she? Bring her home to me, please, please, bring her home! I'm so sorry for everything I've done. Forgive me and bring her home.

Alexandra was then missing nine weeks and two days.

•◦•

If you enjoyed this chapter from
So What if I'm Broken by Anna McPartlin,
why not order the full book online
@ www.poolbeg.com

•◦•